Hearts

Also by Ry Herman

Love Bites

Bleeding Hearts

RY HERMAN

Jo Fletcher

BOOKS

First published in Great Britain in 2021 by

Jo Fletcher Books
an imprint of
Quercus Editions Ltd
Carmelite House
50 Victoria Embankment
London EC4Y 0DZ

An Hachette UK company

A CIP catalogue record for this book is available from the British Library

PB ISBN 978 1 52940 631 3

10 9 8 7 6 5 4 3 2 1

Typeset by Jouve (UK), Milton Keynes

Printed and bound in Great Britain by Clays Ltd, Elcograf S.p.A.

Papers used by Jo Fletcher Books are from well-managed forests and other responsible sources.

Dedicated to Entropy (1998–2019)

You were the best cat.

THE EARTH DRAGON

Chinatown, San Francisco, California
18 April 1906

The first tremors wake Meijing from a restless dream. Traces of it linger in her mind, a fading memory of sprinting up and down the city streets, pursued by a creature she cannot name. She comes to consciousness with a gasp, short of breath, her heart racing.

She's one of the first to open her eyes, but it takes a few more disoriented moments before she wakens fully. The scant hours allotted for her sleep have been shortened further by the disruption, and her thoughts are muzzy, her limbs heavy on the mattress, leaden with fatigue. The bruises around her throat ache. She coughs, as if that will soothe them. It doesn't.

A hard jolt from below makes the earthquake finally register on her bleary senses. Through the thin mattress, she can feel the floor shake and vibrate. A rumbling noise fills the air, almost identical to the low-pitched clatter of a streetcar passing too close. Basins and chamber pots are crawling across the bare planking, moving in little jumps, making tinkling sounds as they circle each other like dance partners. Cries of '*Ai ya!*' rise up throughout the room. Someone shouts, '*Dai loong jen!*' – the earth dragon is wriggling.

Most of the other girls are already up, staggering towards the centre of the room, where the heavy crossbeam supports the ceiling. Meijing has always doubted that would do any good. What chance does a stick of wood have against the might of the world? If the ceiling collapses, a crossbeam or door lintel would smash down on them along with everything else above their heads. Not that they can seek shelter under the door lintel. The only door is locked from the outside.

Instead of joining the others, Meijing hauls herself up and takes an unsteady step towards the window, lacing her fingers through the metal bars. In all likelihood, this won't be a bad quake, anyway. The restive earth rattles the city a handful of times every year, but never causes much harm. It's a commonplace fact of life, like the brushfires and mudslides and floods that sweep through the state every now and then. Another ordinary day in California.

The buildings across the way are quivering, wobbling back and forth on their foundations. A chill early morning breeze blows across her face; the sun has not yet risen, although the eastern sky is beginning to brighten to a placid blue. On the street below, the few people out and about at this hour are lurching across the unstable ground, looking for somewhere safe to crouch down. The rumbling and shaking go on and on as if they will never end. A city trapped in an eternity of noise and motion.

In truth, though, the earthquake peters out in less than a minute. Meijing sees little if any damage to the shops and houses. Exactly as she expected.

Behind her, the sound of chatter starts as the other girls sort themselves out. Meijing rests her forehead on a cool metal crossbar, not bothering to participate. She will be forced to move soon enough. It will be their job to mop up whatever has spilled and sweep up whatever has broken, no matter how red-eyed they are from lack of sleep. She is awake, so she must work, whether here in the rooms above or down in the bathhouse below. So says her contract. There are four years left on Meijing's contract. There will always be four years left on her contract.

In the months since she became old enough to whore, it has been extended again and again. Penalties are applied when she doesn't make enough money, when she falls ill, when she irritates customers. The latest penalty came last night, when a French sailor became enraged upon discovering that her *hai* is like any woman's, not twisted sideways as he'd heard. He'd throttled her until the world went dim. Bad luck. Most men don't mind when they find her privates do not really run east–west, at least not by the time they realise their mistake.

She is unlikely to survive long enough for the penalties to matter. In far less time than four years, she'll be broken by the beatings and riddled with disease. There will be no chance for her to marry out of the profession, as so many others have. Not when her clientele is exclusively white.

She wonders why anyone bothers to pretend the contracts are fair. Maybe it fools the *mui tsai* girls fresh off the boat from Guangdong. Although there are precious few of those these days.

In fact, there are so few new girls that the men who hold her contract are growing desperate, although they would never admit it aloud. But everyone knows that the prostitution trade in Chinatown has been dwindling for years, the brothels closing, the profits shrinking. The endless turf wars of the tongs have harmed too many, and the criminal gangs are losing their grip. Their members are ageing, the older highbinders unreplaced by new blood, and more and more of the neighbourhood's residents are turning against them with each passing day.

Meijing has only to look around the room to see the results – a scant handful of girls sharing her sleeping quarters. Not every woman in Chinatown is a whore; that was never true, and is less true now than ever, no matter what the rest of San Francisco, and the rest of the world, might believe. The vast majority are ordinary people living ordinary lives.

Although this fact does not do much good for Meijing. The trade may be dying, but it is far from dead, and she is her mother's daughter. Both of them sold into servitude, one generation after the next.

Meijing is still standing at the window, looking at nothing, when the second wave of tremors nearly knocks her off her feet. Her clutch on the window bars is all that prevents her from toppling straight to the ground.

If the earlier sound was a streetcar, this one is a train, heavy with freight and hurtling down the track. Outside, she can see the sloped street undulating, solid earth heaving like the sea in a storm. Fissures crack open and slam shut. Her eyes widen with shock as she stares through the ironwork, clinging tightly to keep from being tossed across the room. Behind her, something shatters. A girl screams.

The earth dragon is no longer merely wriggling; he is writhing, bucking, throwing off the itchy city that has grown upon his back.

Her view tilts crazily, and for an instant she believes the ground is raising itself up to punch the bathhouse like a mighty fist. But then she realises she is falling, that the wall has pulled away from the building and is carrying her with it, sweeping her out and away and down, rushing to meet the convulsing pavement below.

The seconds she spends suspended in mid-air last a lifetime. Long enough to stare death in the face.

Meijing blinks her eyes open, coughing, choking on the gritty dust that hovers in the air. She has no memory of hitting the ground. After those panicked seconds plummeting down, she can recall nothing but black silence.

The runaway train noise of the quake has ceased, and the earth is still, but a siren is wailing somewhere in the distance – no, several sirens, their caterwauling shrieks overlapping eerily. The fires have already started.

Meijing is lying on a shattered surface of cracked plaster and broken planks, all that remains of the wall that bore her down. The metal bars she clung to lie scattered nearby, knocked askew to form some unknown symbol.

Her whole body throbs with dull pain, and there's a sharp sting where a scrape along her side has left her night clothes torn and spotted with blood. She pushes herself upright and looks around cautiously, unsteady on her feet.

The bathhouse she has lived in for the past three months is gone.

A thick haze floats over the remains. Peering through it, she can make out a low, uneven pile of wood and brick, sloping down from the edges until the centre is well below street level. The building has collapsed into its basement.

Not far from her, an arm pokes out of the rubble, pale where it isn't red-brown with cooling blood. She runs to it and takes hold of the hand, bracing her feet against the wreckage to pull the buried victim free. After a few tugs, she realises that there's no point. The arm is limp and lifeless, and bent in a way that no arm should bend. A jagged shard of bone pokes out through the skin.

She lets the arm drop and listens for any noise from within the wreckage. She hears none. No one screaming for help. No one shifting aside the timbers, scrabbling to get out. Nothing but the distant sirens.

Is everyone else dead?

The highbinders will surely be here soon. They will want to look for any survivors and bring them to safety – and they will also want to check on their investment. Secure the girls. Make certain no one runs away in the confusion.

If she stays to help, they will find her. But where else can she go?

Meijing's mother died in the tiny room where she'd spent her life calling for customers through a sliding panel. Two bits to look, four bits to feel, six bits to do.

If there is anyone alive under the fallen beams, they'll be dead soon enough. It might take minutes if they are left beneath the debris, or it might take a few years if they are unearthed and brought to shelter, but they will die. Crushed, suffocated, or bleeding their lives out; coughing up their lungs in a room with a sliding panel, or beaten to death in a bathhouse that caters to white customers. It makes no difference.

She turns her face from the ruins and drags herself away.

Chinatown is stirring now, rousing itself into shouts and motion. Merchants and their families, servants, lodgers, dragging whatever possessions they can salvage out into the street. Here and there, figures stand motionless, tears streaking through blood and plaster dust as they stare at the wreckage of their lives. Many are half naked; Meijing was not the only one forced outside in sleeping clothes. She passes a woman who clutches a legless, headless doll in her arms. Her face is as blank and empty as a sheet of unused paper. Another man sits, his hands pressed against his eyes, on a stoop which is all that remains of his home. Far to the south, a dark pall of smoke rises into the sky as a distant fire burns. Even now, though, Meijing can see the beginnings of an organised evacuation, neighbours helping each other search the rubble, groups gathering together at the street corners to discuss what to do and where to seek shelter.

'*Siu jie, mat ye si ah*?'

It takes Meijing a long moment to realise she is being addressed, that someone nearby is asking if she is hurt. She looks to her left and sees a stranger, a woman, already dressed for the day.

The woman's clothes are sturdy but well worn; she might be a labourer's wife, or perhaps a seamstress or a waitress, up early to get a start on the day's work when the earthquake hit. She has a kind face. Her eyebrows are raised in question. Her arm is half extended towards Meijing.

Meijing cannot trust a kind face. There is no one here she can trust. She spins away from the woman, giving no answer, and walks on without looking back.

She avoids passing too close to anyone else. Appealing to her neighbours is too dangerous. To ask for help is to invite recapture; anyone might turn her back in to the men who hold her contract. Although many despise the gangs, many others profit from them, or owe them, or fear them. It is impossible to know who she can confide in, and who she cannot. She must be careful. Careful who she talks to, careful where she goes.

And careful how she steals, as well. The authorities will not look kindly upon thieves right now, however great their need. At the best of times, the law never does anything for Chinese whores except jail them. Today she might simply be killed.

But she will need shoes if she wants to go anywhere. Her feet already have cuts and bruises from the jagged fragments of brick and stone that litter the pavement. Shoes, and clothes, and food.

Once she has gathered her supplies, she will run. She will not stop until she's somewhere safe. Or at least somewhere better. Wherever that might be.

Whatever happens, she will survive.

PART ONE

Ishtar Could Be A Real Bitch Sometimes

CHAPTER ONE

Cambridge Common, Cambridge, Massachusetts
1 November 2000

In the dead of night, a witch and a vampire creep towards the old graveyard.

'Are you absolutely certain this is a good idea?' Angela whispers as a lone taxi turns the corner and trundles down Garden Street, forcing them to crouch down behind a tree.

'No, not at all,' Chloë answers. 'In fact, I'm pretty sure this is really, really stupid.'

Angela smiles and tucks a loose strand of blonde hair back underneath her bandana. 'Well. As long as we agree.'

Angela is still dressed as Dread Pirate Roberts from *The Princess Bride*, mask and gloves and boots and all, although she left the plastic rapier behind. When they first set out, Chloë worried that Angela wasn't taking this seriously enough. But now that they're huddled up against a tree trunk, hiding from the traffic, she has to admit the outfit has practical benefits. It's easy to move in and hides Angela's face, and the bandana keeps her hair from glowing like a beacon in the passing headlights.

Besides, Chloë never minds seeing Angela in tight trousers.

Chloë changed out of her own costume as soon as the Halloween party was over. Dressing up as her pet cat might be many things, up to and including psychologically troubling, but 'practical' would not be at the top of the list. The tail got caught in a door twice when they were safely inside; God knows what would happen to it climbing a fence.

As soon as the taxi disappears around the bend, Chloë rises to her feet. After a quick check down the street in both directions, she starts stalking towards the cemetery again. Angela shrugs the strap of her giant duffle bag back up onto her shoulder and pads along silently behind.

Chloë wishes they hadn't had to park so far away and walk so many blocks to get here. She feels exposed every minute they're out doing this. If they're caught, if they get thrown into a jail cell even for a few hours, it will be a death sentence for Angela. Chloë has a sudden nightmare vision of clutching Angela's hand while the first rays of dawn peek through a barred window, nowhere to hide from it and no way to run. Of Angela catching fire, screaming, burning away to nothing while she watches.

At least there aren't a lot of people out tonight, despite how close they are to Harvard Square. There's a reason they're doing this after 3 a.m. on a Wednesday morning. The bars closed over an hour ago, and the holiday revellers have long since departed. For once, the sidewalks here are emptier than the ones in the residential outskirts, where all-night parties will drip drunken X-Men onto the streets until dawn. But no matter how late the hour is, central Cambridge won't stay vacant for very long. They have to keep an eye out for cars full of tired partygoers heading home on Mass Ave, and cleaning trucks, and police patrols. Especially police patrols.

Everything remains quiet and still as they emerge from Cambridge Common – everything except for the whistling drone of the wind and the rattle of the tree branches as it passes. It's a clear night, only scattered wisps of cloud scudding rapidly across the sky.

The smattering of stars that can be seen past the city lights gleam like pinpricks on a black screen. Angela would know what constellations they belong to. Chloë has no idea.

'This may not be my greatest plan,' Chloë says, resuming their earlier conversation, 'but it's the least terrible one I could think of. The book said it should be done at crossroads or a burial ground, the older the better. This is both, plus it's about as old as you can get around here without trying to find something Native American.'

'Why not use a Native American site? Shouldn't we? I mean, they were here first.'

'Yeah, they were. Which means I'd be an interloper.' Chloë squints as they turn into the stiff breeze, and pulls her jacket around herself more tightly to ward off the chill. 'It's not my heritage or my tradition. That'd be pretty much the definition of cultural appropriation, wouldn't it?'

'I guess so.'

'And think about this for a minute – you've literally just suggested that we go mess around with the occult on an Indian burial ground. Have you ever seen a horror movie?' Chloë grins bright and wide to hide her nervousness. She suspects she's only made herself look manic.

'If this were a horror movie, we wouldn't be the victims,' Angela points out. 'We'd be the monsters.'

'That's no reason to press our luck. It's tempting fate. It'd be like making out in the abandoned cabin and then going skinny-dipping in Murder Lake.'

'Sounds nice. I'm game if you are.'

Almost a year after they first met, and Angela can still make her blush. 'Maybe when the weather gets warmer. One of us feels the cold, remember?'

With that, they've arrived at the Old Burial Ground, a grassy pentagon stretching between Christ Church and the Unitarian First

Parish. It also bumps up against the back of a Starbucks at one corner; time marches on and Cambridge real estate values only allow for so much spare room. In the spirit of the holiday, someone has attached cotton cobwebs and plastic ghosts to the iron fence posts. The ghosts dance jerkily where they hang, buffeted by the cold gusts of blustery air.

Chloë peers through the gaps between the bars. The graveyard holds a haphazard assortment of thin, crumbling headstones. They poke out of the ground at odd angles, like a mouthful of smashed and jagged teeth. *Which is probably less ominous than it sounds*, Chloë reassures herself. Every ancient graveyard is going to look like that when you're breaking into it at night. It's not like she would have discovered a cheerful, cosy ancient graveyard if only she'd done more research.

There's been a cemetery on this spot since at least 1635, according to a blue plaque affixed to the fence. Settlers and slaves are interred beneath the ground here, Harvard presidents and paupers, ministers and poets and heroes of the Revolutionary War. She hopes it's enough dead bodies for the purpose.

'Give me a boost?' she asks.

Angela obligingly grabs her by the hips and swings her up, hefting her as easily as a sack of potatoes. Easier, really – it's hard to hold a sack of potatoes at arm's length, and Angela doesn't strain against her weight at all. Chloë grabs the top of the fence and pulls herself the rest of the way over, stumbling a little when she lands on the other side. Angela follows, flexing her knees deeply and leaping without any need of a running start. She lands next to Chloë in a graceful crouch. It's a much more efficient method. Inhumanly efficient.

Sometimes, dating a vampire can be unnerving.

The milestone doesn't prove difficult to find. The half-shattered, boulder-sized marker rests in the northeast corner of the graveyard, not far from where they came in. Most of the inscription is legible in spite of the damage, although the part bearing the B in Boston broke off sometime long ago:

OSTON
8 MILES
1734
A.I.

The stone marks the meeting place of two eighteenth-century roads to the city, and in the present day it sits next to newer crossroads. Although, since that's nothing more than Garden Street crossing from one lane of Mass Ave to another, it might only count as a T-junction instead of crossroads. Chloë isn't sure. She does know there have been routes for travellers here since well before the stone was set in place, before any Europeans ever got here. Which, she belatedly realises, means that if she wanted to avoid anything Native American, she's failed. Maybe there's no way to avoid the messy tangle of history when meddling with forces this old and complex. She hopes if anything is actually listening when she casts the spell, it doesn't mind too much.

Chloë worries her lower lip with her teeth. As usual when it comes to this sort of thing, she doesn't have the best handle on what she's doing. So much of magic seems to involve playing things by ear.

'Shall we get this started?' Angela drops her bag to the ground with a thump, startling Chloë out of her thoughts. She drags the pack behind a low brick wall inside the fence, and kneels down to fiddle with the zipper. The wall doesn't look like it'll do much to hide them from the road, but it's better than nothing.

Chloë watches with growing amazement as Angela starts lifting out flat stones and laying them in two neat circles.

'You didn't just jump the fence, you jumped the fence carrying a sack full of rocks?'

'Safety first. I didn't want us to burn the whole graveyard down. It's a historic site.' She stands up again, flashlight in hand, and clicks it on. 'Want me to read while you do the spell?'

Chloë nods, and takes the piece of paper with the instructions out of her jacket pocket. Angela unfolds it after Chloë passes it over, peering at the writing, holding the flashlight close.

'"Using a need-fire, light two . . . blinfries . . ."'

'Bonfires. That word is obviously supposed to be bonfires.'

'Your handwriting is terrible. "Light two bonfires of sufficient size, one of fir and one of willow."' Angela frowns. 'How big is "sufficient size" supposed to be?'

'I don't know, exactly. My guess would be big enough that I can get around the place three times while they're still lit.' Chloë glances at the graveyard. It isn't huge, as cemeteries go, but the area she needs to cover isn't what she would call tiny, either. 'I hope we brought enough wood.'

'Gah. I hate the descriptions in these spells you dig up. "Add a measure of water", "stir in a quantity of sheep's blood". It's such obvious ass covering. If it doesn't work and someone complains, whoever wrote it can just say, "Well, it's not my fault, the quantity of your quantity was the wrong quantity." Try getting away with that in a scientific paper. You'd never hear the end of it.'

Chloë waits patiently for the rant to finish. Angela has a tendency to grouse when she's feeling stressed. 'I think the amounts can change. Witches are supposed to have some kind of instinctive feel for how much to use each time.'

'Magic needs a peer-review system.' Angela returns her attention to the paper. '"Toss the bones of the slaughtered heifers onto the fires. Don a garment of cow-hide, and pass between them."'

Chloë uncomfortably fingers the leather jacket she's borrowed from Angela for the night. Her own tatty synthetic overcoat wasn't going to do the job, but she doesn't like how dead-cow focused this particular ritual is. Ever since a traumatising attempt at a spell involving animal sacrifice earlier in the year, she's been leaning more and more towards vegetarianism. At least she only had to buy the bones for this one, not obtain them firsthand. She hopes the butcher who assured her they were heifer bones wasn't lying.

'"Walk midway between the fires,"' Angela continues, '"and circle the site three times, either widdershins, walking backwards, or forwards and deosil. Do not stop. Do not turn around." You underlined "not" both times.' She looks up. 'Deosil?'

'Sunwise. That means clockwise, at least in the northern hemisphere. It's from Gaelic, I think.'

'Gaelic? Is this a Celtic thing?'

'Well, yeah. I mean, it's a Samhain rite.'

Angela tilts her head, considering. 'That's not your heritage either, is it? Wouldn't that be off-limits for you, too?'

'I don't think it has exactly the same issues,' Chloë says hesitantly. 'We're not doing this on land that was stolen from the Celts. And I don't think the Celts are being systemically oppressed in Boston, not anymore.'

Angela ponders that for a few moments, then nods. 'OK. I suppose that makes sense.'

'Look, I'm kind of grasping at straws, here. I've tried using the traditional Jewish stuff. I made that Kabbalah amulet, but we've got no idea whether it's having any effect at all. It's supposed to take years to master Kabbalah, God knows I still don't understand most of it, and . . . and I don't know what I'm doing, and I'm probably going to screw everything up . . .' She chokes on the words, unable to continue.

Angela's eyes widen at Chloë's distress. She slips an arm around Chloë's waist and murmurs in her ear. 'Sweetie, it'll be fine. I'm sure you'll do fine.'

'I'm the wrong person to be doing this, I–'

'Better you than me. I'm an atheist, I've got to have offended every god from every culture there is. You're going to look great in comparison.'

Chloë bites back a laugh, beginning to calm down. She always feels less panicked when Angela is holding her.

But it doesn't keep her doubts completely at bay, not tonight. They're running out of time. She needs to find a solution, something, anything, or she's going to lose Angela. And she can't lose Angela.

She can't.

CHAPTER TWO

Old Burial Ground, Cambridge
1 November 2000

Angela lifts her chin and looks into her girlfriend's eyes. Green, green eyes like two perfect slices of lime. Angela can see her own worries reflected there.

They've got two months left. The end of the year, that was the agreement. Then they break up and go their separate ways. Unless they can find something that will ward Chloë against the effects of Angela's bites, some way to protect her from the potentially deadly risks involved. It's terrifying how much the bites affect Chloë, leaving her shaky and pallid, clammy with sweat every time Angela drinks from her veins. Chloë's symptoms seem far worse than what Angela remembers of her own reaction to it. Back in the days when a vampire was feeding on her, she was able to shrug it off most of the time.

They need to come up with a solution, and they need to do it soon. But time keeps passing, and not a single thing they've tried has worked.

Chloë's unearthed spell after spell, poring over every source she could find, from medieval texts buried in university libraries to dog-eared New Age paperbacks she buys at used bookstores. None of her attempts at casting them have produced so much as a flash or a tingle. For all they know, every last one of the 'spells' have been nothing more than smoke and mirrors. As ineffective as waving their arms in the air and shouting 'Abracadabra!'

And in the meanwhile Angela, for her part, has been experimenting on herself in every way she can think of, trying to discover exactly what her blood-drinking does, how it works, what mechanism allows human blood to give an unbreathing corpse the power to walk and talk as long as the sun is down. None of it has produced any useful results.

They're scraping the bottom of the barrel at this point. If this graveyard ritual fails as well, they've got no back-up plan. They're out of ideas.

Or almost out.

There is one person they know who might have more information, even if it's someone Angela would rather not see ever again. But she's been hesitant to bring up talking to Tess as a possibility. The dangers are greater than any potential benefits; Tess is far more likely to murder Chloë herself than tell them anything useful. She tried to do that once already.

Angela watches Chloë's hair rise and twist in the wind, the curls writhing around her head like living creatures.

'Come on,' Angela says. 'Let's do this. Hey, I'm half Irish, right? If it's something to worry about, then maybe having me around will be enough to keep things respectably Celtic.'

Chloë nods, looking hopeful. Angela turns back to the bag and digs out the fire-lighting equipment. Board, stake, bow drill, dry grass for tinder. It has to be started by hand in the traditional manner, no lighter allowed. She passes it all over to Chloë and starts readying the firewood, building neat pyramidal frames of fir and willow over the stones. Fallen branches, gathered by moonlight. That had taken a long night of picking up sticks.

Apparently, magic is hyper-specific about annoying things, like fire-starting and wood-gathering, but never about anything useful. 'Sufficient size' – what kind of nonsense is that? No wonder they haven't been getting anywhere. One early attempt to make a protective sachet had them scouring the countryside looking for monkshood and wild garlic, trying to identify the plants using the pictures in a botany text – in the dark. Chloë collected a whole bag full of lily of the valley before Angela pointed out that garlic should probably smell like garlic.

It might not have been such a bad thing that they didn't find any, though. The stench of garlic has been making Angela gag lately, much more than it did when she first became a vampire. She has no idea why it's getting worse. One more mystery to investigate.

'So,' she says as she leans another branch against a woodpile, 'what's your strategy for this? Are you going to walk widdershins or deosil?'

Chloë pokes dry grass into the indentation in the board. 'Definitely deosil. Widdershins is more to put stuff to rest.' Using a block, she presses the stake into the tinder, and takes a moment to ready herself. 'Here goes nothing.'

Angela gives her girlfriend's shoulder a comforting squeeze. 'You can do it. Starting a fire with friction is primitive technology. How hard could it be if a caveman can figure it out?'

'Cavemen had mad skills. Can you make a hide-scraper out of a flint rock? I can't. I couldn't even tell the difference between a hide-scraper and an eye-gouger.'

'You got it lit in the practice session.'

'Sure. Once.' Chloë draws in a deep breath, and begins spinning the stake with the bow drill as fast as she can. 'Anyway. You go deosil if you want to bring energy up from the earth. It builds power. Ocean currents and winds move deosil. Hurricanes turn that way.'

'That isn't magic. That's the Coriolis effect.'

'Don't you mock my mystic art. It's all one. I am a witch, and therefore have a powerful and mysterious connection to nature. Crap!' The stake pops out of the hole and somehow escapes the bow drill altogether. They watch it bounce away across the grass.

'You should be careful with that thing,' Angela says. 'There's a vulnerable vampire present.'

Chloë winces. 'Oh, right. Sorry. I won't let it happen again.'

'Relax, I'm joking. If I can't stab myself with a wooden stake on purpose, it's not going to injure me accidentally.' During the cautious experiments she's conducted with Chloë's help – and the single incautious attempt she made by herself, late last year – Angela hasn't been able to get a stake through her mostly impenetrable skin. It's touching that Chloë is still worried about it, though. Angela smiles affectionately at her girlfriend.

Chloë doesn't return the smile, however; she's turned a gloomy gaze on the unlit fires. 'This is what I was afraid of,' she says. 'It's a lot harder out here than it was inside. There wasn't any wind indoors, for one thing.'

Angela sticks a final piece of crumpled newspaper in at the base of one of the woodpiles and picks up the stake. She twirls it thoughtfully in her gloved fingers. 'Do you have to be the one doing this part?'

'Maybe? It's not entirely clear.' Chloë taps her fingers against her thigh, frowning in thought. 'There's a Scottish tradition that says it has to be done by two chaste boys, and a German one that calls for eighty-one married men. I'm improvising a bit here, if you hadn't noticed.' She exhales a long breath, not quite a sigh. 'My gut instinct says that isn't one of the points that matters.'

'Your gut instinct?'

'It's not like we've got anything better to go on, is it? So if you want to give it a shot, go ahead. We've wasted enough time as it is.'

'All right. It couldn't hurt to –'

Chloë's gaze jerks up over Angela's head. 'Car!' She looks around wildly, her eyes darting to the piles of sticks, the duffle bag, all the evidence lying out practically in the open, hardly concealed at all by the small brick wall. Angela pulls Chloë down, ducking them out of sight as best she can just as she starts to hear the sound of the engine, a throaty growl growing steadily louder.

'There's no time to hide it any better,' she whispers quickly. 'We'll just have to hope they don't notice.'

'It's a cop car, shit, it's a cop car,' Chloë hisses back.

Whoever's in the patrol car only has to turn and take a careful look to see everything needed to convict both of them for trespassing, lighting illegal fires, who knows what else. Definitely enough to keep them tangled up at a police station until dawn.

The car comes close enough for them to hear the squawk of a radio and an unintelligible mutter in reply. Angela doesn't poke her head up to check whether they've been spotted. She waits, huddled tensely against Chloë in the moving shadow the headlights throw behind the wall. Both of them stay frozen in place as it takes what feels like an age for the car to pass. It must be crawling.

But there's no sudden flash of red and blue lights, no wail of a siren. The cemetery returns to darkness and the engine noise fades with distance.

'Do you think they'll come back?' Chloë asks.

'Maybe. We should hurry.'

Angela takes a quick glance to the east. There are still no traces of pre-dawn light colouring the sky above Harvard Yard. The white half-moon is high overhead, a semi-circle so perfect that its outline might as well have been traced on the darkness with a compass and a ruler. They've got a couple of hours left before the sun comes up to chase it across the sky, but she never feels completely at ease if she's outside when 'last night' starts to creep its way towards 'this morning'.

She wraps the cord back around the stake and slots it into place, then shuttles the bow drill back and forth, faster and faster, picking up speed until her hand becomes a blur. There's a quiet, constant whirring sound as wood grinds against wood. Smoke rises from the tinder.

There are benefits to being what she is. They don't make up for the drawbacks, but they do come in handy sometimes.

'Keep an eye out while I'm making the rounds, OK?' Chloë leans in close, her lips pursed, ready to blow encouragingly on any nascent flame. 'For the police. Don't watch me, watch the road.'

Angela keeps her gaze locked on the smouldering grass. 'All right. What do you think we should do if I see them while you're out there?'

'Run,' Chloë says flatly. 'Leave me behind. I can't stop before it's done. So get yourself out of here.'

Angela's eyes shift towards Chloë, her brows drawn down in puzzlement. 'Running makes more sense than trying to pretend the blinfries aren't ours, sure.' She's very much aware of how great the danger is. Vulnerable vampire indeed. 'But why can't we run together?'

'Oh. Well. I'm raising a lot of energy. If it doesn't go into the spell, it still has to go somewhere.'

'Like where?' Angela frowns as she sees Chloë hesitate. 'Into you?'

'Maybe.'

'So this could, what, electrocute you?'

'Something like that.'

The noise from the spinning stake stops abruptly as Angela's hand goes still. 'Chloë, what the hell? How dangerous is this?'

'Agh, no, you almost had it! Look, it'll only be a problem if this actually works–'

'Which is the whole idea!'

'–and if I give up in the middle, which I'm not going to do,' Chloë continues without stopping. 'I shouldn't have brought it up.'

Angela stands and glares at Chloë, her hands balled into fists at her sides. 'I think you should have brought it up a while ago. Not right before we start, with a casual, "Oh, by the way, I might get zapped if I do this wrong." How bad could this be for you?'

'I don't know. But you're making it sound more dangerous than it is.'

'You just right now said that you don't know how dangerous–' Angela bites off the rest of the sentence. She has half a mind to pack up and leave. She has the bow drill clenched in her hand. If she tosses it back in the bag, the night's over. 'This isn't even supposed to do what we need. It's only asking for advice.'

'I need the advice. We need the advice.' A pleading note enters Chloë's voice. 'This is all I've got. I've tried every protection spell I could find that didn't make me want to throw up. And I am not attempting dark magic again, I learned my lesson with the guinea pig.'

Angela scuffs the toe of her boot across the ground. The grass, wet with dew, squishes beneath her foot like a damp sponge. 'That isn't the point.'

'I've got to find something that works. This might help.'

'There has to be something else. You could use the cards. Or try talking to Esther again, if you can get a hold of her.'

Chloë snorts. 'Because one of them might tell me something they didn't the first ten times I asked?'

Angela doesn't answer. It's true that neither has been of much use. The ancient deck of piquet cards Chloë uses to read the future has proven worthless when it comes to the problem at hand, giving card combinations Chloë translated as either 'seek out the dragon that guards the red path' or 'follow the vanishing tail'. Which probably means something, but Angela and Chloë have no idea what that meaning might be. And Chloë's great-aunt Esther, the only other witch they know, has never been forthcoming with practical advice. They haven't heard from her in months, anyway, not since she took herself off to Timbuktu. Which isn't a metaphor – she went to the actual city in Africa, following some witchy urge. Their options right now, Angela has to admit, are limited.

'Look,' Chloë says, 'we both agreed that this is worth a try, and tonight's our only chance at it. Samhain only comes around once a year.'

And next year, as Angela well knows, will be too late. 'When I said it was a good idea, I didn't realise it could be hazardous to your health,' she grumbles.

'You didn't have a problem with it when you thought you were the only one who might get in trouble. I could have hauled the wood here myself.'

'I can outrun the police,' Angela says obstinately.

'And I can walk around a field. Seriously, that's the only way it could possibly be an issue, if I fail to walk around a field. Can you trust me to do that much?'

Angela wants to say no. None of this seems fair. Not when Angela is the sole cause of the problem. In a just world, she would be the one taking on all the risk.

She kneels back down on the grass and turns her attention to the bow drill. The sound of wood scraping against wood fills the air once again. Chloë gives her a grateful look. Angela's lips tighten. She doesn't think Chloë should feel grateful. Not to her, not for this.

This time, Angela bears down harder and moves faster. It doesn't take long before a small bright glow sparks in the tinder.

'Get it to the kindling, get it to the kindling!' Chloë shouts, then immediately lowers her voice to a hush. 'Come on, let's do this quick, before it goes out.'

After a bit more fumbling and a lot of coaxing, they manage to get the willow fire lit. The fir fire is easy after that, and soon both bonfires are big and blazing, the branches popping and crackling in the heat, showers of sparks cascading down onto the flat stones underneath. The light sends elongated shadows stretching across the graveyard, but they fade into the surrounding darkness well before they reach the other side.

Chloë throws the bones into the flames. The bits of gristle left on their ends quickly start to blacken. 'All right, time to go,' she begins, but before she can say anything more Angela wraps her arms around Chloë and kisses her, holding her close, pressing their bodies together for a long still moment. Chloë warmly returns the kiss.

'For luck,' Angela says when they break apart. 'I love you.'

CHAPTER THREE

Old Burial Ground
1 November 2000

'I love you, too.' Chloë lets go of Angela reluctantly, trailing her fingers across the loose, slippery fabric of the pirate shirt as she steps back. She holds Angela's gaze for a few seconds longer, giving her girlfriend a reassuring smile before she turns to face the fires.

Their heat makes her face uncomfortably warm, though her back remains cold. Smoke rises from the bonfires in two teetering columns, leaning slantwise in the wind at a sharp angle, their bases lit to a grey glow and their tops vanishing into the night sky. It looks almost nothing like a gate, but Chloë can't keep herself from feeling that it is one. After taking one final deep breath, she walks through.

The first steps are the easiest, the way forward clear in the firelight. No chance yet of stumbling on unseen, uneven ground or slipping on the grass. Isolated inscriptions on the tombstones jump out at her. *Here lyes, wife to, departed this life, pale ghastly death hath sent his shaft.* Some words are nearly worn away by time, faint scratches in the tilted, weathered rock. The oldest stones are covered with memento mori, reminders to the living of their own mortality. Winged skulls, crossed bones, coffins, hourglasses. The more recent markers bear different images – cherubs and flowers and faces. People don't want to be confronted by their encroaching death anymore.

Further away from the fires, the carvings become harder to see. Unreadable hieroglyphs, barely visible in the flickering, distant light, or obscured into nothing but murky blankness by the shadows of trees. Once she rounds the corner by the First Parish Church, she can only make out the dim shapes of larger blocks set into the earth, table tombs covering the hidden steps which lead down to the underground vaults.

This is a boundary place, the living above and the dead below. Crossroads where two pathways meet. Tonight the boundary is at its thinnest, and Chloë means to push through. She has a question for whatever waits on the other side.

If they're inclined to answer. If this works.

Chloë's own mortality has been very much on her mind lately. Not because of the potential risk of screwing up the spell, though, no matter how much Angela overreacted. Chloë lets a slow breath out through her nose. That protective streak her girlfriend has can be a royal pain in the ass sometimes. It can take hours of cajoling to convince Angela to bite her. The stubborn, cautious vampire always puts it off until she's on the verge of starvation.

Although Angela has a point when it comes to the biting. It's always a risk, even if Angela never again loses control and drinks far more than she should. Chloë can feel the process sapping away at her, each time her blood is taken.

When Angela hasn't let herself get too thirsty, she usually swallows no more than a few gulps. Much less than a donation at the Red Cross. But even then, the bites leave Chloë feeling weak and nauseous. Drained. There's some unknown chance that someday, after enough exposure to enough bites, they could prove fatal. And there's no guarantee that she'll wake up as a vampire. At least not according to some cryptic hints that were unintentionally dropped by Angela's ex-girlfriend, Tess. No one she fed on before Angela successfully made the transition. So what happened to them instead?

Angela is convinced that if Chloë dies, she's far more likely than anything else to just stay dead. And given how Chloë feels after a bite, it's hard not to wonder how long that's going to take.

That's the real reason dying has been occupying her thoughts. Still, it's a risk Chloë might be willing to take indefinitely, in the hopes that they'll find a solution before it gets to that point. But Angela won't. For her, the end of the year is an immovable deadline.

Chloë's more than halfway around the graveyard now. There's a parking lot across the fence to her left, chained closed at this hour, dark and empty. The eighteenth-century bulk of Christ Church looms ahead of her. It's pretty during the day, a graceful wooden building painted in soft off-whites. At night it's a massive shape blocking the sky, a monstrous crouching creature eclipsing the stars behind it.

She can't rid herself of the nagging worry that this whole ritual will end up being a waste of time. All the preparation, all the risk, and nothing to show for it. Again. It's not that she doesn't believe in the power of the supernatural, not these days. Not considering the things she's seen. But it's hard for Chloë to have much faith in her own flighty, inconstant abilities.

The twin fires come into view once more as Chloë turns and makes her way down the last segment of the pentagon. She can make out the black-clad figure of Angela keeping watch next to them, a silhouette outlined by the glow of the flames. The snaps and pops of burning wood gradually grow louder as Chloë approaches, and she smells a tinge of smoke carried by the cold breeze. She hurries to get the rest of the way there. Angela has got to be bored out of her mind hanging around like that.

Chloë is about to say hello when Angela looks up at her. Chloë's greeting remains unspoken, her mouth left hanging open.

The skin that's visible beneath the black mask is blotchy with rot and decay, like the flesh of a body many years dead. There's a hole next to Angela's mouth the size of a large coin, with brownish teeth grimacing through it. The plastic ghosts tied to the fence twist in the wind behind her.

If Chloë hadn't been mid-stride, she would have ground to a halt. Instead, her raised foot thuds to the ground, her teeth clacking together as it hits. Don't stop, she remembers. Somehow, she raises her other foot without any pause, and brings it forward.

That can't be real, Chloë tells herself. *This can't be happening.* It has to be a vision, a phantasm caused by what she's doing. She hopes it isn't a premonition.

'I don't know what's going on,' Chloë says to Angela – if it is Angela – when she finds her voice again, 'but I think I'd better keep going. I think . . . I think it'll be worse if I stop.'

Angela opens her mouth, black lips peeling back from shrivelled gums. A tongue like a desiccated slug moves inside the cavity, but no words come out, only a dry rasp. Something is moving behind her mask, a wriggling motion that Chloë at first takes for the flickering shadows cast by the firelight. But then she sees the writhing nests of maggots where Angela's grey eyes used to be. The sickly white larvae squirm their way out of the socket. One makes its way to Angela's cheek and drops off, falling to the grass below.

Keep going, Chloë thinks as she makes her way between the fires a second time. *Walk forward, deosil, and don't stop. Keep going.*

As she ducks her head to avoid breathing in a plume of smoke, it suddenly occurs to her that whatever is going on right now, the ritual is working. It's doing something, even if she's not sure what.

Holy shit. She's actually casting a spell.

What she just saw was nothing like the insights she gets from reading the cards, or the commanding power that sometimes comes out through her voice. Those are both in some way prosaic and deniable, no matter the fact that the second one saved her from a couple of violent vampire attacks last year. But this? This is different. This is something irrefutable, something extraordinary and uncanny. Maybe the ritual won't be a waste of time after all.

As long as it doesn't end up permanently putrefying her girlfriend.

It takes a few moments for her eyesight to adjust to the darkness once the flames are behind her. When she can pick out shapes again, she notices there's no longer a fence to her left.

Instead, two rutted paths cross in a landscape of rolling grassy hills, thickly dotted with trees. The red-brick buildings of Harvard are gone. There's nothing across the way but bare branches swaying in the wind.

But on her other side, there's marble and granite as far as she can see. Pillars and columns and obelisks. Monuments and mausoleums, catafalques and cenotaphs, statues of angels. Tombstones dense on the ground like ranks of soldiers. The polished stone shines white or black with reflected firelight close by, and fades into amorphous dimness further out.

It's not so much a cemetery anymore as a necropolis, a sprawling city of the dead. It looks vast enough to hold every memorial stone or sculpture that's ever been carved. In the far dark distance, Chloë thinks she can make out huge structures that might be pyramids. How is she supposed to go around that?

Moving forward is harder now; there's some kind of resistance fighting against her, like she's trying to shove two magnets together the wrong way. Is that something that's supposed to happen? She starts to sweat with exertion, the moisture lying cold and clammy on her skin.

There are half-seen flutters at the edges of her sight, diaphanous glimmers hovering above some of the graves. She ignores them, pressing ahead, moving as if she's underwater.

She can't help wondering if the things she's encountering have a meaning, a message that she's supposed to interpret. Why the necropolis? Has she passed all the way into the land of the dead already? And why did Angela look like that? Was it because of what she is, an effect of her strange resurrection from corpse into vampire two years ago? Angela sometimes calls herself a dead woman walking, when she's in a black enough mood.

The fires swing into view again, on the other side of a peninsula of sarcophagi etched with horses and chariots. There's no sign of Angela at all this time around. Chloë tries not to let it trouble her. It's been obvious to her for some time that wherever she is, it isn't anywhere near where she started. Some part of her is relieved that she hasn't come upon a pile of Angela's bleached bones, the jaw hinging open and shut as it tries to make its voice heard.

The fires are smaller now, the cracked, chalk-white heifer bones poking out from two piles of glowing embers, with only a few sticks of wood left ablaze on top. She tries to pick up her pace again as she passes between them for the third time, forcing her way forward against the inexplicable drag on her feet.

A bell jingles merrily as a door swings shut behind her. She's anticipating a certain amount of weirdness by this point, so she manages to continue without pause along the twisting walkway between the tall shelves.

'OK, you've lost me now,' Chloë says aloud. 'With the symbolism, I mean. If this is symbolism. The pyramids and everything fit the theme, but I'm not getting the books.'

No one answers. Which doesn't really come as a surprise.

The place looks exactly like the kind of used bookstore she likes, a cluttered labyrinth with so many books crowded inside that they overflow the shelves and end up in cardboard boxes or haphazard piles on the floor. She has to step over them to keep going. The air is thick with the scent of old paper and dust. There isn't a window anywhere to be seen. Or walls, for that matter. Only shelf after shelf after shelf. The place doesn't have a ceiling, either, she notices when she glances overhead. The bookshelves rise up into an impossible distance that hurts her eyes when she tries to focus on whatever's beyond it. There's something up there that isn't a colour or black or white. Like it's transparent, but all the way through, with only more transparent behind. She tears her gaze away from the disquieting non-colour of it.

Just as she starts to wonder how she's supposed to navigate clockwise through the maze of connecting corridors, she spots the flick of a cat's tail as it disappears around a corner.

The piquet cards, she remembers, told her to follow the vanishing tail. Over and over again, in every reading that didn't tell her to go find a dragon. It's as good a clue as any, and for that matter it's the only clue she has.

She turns the corner, frowning in thought. During the brief look she got, she was sure she saw bands of grey and black stripes on the cat's tail. Exactly like the markings of her own cat, Entropy. Does that mean something?

She catches further glimpses, always a rear paw or haunch or the tail again, always the moment before it retreats beyond a further shelf. And she follows.

The light is dim and many of the titles and author names are unreadable, but she's able to decipher a few. Prudence Hancock. Margarit Holyoke. As she steps over another pile, she manages to get a clear look at the cover of the volume on top:

SAMUEL SPARHAWK

*Decd Novembr y^e^*

2nd 1713

Aged 49 Years

She's particularly careful not to knock over any of the stacks of books after that.

This place is, if anything, more disorienting to her sense of time than the necropolis was. She has no idea how long she spends walking between the shelves before she hears the distinctive crackling sound of fire and catches the scent of wood smoke.

She doesn't think a fire in a bookstore is a good idea, but it's not like any of the rest of this has made much sense.

She rounds a sharp corner where she recently glimpsed a tail-tip and finds herself emerging into a parlour-like chamber, with small fires dying in two fireplaces facing each other on opposite walls. Her route dead-ends at a book-covered table that nearly spans the room, and she stops short so as not to crash into it before she realises what she's done. She doesn't get zapped by any energy build-up, though, so either that was never going to happen or this is where she was supposed to stop. She has a sneaking suspicion it's the latter.

One of the three women on the other side of the table – the one with the eye – puts down the book she'd been reading without marking her place in it, and looks up at Chloë expectantly.

The one with the mouth uses it to frown. 'Well,' she says. 'It's about time you got here.'

CHAPTER FOUR

The First Witch

You weren't expecting something so Greek, is that what you said? Well, we're not Greek. Or rather, we're not exclusively Greek. We come from many lands. Witches have been around since the beginning of the beginning, after all. Lilith was already going about her business before Eve got out of bed.

Pass me the eye, would you? We should all get a good look at her. Ah, that's better. She's a tall one, isn't she? Yes, yes, I'll hand it over to you soon, sister, there's no need to become agitated. I'm keeping the mouth, though, it's my turn to answer.

Here, you can have it now, I've seen quite enough. Poke me if she does anything disrespectful.

Eh, what was that? What is this place? Is that really what you want to ask, young witch? That was rather a waste of your first question. You don't have very many, you know.

Good, that's good, now you're getting it, keep your lips clamped tight. Don't ask until you know what you need to know. Although I can tell you're just bursting with curiosity, aren't you? All those questions pressing against your teeth, trying to fly out of your mouth. You want to know who we are, don't you? You want to know how many questions you get.

Tell you what, I'll give you that one for free, a lagniappe. That's how kind I am. You may ask three questions. Those are the rules. There are three of us, and we're not about to hand out more than one answer apiece. Any more than that and it'd be nothing but questions, questions, questions all day and all night. We have other tasks that need seeing to. Boiling newts' eyes, hovering through fog and filthy air. It's a packed calendar, I can tell you that.

Now, as to the question you did ask so foolishly, I'll give you the answer in the form of a story.

I'm being poked, so you must have made a rude gesture. Don't be impertinent with me, young witch! I'm doing you a favour. I could give you a straightforward answer if I felt like it. And then it would be entirely useless to you. Try this – you're on the borders of the land of the dead. There, was that helpful? Got you further along in your quest? Chock-full of information you can use? I didn't think so.

Here's a lesson for you: magic is metaphor made manifest. Signs and symbols, sympathy and synchronicity. There's nothing straightforward about it, and trying to make it straightforward is like trying to hammer a nail with a haddock. It isn't the wrong tool, it's not a tool at all. So settle down and listen to your story.

All right, then.

There are as many legends of trips to the underworld as there are peoples upon the earth. The journey has been made by heroes and goddesses and initiates, by voyagers seeking power or knowledge or love. I could tell you the tale of Hercules, or Lemminkäinen, or Blue Jay. But I think the best one for you is the story of Ishtar. She, too, ended up with a lover who was dead but still walked around half the time.

Why are *you* poking me, sister? You can't even see her! You don't have to poke me when she interrupts, we can all hear her talk, we've got six good ears among us and an extra one in the cupboard.

Sister, give our other sister the eye again, would you? I think she's feeling left out.

And as for you – your lover most certainly is dead, for all that she's still gallivanting around up there rather than coming down here where she belongs. You saw that yourself, when you gazed upon her from the other side of the veil. I may not be giving you an exact parallel for your situation, but there is no myth of The Woman Who Agreed to Break up With Her Girlfriend After a Year Because of the Biting. You're going to have to take what you can get.

Where was I?

Ishtar, yes. Thank you, young witch. Now shut up.

Ishtar, goddess of love, goddess of war, goddess of sex, goddess of power, left her lover Tammuz, god of the harvest, to seek the knowledge held only in the realms below. Ishtar turned her thoughts to the road without turning, to the house with no exit, the house of shadows where clay is their food and dust is their wine.

She travelled to Irkalla, the land ruled by her sister Ereshkigal, goddess of the dead. Irkalla was encircled by seven walls, each pierced by only one gate, and each gate firmly locked.

At the outermost wall, Ishtar called to the gatekeeper, shouting, 'Open the gate and let me in! Or I will break the lock, and smash the door, and shatter the doorposts, and bring forth all the dead to drink the blood of the living! The dead will outnumber the living, and rule the earth!'

Ishtar could be a real bitch, sometimes. And she never got along with her sister. Which wasn't entirely her fault, of course; Ereshkigal was a piece of work herself. I think she had some jealousy issues. You can talk as long as you want about how they were two sides of the same person, conscious and subconscious, ego and id, the varying aspects of femininity or what have you, but when your sister is the goddess of war and sex and you get clay for your food and dust for your wine, you're going to think you got a raw deal. That's what I say, anyway. So. Where did I leave off, exactly?

The first gate, that's right. Thank you. Shut up.

The gatekeeper grew frightened at Ishtar's words, and quickly went to Lady Ereshkigal to explain the clamour outside the walls. When she heard that Ishtar was at her gate, Ereshkigal trembled like a tree struck by an axe, and shook like a reed cut by a scythe.

'Why has my sister come here?' she said. 'Does she mean to dwell in the underworld with me? Then I pity the mortals of earth, who will be without love or sex from this time forward! We must let her in, gatekeeper, lest she try to break open the gates of Irkalla, and bring forth the dead to walk the earth. But as you would with any who come here, deal with her according to the ancient decree.'

The gatekeeper returned to the outermost wall, and said to Ishtar, 'Enter, my Lady. Let the palace of the land of shadows rejoice at your presence!' And he opened the first gate.

But as she walked through, he removed the crown from her head. When she asked him why, he replied, 'Such is the decree of Ereshkigal, and the law of this place.'

At the second gate, he removed her earrings, saying, 'Such is the decree of Ereshkigal, and the law of this place.'

At the third gate, she was made to sacrifice her necklace. 'Such is the decree of Ereshkigal . . .' Well, it goes on that way for a while, but you get the general idea. At each gate, she lost more clothing, until she was buck naked and barefoot by the time she finally stood before her sister.

Ereshkigal regarded her coldly. 'Now imprison her in my palace, gatekeeper,' she said, 'and send against her sixty diseases as punishment. Unleash a headache against her head! Unleash pneumonia against her lungs! Trench foot against her feet! Cirrhosis against her liver! Onychogryphosis against her toenails!' Once again, this went on for quite some time, so I'll skip to the end. 'Send diseases against her whole being,' Ereshkigal commanded. 'Her entire body!'

Ishtar was imprisoned in the realms below, plagued by aches and wracked by agonies and suffering from unsightly toenails, and upon the earth there was great mourning. For all mortals slept alone in their beds, and not a one would approach another with desire in their eyes.

I'm going to have to end it there, though. There's not enough time left for the bit about how her lover Tammuz ends up becoming a part-time corpse, or any the rest of it. We're only halfway through the story, but your fires are almost out.

Ow! Sisters, both of you, stop poking me, and you, young witch, be silent and stop making whatever gesture you're making! It's hardly my fault you didn't use enough wood. You should have made the bonfires of sufficient size. I think you've obtained enough of an answer anyway. Yes, that should prove useful to you.

You're right, though, good point, you do get two more questions. I suppose if you can't stay longer, you'll have to ask them when you find your way back to us. Oh, is the All Hallows' ritual the only one you know? See you next year, then, unless you can find a different one.

Although . . . if you ask right now, I might have just enough time to describe another ritual for you before the fires go out. Maybe. Difficult things to predict, fires. It's why I prefer the snow-based rites, myself. They're seasonal, yes, but a good snowfall will last you all night, and sometimes all week or all month.

But you certainly don't have all night this time around. So don't take too long thinking about it, or the decision's going to be made for y–

CHAPTER FIVE

Old Burial Ground
1 November 2000

Angela knows she should run.

Any further delay could easily become lethal. The patrol car is already pulling up to the sidewalk, blue and red lights strobing across the cemetery, turning it into the world's creepiest rave scene. The warning lights began flashing when the police were close to a block away; the fires are barely bigger than candle flames at this point, but they stood out like beacons in the pitch darkness of the Old Burial Ground. Hiding wasn't possible this time around.

Angela keeps her eyes fixed on Chloë. She's so close to finishing the final circuit. So very, very close. Chloë is walking towards the fires with a steady, plodding trudge. The same agonisingly slow pace she's been keeping all night.

Why doesn't she speed up? Can't she see what's going on? Angela checks a nearly overwhelming impulse to run forward and shake her. She has to wait. Otherwise, Chloë might explode. Or whatever is supposed to happen.

Surely Chloë isn't really going to get blown to pieces by magic if the ritual is interrupted, though, is she? All she's been doing is walking in circles. There haven't been any signs and wonders, no graves cracking open, no visitations by the spirits. Whatever the spell was supposed to do, it hasn't done it. So it obviously isn't working. Right?

But then why isn't Chloë running?

Angela keeps still. Somewhere behind her, a car door slams.

Chloë takes another step forward. And then another.

A hand rattles the fence. Someone takes a breath.

Chloë steps between the fires. One goes out almost at that moment, a final puff of smoke rising from it as the last flicker of flame vanishes. Chloë blinks. She looks around as if not sure where she is, and says, 'What . . .?'

Angela ducks down low and runs, ignoring the shouts coming from behind her.

Her shoulder catches Chloë in the midriff. All of Chloë's breath comes out in a whoosh as Angela hefts her into a fireman's carry. She sprints across the graveyard towards the parking lot on the other side, the glare from the police car lights helpfully illuminating the way. Angela zig-zags, aiming to put as many trees and monuments as possible behind her. There might not be any shots fired over a petty Halloween night trespassing, but stupider things have happened. She isn't going to bet Chloë's life on it.

'What's going on?' Chloë asks as she bounces against Angela's back.

'Cops!'

'Oh.' There's a pause while Chloë takes in the situation. Then Angela feels the muted sensation of a fist striking her side. 'You were supposed to leave me behind!'

'Sorry.'

'You're forgiven. This time. Did you – Ow!' Chloë holds off talking while Angela leaps over the barrier wall. 'Did you see it?'

'See what?'

'The spell. It worked.'

Angela nearly stumbles, only her supernatural reflexes preventing her from tripping and dropping Chloë. 'It did?'

Chloë scrabbles at Angela's back as her weight shifts, her fingers clutching at Angela's shirt. 'Um,' she says, 'thanks for the rescue, Dread Pirate Roberts, but I think it's safe to put me down now.'

'As you wish.' Angela stoops down so Chloë can slide off her shoulder. 'We'd better keep going, though. They can't be that far behind us, not yet.' As soon as she finishes speaking, the wail of a siren pierces the early morning silence. The danger is still right around the corner, hidden from view only by a handful of stores and the First Parish Church.

They grab each other's hands and dash away into the back streets of Cambridge. Away from the streetlights, into the shadowy maze of twisting side roads. Out of sight, and hopefully soon out of mind.

Angela feels hope kindle in her chest, as fragile and fluttery as a hummingbird.

The spell worked. She can't believe it. Something happened. After so many months of trying, they're finally getting somewhere.

If Chloë managed to learn something crucial, they might have a future after all.

'What did it do?' Angela asks. 'The ritual, I mean.'

'You didn't see it?' Chloë lets out her words in short bursts, already short of breath from running. 'Weren't you . . .? Nothing happened to you?'

'No, nothing. What did you find out?'

'I talked to one of . . . There were these three . . .' Chloë takes a long pause, her words trailing off. The siren gradually fades behind them with distance, the quieter slap of boots and sneakers against pavement taking its place. 'It's complicated,' she finally says between gasps for air. 'I talked to someone.'

'But did you get an answer?' Angela asks. 'Do you know what we need to do?'

Chloë hesitates again before replying. 'No. Not yet, anyway.'

'Not yet?' Angela echoes. 'Did whoever you talked to point you in the right direction, at least? Tell you where to look?'

'Not exactly. I mean, maybe? I'm not sure.'

Not yet. Not exactly. Maybe. Angela can feel her surge of hope flicker and dim. They don't have a lot of time left. Certainly not enough time for not-yets and maybes. Did Chloë's magic give them anything useful at all?

'It's a long story,' Chloë continues, her voice getting more and more ragged. 'Literally.' She starts to lag behind; Angela slows down while Chloë puts her hands on her thighs and tries to catch her breath. 'I'll tell you when we're in the car, OK?' Chloë says.

'Sure.'

'We need to keep going.'

'Yeah,' Angela replies. 'Tell me later. First things first.'

Chloë straightens up and runs. Angela takes her hand again and pushes their pace a bit faster than before, keeping an eye on Chloë, ready to scoop her up and carry her a second time if she needs to. But Chloë seems to have found a second wind. She's grimacing with the effort, the muscles in her jaw tightly clenched, but she matches Angela's speed.

Angela hasn't heard all the details of what happened yet. Which means, she tells herself, that she shouldn't jump to any conclusions. Surely Chloë found out something important. Something valuable.

Surely she must have.

This ritual might very well have been their last chance. How long will it take to find another spell that works, when it took them so many months to find this one?

So it has to have helped. It has to have brought them closer to their goal. All of their time over the past year, all of their efforts leading up to this point – the endless research, the useless, pointless incantations, the wasted nights digging up plants – it can't have been for nothing. It can't.

Hand in hand, they run together into the darkness. Heading away from the graveyard, towards safety, and towards home.

PART TWO

The Top Of The Axe-Murdering Charts

CHAPTER SIX

Nob Hill, San Francisco
18 April 1906

The inferno burns bright orange against the darkening sky, entire city blocks feeding the flames. It roars like a giant, demented beast. A beast that is devouring San Francisco, building after building stripped down to skeletons, vast swaths of the town charred to ash. By now, the fire must have destroyed more of the city than the earthquake that sparked it.

Glancing behind her, Meijing can see it crossing another street. Embers fly across the gap in glowing fragments, while a foxfire gleam crawls across the detritus on the ground. A strong wind plucks at her stolen clothes, trying to pull her into the maw of the flames. The turbulent air carries a thick, choking haze of smoke. She coughs as she stumbles over a tangle of rucked-up steel. The earthquake has left the cable car tracks as bent and twisted as spilled noodles.

She's exhausted from running too long on too little sleep, and her feet ache in their hastily snatched, ill-fitting shoes. The wind is dry, chapping her lips to bleeding, all the moisture sucked out of the air by the fire. She fights against its relentless tug, struggling up the steep slope, fleeing into the heights west of Chinatown. All the wealth of these hillside neighbourhoods cannot keep the mansions from burning.

No one else is out on the street. Everyone has either fled or been cleared away by the cavalry men. They're no longer riding through this part of town. The fire is too close. At least that means she doesn't have to worry about being shot for looting anymore.

She wasted too much of her day hiding from the soldiers, making herself invisible in the narrow alleys and shattered houses. She'd thought to seek refuge in the Mission on Sacramento Street, although she's been warned that they serve poison and eat babies there. Those rumours, she has little reason to believe. More credibly, she's heard they take in runaway crib girls who are desperate enough to convert to their religion, and listen to lectures about their god in his heaven and the demons in their hell. As if any god cared about Meijing. As if she didn't know about hell firsthand already.

By the time she reached the Mission, however, the building stood empty, damaged by the earthquake and threatened by the spreading conflagration. When she turned east towards the docks, she found all the routes to the bay blocked by fire. Not that it mattered. If she had somehow smuggled herself aboard a ferry, where could she go?

Nowhere is safe. Not for her.

The fire swept west, house by house, block by block. Herding her in front of it, all the way through the Barbary Coast, all the way across the whole of Chinatown and halfway up Nob Hill as the day collapsed into night.

Meijing stops and crouches low to catch her breath, hoping the air closer to the ground will be cleaner. It isn't. She inhales in ragged gasps, fighting to hold in another cough. Coughing hurts; her throat is raw.

A sudden, thunderous boom echoes down the street, and her head jerks up again. Are they blowing up another building? Earlier, she'd seen furniture and bodies tossed fifty, a hundred feet in the air by blasts meant to create firebreaks. She'd wondered if the people in those buildings died before the dynamite went off, or perished in the explosions then and there.

A second boom. Ahead of her, a heap of concrete and brick and plaster that used to be a house shudders as if struck by a giant. Pieces of detritus slide off the top and crash onto the sidewalk. But no one else is here; certainly no one is close enough to set off dynamite. Could it be a gas main rupturing? When the fire reaches it, will it ignite? She backs away, looking for a side alley, trapped between the flames and whatever new danger this might be.

The noise comes a third time, louder than before, and a hefty pile of rock and wood hurtles away from the rest of the debris, flying out in a spray that reaches all the way across the street, leaving deep dents in a mostly intact storefront. A stone the size of her head lands not two feet from her and bounces down the hill like a child's lost ball.

There's a hole in the ground where the pile used to be, and a man crawls out of it. His pallid face reminds Meijing of a worm squirming in a rotten fruit as he emerges from the earth. He pulls himself upright and brushes his hands across his soiled clothes.

Only when a wooden door slams back down behind him does she realise that he's come out of a coal cellar. He was trapped in the coal cellar and he . . . what? Shoved against the door until a mound of wreckage as tall as a carriage gave way?

Who is this?

Before she has time to blink, he is beside her, closing the distance between them almost faster than her eyes can follow. A thin man with dark hair and pale white skin. Silver buttons gleam on his waistcoat, bright against the dark and dirtied cloth, and a matching pocket watch chain crosses his chest. His eyes are reddened like an opium smoker's. She can see the fire reflected in his pupils.

'The judgement of God has come upon this city,' he says, looking over her shoulder at the flames. He reaches up to sweep a stray lock of hair from his face. His fingernails, filthy with grime, are as long and pointed as a wealthy Chinese merchant's. 'None shall escape His wrath. Those who were not crushed in their beds shall burn.'

He smiles widely, showing his teeth, and she sees his fangs.

Fangs. Reddened eyes. The strength to move mountains. And those cannot be long fingernails after all – they are his claws.

He is a *geong si*. A corpse that moves. There can be no other explanation.

She knows that she should be shocked and astonished to meet such a creature. But the only emotion she is able to muster is a faint, dark amusement. Has she survived the roiling earth and the blazing inferno, only to be slain by a creature out of legend? She wants to laugh, but laughing would mean more agony in her aching throat.

'It's beautiful in its way, don't you think?' he continues, his eyes fixed on the burning city. 'Fire purifies as it consumes.'

Meijing doesn't answer. She wracks her mind for the traditional protections against a *geong si*. The blood of a black dog is hardly something she keeps on hand. She is neither a scholar to immobilise the monster with a Taoist talisman, nor a warrior to stab it through the heart with a peachwood sword. There's no certainty that such things would work on a *geong si* of this country in any case; the stories told about them are different here. She has heard that they drink blood instead of breath, and bend their knees when they walk, as mortals do. From all that she has seen of this one, he shows none of the stiffness of a dead body.

She can feel the heat of the fire growing on her back. The buildings on either side of them have started to catch. Burning embers float through the air around her, drifting down like petals to land by her feet, where they glow on the ground for a few moments before they vanish.

His eyes flick down to hers. '*Ni sik gong ying mun ma*?' he asks in halting, badly accented Taishanese. The memorised stock phrase of a man who goes to Chinatown to make purchases or indulge vices, but never to stay for long. Surprised, she doesn't answer, and he frowns. 'Do you speak English?' he repeats in his own tongue. 'You are of no use to me if you speak no English.'

She does, in fact – well enough to follow him. She's had to learn; her white customers do not like being misunderstood. But what can he mean? Of use to him? She needs no English to be his meal.

It is that glimmer of possibility which prompts her to answer.

'I do,' she replies hoarsely. 'I speak English.'

'Good. I have shown you my fangs for a reason. Do you know what I am?'

'Yes.'

He nods to her in acknowledgement. 'I find myself in some small difficulty. My wife has died her second and final death, impaled by a falling timber, and our serving man appears to have suffocated sometime during the day. As have the dogs.' His bloodshot eyes stay placid and unruffled until he mentions his pets; a look of sorrow flashes through them then.

Meijing blinks at him. 'I am sorry.'

He shakes his head dismissively. A trace of impatience enters his tone. 'I am in need of a new servant. Immediately, before the next dawn. While I would not normally wish to rush such matters, these appear to be unusual times. I believe that such an arrangement would be' – he makes a gesture towards the encroaching flames – 'mutually beneficial.'

Meijing abruptly understands. He is in danger himself. That is why she still lives.

His *geong si* wife is dead, and the city is on fire. If she remembers correctly, such creatures need to rest in a dark place during the day.

A cave, or a coffin. Or a coal cellar. Who will protect him from the flames tomorrow while he sleeps?

She is far from certain whether she is being offered a second chance, or tempted to a terrible fate. But she is not burdened with an excess of choices. The last time someone reached out a hand to her, she rejected it. She regrets that now. Surely any risk would have been better than the fire.

Judging by his clothes, he is rich. And no matter what manner of being he is, he could hardly be a worse monster than her previous employers.

Besides, if she says no, she is unlikely to survive very long past doing so.

'I agree,' she says.

No emotion crosses his dead face. 'You may call me Master Hiram.'

'Yes, Master Hiram.' She cannot help glancing to the side, where the buildings are now completely ablaze. The heat is growing unbearable. If they don't leave soon, they will not leave at all.

'I am mindful of the present danger,' he says dryly, 'so I will instruct you in the bulk of your duties at a later time. But I fear I have a sore thirst, and I must drink some portion of your blood before we depart.'

Before she can respond, his arms are clamped around her, and his fangs have pierced her neck. She muffles a shriek and tries to jerk back, but his grip holds her solidly in place.

Some portion of her blood, he'd said. Not all of it. She will live through this, because he needs her.

It hurts, but Meijing long ago resigned herself to that as the cost of doing business.

The neighbourhood burns around them while he drinks from her veins. Not far behind them, a building collapses in on itself, gutted by fire. Flooring and furniture, much of it aflame, spills out of its upper storeys, a chair cartwheeling across the street to the other side.

Abruptly, he releases her, and she stumbles, nearly falling.

'Come,' he says.

Before she regains her footing, he is moving west, away from the burning buildings, holding her firmly by the wrist, nearly dragging her as she tries to keep up. She finally gets her feet under her and runs alongside him, dashing up the steep hill. She should be long past the point of exhaustion, half dead from inhaled smoke and lost blood. But from somewhere, she finds the strength to race towards whatever strange new life awaits.

CHAPTER SEVEN

Brookline, Massachusetts
7 November 2000

'Oh, shit,' Angela says as she slaps Chloë's face. 'Oh, shit, wake up. Come on, wake up.'

Chloë's eyes stay closed. Her breathing is shallow. Angela eases her down to the floor, careful not to smack her head against the sink. Chloë came close to cracking her skull open on it when she passed out. Angela only just caught her in time.

'Don't die. Don't die in a fucking bathroom, that would be stupid, that would be . . .' She needs to stop babbling and do something. Something that works. Something that isn't idiotic, like hitting her girlfriend in the face. Chloë's cheek is reddening where Angela struck her, the imprint of her hand already visible. The slap was too hard, too panicked. She's lucky she didn't break Chloë's jaw. Or stave her head right in. She has to be more careful than that. She always has to be careful.

Did she drink too much this time? She'd been so thirsty; maybe she took more than she thought. What can she do? What can she try? Splash water on her? No, she's got to stop the bleeding before anything else. Trickles of blood are still oozing out of the twin punctures on Chloë's neck. Her life pulsing out of her while Angela dithers.

She leans over and licks the wounds.

The taste of blood almost makes her shudder with pleasure. Warm and wet, rich with iron and salt and something else, something she can't quite put a name to. Three weeks and two days since the last time she fed on Chloë. Why is she even thinking about that now?

'Because I'm horrible,' she whispers. 'Horrible. That's why.'

The fang marks on Chloë's neck are sealing up quickly, responding to whatever strange chemical mixture in Angela's saliva heals the wounds. She doesn't know what to do next. How can she wake Chloë up?

How can she keep her from spinning down into the abyss that swallowed Angela two years ago? Or something worse?

A knock on the door makes her jump like a startled cat, her knee nearly banging into Chloë's ear.

'Are you two OK in there?' comes Mike's voice from out in the hallway.

Angela is about answer, on the verge of saying, *No, nothing's OK, call a hospital, get an ambulance*, when Chloë's eyes flick open.

'We're fine,' Chloë croaks, the words slurring. 'Everything's fine.'

There's a slight pause before Mike speaks again. 'All right. *Buffy*'s going to be on in about fifteen minutes. I thought I should let you know.'

'Is there any news?' Chloë asks, her voice stronger now.

'Not a lot. Some southern states went to Bush. Vermont went to Gore.'

'No surprises there. Thanks.' Chloë turns her head to look at Angela as Mike's footsteps recede up the stairway. 'Sorry I fell over. We might have waited a little too long between – *Oof*!'

Her words are cut off as Angela gathers her into a tight embrace, rocking her gently back and forth, holding her as close as she can. 'Mrfl?' Chloë says, her mouth pressed against Angela's chest. 'Rmph!'

Angela doesn't let go, but eases off enough to give Chloë room to pull back and take a breath. 'Air. Good,' Chloë says. 'Not that I mind the hug, but . . . Hon? Are you, are you crying?'

'I thought you were going to die.' She can feel the tears streaking down her face, dripping off her chin and onto her dress, where they leave dark marks on the velvet.

'What?' Chloë's eyebrows squinch down in bafflement. 'I got a little dizzy, that's all. It happens all the time. And my face hurts for some reason.' She gingerly touches the hand-shaped welt on her cheek. 'But I don't–'

'You passed out! You were out for . . .' Angela realises she doesn't know how much time went by before Chloë woke up. Probably no more than a minute or two. Still too long. Much too long.

'Angela, I'm all right now. Whatever happened, I'm all right.'

'You're supposed to stop me!' Angela's voice rises, an edge of hysteria creeping into it. 'You're supposed to use your magic voice thing before . . . Why didn't you stop me?'

Chloë holds Angela now, her hands buttressing Angela's shaking shoulders. 'I don't know. It comes and goes. Maybe it knew I wasn't really in danger, somehow.'

'You were. You were in danger.'

'I'm fine.'

'You didn't even realise it was happening. You didn't tell me to stop because you thought it was normal. You think this kind of thing is normal now.'

'Maybe. I'll try to be more careful from here on out. I'll cut things off as soon as I start feeling lightheaded, OK?'

Angela shakes her head. 'None of this is OK.'

'We'll figure it out. We've got a lead on getting this fixed now. It's finally starting to come together, we only need to work out what the next step is.' Chloë brushes her thumb across Angela's cheek. 'Your mascara is all over the place.'

'I don't care.'

'Let me get you cleaned up.'

Angela sniffles, and tries to keep back another flood of tears. 'Don't treat me like–' She cuts herself off, shaking her head. 'This is all backwards. I should be comforting you. I should be promising to be more careful, not you. You're the one who fell unconscious. I'm the one who caused it.'

'You're also the one who's upset about it.' Chloë sits back on her heels and lets out a slow breath when Angela doesn't reply. 'All right. If you want to take care of me, you know what I need right now? Some food. I just donated blood. So let's clean up, go upstairs, I'll have some snacks, and we'll watch TV with our friends. We can find out what's going on with the election, and then we'll check out the new *Buffy* episode. Is that all right?' She puts her hand on Angela's knee. 'I think we'll find out whether or not Tara's a demon this week,' she adds encouragingly.

After a moment, Angela nods, and lets Chloë wipe the mascara off her face. She tries not to shift uncomfortably under her girlfriend's ministrations. She'd rather do it herself, but it's quicker this way. It isn't as if she can check for any missed smudges in the mirror.

All the while, one thought keeps buzzing in her mind. The magic failed.

Chloë's magic was supposed to protect her, and it failed.

Angela does her best to smooth her face into calmness as she follows Chloë up the stairs. Her housemates don't deserve to have all of this dumped in their laps on a Tuesday night. No one wants their evening wrecked by a sobbing monster.

Mike mutes whatever news show he was watching when they walk into the living room. He turns to look at them, a concerned expression on his face. Angela halts in the doorway. Did he overhear what the two of them were talking about? She doesn't know how well a werewolf can hear; she's never asked him. Surely he couldn't listen in on a conversation from a floor away, over the noise of the television.

Maybe he's noticed the red mark on Chloë's cheek. Oh, crap – are her housemates going to think that she hits Chloë as well as biting her?

Before Mike has a chance to say anything, Shelly bustles in from the kitchen with a laden tray of snacks. 'Everybody here? I've got sausages for Mike, popcorn for Chloë and me, and lettuce for Sacrifice. Nothing for you, Angela, sorry.'

'She already ate downstairs,' Chloë says. Angela turns to stare at her, but Chloë's plopped herself down on the settee with a bowl of popcorn and doesn't notice. How can she be so flippant about it?

Shelly moves over to the guinea pig cage and Sacrifice emerges from her enclosure, making excited *wheek wheek wheek* noises as she senses the approach of iceberg lettuce. She puts her paws against the side of the wire grid cage, her tiny pink nose twitching. Everyone but Angela watches the adorable mound of white-and-brown fluff dive onto her food.

Angela is watching Chloë, who is rapt at the sight of the guinea pig having dinner. She can't resist the sight of anything small and fuzzy, especially if it's eating or wearing a funny hat. Chloë grins goofily as Sacrifice devours a long green strip of lettuce, and Angela has to repress the urge to rush over, crush her girlfriend in another hug, and cry into her hair.

'I can't believe you never changed her name,' Chloë says.

'By the time we started talking about it, we were already used to it.' Shelly reaches down and scritches her pet's head. Sacrifice looks at her hand suspiciously and drags the precious lettuce further away. 'Who's the little piggy who was too cute to die?' Shelly coos. 'You are! It's you!'

It's a good thing, Angela reflects, that Chloë's hastily aborted attempt at blood magic had a happy ending of sorts. Although it says something about Chloë's cat that instead of keeping the guinea pig, they decided that giving her to a household that includes a werewolf was the less dangerous option.

'Did you know that the two of you made the newspaper?' Mike asks.

Chloë looks up from her popcorn, her mouth full. 'Hm?'

'The *Boston Phoenix*. Two lines in the Police Blotter about drunk college kids lighting fires in the Old Burial Ground. I'm guessing they didn't get a good look at you?'

Chloë swallows the popcorn down. 'I suppose. As far as I knew, I was still in death's used bookstore when they spotted us.' She pushes the bowl aside and leans forward. 'It was pretty disconcerting. One minute I'm talking with the weird sisters, the next I'm upside down with my face smacking up against Angela's butt while she jumps over every fence in every back alley in Cambridge. I bruised my nose.' Chloë rubs the injured protuberance.

'Against Angela's butt?'

'She has a very firm butt.'

Mike tears off a piece of sausage with his teeth and turns to Angela. 'What did it look like to you? When she was with the witches?'

'Me?' Angela drags her attention back to the conversation. She'd only been half listening, her mind on other things. 'It didn't look like anything much. I saw Chloë tromping around the graveyard the whole time.'

'Was she in a trance?' Shelly asks.

'I don't know. What would a trance look like, exactly?'

'Glazed eyes? Shuffling step? Mumbling to herself incomprehensibly?'

'That describes Chloë about half the time, anyway,' Angela says, her lips curving up into a fond smile. 'She gets like that whenever she's thinking about a story idea or a spell.'

'That's fair,' Chloë allows, while Angela ruffles her hair. 'I'm just glad we got away. And that we got some answers for once.'

Answers? What answers? Angela feels the smile fade from her face as her attention strays from the conversation again. She wanders over to the guinea pig cage. Sacrifice has made short work of the lettuce and is romping around in her paper bedding now. The guinea pig pauses to spare a glance at Angela, and then goes back to ignoring her.

This corner of the room is scented by the organic odour of animal fur, almost covering the faint, fading smell of new paint on the walls. Not long ago, Shelly and Mike finally got around to scraping off the black crusts of wallpaper glue and sprucing up the living room. A year behind schedule, but still. Progress. At least some people are moving ahead with their lives.

Angela sees nothing ahead of her but dead ends. Heartbreak in two months unless something changes. Her career will fall apart not long after that, when working from home becomes impossible. She's barely let herself start thinking about that yet. Or about the fact that without Chloë, she'll be back to facing the stark choice between assault and starvation.

She doesn't understand why Chloë's been so optimistic over the last week. What kind of lead does she think she has? From everything Angela understands, the witches talked a lot, but none of it was about anything useful. In the end, it was another failed experiment to add to the list. She shouldn't have got her hopes up when Chloë told her the spell had actually worked. She'd been shattered when she realised that there wasn't any remedy at hand.

She shouldn't have expected one in the first place. Spells and magic have never sat comfortably with her as the best approach to their problems, anyway. They make no sense. How can you rely on powers that act according to unknowable whims? The two of them would have been better off if they'd spent more time gathering facts and data, rather than wasting the year hoping that random rituals would somehow violate the fundamental laws of the universe.

And then one finally did, and it still didn't help.

'Show's about to start,' Shelly says, cutting off whatever Mike had been saying. She reaches for the remote.

'Can we wait until the last possible minute?' Chloë asks. 'It's just, I'd feel better if I see something go to Gore other than frigging Vermont.'

'It is the last possible minute,' Mike says. 'And the polls haven't even closed on the West Coast. We're not going to find out what happens for a while yet.'

Chloë looks unhappy, but shrugs her acquiescence. The sound comes back on as Shelly fiddles with the controls. A talking head on the news comes close to echoing Mike's words, only to be interrupted mid-sentence when the channel changes. Angela makes her way back to the settee and slides in beside Chloë, who wraps an arm around her.

Angela nestles against her girlfriend, resting her head in the cleft between Chloë's shoulder and her collarbone. The steady beat of Chloë's pulse is reassuring.

'You know,' Shelly says over a commercial for Sprite, 'I've been thinking that if we were *Buffy* characters, I'd be Xander.'

'No you wouldn't,' Chloë objects. 'Xander's a jerk.'

Shelly shakes her head. 'Xander's the best one. Everyone else has some kind of special power that protects them. Xander doesn't, but he fights evil anyway. He's the bravest one, because he's a totally ordinary guy. Like me.'

'You fight evil?' Mike asks.

'I would, if I had any idea where to find it. I voted for Ralph Nader – does that count?'

'No,' Mike answers curtly.

'Al Gore and George W. Bush are both in the pocket of the big oil companies –'

He rolls his eyes. 'Al Gore is a left-wing hero.'

'Oh, please. No establishment Democrat is a left-wing hero.'

'You know what?' Mike says. 'Forget I said anything. Why don't we just drop it?'

'I'm sorry,' Shelly says sharply. 'I guess I didn't realise that the best way to handle a disagreement is to never, ever talk about it.'

There's a slight pause before Mike responds. When he does, his voice is a soft growl. 'Let's have this out later, OK? And not in front of our friends.'

Angela thinks Shelly and Mike should count their blessings, if that's their biggest political dispute; Angela's whole family is undoubtedly voting straight-ticket Republican. She hasn't asked outright, but it's a safe bet. In their infrequent letters, her parents usually include recommendations for gay conversion therapies.

To be honest, though, Angela isn't sure her housemates' argument is solely political. But she'll have to keep wondering, at least for now. After the commercial commands them to Obey their Thirst in bulging green letters, it fades away into the show. The four of them fall silent as Tara tells Willow a story about a kitten.

Angela tries to push everything to the back of her mind and watch the programme, lose herself in a different, imaginary drama for a while. It doesn't work very well.

She can't stop picturing Chloë's eyes rolling back, her knees buckling. Blood leaking from her neck as she falls. And then that endless time on the bathroom floor when she wouldn't wake up. When Angela thought she might not ever wake up.

The scene plays out over and over again in her mind. Chloë collapsing after Angela sucked too much of the life out of her. Fed on her, like a tick. Like a vampire.

That can't happen again. That can never happen again. Tonight was a blood-streaked warning sign, and she needs to pay attention to it.

Because it might mean they have even less time than they thought.

CHAPTER EIGHT

Quincy, Massachusetts
8 November 2000

Chloë feels like shit.

She has a throbbing pain in her temples that occasionally spikes up into sharp stabs. Her cheek is tender where Angela slapped her, and there's an ache in her lower jaw that feels like a rotten tooth. That one's a low blood sugar thing, most likely. It tends to show up the morning after Angela feeds.

Lack of sleep is probably what set off the throbbing headache, though. She stayed up far too late last night listening to the presidential race results on the radio in her apartment, waiting for a conclusion that never came. No one knows who's going to be running the country when January rolls around; it hinges on a vote count in Florida so close and contentious that the winner is still up in the air. There's an unsettled feeling to the day, a sense that everything is in a holding pattern, waiting for either a landing or a crash.

Her clothes are a mismatched mess grabbed at random from the floor, and her hair is grimy and sticking out every which way. She crawled out of bed this morning long after her alarm went off. There wasn't enough time to wash. Chloë couldn't have taken a shower, anyway; when Angela stays over, she has to get up before sunrise if she wants to have one in the morning. Otherwise, the bathroom door needs to stay shut while Angela sleeps there, away from any dangerous windows.

Well, not sleeping, exactly. Angela doesn't sleep. But Chloë can't bring herself to think of Angela as 'lying dead in the bathtub'. It makes it sound like Chloë lives in a bad horror film and murdered her girlfriend with an axe. Have there been any queer girl axe murderers? Oh, of course, Lizzie Borden. Right at the top of the axe murdering charts.

Chloë's having trouble focusing on work today, even as she puts a loopy signature on a form rejection letter for *Montezuma's Revenge*, a wacky comedy about the conquistador invasion of Mexico. She doesn't bother to add an explanation for the rejection. Telling this author that his jokes about human sacrifice aren't as funny as he thinks is somewhere near the bottom of her priority list today. It ranks a little bit under her need for an Advil, well beneath her worries about the election, and far, far down below her efforts to get back in touch with the dead witches.

The last one has been obsessively consuming her thoughts for the whole of the past week. She's sure she's on the right track at last, that she's found her best chance so far to fix things with Angela. There have to be clues in the story she'd been told, if only she can be smart enough to put them together. Which, as of yet, she hasn't been.

The few ideas she has keep going round and round, like a snippet of a catchy song replaying until it becomes maddening. Is she supposed to find the seven gates? How? And if she does manage to get to them, then what? Should she demand entrance? Take off all her clothes? Catch sixty diseases?

The headache might be a good start, if catching diseases turns out to be the key, but it's making it a lot harder to figure out the rest of it.

God, how much of her blood did Angela drink yesterday? A pint? A litre? Her girlfriend drinks too much and Chloë ends up with the hangover. There's some kind of deep philosophical truth in that, if she could manage to pinpoint what it is. She tries to come up with something clever involving irony and haemoglobin but gives up when the pain in her head intensifies.

She has to remind herself that it's unfair to blame Angela for how she feels. She'd practically hurled herself at her girlfriend's teeth last night, begging Angela to take a bite before she went insane from thirst. Angela had once again pushed things for much too long before she finally fed.

That's because she hates putting Chloë in danger any more often than absolutely necessary, though. It helps for Chloë to keep that in mind whenever her jaw hurts so much from the low blood sugar problem that her gums feel like they're being knifed. After all, that'll go away as soon as she gets some food in her stomach. She can hold out until lunch. A little bit of discomfort is a small price to pay to keep someone she loves, someone who loves her, from starving.

But man. She really, really wishes she could have taken a shower.

'Morning, sunshine!' Shelly says as she bounds in through the office door. The dress she's wearing is such a bright shade of neon green that Chloë flinches away. She barely manages to keep her hand from coming up to shade her eyes.

Shelly looks her up and down, lips pursed.

'Wow. You look like shit.'

'Thanks,' Chloë tells her dryly. 'I'm so glad you noticed.'

'Didn't get a lot of sleep last night?'

'You could say that, yeah.'

Shelly nods and squeezes past Chloë to get to her own desk, inconveniently placed on the far side of the narrow firetrap office. She refrains from bringing up the other most likely reason for Chloë to be in a bad way, thank goodness, although she has to be aware of it.

It can't be hard to notice that Chloë looks the worse for wear every time Angela drinks her blood. Although admittedly, today the effect is probably more obvious than usual.

'How was the staff meeting?' Chloë asks, printing out another rejection letter. Best to act like she's been getting some work done.

Shelly slides into her seat and boots up her computer. 'Interesting. Very interesting.'

'Oh, yeah? What happened?'

'Barry finally decided who's going to take over when he leaves.'

'It's about time. He's what, eighty?' Chloë had been aware that the long-time Managing Editor was planning to retire, but she hadn't been keeping close tabs on the details. She's still too far down on the company food chain for the intrigues of upper management to affect her much – even if last spring her official position rose from Manuscript Reader to the loftier height of Part-Time Assistant Submissions Editor. The biggest resulting change is that she comes to the office three days a week now instead of only one, with additional work to match. 'Who got picked to take his place?' she asks.

'One of the Submissions Editors.'

'Which one is . . . Wait.' Chloë whips her head around, and immediately regrets it. She holds still until the agony in her skull dies back down a little. 'Do you mean it's going to be you?'

'Yep.' Shelly grins.

'That's fantastic!' Chloë tries to figure out a way to get around the protruding filing cabinets gracefully enough to give Shelly a quick hug. She settles for getting halfway up and reaching an arm across to pat Shelly's shoulder. 'Congratulations! How long have you known? Did you just find out?'

'It's been a possibility for a while, but it wasn't, like, finally final until today. Sorry I didn't tell you before, but I didn't want to jinx it.'

'Don't worry about it.' Chloë sinks back down into her chair.

Slowly, so as not to jar anything. 'This is great. I'm so taking you out for a drink later.'

'I'm the one getting a salary increase. I should be taking you out.' Shelly seems about to say more, but pauses, looking thoughtful.

'Is something wrong?'

'No, not at all.' Shelly's gaze clears and the grin returns. 'Enough about me, anyway. How about you? Any more progress on your, uh, situation?'

'What, since last night? No. No sudden insights, no way to get back to the witches.'

'You'll figure it out,' Shelly says with a confidence that Chloë wishes she found more reassuring. 'What about the rest of your life? Like your book. Are you making any headway on that?'

'And again, no. It's stalled. Too much else on my mind, I guess.' Researching spells has become her full-time job lately. More so than her employment at Compass Rose Books, in spite of her expanded duties there, and certainly more than her embryonic career as a novelist. Her free days are spent reading whatever mildewed tomes about magic she can find and making notes in her witch's gramarye. Waiting for the breakthrough. She sighs. 'Ever feel like your life isn't moving forward at all?'

'Sure. I mean, not right now, with the job stuff and all.'

'Yeah, fair enough.'

'Oh! We'll be able to redo the kitchen with the extra money from the raise. Mike will love that.'

'Good for you.'

'Bigger office, better computer . . . Honestly, my life is pretty great.'

'Your boundless empathy,' Chloë drawls, 'is what makes you such a great friend.'

'Also my modesty.' Shelly waves an admonishing finger at Chloë. 'You mustn't forget my incredible, awe-inspiring modesty.'

'You are without doubt the modestest in all the land.'

'Thank you.' Shelly bows from where she sits.

They both return to work, or rather Shelly works while Chloë mechanically performs tasks while thinking about other things. Her thoughts snag on something the dead witch said to her at the very end, tossed off like it was unimportant. What is a snow ritual, anyway? She's never come across that particular phrase during her research. What would go into one? How would it work? She ponders over it for so long that the words 'snow ritual' lose their meaning, become syllables without substance. Snow ritual. Row snitual. Wons Lautir. Sintouwarl.

When she finally glances up at the clock, it's almost time for lunch. She realises that she'd forgotten about her headache while lost in thought, although that realisation makes it come slamming back. She winces and presses her palms against her eyes.

'Are you all right?'

'Just hungry. Should we go get something to eat?' Chloë asks, rising carefully out of her chair and picking up her handbag. 'I'm kind of running on empty here.'

'Sure. Let's get Mike.'

The hallway is more spacious than the office, and Chloë takes the opportunity to stretch her arms out without fear of smacking them into the walls by accident. 'It just occurred to me – when I finally do submit the book here, it won't be to you after all. I'd always pictured leaning over and dropping it on your desk.' She tries to imagine working next to someone other than Shelly. She can't envision it. 'I'm going to miss you in there. Any idea who your replacement's going to be?'

'Well, about that,' Shelly says evenly. 'You want the job?'

Chloë stops short. 'Hold on. What? Me? Are you kidding?' She turns to look at Shelly, searching for any sign that she might be joking. She doesn't see any.

Shelly swings around to face her. 'Yeah, you. I don't know why you're surprised.'

'You're serious.' Chloë wants to feel flattered, but the only emotion she can muster is guilt over the amount she's been slacking lately. 'I . . . I don't know what to say.'

'You've got a good feeling for books, or you wouldn't have the job you do now. I trust your taste. And I'm going to be the one doing the hiring soon.'

'How long have you had this in mind?'

'Since I started thinking about it.' Shelly looks sympathetic. 'Look, I understand why you might not want it.'

'You do?' Chloë feels left behind by the conversation. She didn't think she'd had enough time yet to decide whether she wants the job or not.

'Sure. I'm not stupid. I know a five-day-a-week, nine-to-five job would drop down the time you have for other things. Your writing. Your research into, you know, all the weird stuff.' Shelly takes a quick glance around the hall, and then continues very quietly. 'And I get that it would cut into the time you have to spend with Angela. A lot.'

Chloë opens her mouth to reply, but can't think of anything to say.

It's true, of course. If she has to get up every morning, instead of the thrice-weekly schedule she's on now, that means she's going to have to be in bed at a reasonable hour every night. A timetable Angela can't possibly follow. As it is, Chloë's work necessitates some awkward shifts in her sleeping habits from one day to the next. A real job, one with a long daily commute to Quincy, would end up leaving very little left for a nocturnal love life. During the late sunsets and early sunrises of a Massachusetts summer, it might mean barely seeing Angela at all.

The job offer is tempting, nonetheless. It'd be nice to have a stable career for once. She could certainly use the money; she hasn't had a subletter since Ari left last year, and despite the increase in her work hours, she's barely been making rent. But if it means there's never time for more than a quick nightly kiss as Angela wakes up and Chloë drops off to sleep . . .

'There's no reason you have to make a decision right away,' Shelly says. 'Take a while to think about it.'

'Thanks. I don't know what I'm going to – I mean, I'm pretty sure I'll need the time.'

Shelly flashes her a quick smile. 'No problem. But I hope you can take it. I'd like to give you the raise.'

She turns and strides down the hallway, heading towards Mike's desk, already throwing back suggestions about where they should go to lunch. Chloë follows after, her head throbbing more and more with each step.

CHAPTER NINE

The Castro, San Francisco
8 November 2000

Meijing nudges the corpse with her toe. It squelches unpleasantly, and rolls back into place when she pulls her foot away. Well. So much for that.

It's always such a bother when they die. Although she supposes it's easier to deal with than the alternative, in the long run.

She studies the dead girl's face, the empty eyes staring glassily at nothing. It hadn't been a bad face, once. Perhaps a little sharp featured, the nose longer and pointier than the ideal. Somewhat rat-like. She'd had her good points, though. The heroin addiction had been a pleasant change. It made for a mellow few years. Cocaine was the drug of choice during the eighties, and Meijing spent that entire decade feeling jittery and out of sorts.

She walks over to the pegboard to make sure the tools are in place, running her fingers down the ones that she'll require. Butcher knife, boning knife, cleaver, mallet, pliers. Belt sander for the fingertips. It wouldn't do to leave any fingerprints intact. She will have to fetch the bleach down from the kitchen, and some plastic bags as well. Best to have all the equipment she needs on hand before she starts. Everything necessary to transform the body into something untraceable and unidentifiable, to erase that sharp-featured face from the world.

Her memories of the girl are all so fresh right now; it seems impossible that a time will come when she'll struggle to remember what Tiffany looked like. But after a decade or so passes, Meijing will in all likelihood find her difficult to picture. How many have there been, over the years? Forty? Fifty? The first few are vivid enough. Shy Pearl, cranky Ephraim, handsome Ramón. Not long after that, though, they all blur together, a murky sea of half-remembered fragments, the shape of an eyebrow, the sound of a sneeze or a laugh.

Except for Tess, of course. Meijing absentmindedly fingers the earring dangling from her left ear, the one shaped like a serpent. Feisty little Tess. That one she will never forget. But the rest are only human.

Enough delay. It's fitting to give due regard to the dead, but unwise to waste too much time. A corpse in the basement is a problem that needs to be dealt with before the leaking fluids stain the flagstones. She has a hard task ahead of her as it is. She doesn't need to add any extra scrubbing to it.

She turns away from the body and makes her way over to the stairs, brushing by the locked iron entrance to the chamber where Master Hiram spends his lifeless daytime hours. It's a good thing the girl won't be coming back from the dead; there isn't any chance he would have missed seeing the signs, not when the path to his bedroom takes him directly past the place where they're storing the body. It was easier for Meijing to keep secrets in the last house they lived in, and the one before that. Next time they move, she will have to convince Hiram to choose one with a more convenient arrangement of rooms.

At the top of the stairway, she finds Habakkuk waiting behind the door, his eyes large and expectant. She gives his head a scratch as she passes, but shuts the door firmly in his face before he has the opportunity to dodge around her. He whines, but she cannot let him trot down to the fragrant pile of meat rotting on the basement floor. The days when disposing of a body meant feeding it to the animals is long past. The modern world pays more attention to details. Letting the Dobermans bury the bones in the back garden would be a poor idea in this suspicious age.

The dogs they've had over the years remain vivid in her memory, every last one. They last a good deal longer than the humans, so there haven't been as many.

She finds Hiram reclining on the chaise lounge in the drawing room. He's wearing nothing apart from a brocade dressing gown. Untied. His fish-belly white body is all too visible. His dark hair sticks up in scraggly tufts, unwashed and uncombed. All this when the sun has already been down for hours.

He doesn't look up as she enters. His eyes are fixed on the two slender needles he holds in front of him, one in each hand, their tips rotating around each other in a slow dance above the flame of the spirit lamp. Suspended between them, a small lump of opium paste stretches like taffy and turns golden. He manipulates the needles with practised expertise, his fingers deft and dexterous in spite of their long, sharp nails.

'Tiffany is dead,' Meijing announces without preamble.

Hiram still doesn't bother to raise his eyes. 'As she has been for several days. Does this merit an interruption of my quietude?'

'I meant that she will not be coming back.'

No answer is immediately forthcoming. She waits while he cooks the narcotic, her jaw clenching with barely concealed impatience. The needles spin, around and around.

Quietude indeed. He's spent the past few nights rooted to this very spot, inhaling pipe after pipe of the drug, struggling to achieve the paltry high that one of their kind can get from smoke alone. He acquired the taste for it before Meijing met him, perhaps even before he rose from death to become an undead creature. Half of San Francisco must have had the habit back then. And Hiram is, above all else, slow to change his habits.

'I was aware of your meaning,' he eventually replies. 'Mortal men and women are formed of dust, and unto dust they shall return.'

He wraps the paste back into a lump and pokes it into the bowl of his pipe. Inverting it over the fire, he sucks greedily at the stem until the last of it is gone. His eyes close while he holds the vapour in his lungs. Meijing continues to wait. Long minutes will pass before he bothers to exhale.

She wonders when she started to despise him. Was it as far back as the Great Crash of 1929, when his fortune collapsed and his addictions became uncontrollable? Or sometime in the decades after, when she painstakingly restored their investments and rebuilt their lives, all by herself?

At some point in their long, long history with each other, she stopped needing him. But he still needs her.

And that means she cannot leave.

Finally, he breathes out, a cloud of smoke pouring from his mouth and nose. 'Why do you wait? Go and take care of it.'

'You could help for once,' she snaps without thinking.

She clamps her mouth shut, too late. His full attention is on her now, his eyebrows drawn down, his lips a thin hard line. He half raises his torso off the chaise. Speaking intemperately was a mistake. A bad one.

He is never so lost in his opium haze that he is willing to accept impertinence.

'Am I to do domestic chores now?' he asks softly. 'Shall I perform all tasks, within the household and without?'

She can feel the tendrils of his control binding her to him more tightly, icy and wet like the tentacles of some cold-blooded creature pressing through her skull. A sharp stab of pain behind her eyes makes her vision darken and blur.

'No, Master Hiram,' she says, hating that her voice shakes, ever so slightly, because of the agony within her head. *This is not the time to fight*, she tells herself. Not in a direct confrontation, not when he remains so much more powerful than she is.

'Do I make myself clear?'

'Yes, Master Hiram.'

'You understand your duty?'

'Yes, Master Hiram.'

'Good,' he says, the word a curt dismissal. 'Go do it.'

Her legs march her out of the room as if under their own volition. Before she is out the door, he has sunk back down again, and another lump of opium is already clinging to his needles, heading for the flame.

Once she is out of his sight, the pressure lessens. The pain vanishes, and her legs come back under her control. It was a light disciplining, not the endless torment he inflicts when he is maddened with fury. But the onus he has laid upon her still batters at her thoughts. She must see to the corpse.

She won't resist his will, not now. It would be foolish to expose how much his power over her has weakened. She must bide her time and wait for the proper moment. This is not that moment.

'*Leen hao*,' she mutters under her breath when she is certain she is out of earshot. It's far from complimentary. The one small act of rebellion she will allow herself. She grabs the bleach and the plastic bags, and heads back towards the basement. Habakkuk is still loitering in front of the door. His tail thumps the ground when he sees her.

Go away, she thinks at the dog. *Scram. Play with your brother.*

Habakkuk bounds off to find Nimrod. Meijing smiles in

satisfaction as she descends. He obeys her thoughts more readily now than he did only a year ago. Her strength is growing. Her time will come.

What are a few decades, more or less, to one like herself? She can afford to be patient.

She takes the pliers and the mallet from the pegboard, and hums a little tune to herself as she starts smashing Tiffany's teeth.

CHAPTER TEN

South End, Boston, Massachusetts
13 November 2000

'Djcum by cah?'

Angela blinks. 'I'm sorry . . . what?' She trots up the stairs after the woman from the rental agency, trying her hardest to puzzle out what question she's being asked.

Her interrogator is plump, white-haired, and wears a puffy medical eye patch that makes her look vaguely piratical. She also has the thickest Boston accent Angela's ever heard. Rapid-fire staccato syllables with hardly an R to be found.

'How'dja get downtown? By cah, by the T, what?' The rental agent stops halfway up the stairwell and spins around, her good eye sweeping Angela up and down, taking in the long skirt, spiky jewellery, and heavy eyeliner. 'Not on a bike, I'm guessin', right?'

Angela bristles a little at that. A goth-girls-are-weirdos lecture is the last thing she needs today. 'I came on the Green Line. I didn't think I'd find a place to park.'

'Good thinkin'.' The woman turns around and starts going up the steps again. Either she didn't notice Angela's reaction, or she doesn't care. 'The street pahking sucks, and the place don't come with a spot, don't ask me why 'cause it's stupid, but the buses come all day and it's wicked easy to get around on the T. So if you wanna go shoppin', clubbin' – you club, right? I mean, I'm right, yeah?'

'Yes.'

'Thought so. I don't, I'm too old. I'm tellin' ya, a walk-up like this one would kill me on accouna my knees. But it's only three storeys, you and your girlfriend should be fine. Young lungs. You don't smoke, I'm thinkin', right?'

'I do. Sometimes.'

'Good,' the woman says without missing a beat. 'Too many kids today, it's all, "Oh, no, I can't have any fun, I might die." Live a little until ya do, am I right? Anyway, what's a few flights? I gotta tell ya, it's amazing this place is available at all. Someone died. I'm Moira.'

It takes Angela a few moments to realise that the last two words constituted an introduction. 'Oh. Pleased to meet you. My name's Angela.'

'Yeah, Chloë told me. She's been lookin' around since five. Sorry we didn't wait up, but I'm pushin' it late as it is. You can't come durin' the day, though, yeah?'

'That's right.'

Angela wonders what excuses Chloë made for her, and readies herself to give vague answers to any questions Moira might ask about some fictitious day job. None come, however. The rental agent produces a set of keys and opens a door off the landing on the top floor.

'Chloë, you still inside?' she calls into the apartment. 'I brought Angela up.'

'Hi!' Chloë pops her head around a doorway further in. Her eyes are bright and wide with excitement. 'Thanks, Moira. Angela, what do you think? Isn't this place great?'

'It's old, but, ya know.' Moira gestures expansively. ''S got plenny a chahm.'

Angela takes a glance at the room. Clean white walls with decorative moulding, thick blue carpet, old-fashioned radiator. There's a rounded nook bulging out of one corner, with windows looking onto the street. It's nicer than Angela's small basement bedroom. It's certainly nicer than any of the rooms in Chloë's place. She can picture where the furniture might go. Her work desk against the wall across from the doorway. An armchair in the little nook, where Chloë could read during the day, when the afternoon light slants through the glass.

'Come see the kitchen! There's something I want to show you in here.' Chloë pulls her head away, disappearing from sight.

Angela walks into the next room. Moira follows after, chattering about the countertops. Angela doesn't pay much attention. The kitchen looks fine as far as she can see. Long and narrow, with a gas stove and a dishwasher. Neither of those matter much to Angela; the kitchen fixtures, obviously, don't affect any of her needs.

Chloë walks past the appliances without comment. She stops at the far wall, next to a white-painted door that she opens with a flourish. Angela peers through and sees a small room whose walls are lined with shelves from floor to ceiling. A bare light bulb hanging from a cord is its only other feature.

'A pantry,' Chloë says. 'A nice, deep pantry.'

'Oh, ya like that?' Moira asks, sounding surprised. 'I guess it's kinda nifty if ya do a lot of cookin'. Dry goods, cans, plenny a shelf space. Do ya cook? I tried makin' jam once, but it was borin', so I collect Depression glass. 'S got uranium in it.'

'It's big enough that someone could *lie down in there*.' Chloë looks meaningfully at Angela. 'If anybody had a reason to.'

'OK, now I gotcha,' Moira says before Angela has a chance to respond. 'Yeah, no windows. Totally dahk. Put a cot in it, ya got a nice little place to sleep if the sunlight bothers ya. 'S illegal, 'cause of the fire codes, but' – Moira shrugs – 'if ya need it, ya need it.'

Angela turns to the rental agent. 'Um, Moira? Do you mind if Chloë and I talk about the apartment alone for a little while?'

'Knock ya'selves out. Don't take too long, though, on accouna I got a dog at home.' Moira shuffles out of the kitchen, and soon can be heard humming to herself in one of the other rooms.

When Angela looks back at Chloë, her girlfriend is bouncing up and down with enthusiasm. 'Isn't this fantastic? It would solve so many of our problems! And Moira, isn't she great?'

Angela cracks a smile. 'She certainly is a character.'

'I found her agency in the Pink Pages. She told me she's been renting apartments to lesbians for so long that they weren't called lesbians when she started. I asked what the word used to be and she reeled off a whole list – I didn't even know "homophile" was ever a thing. But anyway, all this space, and this building! It's a real South End brownstone! Did you see the stonework around the front door? And look how high the ceilings are! What do you think?'

'Well . . .' Angela hesitates, not wanting to spoil Chloë's mood. But it's already too late – the bouncing stops as soon as she hears the doubt in Angela's voice. 'I just . . . I don't know,' Angela continues. 'I've been wondering since I got your phone message why we'd be looking at this place right now.'

'What do you mean?' Chloë looks honestly taken aback. 'You hate where I live. So do I. Your room's too small for us, and you've got housemates. We've been talking about finding somewhere better since, what, April?'

'We've talked about it some, sure, but . . .'

'Look, I know this isn't perfect – you haven't seen the windows in the bedroom yet, they're huge and it'll be a pain to cover them over. But other than that it's pretty great. It even allows cats!'

'That's, I mean, that's good, but . . . we can't possibly afford something in this part of town, can we? This place must cost a fortune.'

'Oh, is that what you're worried about?' Chloë visibly relaxes. 'I don't think that'll be a problem. If I take the new job, then between the two of us, we should be able to swing it.'

'I thought you hadn't decided about that yet.'

Chloë nods, the excited light in her eyes beginning to rekindle. 'Because of the timing issues, yeah. But living here would cut an hour off my commute, so I could stay up later and spend more of the night with you. Still not ideal, but at least we'd be able to see each other some.'

'Chloë–'

'I know we could look for a cheaper place down in Quincy, which would be even closer to my job,' she continues without stopping, 'and we can definitely think about that, if you want, but I thought living there would make it a pain to get anywhere else in town–'

'Chloë!'

'–because it's off in the middle of . . . nowhere . . . and . . .' She finally peters out, her words staggering to a halt as she loses her momentum. 'What's wrong?'

'I might not have a job next year.' Angela grinds out the words reluctantly. 'And I don't think you'll be able to pay the rent here by yourself, whether you take the promotion or not.'

It isn't something she's confessed aloud before. Not ever, not to anyone. As if saying the words would somehow make them more real. But that's stupid. A ridiculous superstition.

'Is that what's got you so anxious? Because I think that's probably only nerves,' Chloë says, her chatter getting back up to speed. There's an obliviously empathetic look on her face. 'You'll be fine, because you're brilliant and somebody's going to notice that. I know the academic job market is tough right now, but you're applying for, what, ten different fellowships? Twelve? You'll find something.'

'That's not guaranteed. And that's not the only problem.' Angela's throat feels dry. She wants the conversation to end. 'Even if I get a job, even if it's somewhere around here, I won't be able to take it.'

Chloë hesitates. 'Why not? Do you mean . . . Is it because . . .?'

'Because I can't go out in the daylight!' Angela says at a near-shout. 'I can't walk to work without catching on fire, or disintegrating, or whatever the hell would happen to me!'

That came out louder than she'd intended. She clamps her mouth shut, far too late, as Chloë shoots a nervous glance past her.

In the sudden silence, Moira can be heard humming 'I Put a Spell on You' somewhere else in the apartment. Chloë grabs Angela's wrist and drags her into the pantry.

Reaching up, Chloë yanks the chain on the light, setting it swinging, and pulls the door shut with a click. The moving light bulb makes odd shadows rear up from the shelves and crouch back down. Smaller shadows crawl back and forth across Chloë's face.

'Come on,' Angela says in a hushed voice. 'Are you telling me it never occurred to you that this would be a problem?'

'It crossed my mind a couple of times,' Chloë answers, equally quiet. 'Of course it did. But since you've been sending out all those applications, I figured you had it taken care of. That we'd be able to keep going the way we are now, with you working from home.'

Angela shakes her head. 'No.'

'You never said anything.'

'I know.'

'I thought that if you were worried about it, you'd have–'

'You're right. I'm sorry, I should have been . . .' She should have told Chloë ages ago. It might have prevented what's happening now. 'I've barely been able to get away with it as a student. It was hard enough to convince my advisor to let me do this long-distance, independent thing in the first place, and ever since then, I've had to make up excuse after excuse to miss conferences, meetings . . . I'll never be able to manage it after I graduate.'

Chloë takes that in, her brow furrowing in thought. 'You can't know that for certain.'

'I do.'

'Tell them you're sick,' she suggests. 'Some kind of rare skin condition.'

'If that would have a chance of working at all, don't you think they'd want a doctor's note? Something more than my word that I can't act like a normal person?'

'OK, so I haven't considered every possible difficulty in the last twenty seconds–'

'I have,' Angela says firmly. 'I've had plenty of time.'

'Well, I just found out it's going to be a problem, and now that I have, let's think it through.'

Angela should have known that Chloë would take it this way. Sometimes it seems like her girlfriend only has two modes – bleak hopelessness and relentless optimism. Angela's wondered, on occasion, if the optimism is meant to be some kind of bulwark against Chloë's other, darker moods. If she doesn't want to allow so much as a trace of despair to get in, for fear the depression will come rushing back after it in full force.

It's not that Angela prefers Chloë to be depressed. She absolutely doesn't. But right now the rose-coloured view is hard to listen to. More schemes that won't work. More plans doomed to failure.

Maybe that's why Angela never brought it up.

'There's no point to thinking it through,' she tells Chloë. 'There isn't any way.'

'There's got to be something.'

'Chloë–'

'Other vampires have to deal with this somehow, right?'

'Chloë, would you–'

'And we've got until sometime next year before it becomes an issue, right? So whatever the answer is, we'll work it out together.'

'You and I might not be together next year!' Angela snaps.

Chloë falls silent. Her eyes have gone wide again, this time with shock.

'Have you forgotten?' Angela continues. 'End of the year. I leave you, so you don't fucking die.'

'I haven't forgotten,' Chloë whispers.

'Then what are you doing? What are you talking about? Why are we *looking at an apartment*?'

'I thought . . . I thought we might as well act as if things are going to work out. Not think about, I mean, not focus on . . . I've got a lead now.'

'How much progress have you made on that since Halloween?'

Chloë's lips tighten.

'Anything at all?' Angela persists.

A sudden knock on the door makes both of them jump.

'Ya girls about done with whatever ya up to in the pantry?' Moira asks from the other side. 'It's just, I got a budgie at home I need to feed.'

'Sorry!' Angela calls out. 'We'll only be another minute!'

They listen as Moira shuffles away, mumbling something that fades from incoherent to inaudible as she goes.

The light bulb is still in motion, making small slow circles above them. Angela reaches up and stills it. She looks anywhere but at Chloë. The shelves are painted white and the whole room smells faintly of dust. There's a spider the size of a quarter on the back wall, frozen into stillness by their presence. Waiting for them to get out, so it can proceed with its business.

'We should leave,' Chloë says. 'Have this conversation somewhere else. So she can take care of her dog or bird or whatever.'

'I'm going to go to Phoenix. I think maybe I can get some answers there.'

More silence answers this pronouncement. She counts Chloë's

heartbeats in the quiet. Soft thumps in her lover's chest. It seems to be Angela's night for saying things aloud she'd only been thinking about. She hadn't even known that she'd made a final decision about going, not until the very moment that she said it.

She counts ten heartbeats before Chloë says anything.

'Tess is dangerous.'

'Tess is the one other vampire we know,' Angela counters, turning her eyes back to Chloë. 'There's a chance she might have some idea of what to do. Maybe I can get her to tell me.'

'Or maybe she'll try to murder you. She does that, remember?'

'I can handle Tess,' Angela says with more confidence than she feels.

'Well,' Chloë says grudgingly, 'if you think . . . I mean, it's true that she probably knows more than we do. About the biting. And about how to handle the daylight, too, maybe.'

Angela has her doubts about the second one; Tess was always terrified of the sun. But she lets it pass. If it helps get Chloë on board with the idea, Angela won't argue the point. 'My thesis advisor's been bugging me to come down there, anyway, to check in with him in person for once.' She attempts a smile. 'So I can get the trip paid for by the university. Full funding to solve our personal problems, as long as I'm willing to egregiously misuse Arizona State's money. Which I totally am.'

The bare ghost of an answering smile appears on Chloë's lips. 'All right. I guess I'll have to miss some work–'

'I don't want you to come.'

Chloë stops short. 'What?'

'You said yourself, Tess is dangerous. I'm pretty much invulnerable. You're not.'

'That's ridiculous. You're not invulnerable to other vampires, it's like the one thing we know can hurt you. And I'm not afraid of her.'

There's a mulish expression on Chloë's face that Angela recognises all too well. 'I've taken her on before.'

'Using a power you don't understand and can't control.' A power that didn't work the last time she needed it, last week in the bathroom, when Angela drank her blood until she collapsed on the cold tile floor. 'And you need to be able to talk to use it. What if she gets behind you and breaks your neck before you have a chance to speak?' Angela can see that Chloë is about to say more, already has further arguments marshalled for her case. She rushes on before Chloë finds an opportunity to bring them up. 'Look, the whole reason for going is to find a way to protect you. And of the two of us, you're the one she's seriously attacked before.'

'She did worse to you than she ever did to–'

'Chloë, if you get hurt because it turns out I had a stupid, dangerous idea, if you . . . Please. For me. So I don't have to worry that I'm going to get you killed.'

Chloë's expression softens, and she wraps Angela in her arms. Angela leans her head against Chloë's chest and tries not to cry.

She can't keep herself from picturing Chloë's body, broken, mangled, bleeding. It's far, far too easy to imagine it. And it doesn't require Tess standing over her with blood on her lips to complete the scene. Angela's seen Chloë bleed, and been the cause of it herself. Many times over.

All of Angela's anger tonight has been misdirected. It isn't Chloë's fault that Angela will have to leave astronomy. It isn't Chloë's fault that they're going to break up. It's Angela's fault. All of it.

They're still holding each other when Moira starts pounding on the door again.

'We'll have to finish talking about this later,' Chloë murmurs. Angela nods assent, but she already knows that she's not going to change her mind. Chloë can't come with her. Angela has to keep her safe. She has to keep her away from danger, away from Tess.

And if things go badly enough, Angela reflects, *and I never come back at all, maybe that's another way to fix things.*

One way or another, she'll protect Chloë from vampires. Both the one who hates her, and the one who loves her.

CHAPTER ELEVEN

Somerville, Massachusetts
14 November 2000

Chloë clicks off the radio. Nothing much has changed. Palm Beach County is delaying its election recount. Miami-Dade is starting theirs. She wants to keep abreast of the news, but it's hard to maintain an interest when all she wants to do is crawl back under the covers. There will come a day – there must come a day – when she wakes up and hops out of bed feeling refreshed and invigorated. Today is not that day.

There's a noisy, dark-grey static hovering at the edges of her thoughts. She can hear it there, readying itself to grow louder. To spread across her mind and take up all the space there is inside her head.

Yesterday's argument over Angela going to Phoenix swallowed the rest of the night, and remained unfinished when they both collapsed in separate rooms at dawn. It's become their biggest disagreement since . . . well, since last year, when Angela bit Chloë for the first time and they broke up.

Angela remained unwavering in her position the whole night long. She wants to go and see Tess. She wants Chloë to stay home.

The fight reminded Chloë uncomfortably of her fights with her parents, or her ex-husband; Angela clung fiercely to a pre-determined conviction that Chloë was the one in the wrong. Chloë has a sneaking suspicion that when they were sniping at each other about magic and the three witches, Angela stopped just short of calling her irrational. Although it was difficult for Chloë to make a case against that when her counter-argument boiled down to, 'I've got a hunch.'

Her witch's instincts, those rare, strange urges that nudge her in the right direction, are real and have helped them before. The only trouble is, it's impossible to tell the difference between a magical impulse and a completely meaningless one. So is her hunch real, or is it wishful thinking?

How can she possibly know which of her urges are important and which ones aren't? Whether it's her witch's intuition telling her to steam some asparagus for dinner tonight, or simply hunger?

Across the room, the special box Chloë reserves for magical books and supplies sits closed and waiting. It's an iron-bound wooden trunk covered with heart and flower stickers, helpfully labelled 'MAGICAL SUPPLIES' in black Sharpie marker. She was the one who added the label, but the stickers came with it when she scavenged it off the street after the Tufts students moved out for the summer.

It'll have to sit and wait a while longer, unless it plans on telling Chloë exactly what it wants from her. Right now she's not feeling too thrilled with her stupid magical instincts and their stupid lack of specificity.

Much as it pains Chloë to admit it, Angela made a lot of good points last night. Tess's fangs may be able to pierce through another vampire's nearly impenetrable skin, but Angela is capable of duking it out with her blow for blow. Chloë can't say the same for herself. What abilities she does possess haven't done much good so far. Stories and mysteries, riddles and games. Nothing that will protect her, nothing that's given them any information they can use.

It's especially hard to win a debate when you keep agreeing with the other side's reasoning.

She glances up at the bathroom door. Angela will be in there for a few hours yet, unmoving, unresponsive, and unable to talk. There's nothing to be done until then, and Chloë has plenty of other things she could be doing. It'd be great if she could sketch out a plot outline for the second half of her novel. Which is something she should have done before she got started on the first half. But she didn't, and now she can't progress any further until she figures out what happens next.

She taps her pen against her notebook, shifting to move the page into the square of weak sunlight streaming through the window. Entropy wanders over while she stares at the page and butts his head against the side of her leg. She strokes his flank, and he promptly rolls over to expose his belly.

'Oh, no, you're not fooling me with that one again,' she tells him. Sharp claws await any who would dare. 'So. Any chance you're going to tell me what you were doing in the land of the dead? If that was you. I don't suppose you've got any fabulous mystical secrets to relate?'

She waits. His purr and his soft white deathtrap of a stomach offer her no hints.

Trips to the underworld have been much on her mind lately, for obvious reasons. She's spent a lot of time tracking down all the stories about it that she can. Mostly, they don't end well.

She's read about Orpheus, turning his head to see his beloved Eurydice fading away. Gilgamesh, who tried to conquer death but couldn't even conquer sleep. Izanagi-no-Mikoto, who wanted to see his wife again, and found her transformed into a maggot-ridden mass of decaying flesh. There are a lot that go like that.

Ishtar, she's discovered, managed to escape eventually. But only by making someone she loved take her place down there, so it wasn't the kind of happily-ever-after ending you'd celebrate with a party.

Chloë draws some doodles on the page. A plot outline does not miraculously spring forth from them. She needs to concentrate. She has a book to write.

Somewhere above her, her upstairs neighbours start one of their periodic bouts of noisemaking. Deep rhythmic thuds that make the windows rattle. Their timing is as perfect as ever, right when she's trying to get started on something.

Her doodle turns into seven concentric rings. She draws a little gate on each one.

There are a few exceptions to the 'unhappy ending' rule. Pwyll ended up becoming best buddies with the king of the underworld. Odysseus took the opportunity to have a chat with his mother, which Chloë thought was kind of sweet.

What did you do during your perilous quest through the realms of death, great hero?

I saw my mom.

Aw, how did that go?

She told me she died because she missed me so much and I never wrote.

Honestly, that's what she said. Chloë had found a certain comfort in learning that moms have been laying down the guilt trip for at least three thousand years.

But rare exceptions aside, for the most part the message in the myths has been clear, going back to some of the earliest stories ever written down. The dead have no place among the living, and the living have no place among the dead. Which means that taking the journey down below is a bad, bad idea.

The same could be said about a lot of things, though. Travelling alone to see a murderous vampire, for example.

A particularly tooth-jarring thump from up above breaks Chloë out of her reverie. She glances down at her notebook and is surprised to find that she's continued to draw on the page while her mind strayed. Her pen has sketched an abstract shape next to the outermost gate. If she squints, it looks like some kind of sharp-toothed creature with a long, serpentine tail.

While she peers at it, Entropy takes the opportunity to make a grab for her pen, which is probably what he wanted all along. She lets him have it, and he gnaws happily on the end she likes to gnaw on herself.

Did her scribble come out that way for a reason? Is it supposed to mean something?

Chloë puts the notebook aside and stands up. Work on her novel clearly isn't happening. Not today.

She picks her way across the living room, aiming for her magical supplies box. Getting across the room isn't as difficult as it used to be – she's cleaned up the apartment quite a bit over the past year, and with the exception of the clothes heaped on the bedroom floor, it no longer resembles a city dump after a tornado strike. The improvement is limited, however; she lives in one of those grotty old pestholes that's impossible to clean completely. The grime is permanently embedded in the walls and floors. There's a reason the town gets called Slummerville.

Will she ever be able to move out of here? Get away from the dust and the noise and the history, and live with Angela in a place where she can use the bathroom during the day?

The static in her head is louder now, threatening to drown out the neighbours along with everything else. Sometimes, she wonders if she lowered the dosage of her antidepressants too quickly, too soon. She cried for a solid week the last time she changed up her meds. So did Angela, for that matter, in reaction. Chloë can't have been easy to live with until her mood swings settled down again.

At least Chloë's ex-husband is gone from her life. That helps. She hasn't heard a word from him since before she got together with

Angela. He's vanished like a stone thrown into a pond, with only the ripples remaining – still there, still perturbing the water, but getting fainter and fainter with each year that passes.

Not like Tess. What Tess did to Angela won't go away, and it keeps bringing her back into their lives again and again. Alec might have driven Chloë to try to kill herself, but he didn't force the pills down her throat. Tess came close to murdering Chloë, and she as good as murdered Angela, that final time she drank Angela's blood. If their well-founded suspicions are correct, it was only luck that Angela's death didn't turn out to be permanent.

As soon as Angela can square things with her advisor, she's going to run off and confront a homicidal predator. On her own, unless Chloë can make a convincing enough argument that she should be going along, too. Which isn't looking likely. Because Chloë has failed at everything.

Failed and failed and failed. No wonder Angela doesn't want her to come.

But her witch's intuition is real. Unreliable, incomprehensible, and irritating, but real. It's what led her to Angela in the first place. She has to believe it won't abandon her now.

Chloë kneels in front of the box, searching through it for any inspiration that might turn up. There has to be something in it she can use. There has to be another way to make the journey, and she has to find it. No matter what the myths say, and whether or not it's an irrational idea. A magical solution has to be the best way to deal with a magical problem. Even if it hasn't offered any answers yet. Even if so far she's been utterly useless.

She sifts through the contents – the prophecy cards, her gramarye and other books, votive candles, bags of herbs, the bow drill and the other fire-lighting tools. There are some found objects in the box as well. A piece of sea glass from Lovells Island. A feather that a crow left on her windowsill. A stick. Sturdy and straight, and about a yard long. She doesn't know what makes the stick special, if anything; she picked it up off the ground one day on a whim. She doesn't know if any of it has any use at all, except for the cards. Although those have relentlessly continued to tell her 'seek out the dragon that guards the red path' as if it's something she's supposed to understand.

She supposes the book where she found the graveyard ritual has proved itself worthwhile, although nothing else in it worked. Her one great success to date. A year of intensive research for a single usable spell.

On the other side of the room, Entropy yawns, and licks his paw.

'Some witches get a pet who talks, you know,' she calls over to him. 'They offer helpful suggestions and advice, all the time. That's what TV tells me. Or maybe you could give me a clue some other way? Claw some mystic rune I need into the couch cushions?'

In reply, her cat begins washing himself industriously. If he was the one who helped her out back in the graveyard, that's clearly all the assistance he plans on giving her. She doesn't know why she thought she might convince him otherwise when she can't even convince him to stay off the kitchen counters.

Chloë takes the gramarye out of the trunk and sits with her back against the wall. Her witch's journal, a record of all the spells she's tried to cast. She and Angela came up with the idea together, a kind of experimental log of her attempts at magic. Flipping through the pages, so far it's mostly been lists of instructions and ingredients. Amounts and variations, formulae and forms.

Maybe she's been approaching magic the wrong way. Missing the point.

Instead of formulae and forms, it's time to try out signs and symbols, sympathy and synchronicity. Metaphor made manifest.

Is this her witch's intuition, or a meaningless impulse? Pointless steamed asparagus, or steamed asparagus of deep and weighty significance?

Either way, it's a good time to get some writing done. But not the novel. Not today.

Chloë does her best to tune out the noise, both internal and external, and let her mind drift to where it wants to go.

She opens the book to a blank page and starts a story about a trip to the underworld.

CHAPTER TWELVE

Excerpt From Chloë's *Gramarye*

I don't know what this is. All I know for sure is that it's something I need to be writing right now.

So, here goes.

The First Missing Person
An Eleusinian Mystery Story
by Chloë Kassman

Part One

One day, not long after the beginning of time, Hecate the triple goddess – goddess of witchcraft, goddess of crossroads, goddess of necromancy – was strolling through the fields of Eleusis with her best friend, Astakos the lobster. ('Astakos' means 'lobster' in Greek, but that was all right because he was the only lobster in existence back then, so there was no chance of anyone getting him confused with a different one.) The two of them were discussing the important political issues of the day, such as why Zeus always liked to turn into a swan or a bull or another kind of animal before having sex with mortals.

'It's to disguise his true form,' Astakos insisted. 'So that he doesn't blind the mortals with his Olympian radiance.'

'If that were the only reason, he could appear as a person. A different, non-Zeus person,' Hecate pointed out.

'Huh. You've got a good point, there.' Astakos mulled that over for a while. 'He's getting off on it, isn't he?'

Hecate shrugged, three pairs of shoulders rising then falling. 'Probably. But look, I don't really care if he's into autozoophilia–'

'Nice word.'

'Thanks, I invented it just now. All I'm saying is, I'm a lot more concerned about the consent issues involved.'

At that moment, they came across Persephone, the grain maiden, she who was called the seed of the fruits of the field. She was picking wildflowers by the roadside. Hecate stopped short so suddenly that Astakos bumped into her rearmost ankle.

'Hi, Persephone,' Hecate said, smiling a little stupidly with all of her mouths.

'Oh, hello, Hecate,' said Persephone. 'How are you? It's a lovely day, don't you think?'

'Yes,' Hecate answered, not taking her eyes off Persephone. 'Lovely.'

'Sun shining,' said Astakos. 'Birds singing. Goddesses of witchcraft drooling.'

'Shut *up*!' Hecate hissed at him.

A puzzled look crossed Persephone's face as she laced a flower into her hair. 'Is something the matter?'

'No, nothing at all,' Hecate replied, blushing bright red. 'We have to be on our way now – so much to do, massive amounts of witchy stuff I need to take care of. But it was wonderful to see you, Persephone!'

Persephone waved goodbye, still looking perplexed, as Hecate and Astakos hurried off.

'You could let her know how you feel, you ninny,' Astakos said when they were out of earshot.

'I'm not sure I should be taking advice about my love life from a lobster.'

'Hey, that's offensive! My lobstrosity isn't a shortcoming! It affords me a unique perspective which could be invaluable to you.'

'You're right,' said Hecate, feeling abashed. 'I'm sorry. What do you think I should do?'

'Well, you're going to want to wait until she moults, because otherwise you're never going to be able to pierce her abdomen with your first pair of pleopods—'

Before he could advise her further, he was interrupted by a noise like the loudest thunder, although there were no clouds in the sky. It was followed soon after by a wailing scream, which stopped abruptly as though cut in twain by a sword. Then all was quiet once more. The silence lay so thick about them that it was as if the sounds had never occurred.

'What was that?' asked Astakos.

'I think it was Persephone.' Hecate ran back the way they had come, but the grain maiden was no longer there. They searched for her all through the day, calling her name, but found no trace of the young goddess.

'Where could she have gone?' asked a bewildered Hecate. 'She was right here! We'd barely passed out of sight!'

'I don't know,' said Astakos. 'But, um, maybe we should also be worried by the fact that everything is dying?'

Hecate looked about her and saw that the flowers had dropped their petals, the grapes had withered on the vine, and the grass had turned brown and fallen lifeless to the ground. All plants that grew upon the earth were touched by death.

'We need to go and see Demeter,' Hecate said. 'Right now.'

*

Demeter, the poppy goddess, goddess of the harvest, goddess of agriculture, bringer of law and civilisation, had shed so many tears that they formed a small saltwater lake around her. Hecate had to tread water to keep herselves upright. Astakos busied himself hunting for mussels in the shallows.

'So you heard my daughter's cries for help, but could not see what fate had befallen her?'

'That's about the sum of it, yes,' Hecate admitted. 'I don't know what happened.'

'Then alas for this world,' said Demeter, tears streaking down her face in rivulets. 'For this I swear – so long as my daughter is separated from me, no seedling shall grow from the soil. All that roots in the ground shall perish, rot, and decay, until no more life remains within the boundaries of the earth.'

'I . . . see,' said Hecate. 'Not even a little bit of life? Like maybe a lichen or something?'

'All shall perish,' Demeter confirmed.

'Well. I suppose that means I should probably keep on looking for her, then.'

'I beg you to do so,' replied the goddess of the fields. 'Please.'

Hecate swam back out to Astakos, and they pulled themselves from the lake of tears to sun themselves dry at the edge of the water.

'How'd that go?' asked the lobster.

'Demeter has completely flipped her lid, and unless we find Persephone soon, everything everywhere is going to die.'

'I'm guessing it didn't go well, then.'

'No,' Hecate said. 'No, it really didn't.'

Hecate and Astakos lay in silence for a time, listening to the waves lap against the lakeshore, until Astakos finally spoke once more.

'So, how do we find Persephone?'

'How should I know?' Hecate snapped. 'No one's ever gone missing before. I didn't know anybody *could* go missing.' Her six eyebrows drew down in thought. 'Maybe there was some detail we missed? Some kind of, I don't know, clue or something that would tell us what happened, if only we managed to think of it?'

'Maybe. We could try to reconstruct the events, I guess. What do you remember?'

'Let's see . . . we came across Persephone picking flowers, her hair the gold of ripening wheat, her eyes gleaming like two freshly minted drachmae–'

'Settle down your libido, witch goddess. I don't see how hair and eye colour is going to be relevant to a missing-persons case.'

'All right, then what do *you* remember?'

'Hmm.' Astakos absently clicked his claws like castanets as he searched through his memories. 'It was a lovely day . . .'

'How is that any more helpful than her hair colour?'

'I don't know, let me think. The sun was shining, the birds were singing–'

'Wait, wait! Stop there!'

He swivelled his eyestalks towards her. 'You're really not helping with all the interruptions.'

'No, I mean, I think you've got something,' Hecate said. 'The sun was out.'

'Yeah, but so what? We already knew that.'

'We knew it, but we didn't realise that it mattered.' Hecate looked upwards, squinting at the heavens. 'The sun sees pretty much everything, doesn't he?'

'Nothing unusual happened that I can recall, no,' said Helios, light of life, the radiant sun who gladdens the hearts of mortals, he whose eternal eye witnesses all. 'It was an ordinary day. I went up, and then I went back down.'

'Oh.' All three of Hecate's voices deflated with disappointment. 'So there wasn't anything weird going on?'

'Not that I can think of.'

'No strange noises?' Astakos asked.

'Can't remember any offhand.'

'Sudden disappearances?'

'Nope.'

'Think hard,' Hecate said. 'Not a single thing? Not even in the fields of Eleusis?'

'Well, now that you mention Eleusis,' Helios replied, 'I guess there was that time when a great crack rent open in the ground and a horde of men on black horses poured out of it and they captured a screaming girl and then returned into the depths of the earth and the crack sealed up behind them leaving no trace it had ever been there. But other than that, no. Nothing weird.'

Hecate and Astakos turned to look at each other. 'Hades,' they said at the same time.

'Is that bad?' Helios asked.

'No, of course not,' Hecate grumbled. 'He's only one of the three most powerful gods in all existence, the adamantine and unyielding lord of death and darkness, brother to Zeus himself.'

'Oh, good,' the sun god said. 'For a moment there, I thought you might be worried. Have a lovely, sunny day!'

The sun continued on his eternal round, and Hecate and Astakos waved goodbye. As they made their way back down from the sky, Hecate said, 'So that explains why we couldn't find her. She's in the friggin' underworld.'

'But now that we know where she is, all we have to do is get her out of there before everyone starves to death.'

Hecate gritted two sets of teeth in frustration as her third mouth spoke. 'I don't know if rescuing her is possible. There aren't many people who can travel to the underworld without getting trapped there forever. It's the country from whose bourne no traveller returns, you know? It's not exactly accommodating to tourists.'

'Who do you think might be able to pull it off, then?'

'Let me think . . . Dionysus says he did it once but was too drunk to remember how. Hermes takes messages almost everywhere, I guess, but he travels so much that it'll be really hard to track him down if we want to ask him about it. Other than that, I don't know. Maybe there's some other deity who's in charge of a particularly relevant domain. Like, if there's a god of returning from the realm of death or something. But if there is one, they probably wouldn't do it. They'd have to be an idiot to risk getting on Hades' bad side.'

Astakos curled his antennae thoughtfully. 'What about Hecate, the goddess of necromancy?'

Hecate considered that for a moment.

'Ah, shit,' she said.

PART THREE

The Voice Of The Lobster

CHAPTER THIRTEEN

The Cat's Meow, North Beach, San Francisco
5 May 1928

Outside, San Francisco faces a chilly spring evening, but the basement room is warmed by bodies and breath and sweat, filled to overcrowding with eager customers. The place must be making a fortune. Meijing wonders why. It can't be because of the music.

'Hey, dollface,' someone says, shouting almost in her ear. 'Y'here all by yrsel'?'

The voice is slurred, nearly incomprehensible. Meijing turns to find a pasty-faced man teetering at the edge of her table. His hands clutch at the rim to keep him from toppling over.

'Speakee Engrish?' he asks, leaning in closer. The sour smell of alcohol on his breath is overpowering. 'Can I buy y'a drink?'

Without breaking eye contact with him, she reaches down and carefully bends the table's tall brass candlestick into a rough hoop. 'Leave now,' she says, 'before something unfortunate happens to you.'

He stares at the candlestick, then curses and stumbles away, muttering under his breath about Chinese witchcraft. Meijing suppresses a smile. He's picked the wrong folk tale; she is no *mòu* to curse him with a spell. She is something much less pleasant.

She listens to the jazz band over the roar of the crowd, and winces when the bassist hits another flat note. He's getting worse with each day that passes.

It's not as rare as it used to be for a Chinese woman to be spotted outside of Chinatown. But even as close to the boundary line as North Beach, it comes with hazards. Being propositioned is a minor yet frequent one. It does not seem to matter that Meijing wears expensive and fashionable drop-waist dresses in stylish black these days – nor would it matter if she walked out the front door wearing a burlap sack. It may be decades after the earthquake finally shattered both the brothels of Chinatown and the gangs that fed on their profits, but rich or poor, pretty or ugly, a Chinese woman on her own is considered fair game.

Scaring the man off in such dramatic fashion was perhaps a foolish risk to take. The effort has left her with a mild headache; she had to push back against one of Master Hiram's earliest injunctions to manage it. *Never tell our secrets to those who know them not.* She would not have been capable of it if he were there watching. But since he has not yet arrived, she can skirt the edges of his intent. Bending a candlestick bears little resemblance to telling a tale, and her words themselves revealed nothing. It is to her advantage to test the boundaries of his commands every now and then.

Her indiscretion is unlikely to have repercussions, in any case. The speakeasy is dim and noisy, and the man practically too drunk to walk. In all probability, no one will notice or remember. It isn't as if she showed him her fangs.

Besides, it was very satisfying.

Coming to the blind pig holds more dangers than lecherous men and incautious exposure, of course. Neither she nor Master Hiram can afford to be picked up by a police raid. This one is well safeguarded as they go, however; a clever intercom system links the street-level door with the bar in the basement. If the police come knocking, everyone inside will get ample warning to clear out through the back exit. Perhaps that is why the place is so popular.

As terrible as the bass player might be, the dance floor is packed. Over at the bar, the patrons are crammed three rows deep, throwing down their money, shouting to be heard. All of them knocking back glass after glass of the finest rum and whiskey shipped in direct from Canada. There's no need for anyone in the City by the Bay to make do with cheap booze and bathtub gin.

Meijing isn't there for the drink selection. Her taste in beverages has changed since she became a *geong si*. Although she does like to go to Sam Wo every now and then to order tea. She can't drink it any more than she can drink alcohol, of course, but she likes to inhale the scent and revel in the memories of when she could.

She will probably have to break that habit soon. Or at least frequent a different restaurant for a time. A few years, until she is forgotten. Otherwise, someone will eventually notice she is not ageing. There are still those in Chinatown who know what to do about a *geong si*. The city is modernising more and more each day, but the old tales are not forgotten yet.

It's a pity she can't consult an expert on the restless dead herself, but defying Master Hiram's will to that extent is far beyond her abilities. There is much that she does not understand about her condition. A learned *dou shi* might be able to tell her many things. Whereas Master Hiram tells her very little, barring when he does so unintentionally.

When she died, she had no idea that she'd been more likely to remain a corpse than transform. One of many perils he never warned her of. She does not know how many of their kind exist, or when Master Hiram died, or why her fingernails have not turned into sharp claws like his. Is that a difference between the women who walk after death and the men? Or is there some other cause? She could not say.

The mental control that Master Hiram exerts over her was another piece of knowledge he elected not to share beforehand.

She has managed to learn a great deal from her own observations, though. As well as from Master Hiram's drugged ravings. Not long ago, in a crazed rant, he let slip that peachwood is not necessary to slay a *geong si* of his advanced age. Any sharpened wooden stake will do.

A useful thing to know.

As if summoned by her thoughts, Master Hiram pulls out a chair beside her. It's past time he arrived; he's more than half an hour late. Much longer and he would have missed the band's break and ruined the entire plan.

'Sin,' he announces as he sits, apropos of nothing in particular. As usual. 'This city is steeped in it, and this is surely its very heart. We are surrounded by wickedness.' He shakes his head sadly. 'Generation after generation, they learn nothing. The lessons of the past are wasted upon them, and they seek only their own degradation.'

'Yes, Master Hiram,' she mouths automatically.

His disapproving gaze sweeps over the dance floor, condemning the Lindy Hop and all who partake of it. Men in loose trousers and double-breasted waistcoats, women showing rouged knees beneath their short skirts, all anathema to his sight. His expression takes on a look of particular distaste when he spies a pair of men standing a little too close to each other in a corner.

It is ridiculous that a drug addict and murderer judges them so. He has tried to teach his peculiar religious views to Meijing. As, she has gathered, his dead wife taught them to him. The details are complex and convoluted, but they seem to revolve around one essential principle – Master Hiram has been blessed above all others, in strength and power, in longevity and morality, and therefore Master Hiram is superior to all others. Meijing is wise enough to keep her opinion of this to herself.

'Have you been observing our prospect tonight?' he asks.

'Of course, Master Hiram.'

'And how does he fare?'

She returns her attention to the seven-member jazz ensemble. Specifically to the bass player, Desmond. His tempo is off, speeding up and slowing down arrhythmically while the rest of the band struggles to follow. The pianist levels a dark look at him, not for the first time this evening. Desmond grimaces. Sweat beads his brow.

His fondness for whiskey is taking its toll.

'He fares poorly,' she replies.

Surely he must be near to his lowest point. The moment when he is ripest for the plucking.

Master Hiram grunts contentedly, running his fingers over the head of his walking stick. 'Fetch the man a drink. He'll be wanting one during his break.'

Meijing nods and rises. There is no option to refuse. She shoulders through the press of flappers and sheikhs, making her way to the bar. Fetch and carry, carry and fetch. Such are her tasks these days. She is no fool; she knows that all she has done in her life is exchange one set of shackles for another. She did not even escape an early death by committing herself to Master Hiram's service. Death came for her, and her body is a carcass, animated only by the life essence that she steals from others, the *hei* she extracts from their blood when she drinks.

She elbows aside a flapper in a beaded headpiece. A mere tap, no effort at all on Meijing's part, but the woman topples over with a shriek. Giving someone a push is not the same as telling a tale, either. Another step forward and Meijing has reached the front of the pack. The bartender takes her two bits and hands over a rye and ginger.

This set of shackles does come with some advantages.

The band has finished its set by the time she returns to the table.

Desmond is already seated in the third chair, deep in conversation with Master Hiram.

'Hello, Des.' She smiles and pushes the highball glass across to him. He nods back, barely acknowledging her presence; she isn't the one he's there for. But he accepts the drink with eager, trembling hands, and gulps at it gratefully.

'I've been thinking about your offer,' he says when he sets the glass down.

'It is not an offer, Desmond,' Master Hiram corrects him. 'I merely point the way down a path which you might travel.' His syllables are rich and resonant, ringing with the cadences of a revival preacher. Meijing has occasionally wondered if he was one, sometime in the distant past. 'You will walk in the footsteps of the Redeemer, giving your blood that others might live. And when you are cleansed of sin, then for your sacrifice, after three days you will rise.' He puts his hands on Desmond's shoulders. 'You shall achieve the Kingdom of Heaven while yet upon the earth. You shall be resurrected. Immortal.'

'Immortal,' Desmond echoes.

This is Master Hiram at his finest – his voice powerful, his eyes shining with an inner light. Meijing might not find his religious nonsense seductive, but there are many who are susceptible to it. Who are drawn in by his promise of redemption and renewal.

'And it'll cure my hands?' Desmond asks. 'You give me your word that God will stop the shakes?'

'The redeemed body is physically perfect. You will suffer no more.' Master Hiram lifts the candlestick Meijing bent earlier and straightens it with a single sharp tug before placing it neatly at the table's centre. It's a nice touch, she must admit.

She hopes he did not recognise the bent candlestick as a sign of her rashness earlier in the evening. But the cause of it must be obvious. She should not have left the evidence so exposed. There will likely be a punishment tonight for her show of strength. Her teeth grind together behind her fixed smile. Nothing to be done about it now.

'I'd give anything to play like I used to.' Tears well up in Desmond's eyes. 'Anything.'

'Let us pray.' Master Hiram grasps Desmond's hands in his own and lowers his head. After a moment, Desmond lowers his own.

If Meijing is unimpressed by the theological trappings, she understands the other attractions of Master Hiram's proposals. The benefits he offers are concrete and demonstrable. So much more tempting than vague promises of an unseeable afterlife. Physical might, perfect health, eternal youth. And access to Master Hiram's considerable funds in order to make use of them.

The bassist is unlikely to see any of the benefits being laid out before him, even if they try to be more careful with him than usual. He is already weak and sickly. It is difficult to predict with certainty how he will respond to being fed upon, but many take it badly, and those who are in poor condition to begin with tend to be among the worst. In all likelihood, each bite will leave him frail and trembling, no less so than the ravages of alcohol leave him now.

Meijing does not expect him to last more than a short while, or come back when he passes on. She predicts that Desmond will be dead and gone within a year, perhaps within a year and a half at most. Such a waste. Even a dreadful musician deserves better. Even a drunkard. She cannot prevent it from happening, though. Whatever advantages her shackles might bestow, they bind her far too tightly to let her warn him.

Desmond has not examined the salvation he has been offered too closely, or questioned it too suspiciously. The chances are, he never will. Master Hiram's tactics work best upon the desperate, those who are convinced that they have no other choice. As she had no other choice, at one time.

Meijing watches the two men mumbling words she does not believe, and waits for them to finish. She is not so desperate now as she once was. There are worse lives she could have; that was true when she took Master Hiram up on his offer, and it remains true tonight. For all the many disadvantages of her lot, she knows she has been exceptionally lucky. After her death, she yet survives, and she has attained the strength, health, and agelessness he holds out as a lure.

And as things stand, there is little she can do other than accept the life of servitude that Master Hiram has given her. For now, she will continue to watch and wait.

For now.

CHAPTER FOURTEEN

ManRay, Cambridge
16 November 2000

It's well after midnight, and Angela is still out on the dance floor, untiring and effervescent. She's in her element here, arms raised above her head, eyes closed, a look of bliss on her face.

Chloë leans against the wall, sipping her rum and coke. Watching. ManRay is much the same tonight as it was when Chloë first came here last year. Dark, crowded, and loud. But there's a particular pleasure that Chloë gets from seeing her girlfriend move, sinuous and supple, the circles of fringe on her georgette dress catching and amplifying every shimmy.

They needed the break after days of arguing. Back and forth, around and around. Both of them have realised that Angela will end up having her way in the end, if she wants to. All she has to do, after all, is hop in the car and go. And Chloë hasn't made any further progress on the magic, or even on her Hecate story.

None of this has made Angela any happier than Chloë. She's as wrung out from winning their fights as Chloë is from losing. So there came a point when Chloë decided that arguing wasn't the best way to spend the limited time they had left before Angela heads off. They haven't had much of a chance to go out and have fun together, with everything else that's been going on.

Chloë isn't the only one noticing Angela's preternatural grace; around the room, kohl-rimmed eyes slide over as if magnetised to the blonde woman swaying her hips in the centre of the floor. *Go ahead and look,* Chloë thinks generously. *I'm the one she's coming home with tonight.*

Even if she's leaving me in a few days. For a while.

Chloë is attracting the occasional glance herself, although they can probably be roughly translated as, 'Why are you here? Did you perhaps get lost on your way to somewhere appalling?' She does her best with the clothes she has, but one of these days, she should get herself an outfit more appropriate for their club nights. Is a tuxedo goth?

While she considers, Angela appears in front of her, eyes bright. She looks both more relaxed and more animated than she has any night since Halloween. The goth clubs are her true terrain, and they've always served as her haven.

Although Chloë has plans for the night that go beyond ManRay alone.

'Are you rested enough yet?' Angela asks, holding out her hand. 'Ready to dance some more?'

'Sure.' Chloë sets aside her drink and lets herself be led back out onto the dance floor. She doesn't know the name of the song that's playing, but it's one she likes – the one about not finding the dead body.

Angela slides her arms around Chloë, pulling her close. Chloë settles her hands on Angela's hips. They turn in a slow circle together.

'Are you having a good time?' Angela asks.

'Yes.'

'Good. Me, too.' Angela smiles up at her. 'Thanks for this.'

'I like dancing, too, you know.'

'You wouldn't rather be curled up with a book?'

'Not tonight. I'm choosing you over *The Blind Assassin.*'

'I beat out Margaret Atwood? That is an honour.' Angela moves in closer and rests her head against Chloë's chest. 'How long before we leave for the mysterious second part of the evening?'

Chloë shrugs nonchalantly. 'Whenever you like. There's no rush.'

'Are you ever intending to tell me where we're going?'

'No.'

'Hmph.' Angela doesn't sound displeased.

Chloë is enjoying keeping her surprise a secret. She's enjoying the whole evening. A night to enjoy the calm, before the storm comes in and blows the roof away.

'Also, happy anniversary,' she says.

'Hold on, what?' Angela pulls back. 'I thought that wasn't for another couple of days.'

'That's for our first date. This is for the night we met. Right here in the club, remember?'

'But I didn't get you anything!'

'For the pre-anniversary I made up without telling you? Don't worry about it.'

Angela shakes her head. 'No, that's not fair,' she says. 'I'll think of something. So, are your plans for later some kind of anniversary present?'

'Maybe.'

Chloë steps back and leads Angela into a twirl, catching her around the waist at the end of the turn. The fringes on Angela's dress whisk softly against Chloë's skin.

'Can you at least tell me why I'm wearing a bikini under my club clothes?'

'You'll have to guess.'

'You're full of secrets tonight.' Angela is grinning. She reaches up and traces Chloë's cheekbone with her fingertips. 'I'm guessing . . . that I'm going to get wet.'

'Very wet. And that's all I'm going to say about it.'

'My mystery woman.' She moves her head back to Chloë's chest.

Chloë holds her close, and sways to the rhythm of the song.

CHAPTER FIFTEEN

Revere Beach, Revere, Massachusetts
16 November 2000

The lobster regards Angela warily from its perch on the rock. She takes a cautious step closer. It lifts a claw but otherwise remains motionless except for its antennae, which wave to and fro in the current. The lobster is the first creature she's seen that hasn't swum off out of sight as soon as her flashlight beam brushed across it.

She almost missed it; everything down here gets fuzzy and blurry beyond more than a few feet of distance. Next time she does this, she'll make sure she has swimming goggles. It's the only thing Chloë didn't think of.

What Chloë did think of, however, was thorough. A flashlight that works down to a hundred metres, a waterproof compass, a diving watch. The weight belt keeping Angela from floating up off the seabed. And Chloë had carefully picked a location on the beach where the late-night crowd at Kelly's Roast Beef wouldn't see someone wading out into Massachusetts Bay and not coming back. All to fulfil a fantasy that Angela can't have mentioned more than once. An idle comment she'd made months ago – that since she doesn't need to breathe, she might be able to walk across the ocean floor.

Chloë can't join in herself, not without scuba gear she can't afford. For that matter, the light, compass, watch, and belt probably cost her more than she can spare.

My girlfriend is the best girlfriend, Angela thinks. *Definitely a much better girlfriend than I am.*

She feels a sudden rush of desire for Chloë, overpowering the queasiness she's been feeling since the moment she dipped a toe in the Atlantic. Her longing is so intense that it's almost uncomfortable in its own right.

Well. Nothing she can do about that now. Maybe later.

She takes another long step towards the lobster.

It's a big specimen, with massive claws. The one it raised earlier is still up, as if it has a question it wants to ask. As the lobster comes into sharper focus with her approach, she notices that it's bright blue. That can't be normal, can it? It looked greyish from a little further away.

Angela waves hello, her hand moving in slow motion through the water, and says, 'Hi.' Or tries to, anyway. When she opens her mouth to speak, she only manages to flood the area around her head with bubbles. She gags as she inhales a mouthful of seawater. The air pouring out of her mouth and nose are too much for the lobster to endure, and it hurtles away backwards, its tail whipping back and forth, until it vanishes into the murk.

She tries to cough the liquid out of her lungs, but it doesn't do any good. Only a few more bubbles break free from her throat. Well, of course that didn't work. What did she think she was going to replace the water with, other than more water? Her chest feels odd, uncomfortably full. Almost as if she'd eaten too much, but was feeling it behind her breastbone instead of lower down.

Her stomach isn't any better off, for that matter. It's doing nauseating flip-flops. That's been happening to her a lot these days – it's the same feeling she has every time she crosses a bridge. Running water isn't friendly to vampires, and the ocean apparently counts.

The effect has been getting worse lately; it's always felt like the water was trying to repel her, but it never used to make her sick.

She wouldn't have wanted to miss this, though, even if she'd known in advance that her internal organs would object. There's a stark beauty down here that isn't at all what she expected to find. In a strange way, it reminds her of the Sonoran desert, the dry plains and mountains she'll be heading back to soon. Places where tough, angular creatures scrabble a subsistence out of the rocks.

It's probably time to leave. A quick look at the diving watch tells her that she's not in any real danger yet, but it's a long drive home and dawn is an unforgiving deadline. She checks her compass and plays her flashlight over the landscape – seascape? – until she finds the edge of the kelp forest she passed through on the way out. Her footfalls stir up silt as she walks until she reaches the upward slope on the other side, where the mud and rock change to coarse sand. She trudges onward, swinging her light around in the hopes of catching a last glimpse of undersea life, but there isn't any to be seen. She's all alone in the water now.

Her head breaks through to air, and she sees the broad dark strip of the beach and the streetlamps lining the road beyond it. The upscale condos that cluster around the shoreline are dim shapes beneath the cloudy, starless sky. Kelly's, finally closed for the night, is only a closer silhouette; the bright lights above its windows are off, no longer blazing like miniature suns to chase away the darkness.

A glance behind her shows the eastern sky is a solid jet black, with no trace of early morning rosiness colouring the clouds. She trudges through the breaking waves, her feet sinking deep in the wet sand, until she's far enough out that the foam washes her ankles before it recedes.

Then she drops down and hacks up a couple of lungfuls of seawater.

She retches again and again, for a distressingly long time, but by the end of it she thinks she's mostly got it out. After she coughs a few final teaspoons of salt water, stringy with mucus, back into the surf from whence it came, nothing more comes up.

She scoops up a palmful of water to splash on her face, another to rinse out her mouth, and straightens up at last. A tall, bulky figure is approaching her across the beach, a diagonal line of footprints trailing through the sand behind it. Angela can only tell it's Chloë from the blue knit wool hat with the bobble on it; she's wrapped up in so many coats and sweaters and jackets that she looks twice her usual size.

'Angela? Are you all right?' Chloë asks as soon as she gets close, her voice muffled by a scarf.

'I'm fine,' Angela manages to croak out. 'I already feel a lot better. And I learned a good lesson. Don't talk underwater.'

Chloë tilts her head in puzzlement. 'Who were you talking to down there?'

'A lobster. It seemed friendly.'

'A lobster?' Her eyebrows shoot up in alarm. 'Did it . . . did it say anything back?'

'What? No, of course not.'

'Oh. For a moment, I thought . . .' Chloë trails off. 'It's bizarre,' she mutters to herself, 'the kinds of questions I have to seriously ask these days.'

'I had a great time, other than the accidental water inhalation. Really, it was amazing. Only the very end of it was a problem, and that was my own fault.' The two of them start following the line of footprints back across the beach, Chloë shuffling in her boots and Angela treading more lightly on bare feet. She slips her arm through Chloë's, and smiles crookedly. 'I'll admit that I'd rather have risen like Aphrodite from the water than crawled out vomiting everywhere, but it was worth it.'

whenever we do it at your place, I always think, "Mike's a were- what if his ears are as good as his nose?" '

ıgela blinks. 'I've wondered about his hearing, but not, uh, not ıat particular context.' She tries to remember if there's ever a hint that he can hear them having sex. 'He's never said any- ıg. But I guess he probably wouldn't, would he?'

Could we, could we maybe discuss that later? Because it's just, been quivering with lust for you all night and we were finally ut to mmf!' Her last word is lost as Angela cuts her off with a s. Chloë melts into it, sliding her tongue into Angela's mouth, king a practised, delicate touch against the pinprick sharpness Angela's fangs.

The rest of their clothes come off quickly after that, and Angela kes the opportunity to bring her mouth down to Chloë's enticing easts, her lips rounding into a smile when this elicits a gasp. ıloë's hands are tangled in Angela's still-wet hair, nudging her oser to where she wants the most attention, and Angela obligingly ıifts over to suck on a reddening nipple. She's rewarded with an ven better response, a sound halfway between a sigh and a moan.

'Come over here,' Angela says in a husky voice, drawing Chloë nto her lap. 'I want to try something.'

'I thought I was supposed to be the seasoned pro at car–Ow!' Chloë winces as her head bumps against the roof.

'Whoops, sorry. Can you scootch down?'

'Only if I put my legs around the front seat.'

'Well, that,' Angela purrs, 'will do just fine.'

Chloë manages to get her head a bit lower by resting one leg on the door handle and the other by the gear shift. She leans back to keep her balance, pressing her body up against Angela's.

Angela moves the muscles that make her heart beat. One-two, one-two, a steady rhythm. She likes to do that whenever Chloë is close enough to feel it.

'You're always Aphrodite to me.'

'Right. I'm sure I cut a super-sexy figure back there.'

'It was only water. And the bikini is driving me nuts, honestly. I want to drag you to the back seat of the car and make out with you for the rest of the night.'

'It'd have to be in the car. It'll be too close to dawn by the time we make it home.' Angela bumps Chloë affectionately with her hip. 'You know, I've never done that. The back-seat thing.'

Chloë stops, turning to Angela in surprise. 'Never ever?'

'Nope. I spent my youth shy, studious, and closeted, remember? By the time I was doing anything interesting, there were bedrooms available without any parents around. No cars needed.'

'Sometimes I forget what a late start you got. I always think of you as the experienced one.' The narrow, visible portion of Chloë's face between her scarf and her hat scrunches up in thought. 'Do you want to?'

'What, right now?'

'I mean, not if you're feeling bad.'

'No, I'm fine, I can't even tell I tried to suck the ocean into my lungs. Vampire physiology, I guess.' And the image of a close grapple with a naked Chloë is making her earlier surge of lust come back in force. Tinged with more than a trace of hunger, if she's being honest. 'Wouldn't it be kind of awkward, though? And what about you, won't you get cold?'

'Cars have heaters. And the awkwardness is part of it. Fumbling around is a key element of this quintessential American experience. Which you should definitely not miss out on, even if I have every ulterior motive for saying so.'

Angela almost raises another objection, but then she stops herself. She wants this. She wants it desperately. She wants Chloë. Right now.

She wants to peel her out of all of those clothes, touch her body, make her come. She wonders if Chloë is feeling the same aching need.

The thought flits across her mind that they might not have many more nights together.

Angela nods decisively. 'All right. Let's do this.'

'Yay!' Chloë launches into motion, hurrying towards the car. Angela laughs, picking up her pace to keep up.

When they reach Angela's Corolla, Chloë makes quick work of turning on the engine and sliding into the back seat. Keeping her eyes locked with Angela's, she unwinds the scarf from around her face and starts seductively unbuttoning her outermost coat.

Angela's fangs are out before Chloë gets to the second button. Her mouth grows moist, and she swallows the saliva down. It still tastes faintly of saltwater.

'Are you coming in?' Chloë shimmies out of her coat in as enticing a manner as possible given the limited confines, and gets to work on the jacket beneath it, suggestively tugging the zipper down a tiny bit, and then a tiny bit more. 'You might not feel the wind, but I'd rather have the door closed.' Her shoulders shiver just enough for Angela to see it.

Angela beats back the desire to sink her teeth into Chloë's neck and drink her blood in frantic gulps. It's only been a little more than a week since she last fed; she can handle the arousal without getting too bitey. A week is nothing.

She gets in the car and shuts the door.

'That's better.' Chloë reaches out and touches the side of Angela's face, stroking a thumb across it. This time, Angela is the one who shivers. They move together at the same moment to share a kiss, letting it linger.

Angela will never understand how she found someone willing to be with her in spite of everything. She got lucky, somehow. Lucky,

lucky girl. She pulls the zipper of Chloë's jacket
way and slides her hands across the sweater unc

'How many layers do you have on?'

Chloë grins at her. 'Let's find out.'

The car warms up as they work together to st
Chloë's clothes. They have to go through five layer
contortions before Chloë, flushed and breathing h
her underwear.

'And at last we reach equality,' Chloë says, toyin
holding Angela's bikini top together.

'Um.' Angela puts a gentle hand over Chloë's. 'S
newbie to this, before we go past acceptable beachwe
we be worried about, you know, people walking by?'

'Before sunrise on a beach in November? Probably

'Probably?'

'And it'll be hard to see in, because the window
steamed up,' Chloë points out, blushing a little bit. Sh
that's all due to her. Angela's body doesn't generate m
she only exhales when she wants to.

'OK, but someone could still listen in if they get c
couldn't they? I know I'm being paranoid, but . . .'

Chloë thinks about that for a second, and then leans
the radio on. Music thunders out, crashing guitar ch
heavy rumble of bass.

'There,' she says, raising her voice over the din. 'No sex
getting past that. Better?'

'Much.' She knows it makes no sense, that if anything
is more likely to attract attention than moans and gas
makes her feel more secure, nonetheless. A shield of sound
you. Sorry.'

'Don't worry about it. You're not the only one who . . .

She trails her fingers down Chloë's torso, lingering at her stomach, taking a moment to dip a fingertip in Chloë's navel. Then she moves her hands down to the legs and draws them across her girlfriend's thighs. Chloë draws in an anticipatory breath. Her hips are moving, seeking a closer touch.

Angela strokes her, softly and gently, feeling the wetness. She takes her time, almost teasingly, drawing it out until she senses Chloë is on the very verge of begging.

Then Angela slips a finger inside of her.

Chloë cries out. Almost loud enough to match the electric guitars and wailing vocals from the radio. Angela kisses Chloë's neck. Then adds another finger.

Angela's lips graze lightly over Chloë's shoulder. She keeps her thumb resting on her lover's clit, letting Chloë move against it at the pace and pressure she wants. Chloë is making low moans in between her gasps for breath. She grinds herself into Angela's hand. Angela can feel Chloë's muscles clenching and unclenching on her lap as she writhes.

Chloë reaches back to once again twine a hand into Angela's hair. Angela slides her fingers out, almost all the way, and then back in, twisting them around each other inside of Chloë, curving and straightening, stroking every spot, making sure her thumb never strays too far from its place.

She adds a third finger.

Chloë's body is in constant motion, nearly bucking herself off Angela's lap as she presses forward, harder and faster. Angela's fingers stroke her in ever smaller motions as Chloë tightens around them, almost there. Ready.

When she can feel the moment is exactly right, Angela presses her thumb down.

Chloë grabs Angela's wrist with her free hand and holds her where she is. Her climax comes fast and strong, her inner muscles spasming and clamping down, her stuttering yell making a rhythmless counterpoint to the radio. She clings to Angela's hair and arm, holding tight, as if she'll be swept out across the beach and into the sea if she lets go.

When Chloë finally relaxes, Angela wraps her arms around her. Chloë is still panting, although in slow, deep breaths rather than hurried gasps. Her body is covered with a light sheen of sweat.

'Good?' Angela asks.

'Very good. Better than good. Do you want to, um, switch around?'

Angela is tempted to say yes, but she shakes her head. 'I mean, I do, but I'm getting worried about the timing. We need to start heading back before it gets too early, or you're going to have to throw me in the trunk of the car. Maybe you can make it up to me another time. Soon.' She gives Chloë a playful nip, careful not to break the skin.

'Any time you want.' Chloë manoeuvres herself into a position where she can turn off the music. Once it's silent, she wriggles back around again so she can give Angela another kiss.

In the quiet, Angela can hear a soft, constant pattering coming from the car roof. At some point when they were too preoccupied to notice, it started raining.

'Also, happy anniversary,' Angela says. Chloë grins, and slides off Angela's lap to begin the complicated process of finding her clothes and putting them back on.

She pauses in the middle of buttoning up her shirt and casually tilts her head to the side, exposing her neck. 'Hey, did you want to have a drink before we go? Since your fangs are out and everything.'

'It's way too soon.'

'I know, but I thought you might want to, you know, top up before you went on the trip.'

'I'm not going to–I mean, I can't do that anymore until we've solved this.' Angela looks away from Chloë, watching water droplets slither down the fogged-up window. 'Unless I come back from Tess with what we need, then last week in the bathroom . . . That was the last time I do that to you.'

To Angela's relief, Chloë makes no argument, no attempt at a debate. In the blurred reflection on the glass, Angela sees her nod her head slowly.

Angela reaches down and picks up her top.

'I'm going to miss you so much while you're away,' Chloë says, shrugging herself into her cardigan.

Angela finishes tying her top back on and puts her hand on Chloë's. 'I'm going to miss you, too. Let's call each other every day when I'm gone, all right?'

'I'm also going to worry about you. Heading out there all alone.'

'I'd worry even more if you came with me.' Angela's grip on Chloë's hand tightens. 'Sweetie, please. We've talked about this over and over.'

'I know.' Chloë gets a ruminative look on her face. 'But if I'm staying behind . . .'

Chloë trails off. The rain rattles against the windshield.

'What?' Angela asks. 'What are you thinking?'

'You might not want to mention exactly how his name came up tonight,' Chloë says, popping open the door so she can head to the front seat, 'but how would you feel about asking a werewolf to come along?'

CHAPTER SIXTEEN

The Tenderloin, San Francisco
17 November 2000

Hiram has cleaned himself up for the hunt, after a fashion, although Meijing wishes he'd chosen clothing that was less conspicuous. His long coat is reasonable enough, but beneath its open front lurks a ruffled shirt, mustard-yellow waistcoat, and loosely tied silk cravat. An ebony walking stick with a silver knob on the end completes the look of a well-heeled Pre-Raphaelite poet strolling through the streets of a modern city. While it's true that a wealthy appearance can be an aid to attracting prey, he isn't going hunting a hundred and fifty years in the past. Her own taste in clothing doesn't run to jeans and T-shirts, either, but she makes an effort to dress like someone born after puffed sleeves stopped being in fashion.

At least in San Francisco he blends in a bit better than he would nearly anywhere else. It is fortunate that they live in the land of ostentatious dressers.

His walking stick raps against the pavement with a steady *tap, tap, tap* as they walk. Every now and then, the rhythm breaks so he can sweep aside some small piece of trash in their path. They've plotted a route through the filthiest back alleys in the city, the better to find those in the most desperate of straits. Meijing takes an experimental sniff, and is rewarded with an overwhelming scent of rot and piss. They are certainly in the right place.

She would rather Hiram wasn't out with her at all tonight, but he had insisted. Finding an appropriate long-term companion takes time and effort, a fact he knows full well, but he'd become impatient after her first few forays into the city proved unsuccessful. Impatience, hunger, and the early symptoms of withdrawal are a bad combination for the delicate approach required to entice a willing donor.

His appetites have been increasing as he ages, she has noticed, the intervals between feedings shrinking little by little with each passing year.

He comes to a halt in front of her, raising a hand, and she stops in her tracks. He noticed the grubby sleeping bag an instant before she did. A head of dark hair pokes out of one end, resting on a folded blanket. A small nest of bedding lying in the threshold of a wide, shallow entryway, the loading dock for some closed and locked business.

Hiram motions her forward with a wave of his walking stick. She has to hold back a scowl at his imperious manner. Nonetheless, she moves next to the sleeping bag and crouches down. They both know that she's more suited to the chore than he is, these days. He retains that much self-awareness.

'Hello,' she says quietly. There is no answer but a snore. She reaches out and touches the sleeper on the shoulder. 'Are you all right?'

There's a sharp, phlegmy inhalation as he starts awake, twisting himself around to face her, getting himself tangled in his sleeping bag in the process. He has a thin face with a rough, reddened nose and a patchy beard that crawls all the way down his neck into the collar of a grimy jacket. His eyes are wide with an anxiety that could easily turn into aggression or terror.

'Whaddayou want?' he snarls.

Meijing holds her hands palm out, hoping to calm him down quickly. 'I am very sorry to wake you. We saw you there and thought perhaps you could use some help.'

His expression becomes marginally less fearful, although it remains suspicious. 'You with the government?'

'No.'

'Church?'

'Not exactly.'

He grunts, although whether with approval or disapproval she could not say. 'So who the hell are you?'

'I am Meijing. The man hovering about behind me is called Mast . . . is called Hiram.' She must take more care with her words. Her tongue is too used to the title he insists upon; it will not do, not here. 'And yourself?'

There's a moment of hesitation before he answers, a crease forming in his brow as he takes in Hiram's outmoded clothing. Meijing silently curses. Finally, though, his eyes move back to her and he says, 'Rigo.'

'Interesting name.'

He shrugs. Meijing smiles, genial and friendly, relaxing into her role. The first obstacles have been passed; they have not frightened him into silence, and he is neither too crazy nor too violent to talk.

Properly done, this will be a long dance of seduction, each side testing the other for the qualities they seek. She must appear trustworthy, compassionate, and affluent. He should ideally be discreet, needy, and mostly sane. It would also be a definite perk if he proves to be a drug addict, or someone who could be turned into one – she has nowhere near the craving for adulterated blood that Hiram does, but it does provide them with greater leverage for control, as well.

It might take days before they invite him to stay the night, longer before Hiram reveals their true natures to him, and it could all fall apart at any time if he fails the test in one way or another, or if they do.

'I think there is a late-night restaurant still open nearby,' she begins. 'If you wanted a bite to eat–'

Before she can finish, Hiram leaps forward and drives his fangs into the man's throat, a hand clamped over his mouth to muffle the screams.

'What are you doing?' Meijing asks, exasperated. Hiram, of course, doesn't answer, fully occupied in gulping down blood. Rigo struggles and tries to bite Hiram's hand, which only results in Hiram tightening his fingers, the nails digging into flesh. Trails of blood drip down where they pierce through the man's cheeks.

'We had barely started with him,' Meijing complains. 'He might have turned out to be a good prospect.'

Hiram finally pulls away, gore streaking his chin. Rigo struggles in his grip and flails at the arm pinning him down.

'No matter. We shall begin anew tomorrow.'

Meijing frowns at him. She knows how difficult it can be not to attack the nearest passer-by when the hunger grows too strong. It's always a problem when they're between long-term companions. But she was able to maintain her composure tonight.

'We'll have to kill him now,' she points out. 'That is far from ideal. We cannot leave a trail of corpses across San Francisco. Not anymore.' At this, the noises Rigo is making become higher pitched, and his efforts to escape redouble. He reaches for Hiram's face, trying to press his fingers into Hiram's eye sockets. Hiram bats the groping hands away with his walking stick, but otherwise pays the man no mind.

'One corpse does not a trail make,' he says grumpily. 'No one will pay any mind to a single vagabond.'

One corpse that I will have to clean up, Meijing thinks with some irritation. *And what if your patience snaps again in a week or two, and again after that?*

Saying more aloud would be pushing him too far, though. 'No one says vagabond anymore,' she tells him, contenting herself with a minor gripe. 'You are showing your age.'

'Beggar, tramp, what does it matter? He shall not live to report our eccentricities. Are you going to drink, or allow the rest of him to drain out upon the thirsty earth?'

Meijing glances down at Rigo, whose attempts to break free are growing weaker as the shock of blood loss sets in. She is feeling somewhat peckish, it's true; like Hiram, she's had nothing since Tiffany died. Waste not, want not.

She bends down and sinks her teeth into the side of his neck.

She tries to avoid smelling him, but it's impossible not to breathe in just a little while swallowing. The rank scent of unwashed flesh floods into her nostrils. She would have preferred to get him into a bath before doing this, but there's no point in fussing over might-have-beens. In any case, soon the potent taste of hot blood overwhelms everything else.

It has the distinct, slightly stinging flavour of alcohol in it. Rigo must have been a heavy drinker. She'll be unsteady on her feet for hours after this.

He's barely fighting now, his movements reduced to twitches. She doubts that he's truly conscious by this point, but there's no need to prolong his agony if he isn't. With a quick movement, she reaches around his head and crushes his spine at the neck.

She stands up, letting his head fall back onto the ground with a thump, and contemplates how best to deal with the body. The bite marks will not heal now that he is dead, so those will have to be disguised. Perhaps she should slit his throat? If she does, she will need to move him elsewhere as well; someone might wonder why so little of his blood is splashed around the area if he is left to lie where he died. This will all be much harder without any of the appropriate tools on hand, but she'll have to make do.

Beside her, Hiram is cleaning his face and fingers with a pocket handkerchief. She purses her lips in thought. He will be at his calmest now, replete with blood and mellow from the alcohol. And he surely must feel some regret over Rigo's death, if only because of the added delay in finding a more lasting source of nourishment.

'It's such a bother that we must endure this hardship every few years,' she says, carefully keeping her tone casual. 'Perhaps we should treat our next guest with greater care? We might go decades before we had need to search the streets.'

'This again?' Hiram chuckles. 'You cannot deceive me. I know your true purpose in asking.'

Meijing stills.

'Your tender heart does you credit,' he continues, 'but you must remember, they would none of them thank you for the favour. Only through the risk of death do they gain their chance at life eternal. Such is our promise to them in exchange for their service. It would be miserly of us to hoard that gift to ourselves alone.'

She relaxes, but only slightly. He may not have seen the betrayal that lurks in her heart, but his answer is far from comforting. She knows that he doesn't give a tinker's damn for the aspirations of their victims, and never has.

'You are right, of course,' she says. 'But I find it so heartbreaking when they die.'

'You must not think of them as people,' he chides her gently. 'They are mayflies, here briefly and then gone. Do not take them for more than what they are.'

'I will not, Master Hiram.'

'Only the blessed and the elect are granted life eternal.'

She ducks her head in acknowledgement. 'That is very true, Master Hiram. But still, if we were to be more cautious in how we –'

'Enough.' Hiram frowns. A trace of annoyance has entered his tone. 'You have made your plea for their lives, and I have heard it. Do not speak of these matters again.'

Against her will, Meijing's lips seal shut over her planned response. Until he bids her to speak freely – perhaps next week, or next month, or next year – the subject is closed to her.

Hiram has seldom been inclined to be careful about keeping their companions healthy. In fact, she doubts he is capable of the effort it requires anymore; he lacks whatever vestiges of self-control he once possessed. But so many years of unwillingness to make the attempt goes beyond mere impatience. The sheer obstinacy of his continued refusal can mean only one thing. He wants another vampire of his line to command.

He wishes to replace her. She does not much fancy her chances of living very long if he ever succeeds.

Did he ever see her as more than a momentary servant, the Chinese girl thrown haphazardly into his path during the great earthquake? Or does he seek to rid himself of her now because she may soon become a threat?

It hardly matters, she supposes. All that matters is thwarting his designs. All that matters is survival.

I have been granted life eternal, until he murders me, she muses. *Such a wondrous blessing have I been given.*

The urge to fight back is strong. To resist, break free, test her growing strength. She might throw off his control with a single, unexpected push. She came so close to freedom, once.

But that was many years ago. And she had help, then. An ally. She is alone now.

If she tries and fails tonight, there will be no second chances. Now is still not the time. Not yet.

She nods stiffly. 'Of course, Master Hiram. As you command.'

He replies with a dismissive grunt, and without another word he turns and strides out of the alley, his walking stick *tap, tap, tapping* against the pavement, leaving her alone with the rapidly cooling corpse at her feet.

CHAPTER SEVENTEEN

Brookline
17 November 2000

Angela sits on the kitchen counter, idly swinging her legs, her heels bumping rhythmically against the cabinets below. She can hear canned laughter through the closed door; out in the living room, Chloë and Shelly have turned on the TV. They've left her and Mike alone for this, by some unspoken agreement among the four of them. It's a private thing, this meeting, a conversation about secret and sensitive topics. No rubberneckers allowed. Only the monsters.

Mike is chopping a steak into small cubes and the cutting board is soaked with its juices. There's a red sauce bubbling away in a pot on the stove. Probably it smells delicious. Angela can't tell anymore. Meat and spices and vegetables don't make her stomach growl or set off her salivary glands. There's nothing in the base of her brain telling her that they're something to eat. The sauce smells nice to her, but only in the way a flower or a bar of scented soap smells nice. There's nothing primal about it.

Mike himself, on the other hand? He smells like food.

She has no idea if werewolf blood can sustain her the same way Chloë's blood does. Animal blood doesn't work, in her experience. But her nose has always insisted that he's close enough to a human being to pass. One of several reasons it can be hard to remember that it's not entirely true. Although the biggest one is that he's, well, Mike. Her friend, her landlord, her college buddy's boyfriend. He's got hairy arms, sure, but he's thinning on top and has the slightly hunched posture of a tall man who doesn't want to stand out. Nothing that screams werewolf, especially when he's in the kitchen, looking so completely at home beside the black marble countertops and cast-iron pans. Not exactly the wild beast in his lair.

To be fair, most casual observers wouldn't leap to the conclusion that she's a vampire, either. Not when her fangs are hidden. Without those showing, she could be any pale girl with a fondness for dark clothes and expensive fabrics. Mike figured it out, though. He might smell like a normal person to her, but he was able to detect some kind of strange undercurrent in her scent. Maybe he has a keener nose than she does. Angela has an extraordinarily good sense of smell, at least when it comes to blood-related matters, but all things considered it wouldn't be surprising if Mike's was better.

'If you come with me, you should know we probably won't be getting back until after Thanksgiving,' she says. 'So if you had plans . . .'

'It's OK.' Mike turns to face her, knife still in hand. 'This is more important. My family won't miss it if I don't cook the ham this year.'

'I didn't know anyone had ham for Thanksgiving. Is it a family tradition?'

Mike grins, showing solid teeth the colour of old ivory. 'It's more that my mom's territorial about the turkey, so I'm only allowed to bring a side dish.'

'A ham counts as a side dish?'

'In my family, yes. What about you and Chloë? Any plans?'

'Not really.' She glances down at her swinging feet and makes them go still. Why is she so nervous? It's only Mike. 'We were going to have a quiet long weekend together. No big gatherings. Nothing we can't do another time.' She lifts her head back up and smiles thinly. 'It's a bad year to talk politics with the folks.'

He gives her an understanding nod, and goes back to cutting up the meat.

Angela is still in two minds about bringing Mike along on the trip. It'd be putting someone in danger because of what she is, yet again. The idea leaves a bad taste in her mouth. She's more than a little bit tempted to call off the whole discussion. Leave him to his cooking, go into the living room and play with the guinea pig for a while. Tell Chloë the idea didn't work out.

But if a werewolf is capable of surviving a vampire attack, if the danger to him would be minimal compared to the danger to Chloë, then there's no rational reason for him not to come. None that she's been able to think of, anyway. And during the drive home from the beach, Chloë made a persuasive argument that she needs all the help she can get.

Only if he's able to handle it, though. Beyond a few vague comments he's dropped over the past year, she has very little notion of what being a werewolf entails. It seems almost odd, now, that she and Mike have never talked with each other about any of this. That her knowledge of what he can do – other than smelling vampires, of course – is limited to suppositions, guesses, and jokes made in passing.

Privacy and secrecy are habits that are easy to learn and hard to put down. She understands that as well as anyone.

The secrecy between the two of them has to end tonight. If he's going to come along, she needs to have proof that she isn't going to get him killed. And he should have some idea of her capabilities, too. They've both agreed that it calls for something neither of them is very comfortable with.

A demonstration.

'So,' she says, forcing a bit of playfulness into her voice. 'I'll show you mine if you show me yours?'

He finishes sawing through a last, troublesome strand of gristle and looks at her owlishly. 'All right. I guess we should get on with it. Who goes first?'

Angela shrugs, and holds out her hand for the knife.

'One second.' He scrapes the chunks of steak into a pan, where they sizzle noisily, and brings the knife over to the sink. 'Let me wash it off.'

'It doesn't matter. I'm not going to get an infection.'

'Do you want it to splatter all over your dress?' he asks, scrubbing away the clinging flecks of meat.

'I suppose not.' It's a raw silk midi dress. Definitely a bad idea to dribble steak drippings onto it. It's sleeveless, at least; that should help.

'I had to learn to be practical about this stuff, growing up,' Mike says. 'Once you've ruined a few nice shirts that suddenly have a wolf trapped inside of them, you start to think about things in advance.'

'Sounds like a pain. How do you deal with that one?'

'Velcro. Trousers I can wriggle out of, but shirts I have to prep.' He towels the knife dry, then presents it to her with a flourish, hilt first. 'All right. Show me what you got.'

She takes hold of it and places the edge against the palm of her hand. Then hesitates. No matter how many times she does this, no matter how many tests she's performed, she inevitably feels the slightest touch of uneasiness at this point. What if, sometime, whatever protects her stops working?

It never has before, she reminds herself. Experiment after experiment, all with the same outcome. Trust the science.

She presses down firmly and draws the blade across her skin.

No cut, no blood, no pain. As always. Consistent experimental results validated once again. With a small flourish, she holds up her hand to show him her unblemished palm. 'Voila.'

'I'm impressed. And I guess it's my turn.' She relinquishes the knife to him, and he brings it to his upper arm. 'It works a little differently for me.'

He slices into his flesh, a shallow cut, but he still grimaces in pain as the blood oozes out. Angela watches it snake through the thick forest of hair that covers his arm. She tears her gaze away and looks down at the floor instead when she realises that, embarrassingly, she's salivating.

'Was it supposed to cut you?' she says to her feet.

'Yes. Be patient. Keep watching.'

Reluctantly, she brings her eyes back to the wound, only to discover that the flow of blood is slowing, the edges of the cut knitting themselves back together. Within a minute there's only a red line, then a white line, then nothing at all except a patch of blood dried to tackiness on his skin. He grabs a napkin, wets it under the faucet, and starts wiping his arm clean.

'And now I'm impressed.' She makes a mental note of how similar that looked to what happens to vampire flesh pierced by vampire fangs. The rapid healing, the lack of scarring. Coincidence, or a related process? The better it can be categorised, defined, explained, the better off they'll be. 'Is that how it always works?'

'Yes and no.' He tosses the napkin into the trash and returns to the stove, where he pokes at the steak with a spatula. 'It's faster when the moon is full. Right now, it's about a half-moon.'

'Is that something you always know? What phase of the moon it is? I mean, instinctively.'

'No, I keep careful track. The closer it is to a full moon, the harder it is not to unintentionally go wolf, so I pay a lot of attention to the calendar.' In accordance with some inscrutable cooking-related signal, he starts flipping all the steak chunks over in the pan. 'Anyway, what you saw is pretty much what'll happen unless I'm stabbed with something silver. Or shot with silver bullets, I guess, although I've never seen that happen. Otherwise, cuts and bruises go away, even big ones. Broken bones knit up.' He sniffs the sauce, frowns, and grinds some pepper into it. 'How about you? Any problems with silver?'

'Not that I'm aware of. I mean, I've never tried to stab myself with it, but half my jewellery is silver, and I've never had a reaction.' Definitely an avenue she needs to explore, though, given the similarities she observed. Which, now that she's thinking about it, brings to mind another question. 'Um, what about vampire fangs? For you, I mean. Do you heal from them the same as everything else, or are they different?'

He puts a lid on the sauce and turns down the heat. 'No idea. You're the only vampire I know. Why?'

'They're the only thing that can break a vampire's skin, at least that I know about. They're, um . . .' She hates using the word. 'They're magical.'

'Oh, I see.' He considers for a moment. 'You'd better try biting me, then.'

'I . . .' Angela lapses into silence. She knows he isn't wrong. Considering who she's planning to talk to, it's the obvious course of action if he's going to come along. 'Mike, look, before we do anything like that, are you absolutely sure you want to go to Phoenix with me? It's short notice, you'd have to take time off work–'

'Of course I'll go,' he says, cutting her off. 'It's for you and Chloë.'

'It could be a lot of time. When I said after Thanksgiving, I didn't necessarily mean a day or two later. We'll have to drive cross-country.'

'Why would we have to . . .' The puzzled look on his face clears. 'Oh, right. Sunlight.'

'Yeah. We might be able to find a red-eye flight that works on the way out, but any major delay would kill me. And we couldn't do it at all on the way back. Every flight east is going to hit the sunrise somewhere.' She doesn't mention that if Tess doesn't have any answers for her, she might not be coming back at all. When she said she'd put Chloë at risk for the last time, she meant it. But that half-formed idea is one she hasn't told anyone. 'You need to pay attention to moon phases,' she continues, 'but I need to worry about time zones.'

'I can imagine.'

'So, will that be a problem for you?' she asks. She manages not to sound hopeful.

'No, I should still be able to swing it. I've got time off saved up. And besides . . .' He hesitates.

'Besides?' Angela prompts.

Mike pauses for a moment longer before he says, 'I think maybe Shelly and I could use some space from each other right now.'

Angela frowns. 'Is something wrong?'

'Not exactly. Let's just say it'll be nice to have an excuse not to go to Thanksgiving. You're not the only one having family problems.'

'Mike, if there's something you need to deal with, I don't want to –'

'It's fine.' He tilts his head to one side. 'You should bite me.'

'I mean, if, if that's what you . . .' Angela fights to clamp down the wave of hunger that roils through her at the sight of his exposed neck. If he wanted to distract her, he's picked a good tactic.

She's the last person with the right to give relationship advice to him, anyway. He's not the only one making plans to skip town.

'Does it have to be the jugular?' Mike asks.

'N-no,' she tells him, wishing she'd fed a lot more recently before trying this. 'No. It'd be better if it's somewhere less . . . I mean, ideally I'm not going to be taking a big drink or anything, just a bit of, um, piercing. Let's stay away from the neck.'

She slides off the countertop and approaches him slowly, as if he were the dangerous one instead of her. Her fangs are out, of course. They've been out since he first mentioned biting.

I'm not going to suck his blood, she tells herself as he proffers his hand. *It's only a test. I've held out for way longer than this before. It's been ten days. That's nothing. I will not let it control me. I am the one in control. I am the one in control.*

It occurs to her, suddenly and forcefully, that if this works, if she can drink his blood but can't hurt him, then there'd be no risk of killing him if she ever gives in to bloodlust. He'd be as protected from it as Chloë using her magic, or more so if his healing works reliably. For that matter, can a werewolf become a vampire at all? Is it possible he could be totally immune to her? How would you test for that?

The idea of using Mike for blood makes her queasy in a way she's finding difficult to articulate. If it's safe to drink from him, though, if he'd be willing to help, if they could solve the problem without needing to go to Phoenix at all . . .

She shouldn't get ahead of herself. Try the experiment, collect data first. A nip, a nibble, as brief as she can manage. Bite and release.

Fast as a striking snake, she grabs hold of his arm and sinks her teeth into his wrist.

I am the one in control, she repeats to herself. *I am the one in—*

She lets go. She's already across the room; there's blood in her mouth, blood on her tongue, but it tastes wrong. It's burning her mouth, and she can't swallow it, can't bring herself to drink it down.

She throws herself at the sink and spits into it. It doesn't get rid of the grotesque taste of his blood, not entirely, so she twists the faucet on and fills her mouth with water, directly from the tap without bothering with a glass, and spits again. And again.

'Do I taste that bad?' Mike asks.

'It's not, I can't– You're not human,' she chokes out. 'You, you smell good, but the taste . . . It's pretty awful.'

'Sorry.' He takes a step closer, but doesn't touch her.

'It's not your fault.'

'So, I'm like a heaping spoonful of cinnamon?' he suggests. 'Or a lemon, maybe. I have a nice scent but you shouldn't take a great big bite of me.'

'Something like that.' Since she's still crouched over the sink in case she gags again, he probably can't see her weak smile. 'More like shampoo. Not really food at all.' Clearly drinking from him isn't going to work. So much for that idea. She should have known it couldn't be so easy. Back to Plan A. 'How's your arm?' she asks.

'Take a look.'

She turns her head to see him holding his hand out. The two puncture holes below the meat of his palm are already fading, almost gone.

She comes closer, watching as they disappear. The second, impromptu experiment may have failed, but he's passed the original test with flying colours. 'Well. It looks like you're safe against vampires. As safe as I am, at least. Maybe even more, since once they get a taste of you, no one's going to want to bite you a second time.'

'So does that mean I can come with you?' he asks.

There aren't any reasons left for her to say no.

'Yeah,' she answers. 'Yeah. You can come.'

CHAPTER EIGHTEEN

Excerpt From Chloë's *Gramarye*

Hooray! Werewolf backup!

It's something, at least. Although it's hard to imagine Mike in a fight with anything more threatening than a recalcitrant website. But since she won't take fragile and vulnerable me along with her, better him than no one at all. Two supernatural powerhouses must be a force to be reckoned with, right? Even if they both have desk jobs.

I hope they keep each other safe. I hope they find answers.

And if they don't find any answers, she wouldn't let him drive all the way back alone. Would she?

Anyway, whatever happens on their trip, fragile and vulnerable me isn't going to sit around and do nothing. I mean, I'm sitting around, yes, but I'm doing something.

Is this doing something? Whatever it is I'm attempting here? I really wish I knew.

I keep reading and rereading the myths. The voyages to the realm of death. Katabasis – the descent to the world beneath the world.

One of the first stories I looked up was the one the witches started to tell me. In the end, Ishtar got out of Irkalla with the assistance of Ea, god of wisdom and culture. But for Ishtar to get out, her lover Tammuz had to take her place in the underworld.

Tammuz also managed to get out for half of every year, though – he could come up when his sister Geshtinanna, goddess of the fields, went down there in his stead.

There's something there, if I can find it. There's a spell in that, if I can cast it.

But there's a story that needs to be written first. A story about a journey of katabasis.

If I can write it.

So I'd better do that. Although I wish I had a better idea why.

The First Missing Person
An Eleusinian Mystery Story
by Chloë Kassman

Part Two

'That,' Hecate said nervously, 'is a very big dog.'

The three-headed monstrosity was larger than Elephas the elephant. It might even have been larger than Ketos the whale. The colossal hound's snakelike tail whipped back and forth, and its alert, fiery eyes scanned the rocky plain in three different directions. Behind it stood the brass gates to the underworld in all their forbidding majesty.

The witch goddess and the lobster crouched down further into the shadow of a boulder. Of the many perils they had encountered on their journey thus far, the monsters and the barriers and the terrors without name, this one was without question the most perilous.

'I swear, if I get past that beast, I'm adding dogs and entranceways to the things I'm goddess of,' Hecate muttered. 'I'll deserve it. If anyone wants to argue with me about it, they can try to do this themselves. We'll see how well they manage it.'

'Can you use witch magic on it? Put it to sleep?' asked Astakos.

Hecate shook her heads. 'See, that's the problem with coming down here. Hades is one of the Big Three Gods. In his own realm, he's practically omnipotent. Using my magic directly against any of his stuff would be like throwing a snowball into a volcano.'

'So we're screwed?'

'Well, we got past that river of fire, right?'

'Sure.'

'And the Hydra, and the Chimaera, and the flock of harpies.'

'We did, yes.'

Hecate sighed and sat down on the pebble-strewn ground, resting her backs against the boulder. 'Yeah, we're screwed.'

Astakos scuttled closer to her. 'You should look on the bright side.'

'What bright side? If we don't get past Bowser there, Persephone stays kidnapped for good.'

'Yeah, but if you do manage to pull off a rescue, I bet she'll be super grateful. Persephone will probably throw herself into your arms.'

Hecate quirked up her eyebrows. 'You think so?'

'Well, if you set the mood right. Be seductive. Once you get near enough to her, try wafting a cloud of your urine gently towards her face.'

'I really need to stop getting my romantic advice from a lobster,' Hecate said, rising back to her feet. 'Anyway, first things first. How do we keep ourselves from ending up delicious snacks here?'

'Can we distract him?'

'Maybe. What does a dog find distracting?'

'Dog food.'

'We don't have any.'

'Squeaky toys.'

'Once again, I neglected to bring those along.'

'Small running animals.'

'That,' Hecate said, eyeing Astakos, 'we might be able to arrange.'

'Um.' Astakos's antennae quivered nervously. 'What exactly do you have in mind?'

'I can't cast spells on him, but I can cast spells on you.' Three pairs of hands rose up, fingers contorting into arcane configurations. Glowing patterns and sigils formed in the air around them as they moved. 'How about we make you the world's fastest lobster?'

'I'm already the world's fastest lobster! I'm the world's only lobster!'

'Then your entire species,' she said as the mystical energies shot forward and enveloped him, 'is about to get a temporary turbo boost. Draw him off, get away from him, then meet me on the other side of the gate.'

'This is a terrible idea!' Astakos wailed as he shot off across the barren landscape, swift as a bolt fired from a ballista.

The great dog's heads lifted in startled surprise. A moment later, he launched himself after the lobster with a roar, his footfalls echoing like thunder as he chased down his prey. But each time one of the massive heads bent down to bite, the teeth closed upon nothing but air. The warden of the gate was fleet, but Hecate had made sure Astakos would be the tiniest bit fleeter.

She watched the tiny lobster zig and zag his way through the rocks and boulders, the hound behind him batting the stones out of the way as he pursued.

'He'll be fine,' Hecate muttered to herself as she snuck out of hiding and tiptoed over to the gate. She glanced back across the plain and blanched as a claw missed her friend's tail by mere inches, cracking the ground beneath with the force of the blow. 'Absolutely fine.'

'That was *horrible*!'

'So you keep saying. It got us past the gates, didn't it?' Hecate wished that Astakos would let it go. She wasn't in the mood for an argument. Her arms were aching, and her ankles felt like someone had been stabbing them with a sword.

'That's easy for you to say! You didn't nearly lose your tail to those teeth! And the claws! And the *barking*!' Astakos shuddered. 'Do you have any idea how disturbing it is to get growled at in three-part harmony? That was too weird.'

'Weird?' She tried to adjust her bodies into a more comfortable position, and failed to find one. 'You're saying that having three voices is weird? To me?'

'Er, well, I mean, I'm sure if your heads ever growled together, it would be lovely. Charming. Just the nicest kind of tripartite growling–'

'I'm sorry I said anything. Never mind.'

Half a mile up the side of a wall of bones, Hecate was beginning to wonder if their plan had some terrible flaws in it. It wasn't a particularly difficult climb, since the irregular surface offered plenty of handholds and footholds, but it was a very, very long one.

The Palace of Hades was made out of bones and sinew, millions upon millions of femurs lashed to tibias, skulls nesting in pelvic girdles, grinning mouths and empty eyes spiralling up to impossible heights. The tallest of the towers nearly scraped the roof of the vast underworld cavern, miles above, and the lower levels spread out into an uncountable number of chambers, wings, balconies, gatehouses, and courtyards. Pale, wispy ghosts flitted about its walls, but the shades ignored Hecate and Astakos, and they returned the favour.

'Are you sure we're going to the right place?' Astakos asked. 'How do we know she's in the palace at all?'

'We don't. But it seems likely. He wouldn't piss off the other gods on a whim, which means he kidnapped her for some purpose. Whatever it was, he'll want to keep her close. Besides,' she added, 'umpteen thousand rooms, but only one where the lights are on? I'm thinking that's where the living girl is.'

From below, they had noticed the barest, faintest flicker illuminating a window midway up a slender tower. In the world above it wouldn't have been noticeable, but in the unrelieved darkness of the cave, it stood out as clearly as a lit flare.

At the time, climbing up to it had seemed like a better strategy than walking through the front door and encountering any guards Hades might have posted, or perhaps running into Hades himself. But she'd long since started second-guessing the idea.

'Can you climb any faster?' said Astakos. 'This is taking so long.'

Hecate threw three glares at the lobster riding on her shoulder. 'Why do you care? You're not doing any of the – Ow!'

Hecate winced as a bone – an ulna by the look of it – dropped from somewhere above and hit her square on a head. Two of her hands lost their grip on the smooth surface of a skull, and she felt her middle body slipping down. Only a quick grab from the ones on either side kept it from a long, shattering fall to the cavern floor.

Her shoulders burned, wrenched almost out of their sockets by the sudden strain, and she scrabbled at the wall with her free hands to regain her purchase.

'What was that?' Astakos said as he scrambled off the endangered third of her and onto a safer perch. 'Are we being attacked?'

'If that was an attack, it wasn't a very impressive one,' Hecate replied as she finally got a good hold on a ribcage. 'I'm thinking that Hades, lord of the underworld, the unseen god who carries away all that lives, could probably do more than fling body parts at us.'

As soon as she was done speaking, a fibula plummeted down past them, followed by a femur. Hecate and Astakos watched the bones fall. It took a good twenty seconds before they broke into pieces on the ground below.

'Let's find out what's going on,' Hecate said, and resumed her endless climb.

The endless climb ended about fifty feet further up, where they found Persephone sawing away with a fruit knife at the last of the bones barring her window. She cut through the tendons holding it in place and it fell from the embrasure, coming close to braining Astakos.

'Hey, watch it!' the lobster cried.

'Astakos?' Persephone said in surprise. 'Hecate? What are you doing here?'

'We've come to rescue you! Which is apparently entirely unnecessary,' Hecate answered, eyeing Persephone's nearly complete escape attempt.

'Not if you know the way out of Hades, it isn't,' Persephone said. 'Because my scheme for getting away stopped at "crawl out of the window, climb down, and get hopelessly lost".'

'Oh! Oh, good. I mean, not good, that would have been bad, but I'm glad that I . . . That is, I'm sorry that you . . .' Hecate coughed. 'Er, can I come in for a minute? Just to rest my arms?'

Persephone stepped aside, letting Hecate and Astakos enter her prison, which proved to be a sumptuously appointed chamber. There were so many gilded decorations festooning the walls that it looked like someone had savagely murdered a jewellery shop and splattered its innards around the room. An enormous feather bed took up the whole of one side, and across from it was a long table laden with delicacies and jugs of wine.

'Nice digs,' said Astakos.

Persephone's lips tightened into a grim line. 'Hades was trying to impress me. He wants to marry me.'

'He thought that kidnapping you was the best way to propose?' Hecate asked.

'Apparently. So as you can probably imagine, I'd love to get the heck out of this place.'

Hecate nodded. 'Then let's get going. As long as you didn't eat or drink anything while you were here, you shouldn't have too many problems.'

'Ah.' Persephone glanced down at the fruit knife in her hand, sticky with red juice. 'How big of a problem would it be if I ate something?'

A look of concern crossed Hecate's faces. 'The food of the dead isn't meant for the living, and marks you as being part of death's domain. The plants in this realm grow without light or warmth, and are not of your mother's making. Eating food in the underworld traps you here.'

'Forbidden fruit,' Persephone said darkly.

'Nice phrase.'

'Thanks, I invented it just now. But look, it wasn't even a whole piece of fruit that I ate.' Persephone gestured towards the table, where a halved pomegranate sat, a single spoonful of seeds missing from its exposed flesh. 'I had part of a food. So maybe I'm not trapped? Or I'm only partially trapped? What would that even mean?'

'How about we ask the other gods for a judgement call on that,' said Astakos. 'Perhaps sometime when we're not, I don't know, hanging around inside the home of the guy who took you captive?'

'He's right,' Hecate said. 'Let's get this sorted out later.'

Persephone tucked the knife into her belt and strode towards the window. 'So what's our route out of here once we get down, Hecate?'

'First we have to get past the giant three-headed dog guarding the gate.'

'OK.'

'Then a nine-headed serpent.'

'All right.'

'Then a monster with the body of a lion and the heads of a dragon, a lion, and a goat–'

'What is it with this place and multiple heads?'

'There's nothing wrong with multiple heads,' said Hecate as the three of her eased themselves over the windowsill and started climbing down. 'What has everyone got against multiple heads?'

'You're absolutely right,' Persephone said, smiling up from below her. 'In fact, some of the nicest people I know have multiple heads.'

Hecate smiled back. 'Oh, do you really think so?'

'I do.'

'You know, one of the big advantages of having three mouths is–'

Astakos, once again perched on Hecate's shoulder, whapped her on the head with his crusher claw. 'Maybe right at this moment, less flirting and more escaping from you two? Because it'd be a little too ironic if Hades overhears our getaway before we've actually got away.'

'I wasn't–'

'We weren't–'

'Not that I wouldn't–'

'I mean, if she–'

Astakos rolled his eyestalks. 'It's fine, it's great, I hope you two hatch thousands of healthy larvae together. But please save it until we're at least past the dog.'

Blushing furiously, Hecate and Persephone climbed down in silence.

Hecate paced to and fro across the antechamber, her bodies weaving around each other, sandalled feet slapping the marble floor.

'Would you please stop twiddling yourselves?' said Astakos.

Hecate glanced at the doorway leading to the Olympian throne room. 'I want to know what the decision is.'

'It's not like you can do anything about it.'

Hecate resumed pacing as Astakos sighed. Soon, however, he was distractedly tapping his claws against the marble himself. She wasn't the only one concerned about how things might turn out.

Not much later, though, Persephone flung open the doors and emerged, her expression unreadable. Hecate immediately surrounded her.

'Well? What did he decide?' she asked.

'Almighty Zeus, god of the sky, god of thunder, bearer of the aegis and king of all the gods, went for the split decision. I ate six pomegranate seeds, so I have to spend six months of every year in the underworld.'

'Could have been worse,' Astakos said. 'I guess Zeus is tough but fair?'

Persephone snorted. 'Zeus is a sexual predator. This was the compromise between his actual goal of giving me to his brother as a sex toy and my mother's threat to destroy all life if he went through with it.' She leaned her back against a Doric column. 'Mom says she's going to make things miserable for everyone every time I'm down there, and I'm not about to let the creeper death god touch me, so we'll see how long this little arrangement lasts.'

'Sounds like it'll be no fun at all for you for as long as it does,' Hecate said sympathetically. 'Half of all your time trapped in a bone palace with your kidnapper and a bunch of ghosts.'

'My biggest worry is that it's going to be astonishingly boring. There's not a lot to do down there. I'm thinking of asking the Muses to invent the novel so that I'll have something to read.'

'Do you want company?' Hecate asked.

Persephone blinked in surprise. 'What?'

'Well, I mean . . .' Hecate looked down and scuffed the floor with the toes of a couple of her sandals. 'Turns out that as the goddess of necromancy, I can go down there and come back if I want to. I mean, obviously, since I was there looking for you and now I'm here.

But I thought, since I can, if you wanted someone to talk to who wasn't dead or creepy or a three-headed dog . . .'

'I'd like that,' Persephone said.

'Yeah?' asked Hecate, raising her heads.

Persephone took Hecate's hand, lacing their fingers together. 'Yeah.'

Astakos rubbed his maxillipeds together in satisfaction, and scuttled off to leave the two-to-arguably-four of them alone. Even though their courtship had been urine-free and sadly lacking in moulting, it seemed to be working out – and once such a thing had started, it was generally best to let it progress on its natural course without interference.

Besides, Olympus usually served crab cakes at the buffet table, and he didn't want to miss out.

CHAPTER NINETEEN

Brookline
18 November 2000

'Why do you roll up your clothes like that?' Chloë asks.

Angela pauses in the middle of turning a blouse into a neat cylinder. 'They fit in the suitcase better and they don't wrinkle. What do you do?'

'I cram whatever I can find into a bag at the last possible minute while thinking, "Oh, God, I'm never going to make it out of the house in time." I can't imagine packing a whole day in advance. Especially not right after waking up. That's not natural. You could at least put it off until later.'

'Absolutely not.' Angela shudders. 'I'd go insane. I'd spend all of today worried that I was going to forget to put in something important.' She goes back to rooting through the vast array of outfits squeezed into her closet, all meticulously arranged by style, fabric, and colour. Or she claims that they're arranged by colour, anyway; however much Angela swears there are vast differences between onyx and jet black and midnight black, Chloë has never been able to see them. The overflowing closet is the only area of indulgence in Angela's room, which is otherwise as spare as a monk's cell.

Assuming the monk also had a fancy computer he used to reduce data from ten-metre telescopes.

Chloë tries to envision her T-shirts and flannels hanging next to Angela's corsets in a closet like this one somewhere. She wonders if she'll ever see that in reality. Although if they do end up sharing an apartment someday, Chloë's clothes are more likely to be flung around on the floor next to the closet door.

She stretches out on the mattress, propping her head up with her hands. 'I don't usually leave anything important behind when I pack. Only minor stuff like toothpaste, boarding passes, and underwear.'

'Please tell me you're joking.'

'Mostly. Have you always played clothing Tetris with your suitcase? How is this the first time I'm seeing it?' Chloë asks. 'I guess we haven't really been on any long trips together.'

'Travelling is hard for me.'

'Oh, right.' Of course Angela is going to avoid extended journeys through uncontrolled environments. The further she strays from her tinfoil-covered bedroom window, the greater the risk. 'I should have realised.'

'That's one reason I stick to a carefully organised plan.' Angela slides one hanger after another left to right across the short distance available, glancing over her clothes, leather and velvet and vinyl shifting by. 'As tempting as your "eleventh hour insane chaos" method sounds.' She holds up a pair of capri trousers for inspection. 'Do these look even vaguely normal? I have to have something I can wear when I meet with my advisor.'

Chloë looks dubiously at the buckles running up the sides. 'Maybe? How normal does it have to be?'

'Enough not to raise any eyebrows, I guess. It's academia, so it isn't like I need to put on a business suit.'

'Then it's probably fine.'

'I suppose it doesn't really matter.' Angela rolls up the trousers and tucks them into the suitcase. 'What's he going to do, write me a bad letter of recommendation for a job I can't take?'

'Couldn't he refuse to sign off on your thesis or something?'

'Over a pair of trousers? I hope not. Anyway, who knows if I'll even finish the thesis?'

Chloë sits upright, frowning. 'I thought you were 90 per cent done.'

'I am. Sometimes it feels like there's no point, though, you know? I mean, if I don't . . .' She pauses and shakes her head, not speaking the rest of the thought aloud.

If you don't what? Chloë thinks. *If you don't get a job? If you don't get any answers out of Tess?*

If you don't come back?

'You've put in so much work already,' Chloë says. 'Wouldn't you hate tossing it all aside now?'

'I would,' Angela admits. 'But I also wanted to leave more behind than a couple of papers and *The Role of Planets in Shaping Structure in Transitional Disks – a Dissertation by Angela Ryan.*' She shrugs. 'I might as well not horrify my advisor with my clothing choices, though.' She pulls a pair of lace thigh-high stockings out of a drawer and examines them closely.

'Those might be a bit much,' Chloë tells her.

'They aren't for the meeting. I'd be using these for regular evening wear. Do you think they go with the miniskirt with fake fur trim?'

'The one that looks like someone killed and skinned a muppet?'

'Yeah.'

'Probably.' Chloë hesitates, then asks, 'Do you ever wish I dressed up more?'

'What do you mean?' Angela says, absently coiling up the stockings. 'Of course not.'

'Even when we go clubbing?' she persists. 'Because I was thinking I could let you pick out clothes for me sometime.'

The stockings drop to the floor as Angela turns, her eyes going wide with surprise. 'You thought what?'

'That I could let you dress me up. In whatever.'

Angela is immediately kneeling down in front of her, her hands on Chloë's shoulders. 'Sweetie. You know I love you just the way you are, right?'

'I know that, yes. And I also know, even though you've never said anything, that you'd prefer it if I wore something a little, I don't know, fancier when we went clubbing.'

A look of distress passes across Angela's face. 'It isn't, I mean, I'm not trying to . . . but when we went last month, your jeans had holes in them.'

'Oh.' Chloë tries to remember. 'Did they? Probably I didn't have anything else clean.'

'Holes at the knees,' Angela confirms. 'And not intentional holes. Just, just knees, wearing through the fabric, until there are holes. I know you like those jeans, I would never tell you not to wear those jeans, I'm sure they're very comfortable jeans –'

'Angela,' Chloë says firmly. 'I am offering. You are not making me throw away my jeans. I am voluntarily saying that you can put me in something that doesn't leave my knees hanging out for all the world to see, OK? Next time we go out.'

'Next . . .' Angela trails off. Her hands drop from Chloë's shoulders, and she turns back to the suitcase. 'We probably shouldn't plan too far . . . I mean, this is, it was very sweet of you, and, and let's talk about this when I get back, OK?'

Chloë curses silently to herself. She thought she'd been subtle. 'Sure.'

'How was your day today, anyway?' Angela asks, in an obvious attempt at changing the subject. 'Anything interesting happen while I was dead to the world? Do we have a president yet?'

'Nope. Everyone's still arguing over hanging chads.'

'Ugh. Do you think Bush is going to end up winning?'

'God, I hope not.' Chloë shudders. 'That would be a disaster. For everybody.'

'Do you think he'll start a war?'

'Maybe. His dad did.'

Angela sits on the suitcase so she can zip it up. 'Gay rights would head right back to the eighties.'

'Yeah. We could forget about legal marriage.'

'That's for sure.'

'It'll have to be a commitment ceremony, or a Vermont civil union or something. I mean, not that the Democrats are so very enthused about gay marriage, either, but I thought a civil union here in a few years might at least be . . .'

Chloë trails off when she notices that Angela has gone completely immobile, the zipper stopped only halfway up the side of the suitcase. She's become so inhumanly still it's as if she's turned into a statue. Not even the telltale twitch of an eyelash gives away that she's capable of motion.

'Angela?' Chloë asks. 'Are you all right?'

'Did . . . Was that . . .?' Angela stops, gathers herself together, and starts again. 'Did you just propose to me?'

'I . . .' Chloë takes a moment, trying to figure out how to respond. 'I guess I did? Yes?'

Silence answers her. Silence and an eerie lack of movement.

'Is that, is that a no?' Chloë blurts out once the lack of response has gone on far too long to be comfortable.

'No, it's not a no.' Angela's voice is very quiet. 'But it is a why now? If we can't, if I can't plan our next date, why did you think . . .?'

'I'm sorry,' Chloë says. She can feel tears slipping down her cheeks. 'That was stupid. But you're going away, and it feels like you might be . . . going away. So I'm, I'm clinging.'

Angela walks over and sits down next to her on the mattress, her arms open in invitation. Chloë eases herself into them. Angela holds her close and gently runs her fingers through Chloë's curls.

'It wasn't a no,' Angela says, 'and we'll talk about it more when I get back.'

Chloë sniffles. 'Right. When you get back.'

Angela doesn't say anything further. All she does is stroke Chloë's hair.

PART FOUR

The Wolf And The Snake

CHAPTER TWENTY

Chinatown, San Francisco
17 February 1969

the dragon has the face of a lion and the body of a centipede a hundred legs a thousand legs and it skitters towards Tess roaring with the sound of drums and explosions eyes rolling mouth open saliva dripping from its sharp sharp teeth

You should pet it, says the snake in her left ear. *It looks friendly.*

Are you out of your tree? asks the wolf in her right ear, its voice gruff and low. *That thing'll bite the arm right off your body. Bite the body right off your arm. Swallow you whole, chew on your soul.*

Says you, the snake in her left ear hisses, sibilants drawn out to impossible length. Sssaysss you. *Touch it and you'll get magic powersss. Touch it and you'll live forever. Fortune favourss the bold.*

Touch it and you'll end up as a vitamin-rich snack, says the wolf in her right ear.

she's more inclined to believe the wolf because everything is shit the world is shit this trip is shit what the hell was in that acid it can't have been just acid because that dragon is a million miles long circling the earth like a boa constrictor and if it squeezes too tight it'll crack open the goddamn world

she should leave she should get away right now but it's hard to move it's hard to think past the smoke in her nose and the people jostling into her and the tingling itching burning in her fingers in her toes and the noise all the noise all the singing and shouting and drumming and screaming

happy fucking chinese new year

instead of crushing the world the lion centipede dragon thing rears back and breathes fire into the sky and the fire spouts up and rains down in a fountain and fish are jumping in and out of it fire dolphins and fire whales and her hand reaches up for the camera hanging around her neck but the camera is gone haha that's right she hocked the camera at the pawn shop on mission street fuck everything

the monster slams back to the ground with a sound like a bomb exploding and its rolling eyes spin round and round until they fix on Tess the pupils are black holes dilated like a teenage mod kid high on purple hearts and it blinks its long lashes down over its enormous eyes the better to see you with my dear

I think you'd better flee the scene, sweetheart, says the wolf in her right ear. *Beat feet before the early wyrm gets the bird.*

enormous teeth the better to eat you with my dear

it's time to go so she turns and pushes through the crowded figures shoving them aside and they shatter into starlings and flap away shrieking more bombs are falling and they arc across the sky leaving traces of light that hang there and burn and the street is a river of smoke and she's drowning in it

napalm is burning up the jungle plants the fronds and creepers crawling up the sides of the buildings they smell of burnt marshmallows with a hint of rotten egg

the napalm is having a cookout and we're all going to die because nixon is in the white house and he's going to drop the big one the nukes are going to start flying any day now everybody says so except the hippies they think they're going to heal the planet with flower power morons

everything is shit the summer of love is over it was over long before she got here and it's been replaced by the winter of shit nothing but shit everything is shit hurray let's have a fucking party for the shit

she hits a clear patch at last out of the crowd and tries to run but the air is thick as tar so her knee comes up slowly

then her foot goes down inch by inch

she can hear the dragon behind her

eating the people behind her chew slurp smack

her toe finally touches the ground and time snaps back with a crack like a whip and Tess is running running running because she has to survive that's the only thing that really matters no matter what happens you've got to survive

running up the hills and down the hills and the buildings lean over to stare at her arching over her head and blocking out the comets and mandalas and pinwheels and explosions in the sky

Relax, says the snake in her left ear. *Turn off your mind. Float downssstream. The belly of a dragon is warm and sssafe. Curl up and sssleep and let it all go.*

The wolf in her right ear laughs. *That's what the junkies say. Turn on, tune in, drop dead.* Its voice drops down to a rumbling growl. *Don't sleep. Never sleep. Never close your eyes. Run.*

why did she even come here it was all bullshit everything she'd heard everyone who said go to san francisco live in haight-ashbury free food free love free drugs all there for the taking bullshit bullshit

nothing is ever free and now she's got nothing no camera no money and there's a monster behind her devouring the fucking city block by block and she doesn't think it's going to look a whole lot better when it gets shat back out

how long has she been running

the bombs aren't falling anymore it's quiet and the buildings twisting overhead are darker broken windows with shards of glass around the fringe they're leech's mouths with teeth made of glass and there are tongues lolling out of the doorways dripping saliva into the gutters

she slows down because her calves are aching and she can't get enough air fuck this city with its fucking hills at least back in the midwest everything was flat

her eyes are on the mouths and the tongues even though they're not doing much only whispering but you never know so Tess isn't looking where she's going and she walks right into him

Hey, he says, watch where you're going, freak.

sorry sorry there was a dragon and the bombs and she explains to the men gathering around about the city how the city is being eaten and they'd better get out of here she doesn't know how far behind her it is

Oh my God, he says. This chick is stoned off her ass.

Oh, yeah? asks another one. What's she on?

Beats me. Here, want to take a look?

he shoves her and she stumbles and the other one catches her and then he shoves her to someone else and they start tossing her back and forth like it's a game and she's the ball

oh shit oh shit oh shit shit shit

the shoving is getting rougher now and her legs aren't holding her up she's limp and one of them hits her in the shoulder hard enough to bruise and she drops to the ground and she can see the bruises spreading like mould across her skin under her clothes and then a cool voice says

Pardon me, Miss. Are these men bothering you?

yes she says yes they are help

then one of the men pushing her says, Do you want some, too, you slant-eyed bi–

and the air becomes tar again

the men are flying in a graceful ballet blood blossoming from their bodies and turning into poppies and soon they are covered in flowers and they drift into the jagged glass mouths

Tess blinks her eyelids going down her eyelids going back up it takes thirty years

there's a crunching noise and Tess can move again and there's a woman kneeling down asking, Are you all right? What's your name? I am Meijing.

it's some chinese or maybe japanese chick no it's a safer bet she's chinese in this part of town and behind her there's a guy with a sword no it's a sceptre no it's a stick with a knob on the end he's cleaning it off with a cloth wait no they're both rotting corpses held together with gristle and skin she blinks again and no they're not they're fine and behind them far in the distance the dragon is breathing fire into the sky maybe they frightened it away

The last of the fireworks, says the man with the stick. Tonight's festivities are almost at an end.

They ssseem nice, says the snake in her left ear. *Asssk if they have candy.*

The wolf in her right ear growls cautiously but she can tell his heart isn't really in it. *They've got moves, sweetheart, I'll say that much for them. They are moving and grooving and I may be in love.*

Who are you talking to? asks the chick kneeling beside her Meijing that was her name Meijing. Are you on something?

oh yes yes absolutely yes I am Tess and I am on something something is on me we are on each other and it is on

Good. That's good indeed. I am very pleased to make your acquaintance, Tess.

Meijing smiles

and her teeth are beautiful knives

CHAPTER TWENTY-ONE

Spleen, Phoenix, Arizona
22 November 2000

Angela pushes her way through the press of bodies. The club is more crowded than she likes, and the music is turned up way too high. The noise is ear-splitting right next to the speakers, where she's somehow managed to end up. Still, it could have been worse. At least there aren't any Thanksgiving decorations up. She tries to imagine what that would have entailed. Zombie turkeys? A cornucopia with severed heads spilling out of it?

She hasn't caught sight of Tess here, and she's been around the entire space twice. A final glance around yields no sign of a short, slender figure in a ruffled dress, hair dyed a dark cherry red. This has been another waste of time. Angela tries to keep her frustration in check as she manoeuvres towards the door. If she stomps recklessly through, she could hurt someone. Or even knock the whole dancing, drinking mass over like a bunch of black-clad bowling pins.

She automatically looks around for Chloë before she remembers that she came in alone. The realisation makes Angela feel almost physically empty, like her torso has been hollowed out. Tonight marks the first time in almost a year she's been to a club without

Chloë. There's no one waiting for her on the fringes of the dance floor, sipping a Fuzzy Navel, wearing clothes only just passable enough to get her inside.

It's ridiculous to feel so bereft without her there. She's hardly unreachable; the two of them talked on the phone earlier tonight. *It's better that Chloë's not here,* Angela tells herself. *Better that she's home, and safe.*

Although safety won't be an issue if Angela never manages to find Tess.

The first part of the trip to Phoenix went well enough; Angela and Mike made the cross-country drive in only a few days. The long hours on the road meant that Angela needed to spend some of it stored in the car trunk, but she'd been functionally dead while that was going on, anyway. They arrived before the holiday break, and Angela quickly arranged a dinner meeting with her academic advisor. With that business taken care of, gas, tolls, and lodgings became officially reimbursable by Arizona State University.

At the meeting, her advisor had waxed enthusiastic about the research she could get involved with as a postdoc. Really interesting projects, too, with a good chance of capturing the first true picture of an exoplanet. Proposals to use adaptive optics, telescopes with deformable mirrors to correct for atmospheric distortion, allowing ground-based observatories to get better resolution than the Hubble out in space. One group was planning to set up a double Wollaston prism to split the incoming light as well, and then employ quad filters to take images at multiple wavelengths. With a lot of work and a few lucky breaks, subtracting those images from each other might make any planets in the field of view pop out from all the random patterns of noise. Cutting-edge science. She hadn't had the heart to tell him that she won't be able to take any post-doctoral jobs after she graduates. If she bothers to graduate at all.

But at least the meeting had happened, which is more than she can say about her real reasons for coming to Phoenix. She'd tried to phone Tess, but the number had been disconnected. When she and Mike drove out to the house in Scottsdale, they were greeted at the door by a surprised middle-aged couple who'd bought the place in the spring. They'd had no idea where the previous owner had gone.

Angela's been trying to stay calm in her calls and e-mails back to Chloë, but the longer they've had to search, the more her anxiety has grown. It's possible that Tess doesn't even live in town anymore. Angela couldn't think of anyone she could ask. Tess didn't have any close friends, by choice.

If she's still around, though, the clubs might be their best chance of finding her. They'd been Tess's home as much as her house was, back when she and Angela were a couple. But this is the second one Angela has searched through with no sighting of Tess, and there aren't that many goth nights left to check on a midweek evening.

Angela stalks out the door into the dry, breezeless air. She flips open her phone and speed-dials Chloë again.

'Hi, you,' Chloë says when she picks up. 'How's the hunt going? Any luck?'

'No. There wasn't any sign of her at Spleen. I'm starting to think Mike and I are going to have to stay in town over the weekend.' If they don't find Tess soon, the holiday tomorrow will shut all of the clubs down for days. They'll have to hang around in Phoenix until everything opens again. Waiting and waiting, without any idea if they'll ever find her at all.

'How long do you think you should look before you give up?'

'I don't know. I haven't decided. It might not be an issue, anyway, right? Maybe things will go our way for once, and she'll turn up at the next place we look.'

'Sure.' There's a pause before Chloë hesitantly adds, 'But we should start discussing back-up plans now, shouldn't we?'

'I think it's a little early for that.'

'Is it?' Chloë asks. 'You don't know where she is. We need to figure out what we're going to do if you come home with nothing.'

Angela doesn't say anything, which probably tells Chloë just as much as if she'd spoken aloud.

'When you come home,' Chloë says sharply, 'and we talk about all those things we were putting off until you get back. Remember?'

'Can we not do this right now?'

'If not now, when?'

'I don't know, Chloë,' Angela snaps. 'I don't know when we should talk about it, or what we should do, or whether it'd be better if I didn't . . .' She can't bring herself to finish.

On the other end of the phone, Chloë lets out a long exhale. 'You said we'd have until the end of this year. We agreed on that when we got together.'

'And you're going to hold me to that? You're going to hold me to that even if it kills you?'

'We don't know for sure that it'll kill me.'

Angela's grip on the phone tightens. She has to stop herself from clenching it so hard that it'll crack. 'Is that supposed to be reassuring? I said I wasn't feeding on you again until we'd fixed this. And I meant it.'

'So don't!' Chloë shouts. 'Don't drink my blood anymore! But come home.'

'Chloë–'

'We know how long you can hold out, right?'

'And it's not long enough!' Angela yells back at her. 'Do you want to push it until I snap and rip out your jugular vein? Is that how you want this to end?'

'Just come home! Look, if I can figure out the snow ritual–'

'I'm not listening to this anymore.'

'But if–'

Angela hangs up.

When her phone rings, she ignores it. When it rings again, she turns it off.

Once she's calmed down enough, she walks down the block to the car. Mike is waiting there patiently, leaning against the hood. He raises his eyebrows as she approaches.

Angela shakes her head. 'I didn't see Tess.' She doesn't bring up her phone call with Chloë. What would be the point?

'Is there anywhere else we can try?'

'There's one more place I can think of,' she tells him. 'It's a few miles north on 7th Ave. If it's still around. After that, I don't know.'

Mike nods and opens the driver's side door, ducking down to get inside. 'We passed 7th on the way here, right?'

'No, that was 7th Street. 7th Avenue is on the other side of Central. Don't ask, it doesn't make sense.'

Angela buckles herself into the passenger seat, and Mike pulls the Corolla out into the sparse traffic. Outside, a bleak landscape of concrete walls, beige buildings, and grey dirt rolls by. As beautiful as Angela finds the desert outside the city boundaries, most of downtown Phoenix looks like a cinder-block termite mound.

'Are you sure you don't want me to come in with you next time?' he asks.

She eyes his white button-down shirt, neatly tucked into his blue jeans. 'You're not dressed for it.'

'Is that really important, considering?'

'They probably wouldn't let you through the door. But it's all right. Tess isn't going to attack me in front of a crowd of people. And I'm guessing a club wouldn't be a great place for you to, um, change, if you need to?'

'That's true,' he acknowledges. 'Although I'm hoping it won't come up.'

'Yeah. Take the next right.' She waits while he steers the car around the corner, then adds, 'I have to admit, I'm kind of interested in seeing what it looks like. You must be an enormous wolf.'

His eyes flick over to her before returning to the road. 'What makes you say that?'

'Well, you have to weigh, what, two hundred pounds, give or take? That'd be huge.'

'Nope. I'm a normal-sized wolf.'

Angela frowns. 'Do you get especially dense, or something? Like, you're not big but you still weigh as much as a person?'

'Not really.'

'Gah!' Angela can't keep the disgust out of her voice. 'That makes no fucking sense! Where does the mass go? Mass doesn't just disappear. You should be causing nuclear explosions every time it happens.'

She crosses her arms and glares out at the drab scenery. The dull colours are now at least occasionally interrupted by motionless palm trees or patches of tough-looking grass in the centre divider. The growling hum of eighteen-wheelers fills the car for a few seconds as they pass over I-10, then fades away as they leave the freeway behind.

'Maybe the mass goes into another universe,' Mike says.

She turns back to look at him. 'What does that even mean? You might as well be saying, "It goes to Narnia."'

'That kind of is what I'm saying.'

'All right, then what's the mechanism by which it travels to this other universe? How does it work? Where does the energy to make the transfer come from?'

'I suppose you have a point.'

'And,' she continues, her voice rising, 'what happens to the muscle and fat you're sending there? Is it the meat universe? Are there piles of meat lying around? Are there people living there, and every now and then a big mess of werewolf guts lands on their heads?'

'You seem really angry about this.'

'Yes!' she shouts. 'Obviously! You don't make sense! I don't make sense! Why don't I have a reflection? What if you were on Venus where there isn't any moon? None of it makes sense because we are some kind of unscientific *bullshit*.'

She slams her fist into the glove compartment, leaving a dent in the plastic she imagines she'll regret later, and slumps back in her seat. Suddenly exhausted, she closes her eyes.

'Thinking about it too deeply never helped me a whole lot,' Mike says. 'I was born this way, and at some point I kind of figured, "OK, this is me."'

'Different childhoods, maybe,' she murmurs. 'I was forced to accept all kinds of things without question, growing up. I rebelled against that pretty hard.' After a moment, Angela cracks her left eye back open. 'Wait. You were born a werewolf? You didn't get bitten?'

'No. The children of werewolves are always werewolves. You can catch it from a bite, too, but I didn't. My family's very careful about that kind of thing.'

'Oh. Well . . . good to know.'

She watches the street signs as they pass, trying to get a sense of how much further they have left to go. The city is greener north of the freeway, with aloes, creosote, and cottonwood trees adding their colour to the palms. The desert plants look strange under the orange glare of the streetlights, alien creatures crouching in wait. Beyond the foliage, an endless succession of strip mall parking lots unfolds to the horizon.

'What's it like, being a werewolf?' Angela asks. 'Do you have a pack? Is there an Alpha?'

'I have a family. The whole Alpha Male thing is a myth based on shoddy research from the 1940s.'

'So is anyone in charge, or is it more like–?'

'My mom.'

'Really? Why?'

A wry smile slips onto Mike's face. 'You wouldn't be asking that if you'd ever met my mom.' He glances at her sidelong. 'The scientific consensus can change, right? Like the Alpha Wolf thing. You can always get new information. Isn't that the whole point of science?'

'Sure,' she agrees. 'But there's a big difference between "wolves are more complicated than we thought" and "everything we know about light, energy, and matter is not only incomplete but totally wrong". It takes away our whole basis for understanding the universe.'

'And what if it does?'

She fingers the dent she left in the panel in front of her, then brings her hand away and puts it in her lap. 'That's a question I've been wrestling with every day for years now.'

They lapse back into silence.

They don't have too much further to drive. Another mile, maybe. Outside, the city shifts into a residential neighbourhood of low-slung ranch houses, hunched close to the ground to evade the rising heat of the Southwestern days. A few blocks later, the homes surrender to the strip malls once again. Unable to keep still, Angela alternates between picking at the faux-fur trim of her miniskirt and smoothing it out.

'What's the downside of being a werewolf?' she asks as the car begins to round Melrose Curve. 'We're almost there, by the way.'

'Why are you so sure it's got a downside?'

'Cynicism.'

'Werewolves crave the taste of human flesh,' he says. 'The urge waxes and wanes, but it never goes away completely.'

'Oh.' Angela wonders if she counts as human. 'How do you deal with that?'

'Training. My family's been under the curse for a long, long time now. We use a lot of tricks to keep us all, well . . . to keep us domesticated, I guess you could say. Part of me still expects a treat whenever I hear a clicker.'

'Does it work?'

'Mostly,' he says. 'I've never bitten Shelly. But it's always at the back of my mind, you know?' He drums his fingers against the steering wheel. 'The need for it, the worry that you might just lose it one day.'

'Yeah,' Angela says quietly. 'I know what you mean.'

'My mom thinks it's important to keep werewolfkind alive. Have children. Keep the traditions going. I'm not sure I agree. You can probably guess why I was happy to have an excuse to skip Thanksgiving.'

'What does Shelly think about all this?'

'We haven't really discussed it.'

'You haven't? Mike–'

'Well, I mean, she's been trying to talk to me about kids for a while now, but I keep putting her off. I haven't told her why.' He grins humourlessly.

'Mike, you need to talk to her. You need to tell her what's going on.'

His eyes slide sideways to meet hers. 'Do you tell Chloë everything? When you're struggling with the vampire stuff, do the two of you always sit down and have a nice, calm conversation about it?'

'I . . .' She trails off without answering.

'Should I start looking for a place to park?' Mike asks.

Angela blinks. 'What?'

'It's somewhere right around here, isn't it? Should I park?'

There's more she wants to say. She'd like to let him know that he can talk to her any time if he needs to, one monster with problems to another.

But it's pretty clear he doesn't want her advice. His last comment showed exactly how much it'd be worth, anyway.

'Yeah,' she says. 'Park here. Pull into the suicide lane.'

'The what now?'

'The centre lane. You'll want to turn left in a minute.'

He turns on the blinker and eases the car over.

Angela walks the rest of the way to the club, leaving Mike behind again. The streets are empty, the stores closed. There aren't that many stores around to begin with. The area is a mess of shuttered businesses and empty lots. Noises were being made about revitalising it when she moved away from Phoenix. She doubts the plans will ever come to anything.

The lights outside the venue are the single spot of brightness in the neighbourhood. She can hear the pulse of the music long before she gets there. Pop Will Eat Itself's 'Eat Me Drink Me Love Me Kill Me'.

She should take her own advice and call Chloë. She needs to apologise for hanging up on her, at the very least. But she can't think of any way to do that without being asked a question she doesn't want to hear.

What should she do if she doesn't find Tess here, either? If she doesn't find Tess anywhere in Phoenix? Chloë wants her to come home and . . . then what?

There is no next step Angela can think of. No plan, no tentative hypothesis. No idea at all. Only things that don't work, can't work, don't make sense. Mazes with no exit points, every pathway leading to a dead end.

And if she does goes back, will she be able to bring herself to say goodbye?

The other option, the one that's been on her mind more and more lately, would avoid the danger of being near Chloë when her thirst gets overwhelming. Avoid having to say goodbye altogether. She could vanish without a word, leave everything behind. Let her career fall to pieces a few months early; it doesn't matter now, anyway. She'll let Mike take the car. He'll have to drive it back alone.

Chloë already knows she's thinking about it. So it won't be as cruel as it could have been. Only a little cruel. Surely not as cruel as risking Chloë's life.

But once again, what does she do after that? What can she do other than go back to assaulting strangers for their blood, betraying everything she's promised Chloë, promised herself?

What can she do other than starve?

Angela pays the cover charge to a woman with a shaved head and impressive biceps, who gives her an unwelcoming look. Or maybe it's a bored one. The lyrics of the song blast her as soon as she walks inside, Clint Mansell welcoming her to hell. The crowd is thinner here than it was in the downtown clubs, with almost everyone clustered around a long, L-shaped bar. Only a few people are out on the dance floor, alone or in small groups under the dim, coloured lights. One or two faces turn to look at her when she comes in, but most ignore her. Angela's gaze jumps rapidly from one person to the next.

After no more than a few seconds, her search comes to an abrupt stop at a small woman draped in falls of black lace, slow dancing with some guy who looks no older than nineteen and vaguely familiar. The woman's hair is dyed the dark red of a ripe cherry. It wasn't hard to spot her. In spite of how short she is, she always stood out in a crowd.

Tess.

CHAPTER TWENTY-TWO

Somerville
22 November 2000

Chloë listens in disbelief as her call goes to voicemail once again. She slams the phone back down on its cradle. From across the room, Entropy looks up in alarm.

Outside the window, a snowstorm has begun swirling down, fat fluffy flakes dancing in the wind and screwing up everybody's holiday travel plans. Chloë stares blankly as snow slowly gathers on the sill.

Angela hung up on her.

Angela hung up on her.

Chloë isn't certain whether her reaction should be screaming rage or hurt bewilderment. It came out of nowhere. Angela's been painstakingly conscientious about staying in touch, calling every night and sending e-mails whenever she manages to find an internet café. So what the hell is this?

Maybe it isn't true that it came out of nowhere, though. Maybe it shouldn't have been such a surprise. Angela has never done exactly this before, but there have certainly been times when she went silent, or stopped listening. When she'd run away from Chloë rather than face their problems head on. Once, she ran straight out the front door.

That was last year, before the two of them broke up for a week. Chloë doesn't think that everything will be patched up after a week if it happens again.

She's trying to decide whether she should call Angela one more time, to yell at her or plead with her or both, when the doorbell rings.

Entropy hurtles off the couch and races to the door so he can offer his greetings, in exactly the way that normal cats don't. After a moment, Chloë trudges after him, hoping she can shoo away her unexpected visitor quickly; whatever they're after, she doesn't want to deal with it right now.

A blast of cold air and a puff of snow blow in through the door. 'So,' Shelly says as she steps inside. 'Why a lobster?'

'Shelly, why are you . . . What?'

'I'm not saying I don't like the lobster,' Shelly continues, unbuttoning an eye-searingly pink coat. 'What I'm asking is, does making him a lobster add to the story? Or am I missing something?' Entropy butts his head into Shelly's leg, and she reaches down to scratch him behind his ears. 'Is there a mythological connection between Hecate and lobsters?'

Chloë's mind has finally caught up to the conversation. 'Wait – we're doing this tonight?'

Shelly glances up. 'You forgot.'

'I didn't forget,' Chloë says defensively. 'But I thought you were coming over on . . . Oh. Right. Wednesday is today.'

'All day long,' Shelly confirms. 'Is this a bad time? Should I come back another night?'

When Chloë asked Shelly to give the Hecate story a look-over, she'd figured that having a professional editor's eye on it couldn't hurt. As shy as Chloë is about her writing, she didn't want to miss out on any ideas that might help make this one work. If anything can make it work. She's having doubts about her ability to master the intricacies of witchcraft when the days of the week are beyond her grasp.

'No, it's fine. Come on in.' Chloë might not be in the best mood for an editing session tonight, but she isn't about to send Shelly back out into the snow. 'Do you want something to drink?' she asks. 'Coffee, or water, or . . . coffee? I'm pretty sure those are the choices.'

'Coffee would be great, thanks.'

'I'm keeping the lobster no matter what, just so you know,' Chloë adds over her shoulder as she heads for the kitchen. 'The lobster is my favourite character.'

'We'll see.'

It isn't long before they're ensconced upon the couch, sipping their drinks, with a purring Entropy curled between them. Chloë tries to listen to the notes that Shelly is giving her. But she isn't really hearing them. The words all slip past her without registering. Her mind keeps straying back to the phone call with Angela.

Is that how you want this to end?

I'm not listening to this anymore.

Chloë should be paying closer attention to Shelly, she knows. Especially considering the weather tonight. If there is such a thing as a 'snow ritual', this would be the right time to do it. And considering the argument she and Angela just had, waiting for the next snowstorm might be waiting until it's too late.

I'm not listening to this anymore.

I'm not listening to this anymore.

I'm not listening to this anymore.

It takes a few moments before Chloë realises that Shelly has stopped talking. She belatedly fumbles to fill the pause in the conversation. 'Um . . . that's, what you said, that's an interesting–'

'You're a million miles away tonight, aren't you?' Shelly says mildly.

'No! Not at all, I'm–'

'OK, so what was I telling you right then? You know, the thing you found so interesting?'

Chloë struggles to assemble half-heard fragments into a coherent thought. 'Was it . . . about the pacing, or . . .?'

'I said you should think about turning this into a novel.'

'What?' Chloë's befuddlement is momentarily overwhelmed by surprise. 'But I don't have time to do that! I need it to be finished!'

'As a story, it pretty much is finished, except maybe for the lobster. But I didn't mean for the ritual. I meant just to do it.' She gives Chloë a sympathetic look. 'Listen, I get what's going on. I'm worried about Mike and Angela, too. But there's not a lot we can do from here, you know? They've got superpowers, they'll be fine.'

'It's not that. Or, I mean, it's not only that. It's more because . . . It's because . . .' Chloë finds herself blinking back tears.

'What is it?' Shelly shifts closer to Chloë on the couch, her voice full of concern. 'What's wrong?'

Chloë takes a deep breath. 'Angela won't talk to me about . . . about what happens next with us. If she doesn't find Tess. And I think, I think . . .' She lets her words fade away into silence, unable to say the rest.

'Goddamn it!' Shelly bursts out, startling Chloë. 'Her, too? Christ, what is wrong with them?'

'With them?' Chloë echoes. 'Is . . . is something going on with Mike?'

'Hell if I know.' Shelly abruptly stands up, grabbing her coffee mug from the table. 'He's not talking to me, either. Or, I mean, he'll talk, but he won't say anything.' She takes an angry sip of coffee. 'For months, I've been trying to bring up where things are going with us. If we want to get married, if we want to have kids. I think he went to Phoenix because he'd rather fight vampires than have a conversation.' She puts her mug back down and glares at the wall. 'If your girlfriend weren't a gold-star lesbian, I'd wonder if the two of them were running off together.' Shelly makes a frustrated noise in the back of her throat. 'But I didn't mean to make this all about me. What's going on with Angela? What happened?'

Chloë strokes Entropy for a few moments before she answers. He stretches his head across her leg. She can feel his purr vibrating through her body.

'She hung up on me tonight,' Chloë finally says. 'Then she stopped answering my phone calls.'

'Oof. I'm sorry. I'd say whatever the equivalent of "men suck" is for gay girl couples, if I knew what it was.'

'So now I'm wondering if I'm going to get a break-up message in my e-mail,' Chloë says heavily.

'I don't think she'd do that to you.' Shelly offers a wan smile. 'I mean, if nothing else, she knows you don't check your e-mail.'

'I've started to, while she's away. In case she writes to me. I've been looking at it constantly. Like five times a day.'

Shelly gives her an odd look. 'Do you . . . think that's a lot?'

'I'm using a free dial-up service,' Chloë says in self-defence. 'When I take the new job, maybe I'll be able to afford something better. Then I can be online all the time,' she adds, leaning forward, her voice beginning to rise, 'because once Angela breaks up with me I'll fall back into depression and lose the job because of it and use the money I no longer have to spend all day in my bedroom making sad posts on LiveJournal so I can mope to the whole world!' She inhales sharply, out of breath.

Shelly blinks, taking that in. 'There are a few things we might want to unpack in all that.'

'It's probably not worth the bother.' Chloë collapses back into the couch. 'The most frustrating thing is, neither of us really wants to split up. If I could find my way back to the witches and get an answer, I think I could fix everything. But I don't know how.' She glances out the window again. The blizzard is coming down thicker and faster now. There's a thin white coating clinging to all the cars and rooftops.

'You've got those cards, don't you?' Shelly asks. 'Can't you ask them? I thought they usually steer you right.'

Chloë sighs. 'I've tried. They're no use.'

'None at all?'

'You want to know what they've been saying? Here, I'll show you.'

Entropy gives a disconsolate yowl as Chloë eases her thigh out from under his head and goes to retrieve her cards from the box of magical supplies. She tosses a few handfuls of them down haphazardly in front of Shelly. They land in messy overlapping heaps on the coffee table, the asymmetric figures of the ancient deck pointing in every direction, reversed Kings almost covering the Eights, a Jack peeking out from under a Seven. Nonetheless, the patterns they form are showing her the same incomprehensible message she gets every time she checks these days.

'There you go,' Chloë says. 'See the line of hearts and diamonds leading to the Ace? That means, "Seek out the dragon that guards the red path."'

'I'll take your word for it.'

'You know, metaphor, symbolism, and ineffable numinous transcendence are all right as far as they go, but just once it'd be nice to get a straightforward answer.'

The two women stare down at the jumble of cards.

'It can't be completely meaningless, can it?' Shelly asks.

'Oh, it means something. The problem is, I don't know what it could possibly be.'

'Well, what do you know about dragons?'

Chloë pauses, thinking it over. 'I suppose . . . they breathe fire and hoard gold?'

'And they can fly. What else? There's a dragon in the Book of

Revelation with seven heads. Is that kind of thing worth thinking about? Are there any other famous dragons?'

'Lots,' Chloë answers. 'Fafnir, Tiamat, Smaug. Norbert.'

'Norbert?'

'From the Harry Potter books. The one Hagrid hatches. Oh, and there's Falkor from *The Neverending Story*, and Zmey Gorynych, who causes eclipses by swallowing the sun.' Chloë stumbles to a halt as Shelly raises her eyebrows. 'He's Russian,' she says. 'I read a lot of mythology. Witch research.'

'Sure, fine, throw in the Russian sun-eater. Is any of this helpful?'

'I don't know.'

The two of them fall silent. Shelly frowns at the cards. Chloë puts her fingertips against the windowpane and watches the snow come down. The glass is so cold that it stings. Somewhere out there, far to the west, Angela and Mike are trying to find Tess.

'What about the red path, then?' Shelly asks. 'Any clue what that could be?'

'Well, I thought of the Red Line, but I take that all the time to go to work. If there was a dragon guarding the subway, I'm pretty sure I'd have noticed by now. Maybe it means a real road somewhere.' Are there any red roads? Only half-remembered images are coming to mind. Is there one in Hawaii, maybe? Or Rome? 'Or maybe it's completely symbolic,' Chloë offers. 'Like a trail of blood. Or lipstick. What else is red? Apples? Bricks?'

'Follow the red brick road?' Shelly suggests.

'I wish there was one. That'd make this easy, right?'

'Sure. As long as there's a handy tornado to get you there.'

'Speaking of which . . .' Chloë motions her head towards the window. 'Should you maybe start heading home? I don't think this is getting us anywhere, and the streets are going to be a mess if you wait much longer.'

Shelly looks like she's about to protest, but then she reluctantly nods. 'You're right. I'd better start driving while it's still safe. I'm sorry I wasn't more help.'

'Don't worry about it. I've been banging my head against this for three weeks without any luck. Thanks for giving it a try.'

'Call me if you want to talk, all right?'

'Yeah. You, too.'

After Shelly leaves, Chloë gathers the cards together and puts them back in the magical supplies box, tucking them in next to her other objects. The sea glass, the feather, the completely ordinary stick. Why did she collect them? What are they for?

Entropy jumps off the couch and twines around her ankles. She pets him until he gets bored and races away to check on the kitchen. Chloë considers following him and making dinner, but she doesn't feel very hungry. She turns on the radio and listens to the news.

It's all about the election, as always. It's like the whole country is trapped on the seventh of November and can't move past it. Republican operatives staged a riot at one of the recount sites in Florida. Men in suits, screaming, punching, trampling people to stop the vote from being counted. They succeeded.

Everything is terrible.

She shuts off the radio.

She won't try calling Angela again until tomorrow, she decides. Even if Angela bothers to answer, calling tonight might only make things worse. Both of them are upset, and neither of them have any good news.

Although that might be just as true tomorrow. Most likely, there'll be no sighting of Tess, and no progress on the ritual. Nowhere to go, nothing to be done. No good witch is coming to show her the red brick road.

Wait.

There is a red brick pathway in the middle of Boston, isn't there?

There's a red path in Boston. A red path with *a dragon sitting next to it.*

With a silent thank you to Shelly, Chloë grabs her coat and throws it on. Something is buzzing in the back of her mind that might be witch's intuition. This feels right. This has to be right.

Her foot is almost outside the front door when a plaintive meow from Entropy stops her. After a moment of thought, she turns around, goes to the kitchen, and pours an extra-large heaping of food into his bowl. There's no telling how long a 'sufficient' amount of time will be for a snow ritual, if that turns out to be what she's about to do. Her cat has ways of making his displeasure known if his dinner is late.

Entropy, however, doesn't come trotting up to the bowl for his meal, and continues meowing loudly. She finds him pacing back and forth in front of the magical supplies box. As soon as she comes close, though, he stops caterwauling and races back to the kitchen to eat.

Chloë stands there for a little while, staring at the box, then opens it and takes out the stick.

She isn't certain why she wants it, but she decides to trust the instinct. Maybe she'll need to use it as a hiking pole if the weather gets bad enough. Maybe it's magic. Maybe it's Maybelline. Who knows?

On her second try, she finally gets all the way out the door.

CHAPTER TWENTY-THREE

Phoenix
22 November 2000

'You wanted to talk,' Tess spits at Angela. 'So talk.'

'In a minute. We're almost there.' Angela walks faster, hurrying to make it down the block and around the next corner, where she left Mike waiting. She wishes she'd asked him to stay right outside the club instead. She didn't think this all the way through. After so many failures, she hadn't really been expecting to find Tess there.

She glances back at the two people following her, trying to place the guy trailing a few paces behind Tess. He's barely said anything so far tonight, staring morosely at the cracked sidewalk the whole way. After Chloë's encounter at the art gallery last year, she'd mentioned that Tess had acquired a new . . . accomplice? Minion? Lover? Angela wonders if it's the same one. She's sure that she knows him from somewhere.

His shock of acid-green hair hangs down above a long nose and wide mouth. He's dressed in heavy boots and vinyl trousers which are probably too warm for the Sonoran desert, even in late autumn. Maybe the mesh shirt he's wearing lets out some of the heat. Angela wouldn't know; she's never worn mesh, much, herself – it's too easy for her belly piercing to get caught in it.

'Quit checking out Russell,' Tess says.

'Don't be ridiculous.'

Russell. Hearing the name makes it finally click into place. The teenager that Tess was trying to seduce – that Tess had wanted Angela to hit on, as well – on the night they broke up. His hair had been lavender back then. She wonders if Tess ran into him again later, or went back to find him immediately after watching Angela jump into the canal.

'What are you doing here, anyway?' Tess asks. 'We were supposed to stay out of each other's territories. That was the deal.'

'There wasn't any deal. I told you not to come to Boston. I never said I wouldn't come here.'

'Well, that definitely sounds fair. Who the hell made you the queen of Massachusetts?'

'Tess.' Angela makes an attempt at keeping her voice even. 'Could you maybe try not being an asshole for five minutes? Then we can get this over with and I can go home.'

'Fuck you.' Tess grabs her shoulder and spins her around. 'You have a lot of fucking nerve to come here and say that to me.'

They've stopped on a corner by a restaurant that's been closed for so long that thick layers of graffiti cover its windows like an impasto oil painting. Behind Tess, Russell takes a few hasty steps back.

Angela isn't the only one who recognises the red flags her ex is raising.

Tess leans in closer, until their faces are only a couple of inches apart. 'I don't want you here. I don't like you here.'

'I just want to talk.'

'And you were thinking we'd have a nice little chat? After everything you've done?'

'After everything *I've* done?' That's too much for Angela to take. 'You tried to murder my girlfriend!' She's practically shouting in Tess's face now.

'Oh, please,' Tess scoffs. 'I was only trying to scare her.'

'You can't possibly–' Angela cuts herself off. She tries to force her anger back down to a low boil. 'I don't believe you.' She doesn't know why she's bothering. Accusing Tess of dishonesty has always been useless. Without exception, Tess firmly believes whatever she says at the moment she says it. 'Why would you do that?'

'So she'd go running back to fetch you, obviously.'

Angela shakes her head. 'You took a swing at her. You can bend rebar. It would have killed her.'

'I know how to pull a punch,' Tess says dismissively.

'Is that supposed to be your excuse? Instead of smashing her head in, you would have made it hurt?' Angela isn't shouting anymore. Her words are barely above a whisper. 'Like you did with me.'

'Everything all right here?' Mike's voice, coming up from behind her. Tess's eyes shift to him like a flicked light switch.

'None of your business,' she snaps. 'Who the fuck are you?'

Angela unclenches her hands. She hadn't even realised they were balled into fists. 'This is Mike. He's with me.' Her fingers are cramped from the tension.

'Oh, is that right?' Tess asks. 'Is he in the know, or are we supposed to keep it quiet now?'

'We can talk in front of him, if that's what you're getting at. I mean, he knows about . . .' Angela gestures towards her mouth.

'About what? About your special diet?' Tess grins at them. Her fangs are still hidden, tucked away up in her mouth. 'Is this your latest blood supply? I thought you didn't like them to have dicks.'

'I'm a friend,' Mike says, stepping up next to Angela.

Tess snorts. 'Is that what you're calling it now?'

'Tess, let's just go,' Russell says suddenly, speaking aloud for the first time that night. 'Whoever this guy is, whatever they want . . . They're not worth the time.'

'He's got a point,' Tess says, not bothering to turn to look at him.

'I'm pretty tempted to tell you to – what was it you said a year ago? "Get out of town, and don't come back"? I think that was the gist of it.'

'Look, I want to ask you one question.' Angela has to struggle to keep from raising her voice again. How does Tess get under her skin so easily, so quickly? 'That's all. You owe me that much.'

'I don't owe you shit.'

'Yes, you do! It's your fault I don't know anything about . . .' She lets the words trail away. Tess taps her foot on the sidewalk, waiting. Angela reminds herself there's no reason not to come out and say the word. Not here, when there's nobody listening who doesn't know the truth. 'About being a vampire. Because you didn't tell me.'

'You left. You don't get to come here and bitch about it when you were the one who left me.'

There are a thousand reasons why that's unfair. Angela can feel the arguments trying to shove their way out of her throat. She swallows them down. She's not there to get into another pointless debate with Tess. It isn't as if Angela ever won any of those when they were a couple, and she doubts that's about to change now. Not when Tess is always the one who keeps the score, awards the points, and changes the rules whenever she feels like it.

And not when Tess might have the answer that Angela's looking for.

'I need you to tell me if there's a way to drink blood without . . . without starting the process. Without turning someone into a vampire, or killing them.'

Tess stays silent, regarding her with an unreadable expression.

Angela tries again. 'Tell me that, and I'll leave. I won't come back. I won't bug you ever again. But tell me. Please.'

'Go to hell,' Tess says calmly. 'Why should I tell you anything?'

Angela's fangs pop out, unbidden. Driven by her anger.

Of course Tess won't answer. She's never admitted that her victims might not come back from the dead. Never admitted to anything that might cast her in a guilty light.

Which is the main reason Angela is absolutely certain that it's true.

'You should tell me,' Angela says, her voice tight, 'because I'm trying not to murder people.'

'So what? I don't give a damn what you're trying to do.'

'You'd better give a damn about it,' Angela growls. She can see Tess's body shift a little, getting ready. She can see the glassy, avid look Tess gets in her eyes whenever she's about to throw a punch. This is probably what she's been waiting for since the moment they caught sight of each other in the club.

'You don't know,' Mike says. 'Do you?'

Both of them whip their heads around to look at him.

'What?' Tess says. 'Shut up.'

'You haven't got the faintest idea if it's possible, much less how to do it.'

'I'm having a conversation, dickhead.' She bares her teeth at him. Her fangs are out now, sharp white spikes peeking out from behind red lips. 'You really don't want to interrupt.'

'But you haven't said I'm wrong.' He turns to Angela. 'She's wasting our time.'

'OK, now you've pissed me off.' Before Angela has time to blink, Tess closes the distance to Mike and has her hand around his throat. 'Congratulations.'

Mike smiles at her, and the centre of his face starts growing towards her with the sickening crunch of breaking bones.

'What the fuck?' Tess jerks her hand back and steps away as Mike claws at his shirt, the sound of tearing Velcro adding a strange counterpoint to the awful biological noises coming from beneath his skin. He drops to all fours, kicking off his jeans and shoes as his limbs shrink and twist, dark, thick fur sprouting from everywhere except his bald spot, which grows only a light fuzz.

Within seconds, he's a wolf, crouched low and snarling at Tess, coal black with a mangy patch on his head the colour of old bone.

Tess stares into his yellow eyes. 'Holy shit. Werewolves are real?'

'Mike, don't–' Angela starts, but he's already springing at Tess, a harsh growl coming from somewhere deep in his throat.

Tess only has time to swing her arm around like a baseball bat, but it connects and knocks him away, the force of it flinging him through the restaurant window with a crash of shattering glass. Cracks spiderweb out from the hole he leaves in the centre.

Angela stands paralysed, not sure what to do. Attack Tess? Check on Mike? She brought him because she didn't think he could get hurt, but she only bit him, she never flung him through a window at high speed.

Before she has time to make up her mind, he leaps back out of the restaurant with another spray of broken glass, looking more angry than injured. Angela snaps out of her stupor and moves fast, throwing herself in front of Russell, who's much too close for comfort, hunched down with his hands protecting his head. A few shards of glass bounce off her skin.

'Get away from here,' she hisses at him. Only a few feet down the sidewalk, Mike has knocked Tess to the ground and is clawing at her face. Tess shrieks, a sound Angela's never heard her make before.

'Are you kidding?' Russell says. 'I'm not leaving her here with that thing!'

'Go!'

He doesn't. How stupid can he be? He's the only one there without any protection against thrown werewolves, angry vampires, or flying glass. Against anything at all.

Tess has managed to flip herself on top of Mike and is snapping her fangs at him, trying to bite him somewhere that hurts. Blood leaks from her cheek in neat parallel lines. *So werewolf claws can pierce vampire flesh, too*, Angela thinks with a kind of numb clarity. She hadn't considered testing for that. For the first time, she wonders if Tess might be the one in trouble here.

Mike rakes a hind claw down Tess's side, more blood flowing in its wake. Angela decides she has to do something before this gets out of hand. Or any more out of hand than it already is. With a quick glance to make sure Russell is staying put, she steps towards the thrashing bodies on the ground.

'Hey, you idiots!' she shouts at them. 'Stop it!' She grabs Tess by the shoulders and wrenches her away, tossing her aside. Mike scrambles to chase after her, but Angela puts her foot on him and presses down. He doesn't seem to recognise her. He snarls and slashes at her leg, shredding her stockings and the skin beneath. Angela winces. It's been a long time since anything caused her that kind of physical pain. 'Mike, quit it, it's me.' He tries to claw her again and she catches his paw in her hand. 'Heel!' she yells in frustration.

Much to her surprise, that works. He blinks, and the bared teeth disappear, replaced by a wide-eyed, apologetic expression. He looks so much like a chastised dog that she has to stifle an incredulous laugh.

She turns to look at Tess picking herself up off the sidewalk. 'Are you done?' Angela asks. 'Or do you want to keep going until everyone comes to see the vampire and the werewolf fighting in the street? Maybe you want to wait until the police get here?'

There's a long pause before Tess answers, while she inspects the ripped lace of her dress with a frown; beneath the torn fabric, her cuts are rapidly healing. She glances up, her gaze coming to rest on Mike, her eyes narrowed. 'So you found someone who can chow down on a vampire,' she says. 'That's interesting. That's very interesting.'

'Yeah, it's fascinating,' Angela answers acerbically. 'Let's discuss it when we're not standing in front of the store window you smashed.'

Tess looks back to Angela, and gives her a toothy grin that leaves her eyes cold and hard above it. 'You're right,' she says. 'You're totally right. Let's get out of here. We can all go back to my place, get cleaned up.'

Angela stares at her. That's it? Is Tess seriously going to act like she and Mike weren't trying to eviscerate each other a minute ago?

Tess raises her eyebrows. 'What? You coming?'

Apparently, she is.

Angela doubts she can trust Tess's new-found amiability any further than a werewolf can throw her. No one forgives and forgets that quickly, and certainly not Tess. She's planning something. Plotting something. She has to be. The shift in mood, the empty smile – Angela has years of experience spotting the signs.

The sound of wet pops and snaps comes from below her, and Angela glances down to see Mike's muzzle shrinking, his torso expanding, his fur retracting back into his body. She looks away quickly when she realises her friend is about to become a human being again, and a completely naked one, at that.

'Could you, uh, move your foot?' he asks.

'What? Oh, sure.' Angela takes her weight off of him, still resolutely not looking in his direction as he shuffles over to get his clothes. 'Are you OK?'

'Yeah, I'm fine. A little bruised. But I've been banged up way worse than this without having any problems.'

'Good. I mean, I'm glad you're all right.'

Tess, she notices, is not being so circumspect about looking at Mike, watching him get dressed with a frankly appraising smile on her face. Much to Russell's obvious dismay. Tess, always the charmer.

Angela checks her leg. The bleeding has stopped, although the stocking is a lost cause.

She can't give up any chance to find out what Tess knows. Whatever Tess's scheme is, she'll go along with it, at least for now. At least until she learns whether Tess can tell them anything at all.

'So, am I going to turn into a werewolf-vampire?' Tess asks. 'What would that be, a vampwolf? A werepire?'

'No,' Mike says from somewhere behind Angela. 'Even if that's possible, I didn't bite you. Claws only.'

'Oh,' Tess says. 'That's a pity.'

There's a period of awkward silence while Mike finishes struggling back into his clothing. Tess pulls out a cigarette and lights it, blowing out smoke that hovers like a cloud in the still night air.

'OK, I'm decent,' Mike finally says.

'Great.' Tess drops the cigarette to the ground and grinds it out with her shoe. 'Let's go.'

CHAPTER TWENTY-FOUR

Boston
22 November 2000

Chloë hardly notices her surroundings as she makes the trip downtown, taking them in only in flashes. The wet, slippery steps leading down to the Davis Square T Station. Snow falling into the slate-grey Charles River as the train passes over the bridge. The hiss of the trolley doors closing as she transfers onto the Green Line. She's too focused on her goal to notice anything more.

She's headed for the Freedom Trail. The red brick line in the sidewalk that leads tourists around to all the sites of historic Boston. A route winding through the past, a connection to the dead who lived here before. A passage to their realm. It's the right place. The one where she needs to go. It must be.

The snowflakes are coming down in a wet, stinging torrent when she gets out at Government Center, the wind blowing them almost horizontal. They pelt hard against her face and she slits her eyes, making the few buildings visible through the blizzard go wavery and strange in her vision. She can barely see the concrete monstrosity of City Hall as she makes her way around it, and she has to use the luminescent glass towers of the Holocaust Memorial like a beacon to guide her on the other side.

But then she steps onto Marshall Street. The Freedom Trail is directly under her feet now, invisible beneath the thick white drifts. Which means the Green Dragon Tavern is dead ahead, although she can't make it out yet through the curtains of falling snow. The unofficial headquarters of the American Revolution and the starting point for Paul Revere's ride. Or at least a reasonable facsimile of it, since Chloë is fairly sure the original got demolished a long time ago. But the current one is nonetheless a Dragon on the Freedom Trail, the only one she knows about. If nothing else, it'll be a good place to get out of the wind while she figures out what she's supposed to do next.

When she gets close enough to see the silhouette of the tavern, however, there's something wrong with it. Lines that are curved when they should be straight. Jagged bits that should be smooth. She's trying to figure out what the problem is when the building moves.

That's when she realises it isn't a building anymore.

Its scales are the colour of grass in summer. Its eyelids slide open, uncovering a pair of lambent emerald eyes with slitted pupils, glowing like a cat's on a full-moon night. Predator's eyes.

The giant serpent uncoils its upper body and flexes its wings.

Chloë takes a step back as it lowers its great head towards her, opening a vast mouth to reveal teeth the size of bayonets. Its breath is hot on her face.

She strongly considers running the hell away. But she pauses on the verge of doing so, her body tensed for a sprint. The dragon moves its head no closer. They wait, staring at each other.

'I probably should have guessed there would be something like this,' she mutters, half to the dragon and half to herself. 'But I didn't, and I've got no idea what I'm supposed to do here.' It says nothing in response. She tries again, a little louder. 'If you wanted to give me any hints, now would be a good time.'

'You've had quite enough hints already, I think,' comes a voice from behind her.

Chloë whirls around, her stick raised like a club. She regrets the movement as soon as she makes it, but the dragon doesn't bite her in two, so she can't have startled it too badly.

'You're jumpy tonight,' says the witch. It's the first of the three, the one who told her the story of Ishtar in Irkalla. She looks Chloë up and down with her one eye, the muscles twitching in the other, empty socket.

'Sorry,' Chloë says, lowering her stick. 'I'm just a little, um, you know. There's a dragon.'

'So you've decided to go with the Hecate variant?' the witch says, ignoring both Chloë's comment and the winged serpent itself. 'Hmph. Not a bad choice, I suppose. An old version of the myth, but not without its uses. Some good, reliable tropes there – a kidnapping, a rescue, a return to the light. I don't remember there being a lobster in it, though. I'm not sure that makes sense.'

'Everyone's a critic.' Chloë can feel the dragon's breath huff against her back. She struggles not to take a nervous glance behind her. Did she write her story wrong? Is that going to be a problem now? An eaten-by-a-dragon kind of problem? 'I guess I should have listened when Shelly told me to cut it.'

'It doesn't matter, really. It's the same tale, simply a different telling. The details breathe life into the narrative, but don't change the meaning.' The witch shrugs, dismissing the subject. 'The writing's done now, anyway. Too late to change your approach. All that matters here is descent and emergence. Assuming you make it all the way down without dying. The emergence part rather depends on you not doing that.' She gestures towards the tavern-turned-monster. 'Well, go ahead, get on with it.'

Chloë is on the verge of asking what she's supposed to do, how dangerous it's going to be, but she stops herself. That might, she realises, waste one of the few precious questions she has left.

She pauses to consider her words, weighing the options at hand.

'I don't suppose,' she says, 'that you could tell me the answer I came here to find. Here and now, I mean.'

'Hardly,' the old woman replies. 'You only get one from each of us, remember? Ask me anything now and you'll be throwing it away. You'll have to make your way to my sister.'

So much for that idea. Chloë hadn't been very hopeful that it would work. That doesn't mean there's nothing she can learn, though.

'I would guess,' Chloë says, once again taking care with her phrasing, 'that there's a certain amount of danger involved in all this.'

'What makes you think that?'

'Cynicism.'

The witch chuckles. 'Well, you're not wrong. You could stray from the path and never find your way back. Or you could screw up an offering and a guardian' – she gestures at the dragon – 'might decide to take offence, and gulp you down its gullet. If you're lucky, it'll decide not to chew on you for a while first.'

Chloë glances behind her. The dragon slides its head from side to side with a faint rustle of scale against scale. It looks very much like a snake considering whether to strike. Chloë swallows on a dry throat.

This could fix everything if I can pull it off, she reminds herself. *That's worth taking a few risks, isn't it?*

'I don't know much about any of this,' Chloë admits to the witch. 'Like whatever it is I'm supposed to do next.'

'You should be able to work it out.' Her wrinkled lips curve into a sly smile. 'Where do you think you are?'

Chloë thinks for a minute before she answers. She doesn't want to get this wrong.

Her thoughts turn to the doodle she drew while her mind was on other things. The sharp-toothed, serpentine creature, lurking outside the walls.

'I'm at the first gate,' she says.

'Good luck,' says the witch. 'I have to give the mouth to my sister now, not that she'll use it properly. But it's her turn.'

A sudden gust of snow blinds Chloë for an instant, and when it passes the witch is gone.

She turns back to face the dragon. Its head continues drifting slowly back and forth; its teeth are bared and threatening. She wonders if it's growing impatient, preparing itself to devour her. Of course, she hasn't got the faintest idea what an impatient dragon looks like. Do dragons fidget? Is that what the head-sliding is about?

Get on with it, she tells herself. There's no point in wasting any more time; if she's misunderstood what she needs to do here, she's going to find out soon enough. In a very brief and very painful way.

She unbuttons her coat and slips it off. The wind bites through the fabric of her shirt, and she shivers.

She proffers it to the dragon, as is the decree of Ereshkigal, and the law of this place.

It takes the coat in its teeth and coils itself back up, eyes closing.

Under her feet, a brick walkway extends down Marshall Street, miraculously clear of the snow that mounds to either side of it.

She takes a step, and then another, and starts her journey down the red path.

CHAPTER TWENTY-FIVE

Phoenix
22 November 2000

Much to Angela's surprise, they don't need to use the car to get to Tess's new house. It's only a few blocks away, a single-storey bungalow the colour of an orange sorbet.

'You moved to Melrose?' Angela asks when Tess points it out.

'Melrose is a dump right now, but it's going to be the hip part of town in a few years,' Tess tells her. 'Wait and see.'

'I don't understand why you moved at all. What was wrong with the old place?'

Tess continues down the cracked sidewalk, sidestepping a slope of spilled garbage from a knocked-over trashcan. 'I do it every ten years or so,' she says. 'You should, too. Keeps the neighbours from noticing you're not getting any older. That's what I was taught, anyway.'

It rankles to hear that Tess had been taught anything at all. That's a gift that Angela was never given. 'So we don't get older? We won't die of old age?' She tries to keep her voice casual, conceal how much she wants to know. She's been wondering about that one for years now.

Tess rolls her eyes. 'Duh. We're vampires.'

Angela suppresses the urge to punch her in the face. Now is not the time to start another fight.

Not to mention that lashing out like that would be behaving too much like her ex for her own comfort.

'It would have been nice if you'd mentioned that sometime,' Angela grates out in a low rasp. 'Before you made me one, maybe.'

When they get closer to the house, Angela notices that wrought-iron bars cover all the windows, and the entrance is guarded by a steel outer door. A single prickly pear cactus grows in a garden which is otherwise bare dirt. Tess digs a key out from somewhere in the folds of her tattered dress and steps onto the porch.

'Who taught you to change houses?' Mike asks before she gets it in the lock. 'Did they teach you other things as well?'

'Some,' she says curtly. 'Not a lot.'

'Why not?'

Tess's lip curls. 'I didn't leave like some people did, if that's what you're asking. I got kicked to the kerb. Not my fault.'

'I don't really care,' Mike replies. 'Did they tell you what we want to know?'

'As a matter of fact . . . no. They didn't,' she says. 'But I bet they can give you the answer. If anybody knows it, they do.' Tess once again breaks into that dead-eyed grin. 'And I can point you in their direction. Will that make you happy? Will you leave me the fuck alone if I do that?'

'Sure,' Angela immediately answers. 'It's a deal.'

It's not what she'd been hoping for, but it's still more than she ever truly expected to get out of Tess. It's something, anyway. A signpost, a clue. More than what she had before tonight.

Tess unlocks the door and walks inside, Mike and Russell filing in behind her. Angela steps forward, then stops on the threshold.

'Tess!' she yells into the house. 'You have to ask me in!'

'Oh, yeah. Russell, take care of it, would you?'

Angela waits awkwardly on the porch. She's always found this one of the more irritating drawbacks of her condition. At least it's only people's homes she can't enter without an invitation. If the rule applied to all buildings, every store and bank and nightclub, she might as well give up on trying to have any kind of normal existence whatsoever.

Russell reappears in the doorway and stares at her, saying nothing. He looks oddly smaller than he did before. It takes a moment for Angela to realise that he's no longer wearing his boots, and he's lost a couple of inches in height as a result.

She's been hoping for a chance to talk to him alone. This could be the only one she gets. 'If you want to get away from her,' she says quietly, 'I can help.'

Russell's eyes narrow. 'She told me about you.'

His tone isn't a friendly one. Angela almost flinches back from the naked hostility in his voice. 'Told you what?'

'About what you did. Telling her you loved her for two years, then taking off the moment you got what you wanted.'

'Got what I wanted? What, being a vampire?' She shakes her head. 'That's not what happened.'

'She cried for days after you left, did you know that?'

The conversation is veering rapidly away from where she wants it to go. 'Russell, listen.' She leans forward, speaking with hushed urgency. There's no knowing how long it will be before Tess comes to check on them. 'She's lying to you. She'll say anything, do anything if she wants something from you. You have to have seen that.'

He takes a step away, moving further back behind the plane of the doorway. Getting himself to where she can't reach him, can't touch him without an invitation to come inside. Is he frightened? What else has Tess said about her?

He gives her a look that she thinks is supposed to be contemptuous. 'If she wants something? Did I miss you calling her to say hi sometime in the last two years? You're only here because you need something from her. And you brought your werewolf friend along to beat her up if she said no.'

'Does she hit you?' Angela asks. 'Because she sure as hell used to hit me. If you want to know why I brought Mike with me, there's your answer. And did she even tell you that you might not become a vampire? That you might just die?'

Russell says nothing, watching her from inside the house.

'If you ever change your mind,' she says, 'if you ever want to leave, you can get a hold of me in Boston. Can I give you my phone number?'

'Fuck you.' He turns and walks away from her. 'But you can come in, I guess,' he tosses over his shoulder as he vanishes into a different room.

After a moment, Angela follows him.

He's led her into the living room, where he takes up a position in a far corner and leans against the wall. Mike is already there, perched on a bright-purple sofa, leafing through a thick book. The furniture here is different from anything she and Tess had in the old house. Instead of dusty antiques, everything is brightly coloured and blocky. Yellow chairs next to square green tables. Angela wonders if that represents Russell's taste, or if it came with the house when Tess bought it.

She walks over to Mike and glances down at the book in his lap. It's a photo album, Tess's work, some kind of portfolio. Angela recognises a few of the grainy black-and-white pictures. Phoenix viewed from South Mountain Park, a vast sprawl of city lights extending across the valley to Camelback Mountain and Piestewa Peak. A night-blooming cereus, the flower fully opened into a complicated pinwheel of white petals. Angela was there when both shots were taken. She considers telling Mike that if he keeps flipping the pages, there's a chance he'll come across a nude picture of her. Or of Russell; Tess might have changed her furniture, but she probably hasn't changed her habits.

Angela is on the verge of giving him the warning when Tess comes in, a half-finished cigarette dangling from her fingers. She's changed into a different dress, a crape-trimmed gown that makes her look like a Victorian in mourning. She also took the opportunity to clean the blood off her face.

'The woman you want to ask is named Meijing,' Tess says as she crosses the room. 'She lives in San Francisco. Or at least she used to.' She holds out a hand for the album, and Mike passes it over. Tess turns it to one of the first few pages.

Angela cranes over to peer at the photo. A sturdy-looking Asian woman next to a taller, sickly pale Caucasian man. Both of them are frowning sternly at the camera.

Tess taps the face of the woman. 'This is her. But if you want her to tell you anything, you're going to have to get her away from this guy first.' She shifts her finger over to the other figure.

'Who's that?' Angela asks.

'That's Hiram. And you should stay out of his sight.'

Angela frowns. 'Why?'

'He's dangerous.' Tess looks at Mike with the same narrow-eyed expression she gave him after the fight. 'Send your attack dog to deal with him. He shouldn't have the kind of problems you would.' Tess shuts the book and tosses it on the sofa with a soft thump. She takes a final drag off her cigarette and stubs it out in a garish orange ashtray. 'There, you've got what you wanted. Are you happy now?'

'No. Why is he dangerous?' Mike asks. 'How am I supposed to deal with him?'

'And how are we supposed to even find them?' Angela adds. 'You haven't given us a lot to go on. You think they're maybe somewhere in San Francisco, unless they left?'

'Those two are the ones who told me to move every once in a while, so yeah, they're not going to be in the same part of town.' She spreads her hands in a gesture of apology that Angela doubts is sincere. 'If they're still walking around, though, they probably haven't left the city. Moving too far gets complicated for us.'

'We need more than that to go on.' Mike settles himself deeper into the couch and crosses his arms. 'Think of something.'

Tess glares at him. 'You're a real pain in the ass, you know that?' Two lines crease over her nose as she considers. 'I suppose I could jot down a few places Meijing used to hang out. Some of them might still be in business. But that's the most I can do.'

She glances at Russell and holds out her hand. Without a word, he collects a pen and notepad from a table and brings them over to her.

'I'd also really like to know,' Mike says, 'what you aren't telling us about Hiram.'

Tess hesitates, her pen going still on the page. 'I told you. He's dangerous to Angela, but not to you.'

'Cut the bullshit,' Angela snaps. 'Look, enough with your stupid secrecy. What's up with this guy? Why don't you want me to talk to him?'

Tess taps her pen against the paper, leaving a smeary set of dots. There's a long pause before she answers. 'He's old,' she says at last. 'Vampires, the older we get, the more . . . the more we become what we are. The good and the bad, both. You and me?' She gestures loosely towards Angela. 'We're babies. I bet wooden stakes bounce right off of you and you don't have any problem crossing water. You could probably even survive being in sunlight for a minute or two. Hiram's older. A lot older. He'd burn up like flash powder in the sun. I mean, *fwhoosh*.' Tess mimes a small explosion with her hands. 'But he also has, I don't know, powers. Stuff we can't do yet. He can get into the minds of other vampires, make them do things. Shit like that. Because he's really, really old. Meijing has been under his thumb for a long time.' She looks back down at the notepad, and starts writing where she left off. 'If you don't want the same thing to happen to you, keep the hell away from him.'

'Thanks for the warning,' Mike says. 'Although you maybe could have led with that.'

Angela picks up the photo album and reopens it, looking over the picture more closely. She says nothing, silently seething with anger. In two minutes, she's learned more about being a vampire than she did in two years with Tess, and two more years without her. All of it information that Tess could easily have told her when they were together, if she had cared a little more. But she never bothered to. Even now, when Angela and Mike might be walking into danger on her say-so, they had to pry the answers out of her. Had she ever had any real feelings for Angela? Any at all?

Did she really cry for days after Angela left? Or was that some kind of ploy to win over Russell?

Tess finishes making her notes and rips out the page. 'Here. If there's anywhere else she hung out, it wasn't while I was there.' She hands it to Angela, who takes it in too tight a grip, crumpling it in her fist. Tess looks pointedly towards the door. 'Now get the hell out of my house.'

Angela is tempted to stalk off without another word. But there's something else she needs to say. Tess might have kept everything from her, but she can't return the favour. Not when people's lives might be in danger. She takes an unnecessary breath to give herself a moment to calm down.

'Tess. If we learn anything, do you want us to let you know?' Angela tilts her head towards Russell. 'About how to keep it from happening?'

'I don't need it,' Tess says flatly. 'Russell wants to be a vampire. Don't you, Russell?'

'Yeah, I want it.' He steps up to her side and puts his arm across her shoulders. 'I'm looking forward to it.'

'What if the next one doesn't?' *Or never gets asked*, Angela thinks. *Like me*. 'Or what if Russell does become a vampire, and he wants to know?' She looks at him. 'You might be willing to risk your own life, I get that, but do you want to end up killing someone?'

Russell opens his mouth, but Tess cuts him off before he has a chance to answer. 'Sure, whatever,' she says. 'Send me a postcard or something if you figure it out. You've got my address.'

But not your phone number, Angela notes. *You don't want me talking to Russell too much, do you*? 'Fine,' she replies aloud. 'If that's the only option.'

'Now, really. Get out.' Tess hesitates, then adds, 'Hey. If you do find Meijing, if you manage to yank her away from Hiram, tell her . . .'

'Tell her what?' Angela asks testily when she doesn't continue.

Tess gazes down at the floor. 'I don't know. Tell her I said hi. Tell her I'd like to get back in touch.' When she looks up again, the left side of her mouth has quirked up into half a smile. 'You know something? It was nice to see you again, angel. Take care of yourself.'

Not knowing how to respond to that, Angela gives her a stiff nod in return, and heads for the door.

A short time after that, Mike and Angela are navigating their way back through the darkened streets. The lights are off in all the houses now, the last few holdouts gone to bed.

'She never told me any of that when we were together,' Angela says. 'Not one word.' Their shoes crunch on glass shards as they pass the shuttered restaurant. She tries to decide if she should report the broken window to the police, or if it's better not to draw their attention. Probably they should get as far away as they can, as fast as they can.

First the fire in the Old Burial Ground and now this. She's becoming a vampiric vandal.

'Do you think she was telling the truth?' Mike asks.

Angela shrugs. 'Maybe? I think she must want us to find these vampires. Mostly because I'm pretty sure she's hoping to get something out of it. Although' – she frowns in thought – 'that may have more to do with you than with me.'

'I wondered. She kept staring at me when she thought I wasn't looking. What do you think she has in mind?'

'I'm not sure. But there's not a lot that can hurt a vampire. You can.'

'Yeah,' Mike agrees. 'That's what I was getting from all that, too.'

If Tess is trying to manipulate them, that could explain the weird send-off, as well. It's definitely more appealing than the idea that Tess still has any lingering affection for her. Angela almost shudders, but manages to keep it down to a twitch. Surely their encounter in Boston last December must have made clear that whatever they once had was over and done with.

'What about this Hiram guy? Should we believe that he's as scary as she says?' Mike asks.

'I don't know. I don't think you should attack him just because she wants you to,' Angela says. 'If that is what she wants. But we should probably be careful until we have a better sense of things.'

'Yeah. I agree.'

'And we should definitely go and see what we can find. If Meijing might have the answer, we need to talk to her.'

'Sounds like San Francisco is the next stop, then.' Mike looks up at the moon, a thin crescent hanging low over the dark hump of Camelback Mountain. 'If we leave tonight, it'll be right around the new moon when we get there.'

'Is that bad?'

'It's not great, but it's nothing I can't deal with. I don't think we need to wait or anything.'

'Good, because I'd rather get this over with as soon as possible. It's my turn to drive, right?' They've reached the car. Angela gets behind the wheel and slips the key into the ignition. The engine coughs to life.

'Do you think we'll be able to track them down?' Mike asks as he clambers into the passenger side.

'I hope so. Honestly, it'd be nice to have Chloë along for this part. She can use the cards to do that kind of thing, sometimes.' *Although,* Angela thinks, *card tricks wouldn't have protected her when a vampire and a werewolf were fighting. No matter how handy her predictions might be right now, it's definitely for the best that Chloë's back in Boston and out of danger.* 'One second – I should phone her before we get on the road.'

She gets out her cell phone and turns it back on. She's not looking forward to the call, but it's one she needs to make. Angela is well aware that she owes Chloë a massive apology for earlier this evening. No matter how upset she was at the time, that was out of line.

'Hey, do you think she could give you a card reading over the phone?' Mike asks.

'Oh, crap.' Angela turns to him in dismay. 'I'm an idiot. I should have thought of that when we were hunting all over for Tess.' Chloë's answering machine picks up, and Angela ends the call. 'No answer. She must have gone to bed. I'll try again when she's up.' It's a conversation that merits more than a tape-recorded message.

'No harm done, not using the cards this time around,' Mike says as Angela shifts into drive. 'We found Tess, after all.'

'Yeah, we did,' Angela replies. 'We found her, got in a fight, destroyed some property, and didn't learn the one thing we wanted to know. If we do find more vampires in San Francisco, let's hope it goes better than it did here.'

She pulls out into the street and turns towards the highway. If the traffic is light, they should be able to make it to the California border before she has to hide from the sun.

CHAPTER TWENTY-SIX

The Castro
22 November 2000

Meijing screams.

The boards crack beneath her head as Hiram slams it into the floor. She hardly notices the impact. The pain comes from his presence in her mind, firing all her nerve endings into agony. Knives in her joints, flames crawling up her legs and down her arms, a pressure in her head that threatens to burst her skull. None of it is real; every burn and laceration is a phantasm conjured by his anger.

That makes no difference to her suffering.

'It's all your fault,' he growls, his face close to hers, his fangs out and ready to pierce her flesh. 'You're a curse. A curse upon me for my sins.'

He's in deep withdrawal, his hands shaking, his head twitching with an uncontrollable tic. The opium pipe has not been able to keep pace with his needs, and the alcohol in Rigo's blood had barely any effect on him at all. His hair and pallid skin are damp with foul-smelling moisture. This is the only time he ever sweats, when the drugs are leaving his body.

She curls into a foetal ball as he rains meaningless blows down upon her. She tries to speak, tries to offer whatever defence she can, but her body spasms into rigidity, her mouth snapping shut, her muscles clamped into a lockjaw rictus by his will. The last time he did this to her, she bit clean through her own tongue with her fangs.

'Why are you the only one who ever returned from death?' He points an unsteady, accusing claw at her eye. 'Of all the good, godly people who have served me . . . Only you. The whore I pulled out of the gutter.'

Knives in her joints. Her bones burning to ash. Meijing wonders if he will kill her this time. He's come close before. Very close. In this condition, he is far beyond the bounds of rational thought. He forgets how useful she is to him.

With a sob, he withdraws from her and collapses in a corner, wailing about the afflictions heaped upon him by his God until he lapses into babbling incoherence.

Slowly, the agony abates. She uncurls inch by inch as her muscles unfreeze and the pain fades into sharp cramps, then dull aches, then pins and needles. Her limbs tremble in the aftermath.

In another room, she can hear Nimrod whining disconsolately. The dogs don't like it when they fight. Meijing has no comfort to offer him, though, not right now. Her torture may be over with, at least for the moment, but it has left her completely exhausted. It will be some time before she is capable of rising to her feet.

Over the next few days, his ravings will lessen. *Geong si* are hardy, and he is always quick to throw off the effects of drug withdrawal, no matter how much he has ravaged his body with his addictions. Tomorrow night, or perhaps the night after, the worst of it will be past and she will no longer be at such risk.

Tonight, though, he might well attack her a second time. With an effort, Meijing stills her twitching limbs and lies motionless on the floor, hoping to avoid his attention.

Someday she will break free of him. Someday this will end.
Until then, she must survive.
She must survive.
She must survive.

PART FIVE

The Centre Of The Labyrinth

CHAPTER TWENTY-SEVEN

Russian Hill, San Francisco
9 May 1969

The patterns in the wallpaper are still shimmering and swaying, but less so than before, gradually resettling themselves into fixed, immobile shapes and lines. Meijing relaxes, letting herself sink into the mattress. She always enjoys the warm, hazy feeling that comes at the tail end of a good acid trip.

She pulls Tess closer into her arms, cuddling her and stroking her light-brown hair. Tess rubs her cheek against Meijing like a cat that wants attention.

'Are you having a good time here?' she asks Tess.

'Eh.' Tess moves her shoulders in a languid shrug. 'I'm starting to get bored of being high, to be honest. It's never been my main thing. I just like to experiment.'

Meijing pulls herself up into a sitting position on the bed, letting Tess's head rest in her lap. 'I meant overall. Living in this house, with us.'

'Oh, sure. Mostly. I mean, why wouldn't I be? New camera, new clothes, free food, a place to crash, and, you know, immortality once the vampire thing takes.' She smiles her curious lopsided grin. 'Goddamn right I'll put up with dropping acid once every couple of weeks for that. And donating blood, too. Don't worry, I'm not about to start complaining.'

Meijing continues to run her fingers through Tess's hair, pausing once in a while to toy with the girl's earrings. Hiram's edicts make it impossible for Meijing to mention how unlikely a fate immortality is for her. *Never tell our secrets to those who know them not.* His words hammer through Meijing's skull, even now, so many years later.

Tess has shown a healthy response to the drain on her life essence, but many others over the years have been as strong, and not one has returned from the grave. Not since Meijing herself did, when the century was still young. She wonders how long Tess will last. She wonders if she'll feel anything when Tess dies.

'I'm pleased to hear you are content,' she says. 'We want you to be happy here.'

'*You* make me happy. But . . .' The smile fades from Tess's face as she glances over to the other side of the room. Meijing finds her own gaze following, lighting upon Hiram in his armchair. He's babbling in a quiet, constant stream about the magical caterpillars of caterpillar land. Meijing is so used to his noises that she'd only been dimly aware he was in the room.

'The acid gets him totally wrecked. Way more than you or me,' Tess says. 'Why is that?'

'I do not know. It has always been so, with every drug. Perhaps it is an effect of his advanced age as a *geong si*.' That much, at least, she can say; his longevity is no mystery to Tess. In tempting her with eternal life, he has revealed that he is far older than he appears.

Tess takes hold of Meijing's shoulder and pulls herself up until she's sitting in her lap. She brings her head close and whispers in Meijing's ear.

'The guy's a head-case, you know that, right?' she asks, barely audible in spite of how close she is. 'He's completely nuts, and he's a goddamn useless addict. I've only been around a few months, and I can see that. Can't you?'

'Of course I can,' Meijing says just as quietly, her eyes still locked on Hiram. He gives no indication that he hears or understands them. 'I am not a fool.'

'So how about we split?' Tess's warm breath blows softly against her hair, tickling slightly. 'You and me, Mei. He treats you like a fucking servant. Let's go. Leave him behind.'

Meijing gives a minute shake of her head, her ear brushing back and forth against Tess's mouth. 'I cannot leave. He will not let me.'

'And he has some kind of power over your mind,' Tess whispers. 'Right? I've seen how he jerks you around when he thinks I'm not paying attention. Like you're a puppet.'

Clever, clever girl. 'Yes.'

Merely saying the word is a burden lifted. An almost physical relief, to be able to speak of it, to have someone beside her who knows.

Tess is so close that Meijing can feel her lips curve into a frown. 'Is it always on? Even when he's totally out of it like this? It doesn't loosen up when he's distracted?'

'Never so much that I can break free. Not yet. Perhaps not ever.'

'Let's walk the dogs,' Tess says, sliding off the bed. 'They probably need it by now.'

Jezebel and Zipporah are indeed eager to be outside. They strain at their leashes as soon as they emerge into the breezy night air. Meijing mutters soothing words, trying to calm them, but she doesn't have the kind of control over them that Hiram does. She is not powerful enough to charm a creature as simple as a rat into stillness; dogs are far beyond her abilities.

Tess lights one of her endless Lucky Strikes, and blows out clouds of cigarette smoke that drift away on the wind. She says nothing until they're halfway around the block and the dogs have finished with their business.

They've stopped beside a park bench high on the hillside. Tess gazes out at the double line of street lights marching across the Bay Bridge where it rises up beyond the streets and houses.

'Hell of a view,' she says.

'Yes.'

'I should have brought the camera along.' Then, without additional preamble, she adds, 'If you can't leave him, I'm guessing you also can't kill him?'

Meijing blinks at her, then laughs aloud. 'Such gratitude you show to him!' She tuts in mock remonstrance. 'What a bloodthirsty little thing you are. Is murder your usual fallback plan?'

'Could you do it?' Tess persists.

'It would be difficult in the extreme.'

'Which means you've thought about it.'

Meijing hesitates before saying more, but something in her relishes having a co-conspirator for the first time. No previous human companion has ever made such a suggestion, and she certainly never proposed it to any of them herself. Even leaving aside the near impossibility of the task, there was always too much danger that one of them would betray her to Hiram.

But she has seen how Tess looks at him. She loathes him almost as much as Meijing does.

She is glad that she holds the upper hand in her dealings with the girl, though – the strength, the money, the promise of life everlasting. Someone in the opposite position might not find this ruthless streak quite as appealing.

'Yes,' Meijing tells her. 'I have thought about it.'

Tess nods sharply, as if that settles the point for her. 'If there's any way to get it done,' she says, 'any way at all, we should give it a shot. With him gone, you could do anything. We could do anything.'

'It would involve a great deal of risk.'

'What would it take?'

'Freeing myself for a few moments might be sufficient. Long enough for me to attack him. But it is not guaranteed to succeed. If I tried and failed, he would end me. He prefers to have me at his call, but not so much that he would forgive me for that.'

'What if you pull it off, though? Come on, Mei. You and me.'

'I would be far more likely to die.'

Tess flicks her cigarette over the edge of the hill, looking pensive. She picks up the leashes and leads the dogs away from the bench, Meijing staying close by her side.

'I don't think he's done anything to my mind,' Tess says as they turn the corner onto a steep, winding lane. 'So that means he can only do it to other vampires. Right?'

Meijing tries to correct her, to speak to her about the dogs, but she finds her tongue is stilled. Of course it is. No doubt Tess assumes that the animals are merely well trained. The error matters little, Meijing supposes. Tess is correct that he cannot control a human being yet, if such a thing is even possible. His pets remain his greatest achievement among the living.

'You are free of his command,' she agrees.

'OK, so that's one advantage we've got. But I wouldn't have much of a chance of getting to him during the day, the way he locks himself away.'

'He is cautious, yes.'

'Could I do it while he's tripping?' Tess asks. 'He might not see me coming if he's high enough.'

'Do not underestimate him,' Meijing says sharply. 'He is not a natural creature. For him to fail to notice you, he would have to be more deeply drugged than I have ever seen. If you had tried it tonight, he would have snapped your neck without a moment of hesitation, and then returned to his dreams.'

'Fuck.' That silences Tess for a time. They walk up and down the streets without speaking, while the dogs investigate whatever interesting smells they come across.

It isn't until they've turned around and started heading back to the house that Tess asks, 'How come you don't spend the day down in the vault like he does?'

'I prefer to rely on trust. And affection.' Meijing smiles at Tess, and ruffles her hair. 'Which makes a bedroom with covered windows sufficient for me. A locked door is a temptation. I would rather no one tried to break the lock than count upon the lock itself.' A half-truth, at best – Hiram wouldn't allow her to share his daytime chamber if she wanted to. His sense of propriety does not permit it. Nor does his relish for demonstrating his authority over her.

'Trust and affection. I like that,' Tess says. 'So I don't jab a stake into your heart because I don't want to, and I can't do it to him because he's fucking terrifying and will kill me. Smart. You pet the dog to make it love you, but you kick it when it misbehaves.'

'Is that how you see me? As your owner?' Meijing shakes her head. 'People are not dogs.'

'Aren't we, though, compared to you?' Tess asks. 'How old is Hiram? Five times my age? Ten times? And what about you?'

'Not so old as that.'

'Uh-huh. And how many "companions" have you had before me?'

Meijing does not answer.

'That's what I thought,' Tess says.

'People are not dogs,' Meijing repeats.

'It's all right, Mei. I don't mind being a dog for now. Or a dairy cow, I guess – that'd be closer to what I'm doing for you. Someday, I'll be the farmer. That's the point, right?' As they reach the house, Tess shuts the gate behind them, and takes Zipporah and Jezebel off their leashes so they can play in the garden. The Dobermans race around inside the fence while the women stand and watch for a minute or two.

'But if we don't come up with a way to get rid of him,' Tess says quietly, 'then I'll be under his power, too, won't I? When I become one of you.'

Meijing still cannot contradict the girl's assumptions about the likelihood of her survival. She wonders if she would tell her, were she able. Although there have been many truths shared tonight, there are limits to honesty.

She is unsure she could admit how many she has watched die, how uncertain she is that Hiram is to blame for all of it. What would she do in order to prolong her already long life, if she were completely free of him? What would she do to survive?

'We'll deal with that when we come to it,' she says to Tess, keeping her tone light. 'Perhaps I will be stronger then, and better able to protect you from him. Perhaps I will even be strong enough to –'

'All four of my girls are home.' Hiram's voice from the doorway startles Meijing. The two of his 'girls' that are dogs run up to greet him with delighted yips. 'What is it you are discussing?' he asks as he leans down to stroke Jezebel's head.

'I was saying that I don't have any pictures of you two,' Tess responds immediately, her voice brimming with bubbly cheerfulness. 'I want to try out my new camera. How about I do a double portrait?'

Meijing didn't hear him open the door; he can be as quiet as a cat stalking prey when he wishes. Tess is not the only one who cannot afford to underestimate him.

Hiram frowns. 'I mislike having my likeness taken,' he says. But there's no real anger in his words. He is in a calm and pleasant mood, no doubt, after sating his desires so thoroughly. 'In time, such a thing could raise difficult questions.'

'What, about your age?' Tess asks. 'It's not like I'm going to put a date on it. If anyone asks, you can tell them it's recent.'

'That is true.' He tilts his head, considering. 'Very well. I will permit it. Come inside.' He shoos the dogs back into the garden with a curt gesture, then strides into the house.

Tess winks at Meijing, but she does not respond in kind. When she next gets a chance, she will have to have a word with the girl about discretion. Hiram appears to have taken her misdirection at face value this time. But if they ever discuss such matters again, it can only be when there is no chance whatsoever of being overheard.

Once they're all inside, Tess finds her camera and gets them into position quickly enough, but then laughs when she looks through the viewfinder. 'I can only see the wall behind you. It's like you're not even here. I forgot there's a mirror in there.'

'Will that affect the photograph?' Meijing asks.

'No, it's an SLR. The mirror gets out of the way for the picture.' Tess waves away any further questions. 'Doesn't matter. Short answer, if that's the only hang-up, it'll be fine. Say cheese!'

'Absolutely not,' Hiram replies.

There's a click and a flash, and Meijing has her picture taken for the very first time. It occurs to her that it has been more than half a century since she got a glimpse of what she looks like. She can only hazily recall the last reflection that she saw, back in the distant memories of her youth. When the photo develops, what will she see?

She would like to know how much she has changed. Or how little.

CHAPTER TWENTY-EIGHT

The Freedom Trail, Boston

The buildings are further away from the sidewalk than they should be, and seem distorted and angular through the veil of falling snow. Abstract shapes where there should be bars and restaurants. Everything is askew and wrong in some indefinable way that twists Chloë's vision and makes her sick to her stomach.

This is the Freedom Trail, but it's also not. Downtown Boston, but it's somewhere else, as well. A place between places, the way it was back in the graveyard. She takes that as a promising sign, however nauseating it might be.

The snow doesn't blow onto her as long as she stays on the path. She can see it whirling through the air all around her, but not a single flake ever lands on her body. She can't feel the wind, either, for that matter. It's as if she's walking inside a glass tunnel, untouched by the weather.

It's bitterly cold, nevertheless. Chloë picks up her pace, almost jogging in an effort to keep warm as she heads down a blurry echo of Union Street. There isn't any wind blowing inside a meat locker, either, but that doesn't make it a place you'd want to lie down and spend the night.

If she's still in Boston at all in any meaningful way, and the places and distances haven't changed beyond recognition, then the trail should cross North Street next. It'll turn left once she can see the statue of Sam Adams, and then it will swing around Faneuil Hall.

And sure enough, soon she sees Sam, right where she hoped he would be. The statue is little more than an oblong shadow in the snowstorm, but it's definitely there. This is still the path she knows, which is more reassuring than she would have thought. It's something familiar to hold on to. She starts to follow the trail to the other side of the building.

Even after the dragon, she's taken by surprise when Faneuil Hall shifts around to look at her.

Five eyes fix on her, two of them enormous and three smaller, spread in a curve across a brick-red insectoid face. The old market house leaps closer with its powerful hind legs, landing with a crash that shakes the ground and makes her stumble to one knee. It rubs its legs against the back of its wings, scraping out a banshee screech.

A locust. A colossal one, its antennae as thick as her arms. It spreads its mandibles wide. Some kind of dark, viscous liquid drips from its thorax, giving off a foul smell.

It looks like the grasshopper weathervane on the cupola, Chloë realises. Or the one that used to be on the cupola, when it was a building. Faneuil Hall's most distinctive characteristic has taken over the whole thing somehow, like the Green Dragon Inn becoming a dragon. It all makes sense. A certain kind of sense, at any rate. Metaphor made manifest.

There's no reason to be frightened of it, right? Grasshoppers aren't scary. Unless they're four storeys high. What do grasshoppers eat?

Her, maybe, if she does something wrong here. It hisses like a primaeval locomotive letting off steam, and scuttles closer.

Chloë's still down on her knee. She stands up quickly, stripping off her shirt and holding it out in front of her as she does. The giant insect bends its front legs to bring its head down to her, and she wills herself not to step back.

It takes the shirt in its jaw and retreats back to its place at the centre of the square. And there it stays, motionless. The shirt, tiny against its bulk, blows in the wind like a pathetic flag.

After pausing to make sure it doesn't plan to do anything more, she continues down the trail, warily keeping the grasshopper in her sight until the weather obscures it from view.

Her teeth begin to chatter uncontrollably. She chafes her upper arms, switching her stick from hand to hand so she can rub each of them in turn. It doesn't do much good. Should she be worried about frostbite? Hypothermia? She's only past the second gate, and the cold is going to get worse and worse the longer she walks and the more clothes she loses.

No one gave her a guarantee that she would make it all the way to the final gate. Quite the opposite, in fact. If she doesn't, what would happen? What would that mean? Would she vanish from the real world, never to be seen again?

She briefly entertains the idea of turning back, but she can already feel the same strange physical resistance to her steps that she felt during the Halloween ritual. Energy is building, and it has to go somewhere. Turning back could be even stupider than going forward.

She wouldn't have done it, anyway. Not really. There's too much that might be at stake.

As she passes from Congress Street to Devonshire Street, the unicorn jumps down from the façade of the Old State House and trots towards her. Chloë feels like crying with relief. She could, after all, have ended up facing the lion from the other side of the building. Nothing has attacked her so far, but that doesn't mean she's comfortable with everything she meets being a nightmare of claws and teeth. The unicorn, at least, doesn't seem likely to eat her. It's more beautiful than it is terrifying, with its silver coat and golden horn glowing against the churning eddies of grey and white snow.

It comes close, thankfully not seeming to care that it's been a long time since she was a virgin. It does, however, look at her askance when she unclasps her bra and drapes it over its horn.

'S-sorry,' she manages to wheeze out through her spasming jaw. The bra does look out of place, dangling limply from the lustrous, spiralling spike that juts from the creature's noble forehead. It's not even one of her nicer bras. But if she offers it up now, she can put off removing her shoes for a little while longer.

The unicorn snorts and canters away.

Chloë crosses her arms over her chest, tucking the stick awkwardly under her armpit. So far, it's been more of an encumbrance than any kind of help. As she heads for Washington Street, she wonders if she's visible in the regular Boston. Angela could see her when she was walking around the Old Burial Ground; it wasn't like she disappeared. Are people watching her wander topless through downtown? Is someone going to call the police on her? Or call for an ambulance, more likely, since she's obviously a crazy woman who's going to freeze to death.

God. So cold.

She's able to see what's become of the Old South Meeting House from half a block away in spite of the driving snow. The giant eagle is a bright, burnished gold that hurts her eyes to look at. When she gets close, it moves to block her path, staring down its beak at her with a disdainful air. It takes her a few moments to call up her dim memories of her one tourist trip to the building, back when she was new to the city, and remember the great eagle statuette perched on the gallery clock, staring down at the pulpit.

It'd be smartest to leave her shoes on as long as possible, but she doesn't have anything left she can give up without taking them off at least temporarily. She grumpily unlaces one and pulls it off, planning to give up her jeans next, but the bird leans down and snatches the shoe out her hand with its beak before she has the chance. As it rears back, the shoe vanishes down its throat with a convulsive swallow.

Chloë grimaces. She has one left, anyway. Maybe this is what the stick is for. It's too short to make a good crutch, but she can lean on it to some extent as she hops along, keeping her shoeless foot off the freezing ground.

As soon as she tries to follow the trail to the other side of Washington Street, though, the eagle slams a car-sized talon down in her path, sending her stumbling back.

What the fuck was that for? 'I g-gave you my shoe!' she croaks out in dismay through her chattering teeth. 'Let me go past!'

The talon remains unmoving. Two shining, golden eyes glare down at her.

'What, are we using strip p-poker rules?' Chloë grumbles. 'Shoes c-count as a set? Fine.'

She bends down to remove her second shoe, wincing as she balances on her other foot. Her wool sock isn't doing much to ward off the chill. As soon as she lifts the shoe up, it gets wrenched out of her hand and swallowed, just like the first one.

Chloë begins hobbling her way around the talon, but the eagle leans down until the sharp point of its beak is only inches away from her face and unleashes a deafening shriek. She claps her hands over her ears, nearly braining herself with the stick, and barely manages to keep herself from toppling over. Her head is ringing.

She must be doing something wrong. She's screwing up the offering somehow.

The giant bird looks all too ready to snap her up and send her hurtling down its gullet after her shoes. There's no other way around without stepping off the Freedom Trail, and she's certain that would be a supremely bad idea. Becoming lost forever doesn't sound all that much better than being swallowed whole.

What does it want from her? She's beginning to find it hard to think, with the bitter cold seeping into her body, stabbing at her bones like deeply embedded thorns whenever she moves.

Ishtar had to give up her clothes. It worked at the other gates, why isn't it working here? What had the witch said, exactly, back in the graveyard? *As you would with any who come here, deal with her according to the ancient decree. He opened the first gate, but as she walked through, he removed the crown from her head.*

What was the ancient decree? What did Ishtar end up doing? *At each gate, she lost more clothing, until she was buck naked and barefoot by the time she finally stood before her sister.*

Barefoot?

Chloë strips off her socks and holds them out to the Old South Meeting House. It grabs them in a talon, pinching them out of her hand with surprising delicacy. With a final judgemental look at her, the eagle launches itself into the air, the wind from its wings buffeting Chloë like a cyclone until it vanishes into the grey sky.

Finally. Asshole bird. What the hell was its problem? The other guardians hadn't been such sticklers for the details; the dragon didn't demand she give it a crown.

She knows that the Puritans who built the Meeting House didn't have a lot of fond feelings for witches. Maybe the sentiment lingers. She supposes it makes sense that metaphors can manifest in unfriendly ways, too.

Just her luck to meet a building that doesn't like her, though.

The glacial pavement burns the soles of her feet; her toes reflexively arch away from touching it. She tries to run, but can only manage a kind of lurching stagger. Three more gates to go. Where's the next one?

It had better come soon if I'm going to make it all the way there. And to the one after that, and the one after that.

CHAPTER TWENTY-NINE

Chinatown, San Francisco
25 November 2000

'Hi, you've reached Chloë's answering machine! I have an answering machine now, like a grown-up adult person! Leave a message.'

Angela shifts her phone from one ear to the other while she waits impatiently for the beep. She's heard that message far too many times in the past couple of days.

'Chloë, call me as soon as you hear this, OK? Where are you?' She hangs up and flips the phone shut, staring out into the dense tule fog pouring into the city from the Valley. Watching it as if her girlfriend will somehow wander into view if she only looks hard enough.

'Still no luck?' Mike asks.

'No. I'm really getting worried.'

They haven't heard a single word from Chloë since the night they left Phoenix. At first, Angela left apologetic messages, since she assumed the reason was that Chloë was justifiably angry with her. But as the days passed, the lack of response shifted Angela's mood from penitence to irritation to hurt feelings, and now, finally, to serious concern.

'There's probably a perfectly reasonable explanation.' Mike pats her shoulder sympathetically.

'I know,' Angela says. 'But what if something's wrong?'

'Let me ask Shelly to look in on her. I can do it right now if you want. I bet she hasn't gone to bed yet.'

'Maybe we should go back. What if Chloë had an accident? Or . . .'

Or what if Angela upset Chloë enough to push her back into depression? Is she shut up in her room, unwilling to get out of bed, ignoring the phone when it rings? Or worse? Chloë tried to hurt herself once in the wake of her divorce, a couple of years before Angela met her. Images leap to her mind – Chloë, lying in a hospital bed. Chloë never making it to the hospital at all.

'It'd take us days to drive all the way to Boston,' Mike points out, 'and that's the fastest way you can safely go. Let's at least wait to see what Shelly can find out.'

She makes an effort to convince herself that nothing's the matter, that macabre thoughts are simply the natural result of hunting for a vampire in a fogbound city. The most likely explanation is still that Chloë is pissed off at her. Shelly had reported as much during a chat with Mike a few days ago. And while she'd said Chloë wasn't happy with Angela, she hadn't made it sound like Chloë was in the throes of despair.

'Fine,' Angela says, handing over the phone. 'I'll wait until she goes to check, at least.'

'Are you calm enough to keep looking around while she does?'

'I suppose. Not that it's been getting us anywhere,' she grouses, leaning against an ornately decorated lamp post while he gives Shelly a call.

On top of her worries about Chloë, she's on the verge of despairing that they'll ever find the elusive Meijing. Since their arrival in San Francisco, they've made no progress whatsoever in tracking her down.

Chloë's disquieting silence means they have no way to ask her to do a card reading, and most of Tess's handwritten notes led them to businesses that no longer exist – places that were closed down and replaced so many decades ago that barely a memory of them remains. Some of her other suggestions were useless for different reasons. Golden Gate Park turned out to be three miles long, not exactly a place where it would be easy to spot one particular person. Mike sniffed around for vampires there, but had no luck.

At least Mike's nose won't be affected by the fog; otherwise their task would be even harder. If they were relying on their eyes alone, they could end up across the street from Meijing and never notice she was there. The white mist is a solid wall surrounding them, with tendrils of translucent vapour extending from it like plant creepers. The neon signs and paper lanterns of Chinatown poke through it feebly, and whenever other people pass them on the street, they seem to appear suddenly and then vanish back into nothingness like ghosts. Angela's clothes are sticking soggily to her skin, the filmy skirt of her dress damp and drooping.

Mike passes her phone back. 'She'll go over to Chloë's place tonight to see if she can find out what's going on.'

'All right,' Angela says unhappily. 'I guess that's the best we can do for now.'

They continue down Grant Avenue, heading for the restaurant that's next on their list. Now that they're closer to it, Mike sometimes stops to breathe deeply through his nose, just in case a vampire has passed by recently. Each time, he shakes his head after a few moments and they move on.

'Do you really think you'd be able to smell her out here?' Angela asks. 'I mean, over all the restaurants and dumpsters and' – she gestures around her – 'everything?'

'Vampires have a pretty distinct odour. Or you and Tess do, anyway, and I don't see why another one wouldn't have the same smell.' He leans over to sniff a parking meter that doesn't look especially different from any other parking meter. 'I mean, it'd be easier to do this as a wolf, but then I couldn't talk to you. I should be able to manage it this way.'

'What do I smell like?'

'Dead, but not rotting.'

'Oh.'

She sticks her hands in her coat pockets while she waits for him to finish his examination. After frowning at the meter, he straightens up and starts walking again. 'Nope, nothing there.'

'Are all your senses better than normal?' she asks, picking up her pace to catch up with him as he turns the corner onto Washington Street. 'Even when you're human?'

'For scent and hearing, yes, mostly. Sight is mixed. I've got good night vision, but I'm red-green colour-blind.'

'Then, um, in that case, we'd been wondering whether . . . I mean, when you're upstairs in our house, can you hear what's going on in the basement?'

'I turn the TV up very, very loud whenever Chloë comes over,' he says dryly. 'If that's what you're asking.'

'Ah. Well, thank you for that.' She considers asking if he can smell when they've been having sex, too, but can't figure out a polite way to put it. She decides that she'd rather not know, anyway. 'If it's a problem, I could go over to her place more–'

Angela doesn't notice the other person coming out of the mist until she walks directly into her. The woman stumbles back and nearly falls. As Angela reaches out a hand to steady her, she notices the dark glasses and white cane. She almost knocked over a blind woman.

'Are you all right?' Mike asks as Angela stutters out an apology. 'We didn't see you coming.'

The woman gets her feet back under her and takes a firmer grip on her cane. She's elderly and frail-looking, bent over as if her weight is too much for her bones. Her hair is the same colour as the fog.

There's a monster in the labyrinth, she says
Keep an eye out

She turns and walks back the way she came, her shape soon disappearing from view, the steady tap of her cane fading away not long after.

'That was weird,' Angela says.

'Very.' Mike gazes in the direction the woman walked away, a pair of puzzled wrinkles forming on his forehead. 'Was it just me, or did her mouth not move when she talked?'

'I'm not sure, honestly.'

'I also didn't hear her before you ran into her. Not at all. Or smell her. I should have.' He gives an experimental sniff. His eyes widen. 'I smell a vampire, though.'

'What? You do? Was it her?' Angela tries to peer through the fog, but can't make out anything.

'No, I'd have noticed when you ran into her. Aren't we right by where that restaurant is supposed to be?'

'I think so. If it didn't close down years ago.' Angela fumbles the tourist map open and double-checks the cross streets.

'I can tell you it was around in the eighties,' Mike says. 'I was trying to remember where I'd heard of it. It's in one of the *Tales of the City* books. There was a waiter who was famous for being rude to people, or something.'

'The eighties were a while ago.' She folds the map back up. 'But yeah, you're right about where we are – it can't be too much further on.'

'Let's get a little closer.'

Another quarter of a block brings them to Sam Wo. The little restaurant not only still exists, but is open for business in spite of the late hour.

Angela looks the place over; there doesn't seem to be anything remarkable about it. It's squeezed into a narrow space between two other buildings, and the slope of the street makes it appear to be leaning over to the right. All the signage is written in both Chinese characters and English letters, but that's true of everything around it as well.

'At least one vampire definitely came by here at some point.' Mike says. 'Female. I think it's recent. There's a chance she might still be inside.'

'You can smell whether it was a man or a woman?'

'Yes.' He crouches low to the ground and moves around in an expanding spiral, eyes closed, taking deep inhalations. 'I'm not sure if she was alone or not. There's another scent, but I can't tell how old it is.'

She lets him work. They might not be sure how much of what Tess told them was true, but neither of them wants to run into Hiram until they know more.

Mike takes a long time, going over every inch of the surrounding area while Angela watches. When a bunch of college kids breeze by, she tries to look nonchalant, but it turns out she needn't have bothered. Fully jaded city-dwellers, they studiously ignore the man smelling the sidewalk.

She wonders if she should be more concerned about the strange, apparently scentless – and maybe also telepathic? – old woman. But it doesn't seem like there's much they can do about her, or her warning, other than keep watch for monsters. Although finding a monster was the whole point of their coming to San Francisco in the first place. She's at a loss here. Interpreting mystic warnings from mysterious strangers is far more Chloë's speed.

Where is Chloë? Why doesn't she call?

After an eternity of sniffing, Mike finally stands back up. 'Sorry, but I can't tell,' he says. 'Not like this.' He grimaces. 'If we want to know who's in there, I'm going to have to do it as a wolf.'

'Is there a problem with that?'

'Only that it's the new moon. It's going to take me a while to change.'

'We'd be better off knowing, though, wouldn't we?'

He nods. 'I think so, too. There was an alley a little way back, wasn't there?' They retrace their steps until they find it, and Mike ducks inside. 'Don't let anyone come through while I'm doing this, all right?'

A few feet more, and he's gone from her sight. Not long after, muffled by distance, she can hear the cracking, grinding noises of his transformation. Unlike last time, they continue on as her wait stretches into minutes.

It sounds like it hurts.

'Mike?' she calls into the alley. 'Are you OK?'

Only a strained yip answers her. Unless you count the organic crunches that follow. She isn't sure what splintering bone sounds like, but if she had to guess, it would be exactly like that.

She's about to go check on him when his dark form trots out of the alley.

'Is everything all right? Are you hurt?'

He blinks at her, making no reply. She goes to gather up his discarded clothes, and follows him back to the restaurant. When they arrive, he puts his nose to the ground.

'What do you think? Is she inside?'

After a moment, he looks up and nods, a motion that's strangely unsettling on a lupine head.

'And is it only her? Not the other one?'

Another disconcerting nod. Angela hesitates, wondering if she should ask him to become human again. But if anything bad happens, it might be better for him to be a wolf. Especially on a new-moon night, if it takes him that long to transform. A hostile vampire probably won't hold off for a quarter of an hour while he gets himself ready to fight.

'How about you stay out here and give a howl if Hiram shows up,' she suggests. 'If something goes wrong while I'm in there, I'll scream.'

He turns to face the street, his head thrust forward and his hind legs poised to move. His whole body quivers with alertness.

'You look exactly like a guard dog on the lookout,' Angela says. He throws her an aggrieved glance, then returns to his position.

She hesitates a moment longer, wondering whether she's going to need a guard dog at her back tonight. Wondering what's going to happen when she goes into the restaurant and meets another vampire. Another creature like Tess. Like herself.

But this is what they came to San Francisco for. It'd be crazy to call it quits now. Wouldn't it?

She turns away from Mike, and walks inside.

CHAPTER THIRTY

The Freedom Trail

The cold has penetrated deep into Chloë's body. Her tendons feel tight, stretched to breaking point, and all of her muscles ache with a dull, constant pain. Her feet barely seem like feet to her, more like blocky lumps that have been nailed to her ankles. She can't feel her toes at all.

Her teeth aren't chattering anymore, either. She doesn't think that's a good sign.

The stick is definitely coming in handy now; Chloë leans on it for support as she limps past the Irish Famine Memorial. The desiccated figures of the monument are half visible through the snow, their faces lowered to the ground or raised to the sky in anguish. A few steps more and they pass out of sight.

There's a winged horse standing by the Old Corner Bookstore, whiter than the snowdrifts except for the deep, black pools of its eyes.

No doubt it has some kind of relevant metaphorical connection to this spot, but she's too numb and too tired to figure out what it is. On some level, she knows that she should be thrilled, ecstatic. A deep wish of her childhood is standing before her, quietly nickering. Chloë was always more a pegasus girl than a unicorn girl; she spent a full year of her childhood demanding the winged My Little Ponies as soon as they came out, one of the few instances where her parents bought her non-educational toys rather than listen to her whine. Her dreams were dreams of flight, soaring high over rivers and mountains on some grand adventure, her knees pressed against the warm sides of her steed, its wings piercing the air to either side. Usually she was holding a sword aloft as they flew, which probably would have been tiring after a while.

She can remember all their names – Medley, Firefly, Skydancer, Starshine, and Sprinkles, who came with a duck sidekick and was therefore by far the awesomest My Little Pony.

Get a grip, she reminds herself. *You're freezing cold and you're on a magical quest. Now is not the time to reminisce about the duck.*

Throwing herself astride and flying away would definitely count as leaving the path. There will be no relief from walking, no chance for shortcuts, no time to indulge in old dreams. She's finally on a grand adventure, and it hurts too much for her to enjoy it.

She shimmies out of her jeans and tosses them over. They land neatly on the winged horse's withers, laying across its back like a dark saddle blanket.

The mythical animal takes a few steps closer to her and whuffs into her hair, stirring her curls. Its breath is warm and smells like horse breath, but also lilacs and, in some way, summer. For a moment, only a moment, she forgets the weather.

Then the horse turns and trots away, gathering speed until its hooves leave the ground and it takes to the sky. Its feathered wings must span twenty feet when fully spread. Chloë gazes after it until it merges with the falling snow.

When it's disappeared completely, she shuffles on. But not until then.

The snow on the ground is piled up into drifts on either side of the path, higher than she would have expected for the length of time she's been walking. How long has she been walking, though, really? She isn't sure. She can't have much further to go. Two more gates to pass, only two.

She stumbles forward, past the blurry shops, past the statues of Josiah Quincy and Benjamin Franklin gazing down at her as she passes by. Franklin must be enjoying the view, the old lecher. It's not worth the energy to cover herself up. Besides, he's a statue.

Her thoughts are starting to lose clarity, slipping through her mind like meltwater.

Keep going. Follow the path. She replays those five words over and over again in her mind like a mantra. She paces her steps to their rhythm.

At the corner by King's Chapel, a skeleton peels itself off one of the churchyard tombstones and dances towards her, a candle snuffer in one hand and an arrow in the other. Graveyard imagery again at last, another memento mori to remind her of what awaits. Pale ghastly death hath sent his shaft. She can't help but take the figure as a signal that things are nearing their end. Which sounds far more ominous than she would like.

There's only one thing she has left to give. Off come her panties, down her legs and over her insensate feet. She holds out her last offering, and the skeleton impales them with its arrow and wrenches them out of her grasp. With its prize acquired, it pirouettes back to its grave and resumes its place. Her sense of foreboding is not lessened by this.

She drags herself onward, stark naked and holding a stick. Why didn't she put on a sweater before she went out? Or three?

Tremont Street. Her fingers and toes are an unhealthy-looking bluish colour. She's not in as much pain as she was, though, because she isn't feeling much of anything at all. Except for the cold.

When she was a college student in Michigan, one year there was a winter day where the temperature dropped so low that when she came home from grocery shopping – having stupidly gone out without wearing gloves – her fingers were completely numb. She had to use her eyes alone to guide her as she took far too long fishing her key out of her handbag, manoeuvring it into the lock, twisting it around so she could get inside and run warm water over her hands for ten minutes. It was like playing that game with the claw that drops and grabs the stuffed animals, only with her hand as the claw.

She has to do the same thing now with her entire body. Foot goes there. Other foot goes past it. Move stick forward, lean. Foot goes there. All the way across the broad expanse of Tremont Street. Step after step after step.

First childhood memories, now college ones. As if she's walking through her life, year by year.

At long last, she sees her foot land on sidewalk instead of road, and she looks up.

Park Street Church is gone.

In its place, and roughly the same size, there crouches a three-headed dog with a serpent's tail, guarding the entrance to the Granary Burying Ground. Its body is covered in matted tan fur, with a single dark-brown splotch on one side. All three of its mouths are showing teeth. Thick drool drips onto its three chins.

Of course, Chloë thinks with the small part of her mind that isn't preoccupied with dying of exposure. *Cerberus lies in wait before the entrance to the realm of the dead.*

I really should have written him smaller. Much, much smaller.

She needs to . . . to do something here. What is it? She can't seem to remember.

Clothes. She doesn't have any clothes. All of them are gone already. What happens now? The eagle didn't let her pass until it was satisfied with what she gave it. Will Cerberus do the same? Block her path until she finds a proper offering?

Or maybe he'll skip straight to ripping her to shreds and devouring her. He looks a lot more likely to go with that instead. *If I'm lucky*, she reminds herself, *he won't chew on me first.*

It won't make any real difference whether he stops her or gobbles her up. She's not going to last much longer, either way.

The gargantuan dog's legs tense, poised to spring. Six red eyes are fixed on her with murderous intent.

No, wait. Not on her, exactly. On her hand.

He's focused on what she's holding in her hand.

He's staring at the stick.

Oh.

'Fetch,' she manages to croak, and flings it as hard as she can towards Boston Common. The guardian of the underworld bounds off after it, minor earthquakes shaking the street each time he touches down.

Draw him off. That's right, that's how it went. Since there doesn't seem to be a lobster around at the moment, the stick will have to do. Same story, different telling.

She should go through the gate into the cemetery before he brings it back, though. She doesn't think she has another throw left in her.

The short set of steps leading up to the stone gateway nearly defeats her. She manages to mount the first one, but the second one seems too high up to get her foot on. She isn't sure where her foot is, anyway. How long is this taking her? Time is passing too quickly or too slowly. She can't keep track.

The earthquakes are getting louder and stronger. She can feel the vibrations in her teeth now. Cerberus is on his way. However much time it's been, she's out of it.

Screw it, she thinks, and lets herself fall forward through the gate.

She doesn't feel herself hit the ground.

She doesn't feel cold anymore, either. Which could mean that she's safe. Or it could mean that her body is completely shutting down.

She blinks her eyes open, not sure when she shut them. She sees nothing. Or no, not nothing. The same uncanny, unending, eye-hurting transparency that she saw when she looked up in death's bookshop. Three shapes congeal out of the void, slowly gaining form and features.

The first witch has given both her voice and her sight to her sisters. The witch in the middle has the mouth now, although both of her eyes are empty holes. The third one has their only eyeball. It makes her look familiar somehow. The tune of a hummed, half-remembered song starts running through Chloë's head, but she can't pin down which one it is.

The middle witch – the second witch – studies Chloë with her non-existent eyes.

Welcome, seeker, says the second witch
Walker on the red path
Dancer of the spiral dance

'Hi,' Chloë says. It comes out more as a dry cough than anything else.

You have journeyed
To the centre
Ask your question
Hear your answer

The witch's mouth doesn't open when she speaks, her lips remaining sealed and still. The sentences reverberate in Chloë's head without passing through her ears first.

'How,' Chloë begins, then stops. Any more than that feels like it would be beyond her abilities right now.

No, that's not enough. She needs to get it out. All of it. She has to try again.

'How-can-I-help-Angela?' she says as fast as she can. A single long word.

The witch smiles.

CHAPTER THIRTY-ONE

The Second Witch

In the centre
Of the labyrinth
Is a secret

In the centre
Of the labyrinth
Is a monster

In the centre
Of the labyrinth
Is a prisoner

Take the red path
To the centre
Of the labyrinth

We do not say the name
Of the goddess of the underworld
Her name should not be spoken
Aloud

Instead we call her Korë
The Maiden of the Grain

We call her Despoina
The Lady of the House

We call her Ariadne
The Purest of the Pure
The Mistress of the Labyrinth
(Bring one measure of honey for all the gods
And a second measure of honey for the Mistress of the Labyrinth)

The names become confused
With time
The legends overlap and intertwine
But in the oldest stories
Ariadne is the leader of the spiral dance
Ariadne is the guide along the spiral way

Her red thread unwinding at her feet
The red path showing her the twists and turns
So that she can spiral in
And spiral out
From life to death
And death to life
Threading her way
Through the labyrinth

Such is the nature
Of the goddesses of grain
Of the goddesses of death

When Ishtar fled from Irkalla
The law demanded another take her place
So she let the gallu demons take her lover
Tammuz

But his sister Geshtinanna
Goddess of the fields
Said she would stay in death for half the year
So he could be in life

And thus the grain grows for half the year
Ripening upon the earth
And thus the grain is dead for half the year
Buried in clay pots

Thus the goddess whose name we do not speak
Was taken from her flowers
Thus she ate of the fatal fruit
Red as blood

But Hecate or Hermes or Demeter
(The legends intertwine)
Can follow her along the spiral path
Can follow her unwinding thread
Can help her dance back out
From the centre
Of the labyrinth

From the darkness
To the daylight
From the shadow
To the sun

Free the prisoner
Fight the monster
Learn the secret
Which is sacrifice

Hecate must go with her
Geshtinanna must descend

Half the year, for balance
They must go as well
One must spiral in
So that Tammuz can spiral out
One must spiral in
So Ariadne can escape

Tammuz or Dumuzid,
Ariadne, Korë, or Despoina,
Melinoia, Praxidike, Aristi Cthonia,

The name you call her does not matter
(Although one name we do not say)

Only that you join her
In the centre
Of the labyrinth

Free the prisoner
In the centre
Of the labyrinth

Fight the monster
In the centre
Of the labyrinth

Learn the secret
In the centre
Of the labyrinth

CHAPTER THIRTY-TWO

Chinatown, San Francisco
25 November 2000

The restaurant is set up oddly, with the kitchen taking up the whole of the ground floor and the dining rooms tucked away upstairs, accessed by a stairway barely wide enough for a single person. There's no sign of Meijing after she goes up one flight, but on the top floor Angela spots her the moment she enters the room.

It would have been hard to miss her, even if she weren't almost the only person present. There's something imposing about her that didn't come through in the photograph. She stands out from the scant handful of human customers like a shark in a dolphin tank.

Angela takes a moment to examine the other vampire.

She's dressed elegantly in what could perhaps best be called business goth attire. A black blouse and jacket with embroidered patterns in a lighter charcoal shade, a velvet choker around her neck. Silver earrings that don't quite match each other dangle from her ears, although Angela can't make out their exact design from this distance. She's wearing nothing that would look out of place in either a boardroom or an upscale club. It's a subtler look than anything Tess ever wore. Or Angela, for that matter.

A steaming cup of tea sits in front of her, untouched. Meijing appears to be inhaling its scent, her eyes closed.

If she were human, and Angela were out hunting for prey, this is someone she'd stay well away from. There aren't any cracks in her poise, no visible points of entry that Angela could use to start a conversation. But that's not what she's here for.

She doesn't do that anymore, anyway.

There's no reason to waste more time. Angela makes her way over to the table.

'Excuse me,' she says. 'Are you Meijing?'

The woman's eyes open. Her expression is completely neutral. 'I'm sorry. I think you must have mistaken me for someone else.'

'Tess told me I should talk to you.'

'Tess?' A flicker of emotion passes across Meijing's face so quickly that it can scarcely be seen at all. She looks Angela up and down. 'Who are you?'

'I'm someone who knows her, and she said that you–'

'Are you Tess's child?'

Angela blinks in surprise. 'I . . . No. Or, I mean, maybe?' Although if she's interpreting the question correctly, that's an uncomfortable way to put it. 'She's the one who turned me into someone like you, if that's what you meant.'

'You have to go.' Any vestiges of neutrality are gone from her voice now. Her words are quick, urgent. 'You must leave. Now.'

'Please, I only have one question–'

'There's no time to explain,' Meijing says, cutting her off. 'You are in danger here. Did Tess tell you about Master Hiram?'

Outside, a wolf howls for only a moment before the sound cuts abruptly short. Angela feels a flutter of panic in her stomach.

From Meijing's reaction, she doesn't think Tess was exaggerating the danger.

'Is there a back way out?' she asks.

'I think so, yes, in the kitchen.'

'But not up here?' Angela looks over at the cramped stairs. 'He might already be in the building. Is there another way down?'

'I do not know,' Meijing tells her. 'Or wait, perhaps there is one. They send the food up in a dumbwaiter.'

'Where? Could I even fit in it?' There may not be enough time to find out. She looks wildly around the room. Is there a fire exit anywhere? Surely there must be, but where is it? 'How dangerous is he? I mean, should I jump through the win–'

'Do sit down,' says a voice from the stairwell.

The words exert a pressure on her head; it feels like there's something clamped around it. She finds herself moving to the nearest chair. As soon as she reaches it, her legs give out as if they've been axed. She drops onto the seat with a thump.

The man approaching them looks like he's stepped off the set of a period drama, complete with frock coat, brocade waistcoat, and a silver-headed walking stick grasped in one long-nailed hand. Mike follows behind him like an obedient puppy. One or two of the customers across the room turn to stare at them, but they promptly return to their meals. Angela silently curses jaded city-dwellers, and anyone who can't tell a vampire and a werewolf from an eccentric with a dog.

'Mike?' she calls out to him. 'What are you doing?'

'Is that what you have named him? Michael?' The man reaches down and gives the wolf a pat on his balding head. 'The angel who leads the host of heaven. Apropos for such a noble beast.'

Angela reaches into her handbag and flips open her phone without taking it out. Her fingers trace the keypad until she finds and presses the one number she has on speed dial. *Pick it up,* she wills her faraway girlfriend. *Wherever you've been until now, Chloë, be home and pick up the phone.*

'Master Hiram,' Meijing says, 'let the girl go. This is rude.'

'Rude? Nonsense? She and her pet shall be our guests.' He joins them at the table and relaxes into a chair, ignoring the stiff postures of the two women. 'Do you know how long it has been since I've seen a wolf in the streets of San Francisco?' he asks quietly. 'Well over a century. The moment I laid eyes upon him, I thought, aha, another of us must be about. We are all of us partial to wolves, rats, and bats, are we not? Always the easiest of creatures for our kind to control. I have dogs now, myself. So much less conspicuous.'

Angela wonders if Tess deliberately sent them into a trap, or if she didn't know about this aspect of his power. There's no point in worrying about that now, though. Muffled by her handbag, Angela hears the faint sound of Chloë's voice. She feels a surge of hope until she realises it's the answering machine picking up.

'Your command of your wolf is to be commended. Although it was not so great, of course, that I could not wrest it from you. You must be quite young, still. Tell me–' He stops as a prolonged beep comes from Angela's handbag. His eyes swivel to it, and narrow. 'What was that?'

'My cell phone,' Angela answers unwillingly, the words forcing themselves out of her throat.

'Oh, that won't do. Present the item to me.'

Angela sees her arm reach into her handbag, moving as if it were attached to someone else. It grabs the cell phone, and holds it out to Hiram.

'Help!' she manages to get out before he takes it. 'There's a vam–'

Hiram snatches the phone from her hand and squeezes. It shatters in his grip like a cracked egg.

'Hush, now. No more of that,' he chides her. Angela's mouth snaps shut, and won't reopen no matter how hard she tries. Hiram looks satisfied. 'Do not attempt to call for assistance again.'

She can feel the command settle into her mind, worming its way through her brain. What else can he make her do, with only a few words? Anything at all? Is there any way to resist him?

If there is, she doesn't know how to do it.

Hiram turns to Meijing. 'Let us escort our guest home, shall we? Our hunt can wait until another night. The beggars of San Francisco will still be about when we resume.'

'Yes, Master Hiram,' she replies, her face once again a neutral mask. 'As you desire.'

Angela glances around the restaurant, but if anyone heard her call out for help in the first place, they stopped paying attention when nothing came after. None of them are sitting close enough to see what's happening. All that they could observe would be three people calmly leaving their table. With their dog.

She can only scream silently in her head as Hiram stands back up, and commands her to do likewise. When he goes down the narrow stairway, her legs walk her after him, Meijing close at her back like a prison guard.

PART SIX

Follow Her Unwinding Thread

CHAPTER THIRTY-THREE

Russian Hill
15 July 1972

'I do not like this plan,' Meijing says.

Tess looks up from the pills she's laying in a neat row on the edge of the bathroom sink. 'If you've got a better one, this would be a good time to let me in on it.'

Meijing fingers the wooden stake concealed beneath her clothing. She doesn't, of course, have any other plan to offer, as Tess knows full well. If she'd ever thought of an easier means of escaping from Hiram's grasp, she'd have attempted it decades ago.

But the scheme she's concocted with Tess comes with so many dangers for both of them. Meijing has delayed putting it into practice for months, insisting that they think it over further. All while Tess pushed to move forward, take the risk, make their bid for freedom.

'There must be more precautions we can take,' Meijing says. 'A safer way to go about it.'

Tess's shrug speaks fatalistic volumes. 'Well, honestly, what we really should have done is find ourselves a bigger monster. Something badass enough to put the hurt on him. Something he can't control the way he controls you. But if anything like that exists, I don't know where the hell to start looking for one. Do you?'

'No,' Meijing admits.

'Then pills it is.' Tess goes back to laying them out. 'Look, what's the worst that could happen? Even if it doesn't work, he'll be too out of it to notice that we tried anything.'

'If we are lucky, he *might* not notice. And that is far from the only way this could go wrong. You could take too many pills, he could–'

'I'm not going to overdose. I've done so many drugs with you guys that most times, I have to triple the amount I'm supposed to take just to feel it.' Tess frowns at the Quaaludes. 'I hope this is enough. Do you think I should add one more, to be safe?'

'No.' Meijing is not so confident that Tess will shrug off the effects. Especially considering the likely course of the evening after she swallows them. And Tess is so very, very small. Surely that must affect the dosages.

But delaying further comes with its own hazards. Meijing reaches out and delicately traces Tess's cheekbone, close to but not quite touching the swelling black eye that offers evidence of Hiram's anger.

'Hey, don't get all weepy on me, Mei,' Tess says. 'We have to stay in character tonight.'

'I am not about to burst into tears, I assure you.'

'It was my own damn fault, anyway. I should know better than to shoot my mouth off about vampires. Especially just to freak out some skags in a fucking nightclub.'

'You were drunk.'

'So what?'

Meijing does not answer. She cannot disagree that Tess's behaviour merited punishment. There is little chance anyone paid attention to her booze-soaked prattle, but secrecy is paramount, always.

Tess, however, is no *geong si*. She is human, and fragile. A slight miscalculation on Hiram's part, a bit too much force behind a blow, and she could die. And while Meijing has seen Hiram discipline dozens of companions over the years, Tess is different. A confidant, an ally. Tess shares her struggle.

Tess is hers.

'If it finally got you on board with trying out the plan, a black eye is a small price to pay,' Tess says, turning on the tap. 'I should thank him. And speaking of the big boss vampire, he's going to start getting impatient soon. Let's do this.'

'You are right,' Meijing concedes. 'It's time.'

Tess takes a deep breath and slowly lets it out through her nose. Without hesitating further, she pops the first pill into her mouth and washes it down with a scoop of water. In less time than Meijing would have expected, the pills vanish down her throat one by one.

When none remain, Tess shuts off the water and throws open the door, her mouth a thin, determined line.

They wind their way down one flight of stairs, and then another. Timing is of utmost importance now. Unfortunately, much of the timing is beyond their control. If Hiram makes the ceremony unusually brief tonight, then the drugs will not have time to enter Tess's bloodstream. If he drags it out, then he will surely notice when Tess begins to lose control of her limbs. And they must also pray that he takes the first swallow of blood for himself, rather than offering it to Meijing. He very rarely forgoes the privilege. But very rarely is not never.

There are so many ways for this to turn into a disastrous mistake. So many paths that would end with him killing them both in his fury.

'Here you are at last,' Hiram says, looking up as they descend to meet him in the parlour.

'Sorry about that,' Tess says. 'I was dealing with some, uh, human issues. In the bathroom.'

He nods. 'Your tardiness is forgiven. But let us proceed, before the night grows any older.'

He presses her no further. Hiram has always had patience for the defects of living bodies; their imperfections, after all, serve as further proof of his own superiority.

'Kneel before me,' he tells Tess, and she takes her place at his feet. Meijing moves to her own position by his side as he begins, thankfully without any delay for idle chat. No doubt he is hungry.

Nonetheless, his liturgy tonight is still lengthy. His taste for ceremony, as usual, exceeds even his taste for blood.

'... Grant us power in this life, save us from final death, and count us among the chosen. Bless and approve the offering before us, make it acceptable in spirit and in truth ...'

On and on he drones while Meijing watches Tess closely. Is she swaying slightly where she kneels? Are her eyelids drooping?

'... We shall drink this blood, the blood of a new and everlasting covenant. It will be shed for us so that our sins shall be forgiven.' Hiram motions to Meijing and she proffers the box of blotter paper to him, her sole role in this ritual. He tears off a tab and holds it between two fingers. 'Proclaim the mystery of faith.'

'I will die,' Tess answers, her words slightly slurred. 'I will rise. I will come again.'

He places the paper under her tongue.

More words follow, more bastardised nonsense as Hiram launches into the anamnesis, filling time until the paper dissolves and the LSD takes hold. Tess is visibly having trouble holding herself upright, but Hiram seems to take no notice.

Finally, finally, the prayer reaches its end. 'All glory and honour is ours,' he intones, 'forever and ever.'

'Amen,' Meijing says. A pause follows, but then Tess, dazed and drowsy, manages to repeat the word.

Hiram bends down and bites her in the throat.

Drink deep, Meijing silently urges him as he guzzles down Tess's blood. *Drink your fill.* When her own turn comes, she merely pretends to follow suit. She cannot help swallowing a bit of blood when she licks the wounds to promote their healing, but so small an amount should not impair her much.

Tess is as limp as a ragdoll in her grip. When she releases the girl, Tess slides to the floor, her eyes twitching behind closed lids. By this point in the night, though, that should come as no great surprise to Hiram. They've been feeding upon Tess for years now. If the strain on her body at last appears to be taking its toll, it is only to be expected.

But now the most dangerous part of the plan begins. The part they cannot explain away, if Hiram becomes aware of what she is doing.

Once Hiram eases himself into an armchair, Meijing starts probing at his grip on her mind.

He will not have expected the massive dose of tranquilisers on top of the hallucinogen. He will not be prepared for it. It will drop him deep into his dreams.

Such is their hope.

Slowly, while he remains ensnared by the drugs, she begins to push against his influence on her. It's much like picking apart a difficult knot. All the years of his control are tangled together inside her head, an impossible snarl. But bit by bit, piece by piece, she feels it lightening, lessening as she proceeds.

He sits unmoving in his chair.

When she is close enough to freedom that her fingers are already reaching for the stake, she notices a violent twitch at the edge of her vision.

It isn't Hiram, however. It's Tess.

Meijing turns to see Tess's limbs convulsing, her breath coming in strangled gasps, her arms and heels thudding against the ground as she writhes. There's an awful, choking noise coming from her throat. Her eyes, now open, are rolled so far back that Meijing can only see the whites.

Overdose, Meijing thinks numbly. *Seizure.*

In another moment, Meijing is at her side, grabbing Tess's jaw, forcing two fingers deep into the girl's mouth. Tess's clenching muscles make her teeth clamp down hard on Meijing's hand, but the vampire doesn't feel it. She pushes her fingers further in, until Tess gags and retches.

Vomit spews forth in a thin stream, onto Meijing, onto Tess, onto the floor. A few half-digested pills are mixed in with the bile. Ignoring the mess, Meijing holds Tess, hoping it was enough, that she was in time, that the girl will survive.

Slowly, so slowly, Tess calms. Her arms and legs cease thrashing, and her breathing evens out to a slow, steady rhythm.

By the time Tess has relaxed in Meijing's arms, she can feel Hiram's will once again wrapped tightly around her mind.

She glances up to find him staring at her. His pupils are wide and black. Bottomless pits. She sees neither recognition nor comprehension in his gaze.

She can only hope that he does not truly understand what has happened, and will retain no memory other than his drugged visions. That all he has managed to do is instinctively clutch back at whatever he felt pulling away from him.

Even if she avoids his wrath and survives, however, her chance of killing him tonight is gone. She could no more plunge a stake into his chest now than she could walk abroad in the light of day.

She decides then and there that she will not try this plan a second time. There are far too many risks. Far too many opportunities for a tragedy to occur.

Meijing cradles Tess in her arms while Hiram's eyes drift closed.

CHAPTER THIRTY-FOUR

Boston
26 November 2000

Chloë wakes up in a church pew.

She pulls herself upright and peers over the back of the seat in front of her, finding the rows ahead full of people and a sermon already in progress. There's something familiar-looking about the red carpet, white walls, and fake Corinthian columns. Like the golden eagle, they bring to mind a vague recollection of her first downtown sightseeing tour.

It's Park Street Church, she suddenly realises. She somehow ended up asleep in the rearmost pew. So either it's no longer an enormous three-headed dog, or the dog has swallowed the entire congregation and they've decided to proceed as usual anyway.

There's a sour taste in her mouth and a crust of gunk in the corners of her eyes. She makes a quick assessment and finds that she's not obviously dead, she's fully clothed, her fingers aren't frostbitten, and she really, really needs to pee.

Deciding to work under the assumption that she's alive and not inside the stomach of a mythological beast, she slips out of the pew, crouched low and keeping quiet, and heads to the bathroom to take care of the last problem. While she's there, she also takes the time to confirm that her toes are in as good shape as her fingers. She rinses out her mouth at the tap and peers at her face in the mirror. Nothing appears to be horribly amiss. Physically, she seems fine.

The only emotion she can muster, however, is a kind of blank numbness.

She should have phrased her question to the witches better. She would have, if she hadn't been half dead from hypothermia. As it is, she's come back with an answer and a spell, but not the ones she needed most. She got the wrong answer and the wrong spell. After all that, she still has no idea how to protect herself from Angela's bites.

She failed. Again.

Outside the building, in a hard, pouring rain, she's able to confirm that the church is once again a church, and that downtown Boston looks like downtown Boston. No more giant monsters. Everything is back to normal.

The rain is dissolving what remains of the accumulated snow. In the short time it takes her to cross the street to the nearest T stop, she gets completely drenched, her coat soaked and her hair plastered to her forehead in sodden ringlets. She shakes it out, scattering a spray of drops, as she descends into the relative warmth of the subway station.

The train is practically empty. She picks a seat by the door and drips water onto it during the twenty-minute ride to Davis Square. Spending the whole trip wet doesn't improve her gloomy mood. The rain hasn't let up by the time she reaches her destination, so she gets even wetter as she hurries down the old railroad path to Cedar Street, and around the corner to home.

As soon she as she opens the door, Entropy rushes up to her, meowing frantically, only to recoil back to a safe distance when the water dripping off her coat dampens his fur. He paces back and forth outside the splash zone, yowling without let-up.

'Hi, buddy.' She smiles at him wanly. 'I missed you, too. Give me a minute to get dry.'

She's about to start shedding her clothing when she notices a piece of paper on the floor, just inside the door, already half transparent from the water trickling off of her. She peels it up off the floorboards to take a look.

CHLOË:
WHERE R U?
WHERE HAVE YOU BEEN?
CALL ME IMMEDIATELY THE SECOND YOU SEE THIS.
– SHELLY

Chloë's eyes widen with alarm. She unceremoniously dumps her coat on the floor and hurries inside.

What could be so urgent that Shelly came by herself, rather than leaving a message on the machine? Did something happen to Angela and Mike last night? Or to Shelly herself?

Entropy races ahead of her into the kitchen. Her eyes flick in his direction and she sees him waiting by his nearly empty food bowl, still wailing.

She stumbles to a halt, confusion overtaking her panic. There's something wrong with that picture.

How can his bowl be nearly empty? That can't be right. She dumped enough food in there to last him for days. He can't have gone through all of it, not in a single night.

Wait, hold on. Not in a single night?

Was she away for longer than that?

Connections she hadn't made click into place. She woke up in the middle of a church service. There was almost nobody else on the train. Is it Sunday morning right now? Has she been gone for more than *three days*?

No wonder Shelly was worried. Everyone must be frantic. Chloë needs to call her, and Angela, and Mike. All of them, as soon as possible, so she can explain why she disappeared.

First things first, though. Another minute spent incommunicado won't make that much of a difference, and her cat is convinced that death by starvation is imminent. She refreshes Entropy's water and refills his food bowl while he twines around her ankles impatiently, considerably impeding the process.

'You hadn't even eaten all of it,' she tells him while he crunches down on the kibble. 'Melodramatic kitty.'

Should she feel like she hasn't eaten in days? She isn't all that hungry. For that matter, does this mean she skipped all those doses of her meds? That might be one reason she feels like crap. Not that she doesn't have plenty of cause to feel like crap to begin with.

She missed Thanksgiving entirely. Well, she didn't have any holiday plans. Not with Angela gone. At least the long weekend means she didn't accidentally skip out on any work days.

The light on the answering machine is, unsurprisingly, flashing away when she gets to the phone. But the messages can wait until after she lets everyone know she's all right. She has a pretty good idea of what they're going to say, anyway.

Shelly's number is the first one she dials. She's the one most likely to be up and anxious right now. Angela isn't going to be answering anything until nightfall, and Mike's been mostly keeping to a vampire's schedule while he's on the trip, too.

Chloë hears the phone pick up shortly after the first ring.

'Hello?'

'Hi, Shelly. It's C–'

'Where the hell have you been?' Shelly yells down the line before Chloë can finish getting her name out.

'I'm sorr–'

'We've all been worried sick! Angela and Mike almost drove back from San Francisco!'

'I . . . Wait, they're in San Francisco?'

'I've been calling hospitals!'

'Shelly–'

'I've been calling the police!'

'Shelly!'

'What happened to you? And this had better be good!'

'I couldn't call because I wasn't here!' Chloë blurts out. 'I mean I wasn't, um, I wasn't on earth.'

There's a long pause before Shelly says, 'What's that supposed to mean?'

'I was in a different reality. Or something like that. Another, another realm, maybe? I think I was back in the underworld, at the end of it. It was because of . . .' Chloë tries to think of an appropriate way to explain. 'It was witchy stuff,' she finishes.

'Oh,' Shelly says.

'There wasn't any way to get in touch.'

'Chloë.' She can hear Shelly sigh. 'I get that there probably aren't any phones in the underworld. But you really need to let someone know if you're going to do stuff like this. Beforehand, not after the fact.'

'I didn't know it was going to take so long.'

'That doesn't matter. Think of it like wilderness hiking, all right? You don't go off alone without telling people. When Mike goes hunting in the Fens on a full-moon night, he tells me first. You vanished, and we didn't know where you'd gone. Do you want to do that to your friends? To Angela?'

'You're right. I'm really sorry.'

'Well,' Shelly says gruffly, 'don't do it again, OK? Now, tell me about the underworld.'

Chloë gives a quick account of the journey, dragons and locusts and witches and all. There's another lengthy silence after she finishes.

'Do you ever stop and think about how insane our lives have become?' Shelly finally asks.

'All the time,' Chloë replies. 'Listen, I should probably call Angela and Mike, even if I only end up leaving them a message. You said they've gone to California?'

'Yeah, they're looking for more vampires. Talk to them about it, they can explain it better than I can.'

'I will. See you at the office tomorrow?'

'Unless you're planning on taking the day off so you can get naked in the snow with a unicorn. You will call me before anything like that. Promise me.'

'The unicorn only got my bra off, actually.'

'Chloë . . .'

'Sorry. Yes, I promise.'

She hangs up after they say their goodbyes, and dials Angela's number. As she more than half expected, Mike doesn't pick up and it goes immediately to voicemail. She leaves an apology followed by an abbreviated summary of what happened, finishing a moment before the time limit cuts her off.

That done, she finally plays back her own messages.

The first one comes from early on Thursday night, an apology from Angela for hanging up on Chloë and ignoring her calls. Chloë's anger over that feels like a half-forgotten memory, something from the distant past.

The next few apologies are longer and more agitated, and finally transform into a series of worried queries begging for Chloë to explain where she is and why she isn't calling back. She feels guilt twinge in her stomach, sharp as an ulcer, as she hears her girlfriend's voice growing more and more distressed with every day that passed.

The strange final message, however, is something entirely different. It goes by so quickly she doesn't catch all of the words. Frowning, she plays it again.

Muffled voices, hard to hear. She puts her ear close to the speaker.

'*—t was that?*' A man's voice.

'*My cell phone.*' Angela.

'*Oh, that won't—*' Something Chloë can't quite make out no matter how carefully she listens.

Then, louder: '*HELP!*' Definitely Angela again. '*THERE'S A VAM—*'

Then a brief, electronic-sounding screech. Then nothing.

Something is wrong.

Something is very wrong.

CHAPTER THIRTY-FIVE

The Castro
26 November 2000

Meijing takes a long look around the kitchen. She's always found it the most comfortable room in this house. It's roomy and bright, with the counters and cabinets organised in exactly the way she likes best. The ceiling lights cast soft reflections on the glossy lemon-yellow walls.

So many hours she's spent here in the decade since Hiram bought this place. Evenings spent at the table, chatting with Tiffany or those who came before her. Whiling away the hours together while the one who was still living cooked, or ate takeout, or warmed soup in the microwave.

Angela sits with her arms tightly crossed, offering no conversation. Nimrod and Habakkuk are splayed at the girl's feet, happily thumping their tails on the floor. Hiram has commanded the dogs to accept her as a member of the household, and they've been treating her like a long-lost friend.

Meijing's *geong si* granddaughter, the child of her child by tooth and blood. Angela surely must find the kitchen more pleasant than the basement pallet Hiram gave her to use during daytime hours.

He's placed it outside of his vault door, keeping Angela close by in order to build the mental binds more strongly.

Meijing cannot honestly blame her for her sullen expression.

One advantage the kitchen offers is that Hiram hardly ever bothers to set foot inside. He has no interest in either food or domestic chores. Although Meijing isn't entirely free of him tonight, whether or not he is physically present. She can feel the grip of his mind clutching at her own. He holds her closely right now.

I'll miss this room, she thinks. But of course, that's a foolish notion. She won't miss anything. She will simply be gone.

'First thing in the evening, the Master has a stand-up bath at the upstairs sink,' she says, breaking the silence. 'As soon as you awaken, you must set out a fresh flannel and a basin for his use.'

'Where's Mike?' is Angela's only reply. 'What have you done with him?'

'Your wolf is standing guard in the back garden, where he will remain until Master Hiram is convinced he is fully housebroken,' Meijing tells her. 'Each night, after the Master bathes, he typically–'

'I don't care. I'm not going to be putting out his flannel or washing his socks or whatever the fuck you expect me to do.'

'I can certainly hear Tess's influence on your temperament.' When she sees the look on Angela's face, Meijing regrets her words. The girl seems stricken. Meijing wonders why. 'You will obey him,' she continues. 'If you disobey, he will force you. Which is unpleasant, as you know.'

'You can't keep me prisoner here.'

'If you persist in opposing him, then he will punish you, which is worse.'

Angela has nothing to say to that.

Meijing gives her a reassuring smile. 'You'll have it easier than I did, when I started. You understand, I hope, about how those like us age?'

'I know you must be a lot older than you look.'

'This house has central heating, tap water, a washing machine. I had none of those, to begin with. You will have much of the night to spend as you wish, if you accommodate his habits.'

'Forgive me if I don't exactly leap for joy,' Angela replies dryly.

'Let me show you how to starch his collars. That is one of the only truly complicated tasks. You do not already know how, I assume?'

'He starches his collars?' Angela stares at her, nonplussed. 'Is he going to need me to shine his buggy whips, too?'

'He does not alter his habits quickly,' Meijing says as she bustles around the kitchen, collecting everything she needs from the cupboards, moving aside the cans of dog food and the boxes of Tiffany's preferred brand of pasta.

'Who's the spaghetti for?'

'No one, at the moment.' Meijing fills a small pot with water and mixes in the cornstarch. She sets it on the stove and turns a low flame on beneath it. 'The first step is making the starch solution. Use nine parts water to one part starch.'

'So are you telling me that he's stuck back in, what, the Victorian era? Earlier? How old is he?'

'I do not know. Older than I am, and I was born more than a hundred years ago.' She stirs the pot with a wooden spoon. 'He finds change difficult, but not impossible. He owns no buggy whip, not anymore. I convinced him that his horse carriage had become too conspicuous.'

Giving in to Habakkuk's adoring glances, Angela finally reaches down and pets the beast. His tail pounds the kitchen floor with greater force. 'That makes him worse, though, doesn't it?' she asks. 'I mean, that says to me he could learn to live without you boiling cornstarch for his clothing, but he chooses not to.'

'Never let it come all the way to a boil, that would be too hot. His habits make him easier to please in some ways, really. He is predictable.' She looks Angela over. 'I would imagine that you have worn a corset on occasion, have you not?'

Angela frowns. 'Yes.'

'I thought so.' The girl clearly shares Hiram's taste for romantic and dramatic clothing. At the moment, Angela is wearing the same dress she was in when Meijing first met her at the restaurant, an ebony-and-crimson piece with a gauzy skirt and a laced bodice. It's looking somewhat the worse for wear, having been worn without change for more than a day; they'll need to find her new clothes soon. 'He finds the sight of a woman in a corset comforting. If you wear one, he may treat you with greater respect.'

'You want me to dress up in fetish gear so that a crazy vampire can pretend he still lives before women got the vote?'

'It will make your life easier.'

'You're not wearing a corset,' Angela points out.

'I stopped trying to win his respect a very long time ago.' Meijing examines the texture of her mixture. It's thickened enough, she judges. She starts the iron heating, then drops the collar into the slurry and swishes it around. 'Let the cloth soak up the starch. It helps if you stir it.'

'Is he going to . . .' Angela's voice trails off. She looks down at the floor.

Meijing's hand stills. She should have realised the concerns Angela might have with another person ruling her actions. She should have addressed the matter right away.

'He does not care for . . . amorous relations,' Meijing says carefully. 'Not in all the many decades I have known him. His wife is long dead, and I believe he finds the notion distasteful. A form of immorality.'

'I see.' Angela does not look entirely reassured. 'Does he have a lot of ideas about immorality?'

'Many.' She fishes the collar out of the pot and scrapes off the excess starch. 'Fetch me the ironing board from the corner, would you?'

Angela hesitates, as if she might refuse, but then gets up and brings the board over. The dogs follow her back and forth across the kitchen like devoted lovers.

'This is a lot of work for a piece of neckwear.'

'You should have tried it when the water needed to be fetched from down the street. Smooth out the fabric with your fingers.' Meijing demonstrates as she speaks. 'Then spray the collar with more water, no more than a quick sprinkling. The iron should be on its lowest setting.'

'So what are you going to be doing while I iron his collars?' Angela asks. 'Taking a vacation?'

'No. I will be dead.'

'You . . . What? Why will you be dead?'

Meijing slides the iron across the cloth, twisting it from side to side so that the fabric doesn't ruck up. 'He will kill me as soon as I have finished training you. He has sought to replace me for many years.'

'You're serious.' The girl's pale eyes have widened to the size of silver dollars.

'I am growing too old for his liking.'

'Too old? He's from the buggy whip era. Where does he get off saying . . .' Angela tilts her head, a thought seeming to strike her. 'You get more powerful as you get older, right? He's feeling threatened.'

'Yes.' Clever girl, quick on the uptake. Another way that she reminds Meijing of Tess.

'How can you be so calm about it?' Angela asks. 'Why are you standing there teaching me how to starch his clothes?'

'I am not calm. But he has ordered me to instruct you, so there is little else I can do. Before your arrival, perhaps I stood a chance of defying his bidding. But he has taken a particularly firm hold of my mind since last night.' She flips the collar over and irons the other side. 'He must know, or fear, that I have guessed his intentions. And he is very strong.'

'I know. I did my best to get out of the house as soon as I woke up. I couldn't touch the doorknob. My hand wouldn't move. I kept trying to lift my arm, and it just wouldn't move.' Angela slumps back down into her chair. 'I'm sorry.'

Meijing clicks her tongue. 'No apology is needed. But I do wish you had not come.' She glances up at the girl. 'What drove you to seek me out? Simple curiosity?'

'I was hoping you could answer a question.' Nimrod nudges Angela's hand with his head, and she gives him a desultory scratch behind the ears. 'How to bite someone, how to drink blood, without risking their life or turning them into what we are. If that's even possible.'

'Tess didn't tell you?'

'She didn't know.'

'I see.' So Tess never guessed that piece of information on her own. 'I never did have a chance to complete her education.' Meijing stands the iron on its heel rest. 'The cloth must dry for a few minutes, and then it can be polished. There was much I wanted to say to her that I could not. I hope she has not suffered from the lack.'

Meijing tries to speak further, to answer Angela's question, but no more words emerge from her mouth.

She should have known the attempt would be pointless. On this matter, Hiram's mandate for secrecy has been reinforced by the command he gave the night of Rigo's death. She can say almost nothing that touches on the subject. Not even if Angela stumbles close to the truth on her own.

'He has forbidden me to speak of it,' Meijing says. 'I am sorry.'

'Could . . . could you tell me if it can be done at all?'

Meijing makes another effort, but the interdiction is too strong. She shakes her head.

'That figures.' Angela laughs hollowly. 'I don't know why I expected anything else.'

'Why is the knowledge so important to you?'

Angela looks startled. 'Because I don't want to kill . . . well, anyone, really, but especially not . . . There's someone that . . .'

'There is a person you are trying to protect.'

'Yes.'

Meijing chooses her words very carefully. 'And how do they react to what you do?'

'Badly,' Angela answers, a grim expression on her face. 'She never takes it well. Even from the very beginning. Last time, she fainted.'

'That is not good.'

'I didn't think it was.'

Meijing lays a hand on Angela's shoulder. 'It is difficult for the dead to care too much for the living. Perhaps it is just as well that you must turn your attention elsewhere.'

Angela does not answer, lost in her own thoughts.

'If you are squeamish about taking lives,' Meijing says, 'then perhaps in time, you could guide Master Hiram to take on only those who understand the risk. Those who would willingly face death for what they might gain.'

'What? No!' Angela flinches away, and Meijing lets her hand drop. 'I don't . . . No one should die for that. For me. Whether they know what they're getting into or not, a corpse is a corpse.' Her eyes narrow. 'You don't feel the same way?'

Meijing thinks of all the people she has murdered or watched die, from Rigo to Tiffany to the parade of nameless faces and bodies, back through the years, all the way back to Pearl, when the century was still young. So many.

Surely she hasn't lost all sympathy for those she feeds upon, has she? She was human once.

She remembers an arm sticking out of the rubble. Her mother, dying in a tiny room with a sliding panel in the door. Death meant something to her before she became what she is. Does it still?

It does no good to dwell on such things.

'It makes no difference how I feel,' she answers at last. 'I am not the master of my actions. And neither are you, now.'

'Are you saying . . . He'll make me . . .?'

'Your prey will die by his command. More likely sooner than later. No doubt he'll want another quick meal or two before any long-term prospects present themselves.'

'A quick meal.' The girl's voice wavers like a fluttering moth. 'You mean he'll kill them, after he feeds. So they won't talk.'

'Or he will have you do it in his stead.'

Angela rises to her feet, her body tense. Habakkuk, sensing her agitation, whines from beneath the chair. 'I can't. I can't do that. Please don't let him force me to do that.'

'There is little I can do. He will want to go hunting with you soon. Tonight, I would imagine. He hungers for blood. And for blood-borne drugs.' She gives Angela a curious look. 'Have you never had to take the step of killing your prey?'

'Never. I've tried so hard, I've been so careful. I've hurt people, but I've never, ever . . .' She looks around the room frantically, as if searching for an exit, some way to escape. 'Don't let him take me out to look for victims tonight. Please. I can't do that.'

'Can't do what?' Hiram asks as he enters the room. The dogs go to him as they always do, leaping up to greet him with excited barks. Out in the back garden, the wolf Michael responds to the noise with his own, adding to the din. Hiram stills the dogs with a look, and the wolf's howls fall silent as well.

Meijing suppresses the surge of resentment she feels at his invasion of the kitchen. She may think of it as her territory, but in truth the whole of the house is his.

'The girl was telling me that she cannot go hunting tonight, Master Hiram.' She keeps her face expressionless as she says it.

Hiram crosses the room in three quick strides and cups Angela's chin in his hand. 'Why ever not? Stay,' he adds when she flinches back. Her legs lock in place. 'I was hoping to show you around the town. You are going to be here for quite some time, after all.'

'I . . . I don't . . .' She throws a desperate look in Meijing's direction.

'She should not go outside in such bedraggled clothing,' Meijing says, looking Angela's dress over with disdain. 'It would hardly create the impression we desire. She looks like an urchin. She must have a new wardrobe before we seek any prey.'

It is difficult to lie outright to Hiram when her will is clenched so tightly by his own, but she has made herself a virtuoso of misleading truths.

He glances at Angela's damp and wrinkled clothes. 'What you say is true enough,' he agrees. 'See to her clothing. We can hunt later in the evening.'

'Shall I go make the purchases now?' Meijing asks, resting her hand on the ironing board, drawing his gaze to the half-finished collar. 'I can see to the rest of her instruction on some other night, I suppose. I'm afraid,' she says to Angela, 'that you still have much to learn if you wish to perform the household duties here properly.'

'I'm sure that's true,' Angela says, then wisely says no more. Smart girl. She must not overplay her hand.

Hiram hesitates. Meijing hopes his craving for blood is not too overpowering. It shouldn't be. They fed on Rigo only nine days ago; he will likely be hungry, but perhaps not altogether ravenous yet.

Hiram's desire to drug himself is another matter, but at least he seems to be in a state where he can be reasoned with.

'Continue her lessons tonight,' he says, dropping his hand away from Angela's chin. 'But buy her new clothes soon. We should hunt before our need grows too distracting, and I wish to introduce her to our methods immediately.'

You want to take her hunting before you kill me, Meijing mentally fills in. *So I can show her how best to talk to our prey. Show her what you are no longer capable of doing.* Putting off this hunt for another night may have been to Meijing's own benefit, as well. She will survive that much longer because of it.

'Yes, Master Hiram,' she says.

'Finish her instruction without delay.' With the last, Meijing feels the tendrils of his mind encroaching into hers, pressing the point home.

'Of course, Master Hiram.'

'Proceed.' He leaves the room, Nimrod and Habakkuk following along behind him.

Angela's legs unlock and she collapses to the floor. She lays there unmoving for a time before she speaks.

'Thank you,' she says at last.

'I did very little.' Meijing puts the iron on its maximum setting and turns on the steam. 'I am going to polish the collar now, shape it, and then wrap it around a mould to fully dry.'

Angela pulls herself upright and walks over to stand next to her. 'Thank you anyway.'

'Slide the iron across the collar, steaming it lightly. The finish should get glossier with each pass.'

There is nothing the girl should be thanking her for. All Meijing achieved tonight was postponing the inevitable for a brief time. Tomorrow, more than likely, they will have to hunt.

CHAPTER THIRTY-SIX

Logan International Airport, Boston
27 November 2000

Chloë pushes her half-eaten plate of salad aside, unable to finish it. She'd felt weird ordering a salad at Legal Sea Foods in the first place; it was the one item on the menu that didn't have fish in it. Vegetarian options at the airport are few and far between.

It cost more than she can afford to pay for only half a meal. In the grand scheme of things, though, she supposes that it hardly matters. Not immediately after buying a last-minute plane ticket to San Francisco. When the credit card bill comes in a month or so, it'll be more than she's got left in her bank account. If this all turns out to be a big fuss over nothing, she's going to feel like a complete idiot.

She takes the piquet cards out of her carry-on bag and shuffles them. Again. Obsessively.

At least she's not going to lose her job over the trip. Shelly had been understanding about covering for her at work. Well, not understanding so much as panicked over what might have happened to Mike, once Chloë told her about the phone message. If she'd been able to drop everything and go as easily as Chloë can, they'd be setting out for San Francisco together.

It's a good thing Shelly has her back. Jetting away cross-country to find her missing vampire girlfriend isn't the most auspicious way to get ready for a change to a full-time position. Chloë was already behind on her manuscript reading after vanishing off the face of the earth for a while.

And if there were any questions left about whether or not she'll be taking the new job, there aren't anymore. She can't afford not to now.

She puts the cards down on the restaurant table in the simplest possible spread. Three crossed pairs.

Shelly almost came with her in spite of everything, but Chloë managed to convince her to hold off for a few days. If there's any trouble, a witch is probably better suited for handling it. Chloë had to swear she'd call the moment she found out what's going on, and Shelly will fly over on the weekend if Chloë has no luck on her own.

The Queen of Diamonds is crossed by the Ten of Spades.

They don't, of course, know for certain that anything's wrong. But there's been no word after the cut-off phone call, from either Angela or Mike, no matter how many voicemails Chloë and Shelly leave for them, no matter how many e-mails they send. The scenarios she has to spin to convince herself that nothing bad has happened all sound implausible at best.

The Seven of Clubs is crossed by the Seven of Diamonds.

What else could it be, other than something terrible? Angela going back to not answering calls, in some kind of weird revenge for Chloë's own disappearance? That's the least far-fetched idea she could come up with, and it's insane. It sounds less likely than Angela and Mike deciding to run off together, which is itself less likely than the earth suddenly crashing into the sun.

The King of Clubs is crossed by the Queen of Spades.

Besides, there was Angela's voice on her answering machine. The scratchy, phone-distorted sound of it won't stop running through Chloë's mind on constant repeat. All of her instincts are telling her to go. Go now. Go fast.

Draining her savings and haring off to look for Angela and Mike isn't an overreaction. It isn't an overreaction at all.

Chloë looks down at the divination she's laid out. Peril. Misfortune. A dangerous man and a clever or manipulative woman. An imprisoned animal?

Nothing new since the last time she looked. Or the time before that.

She gathers up the cards, leaves most of her cash on the table, and heads for her gate. Her flight should be boarding soon.

She'll do another reading on the plane. More than one. Bigger spreads, more complicated patterns. As many cards as she can fit on her tray. She'll find out where Angela and Mike are in San Francisco. If they're still there at all.

She'll figure out what the hell has happened to them.

By the time she shows up at the gate, her group number is being called. She shuffles through the line and down the jet bridge. Her seat is all the way in the back, by the toilets. It was probably one of the last ones left on the flight.

After an interminable wait, the aeroplane trundles out onto the runway. The safety instructions wash over Chloë unheard. A child starts crying in the row in front of her, his parents making ineffectual efforts to calm him down.

Acceleration presses Chloë back against her seat and the plane lifts, rising out over the water. The ocean is only visible for a few minutes before the plane turns west and the choppy waves are replaced by the buildings of Boston, slowly shrinking from a city to a map of a city to an abstract painting.

She's already airsick.

She waits until the seatbelt light beeps off, then puts her tray table down. Chloë hesitates, however, before she lays out the cards.

She's tired of seeing the same thing over and over. Finding out what happened to Angela and Mike is too important for her to waste any more time on incomprehensible card readings. She needs more.

Enough is enough.

'All right, you,' she growls at the deck. 'Listen up. I am a witch. I have travelled to the shores of death. Twice. I have faced down Cerberus himself. You are going to give me something I can use. You are going to tell me where they are, or I will *shred you.*'

The man in the seat next to hers is looking at her with a very odd expression. But when she slaps down the cards, the pattern they form is new.

So threats of violence are effective against inanimate objects. Good to know.

The Nine of Spades under the Ten of Hearts, and the Jack of Hearts sideways. *Where people live in the fort.*

A location. That's something, at least. What forts are there in San Francisco? Does 'Alcatraz' mean fort? She should pick up a Spanish–English dictionary when the plane lands. Her credit card isn't maxed out yet.

'Keep going,' she says to the cards as she puts more down. 'Which fort?'

The King of Diamonds crossed by the Queen of Hearts, over the Eight of Diamonds and the Eight of Clubs. *Beneath the crown on the hilltop.*

Where could that be? 'Do you know if there's a Crown Hill somewhere in San Francisco?' she asks the man sitting beside her. 'Or a Crown Mountain? Crown Heights?'

'I . . . think Crown Heights is in Brooklyn,' he says hesitantly. 'I don't really know San Francisco all that well. Are you playing a game, or . . .?'

No help there. She ignores the question and sets out more cards, delicately balancing the last few on the very edge of her too-small tray. The Ace of Clubs beside the Jack of Diamonds, reversed, and the Ace of Spades over the Seven of Hearts. *In the shadow of the tallest tower.*

That's all the room she has.

It's another message high on symbolic meaning and lacking anything as useful as a street address. She's really coming to hate symbolic meaning.

The cards are probably giving her as much as they can, though; clarity will never be their strength. This is more than she had before. It needs a witch to interpret it, but that's exactly what she is. She'll figure it out. She found the red path, and she can find Angela and Mike.

She has to find them. She has to make sure they're all right.

The toddler in the next row down is still screaming. For the first time that Chloë can remember, it's not annoying her. Because she deeply sympathises. She wants to scream along with him.

She needs to get a map. She needs to get that dictionary.

She needs to throw up.

CHAPTER THIRTY-SEVEN

The Castro
27 November 2000

'See, the thing is, I'm on my period,' Angela says, flailing around for any excuse she can think of. New clothes won't work this time around; Meijing has kitted her out for the evening in a ruinously expensive dress, slinky and dark as the skin of a black kingsnake. No corset, though – Angela had flatly refused. 'So I shouldn't go hunting tonight, because . . .'

She can't remember what the bullshit nineteenth-century medical theories said was supposed to happen if she does something physically taxing while menstruating. Her womb will fall out? She tries to say it, but she can't force anything she knows is a lie past her lips. Not when she's talking directly to Hiram. Whatever he's done to her head won't let her do it.

'. . . because I shouldn't,' she finishes lamely.

'Then it is all the more important that you be nourished with good, rich blood,' Hiram says. 'You must replace what you have lost.'

So much for that idea. The question of whether male vampires also have a way of getting rid of used-up blood flits across her mind. Do they piss it out, every now and then? She decides that now is not the best time to ask.

Hiram takes a deep hit off of his pipe, holding the smoke in his lungs. Angela notices a slight tremor in his hands, just enough to make the pipe quiver.

He's summoned her and Meijing to the living room – or drawing room, as he called it, because any phrase that came into use after the Taft administration is apparently too modern for his tastes – to prepare for a night of hunting. For him, 'preparing for a night of hunting' seems to mean reclining on a backless sofa and smoking dope. Angela looks to Meijing, who spreads her hands in a helpless gesture.

So far, he hasn't taken no for an answer. How long has it been since he last fed? How badly does he need blood? And how badly does he need it to be drugged blood, like Meijing said? Trembling hands must be practically a seizure for someone with the unnatural physical control of a vampire.

Angela has been a little high from feeding, herself, at times; she thinks she'd better be careful never to get addicted the way Hiram is. She's noticed the effect when she's drunk blood adulterated with alcohol and sleeping pills, and she suspects that back when Chloë was on a higher dose of antidepressants, they affected her some as well. Certainly she had a reaction when the prescription changed.

She wonders how Hiram squares all the drug use with the weird religious doctrine he keeps spouting. Does he pick and choose his morals like they're on offer at a buffet table? It reminds her of her own parents and siblings, ignoring any of the inconvenient Biblical references to forgiveness and tolerance whenever it suits them better to be cruel. 'Thou shalt not suffer a witch to live' is more their speed than 'be ye kind one to another'.

No one in her family has ever murdered anyone, though, however they might feel about witches and gays. Whereas Hiram clearly justified that to himself a long time ago.

'Tonight isn't . . .' she starts. She can't think of any good way to finish. 'I mean, I can't . . . I don't want to do this.'

He exhales a plume of smoke. 'Come, now. You must be hungry. Your complexion is pallid, and your skin is cold to the touch. It serves no purpose to refrain for so long.'

The terrifying thing is, he's right about that much. She's starving. It's been nearly three weeks since she last fed. That's pushing it. Her craving for blood is a gnawing presence that's always there now, flaring up into a sharp, dry ache in her throat when she gives it any thought.

If she does end up drinking blood tonight, it will be almost impossible not to enjoy it.

'Look,' she says. 'What I'm trying to say is, I haven't ever . . .' *Spit it out*, she tells herself. *Maybe he still has a better nature to appeal to, somewhere in there*. There isn't anything she can say but the truth, anyway; she literally has no other option. She takes an unnecessary breath, and lifts her chin. 'I don't kill people. I never have, and I don't intend to start now.'

'Have you not?' His tone is surprisingly understanding. 'Then I see your difficulty.'

'You do?'

'Of course. You are a young and gentle creature, and so you feel pity even for your natural prey.' He puts his pipe down, blows out the flame of his little lamp, and draws himself upright. 'But you must learn that mortals are ephemeral beings. A life so brief is of no consequence. You do no real harm by making it briefer.'

The merest shadow of a frown crosses over Meijing's face. It's gone before Angela is certain it was ever there.

'I don't agree with that,' Angela says. 'At all.'

'There is no pressing need for her to take such a step tonight,' Meijing says, breaking her silence. 'Let the poor girl become used to the idea. If I may speak freely, Master Hiram—'

'You may not.' He rises from the couch and picks up his walking stick. 'She must learn. And better that she do so early rather than late. Perhaps luck shall smile upon us. There may be no need for a death tonight, if we find a suitable long-term companion before sunrise.'

Fat chance of that, with him jonesing for a quick fix. He won't let Meijing do so much as talk about letting their victims live. Angela's certain that he's going to drain dry the first junkie he finds.

Unless maybe his taste in victims itself is a way out of this. It's worth a try.

'You like them on drugs, anyway, right?' she asks. 'Why can't we dope them up so much they can't remember what happened? I've done that.' And she promised herself that she would never do it again. It would still be better than killing someone tonight. Better than murdering some stranger, some person, someone who had a life and the hope of keeping it before they met the wrong monster.

But Hiram shakes his head. 'There is too much risk in that. A chance memory of a face, and all could be lost. You have been extraordinarily lucky if you have been using that method without dire consequences.'

'But if they couldn't even–'

'Enough. You will not propose this course of action again.'

The words die in Angela's throat, strangled by his power. She tries a second time, and all that comes out is a choked hiss.

She's running out of ideas, and running out of time. 'We could do something else. We could knock them unc–'

'Stand still and be silent.'

Angela freezes in place. It's as if her body has turned to stone, paralysing her with her mouth open to speak but no words coming out. She tries to force herself to move, shift her weight, wiggle as much as a finger or a toe, but her muscles don't respond.

'You must accustom yourself to doing my bidding.' Hiram takes a step closer, his tall frame looming over her. 'You will hunt tonight.'

She can't reply. She can't even shift her eyes up to look at his face.

'And if I say your prey must be killed,' he says, leaning forward, 'then you will kill it.'

PART SEVEN

Zeus Is A Sexual Predator

CHAPTER THIRTY-EIGHT

Russian Hill
30 August 1972

Meijing waits impatiently for Tess to come back from the dead.

There's something moving outside. She can hear it rustling through the decorative blue fescue, and she throws a nervous glance towards the door of the shed. It's almost certainly one of the dogs. She's given Hiram no reason to come and check on her. He hasn't watched her dispose of a body for decades, and he is unlikely to resume the practice now. So many deaths without revival – always yielding the same result, year after tedious year – have left him heedless and inattentive to the details.

It's a hot night. The whole week has been unusually warm, an invasion of dry air from the east chasing away the cooling summer fogs. She's thankful that she no longer suffers from the heat; the toolshed would be unbearable otherwise. In this weather, the sun must beat down on the metal roof from dawn to dusk. Well after it has set, the cramped space remains an oven. It's a terrible place to store a corpse. If Tess hadn't stopped rotting midway through her transformation from death to undeath, the smell would be overwhelming by now.

Poor planning. They cannot rely on that kind of luck to evade notice. The next house they move to will need to have a better spot to conceal a body.

She kneels down and presses her finger into the flesh of Tess's cheek. When she removes it, the skin springs back, pliant yet firm. The signs have been obvious since early this evening. It's fortunate that she has been prepared for such an eventuality for a long, long time. Otherwise, she would have had practically no time to assemble everything required.

Her hand returns to Tess's face, this time to caress it. Her first child. Her only one, in more than eighty years of life. She will never have a human daughter. But lying here before her is, nonetheless, something that is hers.

And Tess is hers and hers alone. A daughter, not a sister; she'll be no child of Hiram's. Meijing was the last to feed when they drank Tess's blood, three nights past. Her bite was the one that brought on Tess's death. The one that sparked her transition to a different kind of life.

Tess never fully recovered from her overdose the month before. As strong as she was – strong enough to survive being fed upon for three and a half years – the seizure and its after-effects proved her undoing. But now she is showing her resilience in another way.

As if prompted by the touch of Meijing's hand, Tess's eyes blink open.

'Good evening, my sweet,' Meijing says.

'I . . .' Tess croaks. 'I think . . . I think I had a really bad trip, Mei.'

'Yes. But you have returned now.'

'I'm thirsty.' Tess tries to pull herself upright, but collapses back down onto the plywood floor. 'I'm so thirsty.'

Ah, yes. Meijing can still recall the desperate craving she felt when she first awoke. Some nights are engraved on the memory like an acid etching, burned deep. She remembers what Hiram did for her then, what she must do now.

She extends her fangs and sinks them into the flesh at the base of her palm. She barely feels the prick; the pain is merely physical, insignificant.

Meijing lowers her hand to Tess's mouth before the wound can close.

'Drink.'

Tess sucks at it hungrily, greedily, taking back some measure of her own blood from Meijing's veins. The sensation of Tess feeding from her is an odd one; a dull, throbbing ache, but she finds it not entirely unpleasant. It is, she supposes, her one opportunity to suckle her daughter.

'Enough.' Meijing pulls her arm away. Tess, ravenous for more, reaches up as if to grab it and drag it back. But she manages to stop herself before she seizes hold, letting her hand drop down to the floor.

It would not do to permit Tess to drain her completely dry. Meijing needs to stay sharp for what lies ahead tonight, and she cannot allow herself to be distracted by hunger.

'So,' Tess says. 'It finally happened.'

'Yes.'

'And I didn't just drop dead.'

'No.' Meijing meets her gaze. So Tess had realised, at some point, that death was a possibility. And she stayed anyway. Interesting. Her longing to become a *geong si* must have been powerful indeed.

'What do we do now?' Tess asks, bringing herself up to a sitting position.

'Now you must leave.'

'Because if I don't, he'll kill you.'

'And enslave you in my place, yes.' Meijing is relieved that she doesn't have to explain the necessity. There is clearly much that Tess knows without ever having been told.

It's a pity that she cannot stay. A pang of loneliness stabs through her, as if Tess were already gone.

'What are you going to tell him?' Tess asks.

'If he does not press me too closely, I will tell him that you died as expected, and I have taken appropriate measures with your corpse. If he is suspicious enough to make lying difficult, I will talk around it. I will say, perhaps, that your body is well hidden, far from the house.'

Tess nods. 'Where should I go?'

'It's better if I do not know, in case he ever realises what we have done. Pick a direction. North, south, east, or west on a ship if you like. It doesn't matter.'

'As long as it's far enough, right?'

Meijing wishes she could tell Tess to be sure to cross water, whether rivers or the ocean. Tess is young enough to do so easily, and it would make it more difficult for Hiram to follow. But she cannot say so, not unless Tess speaks of it first.

'Here.' Meijing retrieves the suitcase from the corner of the shed, where she's hidden it beneath a pile of rotting lumber. She brushes off the spiders and brings it over to Tess. 'Money for your travels. Use it to find shelter in the daytime, use it to obtain a safe home wherever you decide to stop. It should be enough. I also threw in a few changes of clothes, and copies of your photographs. I thought you would want to have them.'

'He won't notice that much money missing?'

Meijing shrugs. 'I have overseen our finances for many years. It was not difficult to embezzle a small portion of it.'

Tess stands up, straightening her clothes. 'Thank you.' Her eyes flick to the tools hanging from the wall. Saws, hammers, pliers, drills. 'And . . . thanks for not taking my head off before I woke up, or something. I know that would have been easier.'

'I did not once contemplate murdering you. Although if you had run to Master Hiram upon waking, I might have reconsidered.'

'Not fucking likely.' Tess grins at her, showing newly grown fangs, sharp as a kitten's claws. Meijing smiles back.

'Go now,' she says. 'He could still come to the shed. Every moment we waste is a risk.'

Tess picks up the suitcase. 'You know, I haven't got a single clue what I'm doing. As a vampire, I mean.'

'You know the most important things. I'm sure you have guessed some of the rest.' She has years of advice to give if she could, dozens of secrets kept from mortal ears. But there is so little she can say. 'Never remain in one dwelling long enough to arouse suspicion. Conceal what you are from all but a few. Do whatever you must to survive.'

Tess is at the shed door, but she hesitates. 'I have a photo to remember you by, but you don't have anything from me. Nothing that matters, anyway.'

'There's no time to find a parting gift,' Meijing says, shooing her out. 'I will pick something that you have left in the house for a keepsake, if you think it important.'

'What, like a toothbrush? Hell, no.' She reaches up and removes the silver earrings she always wears, the wolf in her right ear and the snake in her left. She presses them into Meijing's hand. 'I'll miss you.'

'Go.'

Tess gives her a final, curving half-smile and leaves the shed, moving with a swiftness she could never have achieved in her former life. The dog lying in the grass outside, long used to her scent, doesn't bark once as she passes. Meijing watches until Tess has run far enough away that she can no longer be seen.

She puts the earrings on, and crosses to the house to tell Hiram that Tess is gone forever.

CHAPTER THIRTY-NINE

The Tenderloin
27 November 2000

'You may think me cruel,' Hiram tells Angela. 'But there is no cruelty in it. This is merely the proper order of nature.'

'It's too early for this,' Meijing complains. 'Too many people are out in the streets. The sun set mere hours ago.'

Hiram dismisses this with a brusque motion of his hand. 'We shall be careful, then.'

'I think later would be good,' Angela says. 'Later would definitely work for me.'

'The dangers of being so rash–'

'Cease your hectoring,' Hiram says. Meijing's mouth snaps shut. 'We will need to use all the time we have tonight. You must show the child how best to entice converts to our cause.'

Angela's legs won't let her run away. She's being steered through the stinking back alleys of San Francisco by a man dressed up like an evil duke from a Renaissance Faire. She wonders exactly what his cause is as she shuffles along after him. The cause of feeding vampires? The cause of worshipping Hiram?

Garbage litters the sidewalk, and the occasional spatter of wet, glutinous muck. The dumpsters are filled to overflowing. She can hear the chittering of rats beneath them, scavenging the burst bags for anything that might be edible.

Angela prays that Meijing has amazing powers of persuasion. That she'll be able to convince a random stranger – in a single conversation – that being preyed upon by vampires is a wonderful life choice. Otherwise, somebody will get murdered so the vampires can keep their secrets.

It's an impossible task. Angela's going to have to kill someone tonight.

She won't be doing it willingly. Her body won't under her own control. But it will be her body doing it, nonetheless. Her hands, her teeth. And she craves blood so badly that once she begins drinking, it might stop mattering whether or not she's under someone else's power. If she could stop, would she?

If she can't get away from this lunatic somehow, will a point come when it doesn't bother her anymore? Hiram is nothing but a pitiless predator. Meijing, she isn't certain about, but that hardly puts her mind at ease. After months, or years, when there are so many corpses behind her that another one barely makes a difference to the body count, how much will Angela be able to care?

Meijing's suggestion lingers in her mind. Maybe she could manage it, maybe she could learn to steer Hiram towards people who are eager to gamble for a chance at eternal life. If she has no other choice, she supposes it's better than doing nothing at all.

And what if she did have a choice?

If she wins her freedom back, tonight or tomorrow or months from now, would it make any real difference in the long run? Meijing couldn't tell her whether there was any way to keep Chloë alive, but it didn't sound promising. When there's nothing left for her – no girlfriend, no career, only a long life and an aching thirst – Meijing's proposal might be her only option to survive without murdering anyone unwilling.

Only murdering volunteers. Could she bring herself to stomach it?

She wonders if there's anything she can do to make certain that she never has to find out.

Angela feels an intense longing for Chloë. Her presence, her laugh, the distracted look she gets whenever she's writing something in her head. There's an emptiness in Angela's hand, where her girlfriend's hand should be.

It's a selfish thought. Chloë is thousands of miles away and better off for it. Look at what happened to poor Mike – tied up in a back garden like a dog. She needs to come up with a plan. Some way to save him. She'd better start by saving herself. And she'd better do it before anything irrevocable happens.

On and on they walk, winding their way through one dark, narrow alley after another. Hunting for somebody that no one will ever notice is gone.

It isn't looking like there's a lot of time left before something irrevocable happens.

Angela should have left Mike behind in Boston, too. She should be here on her own. Then if she couldn't find any way out of this, she'd have simply vanished from the lives of everyone she knew in Boston without getting any of them hurt. Out the door and never seen again. All of her unfixed messes gone with her. That would have been better than this.

But still. She wishes Chloë were there to hold her hand.

Hiram holds up his walking stick, halting her and Meijing. 'There,' he says, gesturing ahead. 'Go and see if she is suitable.'

Huddled in a recess formed where one building butts up against another, a woman with stringy white hair rests, wrapped in a puffy coat that used to be beige. Her eyes are closed and her head is leaning against the concrete wall.

Hiram hangs back, keeping Angela with him, while Meijing

approaches. The woman's eyes pop open when the vampire is halfway there.

'Spare change?' she asks. Her voice is unexpectedly deep and silky. Like chocolate milk.

'Certainly.' Meijing roots through her handbag as she walks the rest of the way to the woman. Crouching down, she hands over a few bills.

The woman smiles at her. 'Bless you.'

'You're a bit off the beaten path here, aren't you?' Meijing asks, not getting back up.

The woman shrugs. 'It's quiet.'

'What's your name?'

The two of them continue to talk, but Angela doesn't really hear it. Doesn't catch the woman's name when it flits by. The words have all turned into meaningless noise. She feels sick.

It's not just because of what's about to happen. It's because all of this is so horrifyingly familiar.

Approaching a stranger. Engaging with them. Winning enough of their trust to do what you want to them. The same thing Angela did in club after club for a year before she met Chloë.

Hi. Are you here all by yourself, too? I hate coming to these places alone.

What are you drinking?

What's your name?

Then teeth. And blood.

It would be so easy to fall into it. She vowed she would never do it again. Promised that she'd never hurt anybody that way, not even one more time. Promised Chloë. Promised herself. But here she is. She's going to plunge her teeth into the woman's neck and the blood will flood into her mouth, and the burning itch in the back of her throat will quiet for a while. Not forever, never that, but for a while.

How many dead before she finds the ones who want it?

How long before she starts convincing herself that if they want it, that makes it all right? She's already started thinking it over, weighing the options. It's already begun.

The conversation unfolding in front of her is becoming more animated. Their soon-to-be victim must have been lonely, or bored. Spending her days with too many people passing by without looking, happy to have someone to chat with. At some point, Meijing gestures back to her and Hiram, introducing them.

Angela has to put a stop to this. She has to. Right now. Hiram controls her feet, moving her closer to the woman. He can cut off anything she says with a word. Probably with nothing more than a thought.

Although, it occurs to Angela, Hiram does still need to think that thought.

'If you wanted something to eat,' Meijing is saying, 'There's a restaurant open–'

'RUN!' Angela screams. 'THEY'RE GOING TO KILL YOU! RUN NOW!'

Three pairs of eyes turn to stare at Angela in startled shock. But no one's told her to shut up yet. He's forbidden her from calling for help, but he never forbade her to shout out a warning.

'THEY WANT YOUR BLOOD! LOOK AT MY MOUTH! LOOK AT THE F–'

'Silence!' Hiram roars. The rest of the words die in her throat. The homeless woman is on her feet now, a baffled look on her face, but she isn't moving.

There's a commotion at the entrance to the alleyway, though. Voices. Someone shouting, asking if everyone's all right. Hiram stares in that direction, his eyes narrowed, some silent calculus playing out across his face.

'Too many people,' Meijing hisses. 'Too many bodies.'

Hiram nods sharply and says, 'Come.' He grabs Angela's arm, and runs, pulling her along. Meijing is beside them a moment later, matching their speed.

'When we are certain we have not been followed, we will return home,' he says as they hurtle back through the alleyways. 'You will be disciplined.' His tone is even – a vampire can never be out of breath from running – but Angela can hear the leashed fury behind it. 'Disciplined severely.'

'What were you thinking?' Meijing scolds from her other side. 'You must never expose what we are! Do you want to be discovered? Do you want to die?'

Angela can't answer, the words locked in by Hiram's command. She turns to face Meijing as she runs and nods yes sharply, trying to convey with her eyes everything she's unable to say aloud.

Yes. Yes, I'd rather die. If this is what my life will be, then I will never stop trying to get myself killed. For as long as it takes, until it's done.

From the astounded expression she receives in response, she thinks that at least some of the concept must have come across.

Angela looks away. She has to watch where she's going before she trips. Hiram doesn't look like he plans to stop for anything; if she stumbles, odds are he'll start dragging her along like a sack.

Meijing says nothing further as they race through the dark streets to the house. Towards Angela's punishment, and whatever comes after.

CHAPTER FORTY

Corona Heights, San Francisco
27 November 2000

After a very short time, Chloë has grown tired of trudging up and down hills in the darkness. Why do the streets climb straight up the slopes like this? Why don't they wind around or go between them? Who built this place, and where can she complain about it?

At least it's warmer than Boston. A little bit warmer. It's not the balmy California weather she's been led to expect from movies and TV, but it doesn't feel like it's about to start snowing anytime soon. She'd probably enjoy visiting the city, traipsing past all the brightly painted houses and stunning vistas, if she were here on a vacation. But she isn't. She's here making a panicked, poorly considered, and possibly futile search.

Where are Angela and Mike? What happened to them? They're somewhere in the neighbourhood she's wandering through, she's sure of that much. It's only a few square city blocks in size. The map and the dictionary helped her narrow down the possibilities to the small portion of the Castro that borders Corona Heights, although she's still not 100 per cent certain what the 'tallest tower' is. But Castro means fort, and Corona means crown. Alcatraz, as it turns out, means a pelican. Or a gannet, or possibly a flower.

She's thankful that it isn't a very big area that she needs to cover, but she wishes it were a little flatter.

Chloë keeps looking, a sour expression crossing her face as she starts up another sharp incline. Partway up, the houses give way to scrubby grass and trees, the leaves rustling in the wind off the bay. She must have taken a wrong turn somewhere. She stops, winded, at a spot where the sidewalk becomes mercifully level for a short way.

To her left, past a wire-fenced drop as steep as a cliff, the lights of the city twinkle beneath a cloudy, starless darkness. A broad, glowing avenue cuts through the centre of town like the Milky Way; the earth and the night sky have switched places. She feels a disorienting vertigo, a fleeting, irrational fear that gravity might reverse and send her hurtling up into the blank nothingness overhead.

She takes a few deep breaths of damp, chilly air to clear her head. Wandering through the neighbourhood isn't working. It isn't going to work. She's not going to spot a big sign at some point that reads, 'Angela and Mike Fell into This Enormous Hole – Please Take Elevator Down'.

She needs to do something that makes more sense. Something methodical and systematic.

What would Angela do?

God knows that Chloë should be able to figure that one out by now. Over the past year, her girlfriend has tried her best to augment their spell-casting attempts using the scientific method. Chloë's had a front-row seat to experimental analysis in action.

She watches the cars crawl through the streets below, their headlights glittering speckles drifting in the black. There's some kind of enormous structure rising from a hill across from her, a radio or television mast, dominating the skyline like a three-legged alien sentinel, a tripod straight out of *War of the Worlds*. Could that be the tower?

Chloë can't be certain what happened to Angela and Mike. They might be hurt, somehow. Or worse than hurt. That's not something she can bear to think about too much, though, not now, not yet.

But she isn't entirely at a loss. Angela left her enough of a clue on the answering machine message that she has a good idea of what she's looking for. The last syllable might have been cut off, but there's only one word that fits in any way that makes sense. Angela and Mike came to this city to find other vampires, and it seems likely that they found exactly that.

A dangerous man and a manipulative woman, maybe.

Chloë turns away from the electric glimmer of night-time San Francisco and trudges back down the hill. Back towards the people and the candy-coloured houses. She doesn't think she's going to find any vampires in a park.

There are signs of them you can recognise, though, if you know how to look, and she's been living with a vampire for a year. Someone with no reflection. Someone drinking blood, obviously. Blacked-out windows.

That last one, now that she thinks about it, is something she might be able to spot.

She's going to need to break it down into steps. Testing a theory scientifically means being thorough and methodical. She has to go down every street, every alley, keeping track, not skipping a single one. Look every house over, front and back if she can, for as long as she has to.

The houses on the first couple of streets don't yield anything. A lot of families clustered in front of television sets, blue lights flickering over their faces. Other homes are dark and vacant, and a few have lights on but no one visible inside. She gets as close as she thinks she can without being seen, trying not to make any noise.

Street by street, checking them off on the map as she goes. Finding nothing and then more nothing.

The two of them could simply be dead. The cards didn't guarantee that they were alive. Only that something bad happened, and they could be found somewhere around here. Vampires and werewolves might be difficult to kill, but that doesn't mean it's impossible.

She thinks she spots a house with an oddly dark window, but when she sneaks in closer for a better look, it turns out to be nothing but thick, flat curtains drawn shut behind the glass. Not something that would keep out all the light during the day, useless for a vampire. She slips away again, cursing under her breath as she trips over a planter box. So much for not making any noise. She turns a corner and enters an alley running between two rows of fenced back gardens. The houses on it all look identical, one after another after another like a set of giant-sized school lockers.

The thought that Angela and Mike could be dead keeps sliding back into her mind as she scans the buildings. She tells herself there's no evidence whatsoever to even hint that might have happened. 'Help!' doesn't have to mean 'I'm making this phone call in the middle of being murdered!' It could mean all kinds of things.

None of them good.

If Angela is dead, Chloë will never forgive herself. Not when Angela only went on the whole stupid trip to find a way to protect her. To protect her so that they could be together.

A pair of windows on an upper floor catch her eye. It's hard to tell from this distance, but they seem different from the matching windows in the other houses lining the alley. Darker, no gleam of reflected light in them. She moves closer, pressing herself against the back fence. It could be curtains again, but she doesn't think so. It looks more like they've been covered over with black paint.

Look here, urges a small voice in the back of her mind. *Look closer.*

Witch's instinct?

She tries the gate, hoping to get into the garden for a better look, but it's locked. The fence looks tricky to climb over, but at least it doesn't have anything like barbed wire or glass shards on top. And she can't pass by without checking further. Step by step, house by house.

Chloë grabs hold of the top and heaves herself up, wishing she had Angela here to help her out. After a minute or two of struggle, she lands on the other side with a soft thump.

She feels a sense of rising excitement as she creeps across the garden. There is definitely something odd about those windows. Now that she's nearer, she can see dark dribbles across the wooden frame, where the paint dripped down off the glass.

So, now what should she do? She hadn't thought this far ahead. Should she go around the front and ring the bell? Or smash her way in with a rock, and hope that she doesn't end up terrifying some perfectly innocent family of incompetent housepainters?

As she considers, a growl from the shadows makes her freeze.

The low, raspy sound of it sends a shiver crawling up and down her spine. She'd been so intent on the windows that she hadn't noticed the dark creature lying hidden in the shadow of the wall. Chloë takes a reflexive step back as it rises and stalks towards her.

Deep instincts are urging her to run, run far, run fast from the predator coming for her, coming closer with its sharp claws and its hunger and its . . . bald spot?

'Mike?' she hisses. She's only seen him turn into a wolf once, but she's almost certain it's him. He's pretty distinctive-looking.

He growls again and comes closer, hackles raised.

'Hey, calm down.' She makes a soothing gesture in his direction before giving it up as a silly idea. 'What's going on? Where's Angela?'

His only response is a snarl that bares a muzzle-full of long, deadly teeth. He's given no sign that he recognises her at all.

Could she have been wrong? Does someone happen to own a balding, wolf-like black dog? No, that's ridiculous. This can't be that much of a coincidence.

'What's the matter with you?' she says, shifting her weight nervously from one foot to another. 'Come on, it's me. What are you doing?' He pays no attention to her as he crouches down, readying himself for a leap.

She doesn't think an ordinary human stands much of a chance against a werewolf.

But she isn't an ordinary human, she reminds herself. She's a witch, and her magic brought her here. The cards were hers to command if she was willing to take charge of them, and they're not the only trick she's ever used.

If the others are under her control as well, she imagines that this would be a very good time to make use of one.

The wolf is already springing forward. '*Mike*,' she shouts as his claws stretch towards her, '*snap out of it!*' From somewhere deep in her throat, she wrenches out the power that's been absent from her voice for nearly a year, and forces it back into her words.

He seems to get tangled up with himself mid-air, twisting around as he tries to stop himself in the middle of his jump. He falls short of her, thudding down onto one shoulder and sprawling on the ground.

Chloë dances a few steps back, just in case her powers aren't as mighty as she hopes. But even as she does, the wolf begins changing into something else.

It takes longer than the one time she saw him transform from a man into a wolf, which was nearly instantaneous. This metamorphosis lasts maybe ten or fifteen seconds. Chloë winces in sympathy at the noises made by bones reshaping themselves, cracking and resetting into new and different shapes.

At the end of it, Mike's more familiar human form is lying on the ground, breathing heavily.

'What the hell was that all ab–? Oh my God, you're naked.' She quickly turns away. Other than a leather collar around his neck, Mike isn't wearing a stitch.

'That's really not the most important thing right now,' he says in a voice that sounds strained. 'But could I borrow your coat?'

She unbuttons it and passes it back to him, clenching her teeth for a moment when she feels the sting of the chilly night air. From now on, she decides, she's going to start wearing more layers when she goes on a magical quest.

'How did you get here?' he asks. 'Did you come looking for us? You can turn around now, I'm dressed.'

'Yeah, I did,' she says, facing him. His bare legs poke out from the bottom of her overcoat. He must be colder than she is. 'Long story short, I got worried, caught a flight, and found you with magic. Where's Angela? Is she OK? What's going on?'

'She's in there.' Mike inclines his head towards the house with the blacked-out windows. His expression is grim. 'And we've got problems.'

CHAPTER FORTY-ONE

The Castro
27 November 2000

Meijing watches as Angela writhes on the floor, screaming in agony.

When Hiram grants Angela a brief respite, she lies prone in front of him, silent and shaking. It is difficult to control the body after such pain, as Meijing knows well.

'There is a hierarchy, ordained by providence, which must be observed,' Hiram says calmly. 'As the snake feasts upon the frog, so the hawk feasts upon the snake. It is the nature of things, the divine plan that commands us all. Do you understand the error of your ways?'

'Fuck you,' Angela manages to spit at him.

He shakes his head in sad remonstration, and her screams resume.

Meijing feels pity for the girl's plight – how could she not, having been in the same position herself so many times? – but there is little she can do to help at this point. Angela was foolish to defy Hiram so directly. The best way to influence him is to convince him that an idea was his own in the first place. Angela will learn that, in time, although Meijing will not be there to teach it to her.

Angela convulses, her back bending into an arch so deep it looks like it will snap her spine in two. Meijing's own back twinges in sympathy, memories stirring of Hiram twisting her body into tortuous shapes, holding her muscles locked in place for minutes, an hour, as long as he saw fit.

Perhaps the punishment is merited. Angela's actions could have been catastrophic. However gratified Meijing might be that they did not end up needlessly creating another corpse, there is a reason she has maintained a careful secrecy for more than nine decades. Angela came close to destroying that in a single night. Her ideals could have led to exposure and a second, final death for all three of the vampires, Meijing among them.

Although to be fair, Angela's defiance may have had the effect of once again delaying Meijing's death rather than hastening it. She is now absolutely certain she will remain alive only until Angela has observed her methods of beguiling prey. After that, Hiram will surely be done with her; whatever minor housework lessons are left to impart will not be worth her continued presence.

There is an argument to be made that she should be grateful for her granddaughter's dogged intransigence. A more biddable girl would not have kept Meijing alive nearly so long.

It cannot last, however. Meijing's time is running out, moment by moment. It's almost amusing, in a way, that she sent Tess away so many years ago only for Tess's daughter to return to take her place. It was all for nothing in the end, at least as far as Meijing's survival is concerned. And while Tess herself may remain free, Angela has become a prisoner in her stead.

A tortured prisoner.

Hiram releases Angela's body from its contorted position, but offers her no further rest. Angela presses her hands against her head and shrieks. The expression on Hiram's face is carefully dispassionate. He likes to believe that he derives no pleasure from doing this.

Meijing longs to tell Angela that it is all an illusion; her skull will not shatter from the pressure on her mind, however it might feel. But it would be far wiser to remain silent. Any attempt to interfere would be the height of foolishness. And trying to put a stop to it would be the worst possible mistake.

She knows it would. All of her long years of experience tell her so.

If Meijing does nothing, Hiram might well spend the entire night torturing Angela. Further delay is the only stratagem she has left. Survive until tomorrow, then concoct another plan to put off her death until the next night. See what opportunities present themselves. Whatever happens, she must survive.

She should wait. Protect herself. Let Angela learn her lesson.

On the floor, her granddaughter screams and screams.

Meijing takes a step forward and opens her mouth to interrupt when the doorbell rings.

It's an incongruously mundane sound. Both Meijing and Hiram turn in the direction of the front door and frown. It's rare for anyone to come by the house, but it does happen on occasion – a solicitor out late, or a religious missionary eager to find converts in the sinful city.

'Stand up,' Hiram snaps at Angela. 'When you have arisen, be still, and make no sound.'

Without a word, she follows his commands, rising and fixing herself motionless before him.

After a short pause, the doorbell rings again.

'See to it,' Hiram says to Meijing. She inclines her head and goes to the door, glad to have been granted the postponement. It will give her more time to think.

Behind her, Hiram resumes his lecture. 'Those blessed with power and strength stand at the head of society. Those without such blessings sit at their feet, and serve their needs.'

Meijing has to clamp her mouth shut to hold back a laugh at the sheer sophistry of it. Has anyone ever conceived of such an arrangement without placing themselves at the very top?

She opens the door. Behind it stands a tall woman, with dark, curly hair and bright-green eyes.

'Hi,' she says. 'You must be Meijing, right? I'm Angela's girlfriend. I'll be taking her home now.'

CHAPTER FORTY-TWO

The Castro
27 November 2000

The woman in front of Chloë blinks in surprise. 'Excuse me?'

Chloë steps around her into a room that looks as if the decorator had been told to go all out on the theme of 'expensive, but tasteless'. It's a clutter of vases and tables, paintings with thick frames, clashing rugs lying beneath dark, heavy furniture. Her gaze skips over all the bric-a-brac to light on Angela, or at least on the back of her head. The sight of that sleek fall of blonde hair calms an anxiety that she's been feeling ever since Angela left.

But she can't afford to relax, not yet. The anachronistically dressed man standing next to Angela, lifting his head up to stare, has to be Hiram. Mike's description didn't convey how strange he looks, with his gaunt face and long, sharp nails. He's more inhuman in appearance than any of the other vampires that Chloë's met. Which admittedly isn't a lot. Is it because he's older, or has he always looked that way?

'Hi, there,' she says, walking forward. 'You should know that I stopped at a payphone before I came here, and I let someone know where I am and what was going on. So unless you want a really big fuss here in a really short time, you should let us go on our way.'

Shelly had promised she would call the San Francisco police if she didn't hear back from them. And then the fire department, and the ambulance services, and possibly search and rescue or poison control if she's able to find the numbers. 'After we leave,' Chloë continues, 'we won't bother you again, I promise.' She's finally walked far enough into the room that she can see Angela's beautiful heart-shaped face. 'Good to see you, honey. Are you all right?'

Angela doesn't answer. She hasn't turned to look at Chloë, hasn't moved at all. Her face is as motionless as a carving, her eyes fixed on an empty spot in front of her.

'You are her lover?' Hiram asks, finally speaking.

'Um, yes.' She turns back to Hiram. 'What's wrong with her? Why isn't she moving?'

'I have told her to be still.'

'You've what?' Mike warned her about the control Hiram had over others of his kind, but she didn't expect it to be quite so unsettling. 'Why?'

'She was disobedient,' Hiram says. 'She is being disciplined.'

Chloë narrows her eyes. 'Let her go,' she says, her voice low and dangerous. 'Let her go now.'

His face twists into a sneer. He examines her the same way someone might examine a particularly repulsive insect.

'No.'

CHAPTER FORTY-THREE

The Castro
27 November 2000

Angela can't move. The blinding, shattering pain has dimmed down to throbs and twinges, and her body is straining with the urge to shudder, but she's frozen in place. She can't do anything. Can't scream at Chloë to run away, can't throw herself into Chloë's arms and cover her with kisses, can't fight off the crazy vampire to protect her, can't even raise her head to look into Chloë's apple-green eyes.

She wants to rescue Chloë, but she needs to be rescued herself first.

Run, Angela thinks at Chloë uselessly. *He's not going to listen to you. He's insane.*

'I don't think you understand,' Chloë says to Hiram, anger making her voice shake. 'If you don't let her free, the police are going to be here soon. Do you want to risk spending a day in a jail cell? Because I don't think that would be healthy for you.'

Across the room, a thoughtful frown forms on Meijing's face. It's a good ploy, Angela has to admit. Living with a vampire has given Chloë more than a bit of insight into what they fear most.

Hiram's expression, however, remains stony.

'You can't do this,' Chloë continues. 'Angela has friends, people who love her. There's no way you can just make her disappear, not without consequences.'

'Can I not?' he answers.

'No. Let her go.'

'Master Hiram, this is foolishness,' Meijing says, stepping up to face him. 'We cannot vanish as easily as we used to. This could go very badly for us. If there is trouble–'

'We will depart this house this very night if we must,' he cuts her off, 'but our course is clear.'

On a sane vampire, Chloë's plan might have worked. But Hiram left sanity behind sometime long ago.

He rests a hand on Angela's shoulder. Her paralysed muscles ache with the desire to shake it off. 'This girl, I shall save,' Hiram says. 'The other shall provide an object lesson.' He smiles without warmth. 'And a meal.'

Chloë takes a step back. 'You really don't want to do that.'

Angela's head fills with words she can't say and things she can't do. Her worst fears are coming to pass and all she can do is watch.

'Both of you, hold her still.' Hiram's fangs are extended, wet and gleaming in his mouth. 'We shall all drink from her in turn.'

Against her will, Angela finds her hand rising up and clamping itself around Chloë's arm.

CHAPTER FORTY-FOUR

The Castro
27 November 2000

Before Chloë has a chance to back away, Angela grips her on one side, and Meijing grabs hold on the other.

That isn't good.

She doesn't even try to struggle. She has firsthand experience of a vampire's physical might; if she can't snap chains in two with her bare hands, she's not going to win this one on strength. But using reason on the crazy vampire didn't work, either. The crazy vampire approaching her right now with murderous intent. It's time to switch tactics.

Hiram is hardly the biggest monster she's ever faced. She knows her own strength, now. She doesn't have to ask. She can demand.

'*Let them go*,' Chloë snaps at him, power filling her voice. He flinches back. Angela and Meijing loosen their hold on her arms. The tension in Chloë's shoulders eases down a notch; she might not need to resort to more extreme measures after all.

Meijing turns and stares at her, eyes wide with undisguised shock. 'What are you?' she hisses.

'Keep hold of her,' Hiram says, a fierce scowl crossing his face. Meijing's grip, and Angela's, tighten once again around Chloë's arms.

She inhales sharply, too startled to do anything more. That's never happened before. No one has ever shrugged off one of her magical commands like that.

That isn't good, either.

'She is a witch,' he says. 'One of Satan's harlots. Much is explained. She will not, however, find me such easy prey as an innocent girl newly reborn.'

Did he just accuse her of seducing Angela with witchcraft? Life in the Castro doesn't appear to have modernised his outlook much. However, this doesn't seem like the right time to correct his messed-up assumptions.

'You have no idea what I can do,' she says with as much calm as she can muster. 'So let us walk out of here, before you find out.'

'I do not suffer witches to live,' he replies, reaching towards her mouth with one claw-tipped hand. 'And we'll see how much you can do when I rip out your–'

'Mike!' she screams. 'Now!'

A black-furred shape hurtles through the window, sending glass shards flying across the room. The furious werewolf smashes straight into Hiram before even hitting the ground. The vampire staggers under the sudden onslaught, and shrieks as the claws tear into his face, sending out a spray of blood.

That probably won't help for very long, not once Hiram recovers from his surprise. There's a reason this was the last-ditch plan.

She needs to think of something fast. Her voice didn't work on Hiram very well. But he's not the only one there.

'*Break free*,' she says to Angela and Meijing.

Angela's hand quivers where it grips her, but she doesn't let go. Whatever power Hiram has over her, it has too strong a hold to be disrupted that way.

Meijing, however, releases Chloë and lurches away.

CHAPTER FORTY-FIVE

The Castro
27 November 2000

Nothing that has happened since the strange tall woman came through the door has made any sense to Meijing at all.

Hiram and the wolf Michael are thrashing about the room in a blur of motion, smashing furniture into pieces as they go. Hiram takes a savage bite of the wolf's shoulder with his fangs, but jerks his head back immediately, retching and gagging as if at some foul taste. The animal, in turn, rakes its claws across his flesh, leaving streaks of blood in their wake.

How is the beast managing to pierce Hiram's skin? Meijing has only seen him bleed once in more than ninety years at his side, and that was by his own fangs.

She hears barking from the next room, and the scrabbling of claws on the floorboards. The dogs are on their way to join the havoc.

Meijing's thoughts are coming slowly, like bubbles oozing up through mud. After so many years, the absence of Hiram's domination has left her sluggish and disoriented. Whatever the woman did, the nudge broke his grip on her enough for Meijing's own resistance to do the rest. Could Angela's paramour really be a *mòu*, a witch?

The dogs rush into the room, barking and snarling. Meijing looks again to Hiram, who is stabbing his fingernails at the wolf's eyes as the pair of adversaries roll across the floor. A great flap of torn skin hangs off of Hiram's face like a bloodied flag. Both of their wounds, though, are closing as she watches, even while new ones are being carved into their flesh at the same time.

Surely Hiram will soon recall himself enough to regain his mastery of the wolf.

If he does, he will try to regain control of her.

Hiram bashes the wolf with the silver head of his walking stick, and the animal howls. Meijing can smell the scent of burning flesh.

The wolf stills and ceases fighting. Whether it is dead or back under Hiram's mental dominance, she could not say. Hiram flings its body away. The creature smacks into the wall with a sickening crunch and drops motionless to the floor.

Hiram pulls himself unsteadily to his feet, looking around to get his bearings.

Meijing picks up the broken-off leg of a chair from the floor, and runs towards him.

CHAPTER FORTY-SIX

The Castro
27 November 2000

Two dogs, Dobermans, big ones, are charging towards Chloë from across the room, saliva dripping from their mouths. She tugs against Angela's grip, but it's clenched around her wrist like a vice. Why the hell are they picking on her? They can't know she's the only one here they can hurt, can they? And why is it always dogs?

A room full of supernatural creatures, a vampire and a werewolf ripping each other to pieces a few feet away from her, and she's going to be killed by a couple of slobbering animals. It's just stupid.

Can she use her voice? Probably not. It worked on Mike, but he understands English. She takes a breath anyway, but it's already too late. One of them is leaping, too close, nearly on her, and there's no time left.

She twists around behind Angela, straining her wrist, and the dog clips her statue-still girlfriend with its shoulder and rebounds like it's smacked into a wall. She kicks at the other one and it bites down, its teeth sinking through her shoe and into her foot. She shrieks in pain and tries to shake it off, but it doesn't let go.

The first dog gathers itself for another leap.

CHAPTER FORTY-SEVEN

The Castro
27 November 2000

Hiram is fast, so very fast, even wounded and addled by years of drug use. His arm is already lifting to block Meijing's blow, his mind is already assailing her own. He has recovered from his shock enough to recall his advantages.

She's almost within reach of him, her improvised stake held before her like a spear, but she cannot close the distance before he shouts, 'Stop!'

Her legs lock and she stumbles, only the momentum of her run carrying her forward, falling towards him like a chopped tree. He will never forgive this. He will never let her survive the night.

But her stumble is what saves her.

The stake strikes where Hiram does not expect, the broken tip dipping low as she falls. It passes under his arm and slams into the centre of his chest with her full weight behind it.

The chair leg pierces his flesh with a sound like an arrow striking a target.

He clutches at the wood protruding from his body, but there is no strength left in his hands anymore. His walking stick clatters to the floor. His mouth spasms, and an inarticulate, guttural noise expels itself from his throat.

Hiram drops to his knees.

CHAPTER FORTY-EIGHT

The Castro
27 November 2000

Mike isn't moving, sprawled out at the base of the wall, and immediately behind Angela, where she can't turn to look, Chloë is screaming. Angela hears the Dobermans barking and snarling, savaging Chloë, the only person in the room they haven't been told to leave alone. And her hand is still fixed to Chloë's arm like a shackle.

Chloë is screaming, and there's nothing Angela can do to help. She can't open her hand to let Chloë go. She can't even see what's happening.

Angela wants to scream, too.

In front of her, in the part of the room she's able to see, Meijing throws herself at Hiram and stabs a piece of broken wood into his chest.

The pressure in Angela's head vanishes in an instant. And she can move.

She spins, snatching a dog out of the air mid-jump, its jaws snapping shut an inch away from Chloë's face. She grabs the other one by the collar and yanks it back, hard. Chloë yelps as its teeth tear out of her skin. It still has her bloodied shoe in its mouth.

The dogs make awful, choked hacking noises as Angela drags them away. Maddened by the fighting, they claw and bite at her blindly, struggling to break loose.

But they can't do any damage to her. They only manage to slash up her clothes.

CHAPTER FORTY-NINE

The Castro
27 November 2000

Chloë hops on her uninjured foot and looks around wildly, but no one seems to be attacking her. Angela is restraining the snarling dogs over by the far wall, and Mike is beginning to stir on the floor near the entranceway.

She shifts her gaze to the centre of the room, words of power rising to her lips. They remain unspoken as she sees Meijing step away from the kneeling Hiram.

He collapses onto the carpet, his eyeballs liquefying and running down his cheeks like tears.

CHAPTER FIFTY

The Castro
27 November 2000

Meijing watches, fascinated, as the years catch up with Hiram.

His flesh withers and shrinks, leaving the skin stretched across his bones like a thin layer of dry leather. The lips pull away from his teeth, turning his expression into an enraged grimace. His eyes are already gone, and his nose follows soon after, dissolving into nothingness until all that is left behind is a triangular hole in the centre of his face.

His appearance at long last matches what he has been for so many years. An ancient corpse. But no more than that, now. No longer a *geong si*. No longer a corpse that moves.

The blood oozing out of his heart and onto his waistcoat slows to a sluggish trickle, then stops. There is less of it than she would have expected. The last traces of Rigo, perhaps.

The dogs are barking and making a fuss off to one side. She quiets them with an idle thought.

She attempts to summon any emotion at all over the second, final death of the man who has been her constant companion for nearly a century. The most she can achieve is relief. At long last, she is free.

Strange noises are coming from one corner of the room. She turns her gaze from the corpse and sees Michael the wolf changing, elongating into a different form. Most of his fur disappears. Soon he is a naked man, covered with cuts and bruises. But his injuries are quickly fading away, save for an ugly burn mark on his side which remains unaltered as the time passes.

This is a bizarre night. Although she supposes that this metamorphosis is no more bizarre than everything else she has seen.

'Somebody please tell me,' the former wolf says, 'that I am done fighting vampires and crashing through windows for the week, and can go back to website management.'

The two young women are holding each other; both appear to be on the verge of weeping. After a moment, they seem to sense Meijing watching them. They pull apart slightly, still holding hands, and regard her warily.

'I owe you my thanks,' Meijing says to the pair of them. The three of them, she supposes, now that the wolf is a man. 'I have been in his thrall for a very, very long time.'

'You're . . . you're welcome, I guess,' the witch says. 'And thank you for, uh . . .' She gestures at Hiram's mummified body.

Meijing inclines her head, and walks over to comfort the dogs. The poor things seem confused. She pets Nimrod's flank until he leans into her legs.

'So . . . is everyone OK?' Angela asks.

'I'm all right, I think,' the witch says. 'I could probably use a few Band-Aids. Mike, what about you?'

He touches the burn on his side, and winces. 'I'll be fine in a while. If I'm careful, this should heal up in a few weeks, maybe. I'm glad he didn't have a silver knife, though.' He glances up at Meijing. 'Is his body going to be a problem for us?'

'I will deal with it,' Meijing tells him.

'Are you sure?'

'Yes.' Getting rid of one more corpse is nothing unmanageable. Especially a corpse that no one will be looking for.

'We should probably get in touch with Shelly,' the witch says, 'before she calls the police on this place. Can we use your phone?'

'We've never had such a thing in the house,' Meijing says. 'He saw no need for it.'

'He probably didn't want any of his prisoners calling out,' Angela puts in grimly. 'Mine's a pile of scrap metal now, so that doesn't do us any good.'

'We can go back to the gas station and use the pay phone again,' Michael says. 'Does anybody know where my clothes got to? I'm going to need them soon.'

'Um.' Angela frowns in thought. 'I'm pretty sure I left them in a Chinese restaurant.'

Meijing looks him up and down. 'Hiram's clothing should fit you well enough.' She glances at the others. Their clothes are in little better shape, torn or bloodied or both. 'Leave what you are wearing here. I will burn it all. That will be safer if any questions arise. You can find things to wear among Angela's new clothes.'

'New clothes?' the witch asks Angela.

'It's a long story.'

'I was pretty sure I hadn't seen that dress before, but it seemed like a bad time to ask.'

'We should be swift,' Meijing says. 'I do not think the police arriving would go well for any of us.'

'You're right.' Angela moves towards the basement door. 'Could you get Hiram's clothing for Mike? I can bring up the rest. I'll be right back, I promise,' she calls over her shoulder to the witch.

Meijing fishes the keys to the vault out of Hiram's pocket. He can, after all, no longer object.

On their way down the stairs, Meijing touches Angela on the

elbow to get her attention. Angela turns her head, her eyebrows raised in a silent question.

'Before you depart, I wanted to ask something of you,' Meijing says. 'I would like to hear from you again, after tonight. Would you be willing?'

Angela hesitates, looking troubled.

It occurs to Meijing that she could try to take hold of Angela's mind if she wanted, as she has with the dogs. There is a good chance that she would succeed.

But that seems like a poor reward to give to her grandchild, and to her grandchild's lover, the *mòu*. Who is, after all, largely responsible for Meijing's deliverance. And besides, there are powers here she understands not at all. Meddling with them did not go very well for Hiram.

Setting Angela at ease is probably the wiser course. 'I have been considering what you said to me last evening,' Meijing says to her. 'I do not think I will continue Hiram's practices. There have been enough deaths. This one can be my last.'

Angela visibly relaxes. 'And I think we can chalk tonight up to self-defence.'

So she correctly guessed the source of Angela's concern. Her granddaughter has proven to be decidedly uncomfortable with violence. She is, as Hiram noted, a young and tender-hearted creature. Life cannot have been too cruel to her; if she'd had a harsher time of it, as Meijing did, it would have taught her to be harder.

For all the girl's squeamishness, however, she is nonetheless Meijing's granddaughter. It is not a connection that can be carelessly tossed aside.

And for that matter, a daughter and a granddaughter is a large enough family. She sees no need to chew through the population of San Francisco in an effort to make more. Although of course, if she does have to kill her prey on occasion for one reason or another, there's no reason Angela needs to know about it.

'I'd like to stay in touch, actually,' Angela says. 'It'd be nice to have another person I can talk to. Openly, I mean, about everything.'

'I am of the same mind.' But the thought of her daughter has reminded her of another question she would like to ask, now that Hiram is gone for good. 'Also, can you tell me,' Meijing says, 'how I might get in touch with Tess?'

'You want . . . I suppose you want to hear from her, too?'

'Yes. I miss her.'

'I guess I could do that. I mean, I'm not really talking to her right now, myself, except for when we . . .' Angela shrugs. 'I've got her address. I can give it to you. She's in Phoenix.'

'Thank you.' Meijing wonders again about the circumstances between Angela and Tess. But she motions her head towards the bottom of the stairs. 'We should gather the clothes.'

'You're right. Let's go.'

'I'm impressed with your witch,' Meijing says as they continue on. 'She's important to you, isn't she?'

'Yes.'

'She is very loyal.' The key turns in the vault lock with a dull clunk. 'And quite a handsome woman, as well. I did not catch her name.'

Angela smiles. 'Chloë. And yes, she is. Both.'

Meijing steps into Hiram's lair for the very first time. There isn't much to it. A bed, a dresser, the paraphernalia for his opium. A desk with pages covered in dense handwriting strewn across it. She picks one up and takes a quick glance at the text to see if it's anything important. *Cain was the first to show dominion over other men and so bore God's mark that all might know his right of rulership above them . . .*

His religious ramblings. She will burn it all when she sets fire to the incriminating clothing. The paper will make good kindling.

'The wolf man is more my type, though,' Meijing says as she begins rooting through the dresser drawers for clothing that might suit.

'He's already taken, I'm afraid.'

'I can enjoy the view, nonetheless.'

'This is a really weird conversation to be having when there's a vampire corpse in the drawing room,' Angela notes.

Meijing emerges from the vault with a bundle of clothes in her hands. Angela meets her at the door with a similar pile. 'Are you saying I should mourn him?' Meijing asks.

'No.' Angela looks at the floor. 'No, I wouldn't say that.'

'Then let our conversation be strange,' she says. 'We are strange creatures, after all.'

It will be pleasant to have family to chat with, Meijing thinks. Although it is a pity that they both live far away. But in an age of telephones and computers, that does not mean they need never have any contact. She can purchase those for herself, now that she is her own mistress.

She would like to see Tess in person again, though.

She would like that very much.

'I, I still have something I need to ask you before we go,' Angela says as they head back to the stairway. 'If Hiram is going to be your last . . . that means there's a way, doesn't it?'

Ah, yes – her pressing question. 'A way to feed without causing death, you mean.'

'That's right.' Angela worries her lower lip with her teeth. 'Are you, are you able to talk about it? Now that he's gone?'

'Yes. He has no more hold on me. But I must warn you . . . it will be difficult for you, if Chloë feels the strain of it as strongly as you say.'

'How difficult?'

Meijing stops midway up the stairs. 'I am not sure I could manage it with someone so vulnerable,' she admits. 'It might be wiser to seek a different path.'

'Like what?' Angela scowls. 'I'm not going to massacre any aspiring vampires, if that's what you're getting at.'

'Now that Hiram is dead, there are more possibilities. You could search for prey who do not respond to your bites so poorly. Keeping them alive might prove somewhat less strenuous for you. I could help you look, if you wanted. You would be welcome to stay here with me.'

Angela remains silent for a long moment before she answers. 'You said it would be difficult, with Chloë,' she says quietly. 'Is that what you meant, or was it a nice way of telling me it isn't possible?'

'Difficult,' Meijing replies. 'It will be very hard on you. You will suffer for it every day, and you will never be able to falter or waver, not even once.'

'Then whatever it is,' Angela says, 'I'll do it. Thank you very much for your offer, but I have to try. She came here for me. I want to go home with her.'

Meijing nods. Perhaps Angela and her witch will even succeed. Their love is obvious from the way that they look at each other. Bound together by the Red Thread of Fate, as the Chinatown folktale went. Lovers tied finger to finger by an invisible cord that may stretch or tangle, but never break.

It's better that my granddaughter has a softer life than I did, Meijing decides. *And a softer temperament.* She would not wish her own history upon the girl. She would not wish it upon anyone.

'I suppose that if Chloë cares for you enough to walk into the den of a hostile vampire,' she says, 'then she is worth the price.'

'I know. I hope I deserve her.'

'Make certain you do, then.'

'I will.' Angela hesitates. 'If I can. So how do you do it? What makes it possible? What's the answer?' Her voice is tinged with hope, and more than a hint of desperation. 'What?'

CHAPTER FIFTY-ONE

I-80/US-95 Highway, Nevada
28 November 2000

The freeway stretches out across the desert in an endless straight line. For as far ahead as the headlights can reach, the road bisects the flat, scrubby landscape like a ruled pencil mark running across a piece of paper. The dark hills on the distant horizon are visible only by the way they blot out some of the stars.

A loud snore coming from the back makes Chloë twist around to look behind her. Mike is stretched out across the full length of the back seat, eyes closed, his head tilted at an awkward angle against the door. He shifts a bit, his body seeking out a more comfortable position in the confined space. He'd fit better if he were a wolf. And he wouldn't have to keep wearing out-of-date clothes stolen from a dead vampire, either.

Although maybe he doesn't want to change into his other form so soon after spending days trapped in it. Chloë figures that she would want to keep her thumbs for a while, too, after that.

'Mike's asleep,' she says, turning to Angela. She pulls her dress down further over her thighs. It's sized for someone smaller and shorter than she is, and it keeps riding up whenever she moves. Dresses aren't something she makes a habit of wearing much these days, anyway. It feels a bit like she's going in drag as her girlfriend.

'I'm not surprised.' Angela takes her eyes off the road long enough for a glance in the rear-view mirror. 'It's been a long night.'

'Yeah.'

'Not too much more of it to go, though. Only a couple of hours left before dawn.'

A long night, and a frightening one. Chloë still isn't sure how she feels about what happened. Hiram was a mass murderer, by all accounts. But she's not a TV heroine, and seeing him wither and die isn't something she can shrug off with a pithy quip.

Neither Angela nor Chloë says anything for a few minutes. Everything that's happened since Angela and Meijing came out of the basement has passed by in a whirl – getting dressed, burning their old clothes, calling Shelly, rushing out of town. Now that Mike's asleep, it's the first time they've had an opportunity to talk privately with each other. But they're both, apparently, at a loss for words.

There might simply be too much to say.

Chloë leans her head against Angela's shoulder. Angela takes one hand off the steering wheel and runs it through Chloë's curls, pausing to caress her cheek.

'Thanks for coming to my rescue,' Angela says.

'Hey, you saved me back there, too.' Chloë's wrist throbs where she wrenched it, and the stabbing pain in her foot left her limping around San Francisco until they made it to the car. She needs to get some antibiotic ointment for the dog bite as soon as she has the chance. 'And it's not like Mike did nothing, either. We all helped each other. It would have gone a lot worse for me without you in that room.'

'No.' Angela shakes her head. 'You weren't the one in trouble. If you hadn't come, Mike and I would still be trapped there. I was the damsel in distress, not you. Don't pretend that isn't what happened.'

'Well, either way,' Chloë says, 'you need to take me with you next time.'

Angela half turns to look at her. 'What?'

'If something like this comes up again. Something dangerous. We're in this together, OK? Don't tell me to stay safe at home. Don't decide you know what's best for me.'

'You're right,' Angela acknowledges, her eyes flicking down. 'That was bullshit.'

'And don't you ever' – Chloë sits up straight – 'leave me behind so you can half break up with me, in case you don't come back.' From the back of a car, Mike snorts and contorts himself into a new position. Chloë lowers her voice. 'Don't do that to me. Either break up with me all the way, or take me along.'

There's a long pause before Angela replies.

'I'm sorry,' she says quietly.

'Just don't do it again, all right?'

'I won't. I promise.' Angela puts her hand down behind the gear stick, palm up, offering without insisting. 'I missed you, you know. So much.'

'I missed you, too.' Chloë puts her hand over Angela's and gives it a squeeze. 'So, while we're on the subject.' She takes a deep breath. 'Are you going to break up with me all the way? Or did you find out what you needed to know?'

Angela's eyes widen. 'Oh my God, I haven't told you yet! I'm sorry, everything's been so–Yes! Or, I mean, no. I mean . . .' She stops herself, and tries again. 'Yes, I found out what I needed to know. No, I'm not breaking up with you.'

'Oh.' Chloë sinks back in her seat. She feels dizzy. She clings to Angela's hand, holding it like a lifeline. 'That's, that's . . .'

'Yeah.' Angela grins. 'I know.'

'How do you, I mean, how does it work?'

'It's not complicated. In fact, it's so simple it's almost stupid.'

'Details now, please. I can't handle any more suspense tonight.'

'I can never drink as much as I want to,' Angela says. 'Not ever again.'

Chloë looks puzzled. 'How do you mean?'

'I'm supposed to take only a single small sip of blood from you, once each day. If I can manage it, I'll always be hungry, but I won't ever starve. And there won't be any risk to you at all. If I keep it to a few drops, it's safe.' Angela makes a sound that's almost, but not quite, a laugh. 'I was doing exactly the wrong thing. Trying to minimise exposure, reduce the number of bites . . .' She shakes her head. 'I would have killed you, doing what I was doing. I really would have. It could have happened before we thought it would, too – she said sometimes it doesn't even take a year.' Angela's voice rises in pitch. 'You could have dropped dead, any time!'

'But I didn't. Honey, I'm OK. We're OK.'

'I feel like such an idiot!' Angela thumps her fist against the steering wheel.

'You shouldn't,' Chloë reassures her. 'You didn't know.'

'But it's so easy. I just, I just never thought of it.'

'It doesn't sound all that easy,' Chloë says hesitantly. 'You're going to be hungry all the time? Like, forever?'

Angela shrugs. 'I'm hungry most days now. It won't be that big of a difference. I'll be fine.'

'But–'

'I'll be fine.'

Chloë studies Angela's face. 'If you're sure.'

'I'm sure,' Angela says firmly.

'. . . OK.' Chloë doesn't feel so certain that it's going to be as effortless as Angela is trying to imply. It sounds like a hard, painful way to survive.

But, Chloë thinks, *at least we can be together for it.* Maybe she can help Angela get through it; maybe there's a way to make it easier on her. And even if it's difficult, for the first time in a long time, they have a clear path forward.

They can go down it side by side, and find out what happens.

'Listen,' Chloë says, 'you should know . . . I learned some stuff that might be useful, too.'

'What do you mean?'

'So, remember when I stopped calling for a while?'

'Yes.' Angela frowns. 'What the hell was that about?'

'I went–'

'I was worried sick.' Angela's voice is getting heated again. 'You stopped calling for days. I thought you might be dead! What were you thinking?'

'Really?' Chloë says. 'After Phoenix? *You're* upset because *I* didn't answer the phone?'

Angela immediately looks abashed. 'That's . . . that's fair. I'm sorry.'

'Yeah, well.' Chloë gazes out the window, watching the dark, featureless landscape pass by. 'Me, too. I should have let you know where I was going. How about we call it even?' She turns back to Angela. 'I don't really want to fight. Not now.'

'Me, neither.' Angela offers a tentative smile. 'So, you went somewhere? Where did you go?'

'That's what I was trying to tell you. I figured out how to go back to see the witches.'

'You did? And you were there for . . . How many days were you gone? Three? More?'

'A few, yeah. But that's not the important thing. They taught me something. A spell, sort of.'

Angela gives Chloë a puzzled glance. 'What kind of spell?'

'It's one that'll let you walk in daylight. Well, walk in daylight half the time, anyw– OhshitAngelawatchtheROAD!'

The car swerves dangerously onto the shoulder, the right-hand wheels bumping over rugged desert ground, as Angela whips her whole body around to stare at Chloë. With an inarticulate cry, Angela wrenches her gaze away and manoeuvres the juddering vehicle back onto the asphalt. The tyres squeal in complaint as they slew across the road.

Behind them, Mike mutters in his sleep, and snores again. Chloë lets out a quick, near-hysterical giggle. She tamps down any more of them with a deep breath.

'What do we have to do?' Angela says once she has the car in the lane and under control. Her hands are fixed at ten and two. 'What does it involve?'

'I have to do it with you.'

'Do what with me?'

'Avoid the sunlight. If I spend half of my time awake with you at night, not letting the sun touch me all day, like you do, then you can spend the other half with me in the daylight. It's a whole . . .' She makes a wordless gesture. 'It's a magical balance thing.'

'Wait, won't that totally screw up your life?' Angela asks. 'Your new job and, and everything?'

'I literally just saved my soon-to-be-boss's boyfriend from being enslaved by a deranged vampire,' Chloë answers dryly. 'If I can't negotiate that into some flex time, Shelly and I are going to have words.'

Angela goes quiet, looking thoughtful.

There might be problems with the spell that Chloë doesn't know about, of course. The details aren't entirely clear to her yet – she'll have to learn by doing. It's very possible that she'll have to spend those sunless days dead, like Angela does. It would make sense, given what she's come to understand of how it's supposed to work.

But that's something she can deal with if it comes up. She's not going to let it stop her. Especially not when Angela is planning to spend her whole life hungry for Chloë's sake. A little bit of death seems like a small price to pay in comparison.

'So what about you?' Chloë asks, breaking the silence. 'Your career, I mean. Can you make that work, going in half the time? I mean, are there any astronomy positions where you don't have to be there every single day?'

'Well, if you're positive that it's all right with you . . .' Angela's brow wrinkles as she thinks through the implications. 'Assuming we always stay out of the sun on weekends, and I telecommute sometimes . . .' Her face clears. 'That's doable, I think. I could probably get away with that in a postdoc job, one way or another.'

'And we can be together on both schedules, whether we're doing nights or days. Shifting back and forth is going to be a pain, but I think it's worth messing up some sleep cycles to– Hon? Are, are you crying?'

Tears are slipping down Angela's cheeks in a steady stream. 'I'm sorry, it's just . . . we don't have to split up, and I can have a career, and . . . I don't have to be Angela-the-vampire, I can be Angela-the-astrophysicist, and Angela-Chloë's-girlfriend, and . . . Am I even making sense?'

'Perfect sense.' Chloë reaches over and brushes a tear off of Angela's face. 'It's all OK. Everything's all right.'

'It is, isn't it?' Angela says. 'It really is.'

During the quiet that follows, a green road sign looms up at the side of the highway, white letters flaring in the headlights, announcing the distances to Winnemucca, Battle Mountain, and Elko. Chloë's eyes follow it until it vanishes behind them.

'Let's find a motel in Winnemucca,' she says.

'Do you really want to stop that early? Because we can get a lot further than that before dawn. And even before we get this spell of yours cast, if you and Mike want to drive during the day, you can–'

'We should stop at a motel a nice long while before sunrise,' Chloë says, gently taking Angela's hand and guiding it to her thigh. Her dress has ridden up again, and she doesn't bother to push it down. Angela inhales, a quick, sharp gasp, and Chloë grins at the thought of making someone who doesn't need to breathe have to catch her breath. 'Mike is going to have to get a separate room. We're going to try this blood-sipping thing, and then I intend to have a proper reunion with my girlfriend.'

'I'll pull off at the next exit,' Angela says.

'Perfect,' Chloë purrs.

Maybe she can make Angela's dormant heart beat involuntarily, too, if she tries hard enough. Who knows?

A few miles later, when Angela is switching on her turn signal to warn the non-existent traffic as they approach the off-ramp, she asks, 'Hey, weren't you supposed to get a third question?'

'A third . . . Oh, for the witches, you mean?'

'Yeah, wasn't there a whole big deal about you getting three questions?' Angela eases the car off the interstate, slowing down to what feels like a crawl after so many miles going at seventy-five. The lights of highway-side Winnemucca come into view, garish neon signs blazing in the desert night. 'You've only been there twice. Does that mean you're going to vanish again sometime?'

'I've been giving that some thought, actually,' Chloë replies. 'Because going to see them is, um, kind of a pain. But I think there's something they can do for us even if I don't put myself through another ritual. If I've guessed something right about the third witch.'

'Guessed what? What else can she do?' Angela pulls into the

parking lot of a dusty Motel 6 perched a short distance from the interchange. Mike stirs in the back seat as the car slows and stops. 'I thought we were pretty much set with everything for once.'

'Well . . . If you're OK with the idea, I thought I might call her up when we get back to Boston and ask if she can find us another apartment with a pantry.'

CHAPTER FIFTY-TWO

The Third Witch

This is Kindly Ladies Realty, Moira heah, how can I help ya? Oh, hey, Chloë, how ya been? I'm not bad, can't complain, 'cept my sciatica's actin' up and I keep wakin' up in the night to pee and then when I try to pee? No pee. Y'ever get that? No? That's great, means ya got a strong young bladdah, keep bein' good to it and it'll keep bein' good to you.

So I'm guessin' ya wanna look for an apahtment again? I gotta tell ya, it ain't gonna be easy to find a place. Ya know the occupancy rate in Boston right now? Ninety-nine pahcent. It's wicked crazy. Ya can go up to a guy with a room to let and say, 'I'll pay you a whole yeah's rent, up front, all in cash, small bills,' and he'll say, 'Eh, I'm gonna wait to see if somethin' bettah comes along.' Totally nuts.

Yeah, no, the one ya saw a coupla weeks ago's long gone. Ya shoulda got it while the gettin' was good. South End real estate's hot right now. In the South End, I could show a place wit' rats chewin' on a dead body in the hallway an' I'd get five nice couples askin' to leave a deposit.

So whaddaya want? One sec, lemme write this down. Has to be on the Red Line, got it. Must allow cats. What else? A place with a pantry. Or a big closet, or somethin' like that. Anythin' without windows. 'Cause of the vampire, yeah?

Wait, am I not s'posed to know that you know that I know that? Eh, who can keep track, amiright? The mystical mythical let's-nevah-say-what-we-mean bullcrap is all a buncha bullcrap, if ya ask me.

Hold on, wait, wait, wait. I can thinka one place. 'S a walk-up, top of a triple-deckah, lovely little family just hadda move out. They were cookin' meth. But get a loada this– 's got undah-the-eaves storage space. Nice big storage area, it'll clean up good, ya can make a nice hidden bedroom wit' no windows.

So, how d'ya feel about Cambridge? 'S not gonna be cheap, not since the idiots voted out rent control, but how many vampire-friendly set-ups are ya gonna find? That take cats?

Listen, that reminds me, I gotta go inna minute on accouna I got a boa constrictah needs feedin', but how about we set up an appointment? Aftah hours, I'm guessin', yeah?

I think you'll like the place. 'S got plenny a chahm.

PART EIGHT

The Woman Who Agreed To Break Up With Her Girlfriend After A Year Because Of The Biting

CHAPTER FIFTY-THREE

Tempe, Arizona
19 September 1996

The park is a smear of green in the brown-and-beige city. An interloper from another climate where grass grows wild. Exactly like the blonde girl sitting on the park bench.

She's perfect. Young, awkward, and totally alone.

Tess has been watching her, ever since she spotted her hauling stuff out of a removal van the week before. *Not stalking her*, Tess reassures herself. *Assessing. Appraising.* And so far, this one gets an A-plus rating on all counts.

The girl hardly ever goes out. No friends. New to the city, obviously. And look at how she holds herself – head down, arms tight to the body. Shy.

When she does go out, her eyes follow the women who walk past her like they're goddamn magnetised. Tess prides herself on her ability to spot a closeted lesbian from fifty feet away; she's had a couple of decades of practise by now.

Tonight, her target's been sitting in the park for ages, reading a loose sheaf of papers under a streetlight. There isn't a less subtle way to shout, 'I'm lonely and bored!' without putting it on a T-shirt. This is the moment, right now.

Tess takes her camera in hand and reminds herself, one more time, that it isn't a person she's looking at.

It's a dairy cow.

It's a dog.

Pet her to make her love you, kick her when she misbehaves. Then she'll never betray your secrets. Then she'll be too beaten down to turn on you. As long as you make sure she's alone. As long as you make sure you're all she has.

Hiram screwed that part of it up because Meijing hated his guts. It nearly got him killed. Tess won't make the same mistake. There'll be no one whispering to her new dog when she isn't looking.

It's hard, though, getting it done all by herself. She doesn't have the tag-team advantage that Meijing and Hiram had when they managed to work together. The good vamp, bad vamp double act. But that's all right. Tess can be both. She's had a couple of decades of practise at that, too.

Tess has to do it this way. She has to. She doesn't have any choice. Anything else is too dangerous.

Anything else might make her slip up and start thinking that one of her dogs is a person.

But maybe, someday, one of the dogs will stick around. Transform. Become like her. Then she'll have someone to partner with. She'll have someone who can be with her forever.

She knows why Hiram kept Meijing around, even though she hated him. Anyone is better than no one. It won't be like that for her, though. She'll find someone, and make them hers. It'll be the way it would have been, if she could've stayed with Mei.

Then she won't be so lonely all the time.

All the fucking time.

Tess steps forward, bringing the camera up to her eye. Doing her best to ignore the hunger gnawing at her guts like a feral animal.

'Don't move. Seriously, can you hold completely still for, like, half a second?'

The girl looks up, startled.

'This is going to need a long exposure time,' Tess continues. 'If you move, it'll blur out.'

'. . . all right.'

Tess takes the picture. It really is an amazing shot. The girl's hair looks like liquid gold in the lamplight. 'Perfect.' She lowers the camera and holds out her hand. 'Tess.'

The girl takes it. 'Hi. I'm Angela.'

CHAPTER FIFTY-FOUR

Cambridge
31 December 2000

'I think you should take the guinea pig with you to the beach tomorrow,' Shelly says.

'What?' Chloë manoeuvres a tray full of snacks around a cluster of work acquaintances, trying not to spill everything onto the floor. Even though the living room is almost bare of furniture, the tiny space is crowded with people.

'I've got a theory. She's going to turn out to be the key to the whole thing.'

'Why?'

'Well, one of your witches said the secret was Sacrifice, right? And, duh, that's the guinea pig's name. So what if that's what she really meant? Like a play on words to trip you up.'

'No, that isn't . . .' Chloë pauses. In fact, that kind of pointless misdirection is pretty typical of magic spells, from everything she's seen. She's just reasonably sure it doesn't happen to be the case in this particular instance. 'We're not going to need the guinea pig.'

She finally gets the tray down on the card table. More crudités and dips for the humans, more cocktail weenies for the werewolf – and any humans who like cocktail weenies more than celery, she supposes. She'd felt a little weird about buying and cooking meat when she refuses to eat it herself, but since she gives cat food to her cat and blood to her girlfriend, it seemed hypocritical not to put out something that Mike could snack on, too.

Shelly picks up a carrot stick. 'Maybe that's true, but if you try to cast the spell tomorrow and everything goes wrong–'

'The spell is already being cast,' Chloë corrects her. 'It's more of an ongoing process than a one-off event. Think of it like a book that I'm writing, or a journey we're going on. The beach is just a final check to make sure everything's working right.'

'Whatever. Do you really want to take any chances?'

'Do you really want Sacrifice to catch a chill and get sick? It's going to be freezing cold out there tomorrow.'

'Good point, never mind. You keep your hands off my poor guinea pig, you monster.' Shelly dips the carrot in some hummus and pops it into her mouth.

Chloë looks over the room to check how the party's going. Everyone seems to be having a decent time. Food is being munched, drinks are being drunk, and Angela's computer is playing a constant stream of music that's about as upbeat as goth ever gets.

Next to the kitchen door, Mike is chatting with some of their co-workers from Compass Rose. Chloë figured it was time to start getting to know some of them better. She's going to be working with them a lot more closely once her new job starts. On the other side of the room, Aunt Esther, freshly back from Africa, is leaning in to talk to Moira in a way that can only be read as flirtatious. Which is terrifying to Chloë on a number of levels. At least Moira didn't bring her sisters along, although that might simply be because the mouth and eye thing would be too difficult to disguise with more than one of them there.

Angela has ensconced herself in a corner with some people she knows from the clubs, a little knot of bodies clad in black clothes, their faces daubed with dramatic make-up. Most of them have spent the whole party huddled together, peering out at the rest of the room like foreigners who don't speak the language. Meanwhile, Entropy is holding court smack in the middle of the living room, demanding and receiving attention from all and sundry, showing a completely un-cat-like fearlessness of both the roomful of strangers and his new, unfamiliar living space. Her pet is such a weirdo.

She'd wanted to invite her ex-housemate Ari as well, but she didn't have any idea how to get a hold of him. Somehow, though, he'd known to send a congratulatory postcard. It had a scenic picture of Paint Lick, Kentucky on the front and a long parable about a dog and a lobster written on the back in dense, tiny lettering.

The party is meant to celebrate a lot of different things. New Year's Eve, of course, but also the new apartment, and Chloë and Shelly's new jobs. And secret magic vampire stuff as well, but not everyone at the party is aware of that.

Chloë has the sense that most of the people there are glad to have something to celebrate; the atmosphere's been pretty gloomy in their circle of friends since the Supreme Court handed the presidency to Bush a couple of weeks ago. They'd stolen it for him, frankly, shutting down the recounts with a five to four vote that went along strict party lines. After the inauguration, the US will officially be in the hands of a dimwit, surrounded by cronies champing at the bit to start the next war.

She's hopeful that the world will get through it and out the other side, though. Maybe he'll be gone in four years.

'So, speaking of books that you're writing, how's the novel going?' Shelly asks once she's finished chewing her carrot, interrupting Chloë's train of thought. 'Still chugging along?'

Chloë would rather be thinking about anything other than politics right now, anyway. 'Yeah, actually. Being awake when everything's closed is giving me a lot more free time.'

'I can imagine.'

'Angela and I are racing each other. My book against her thesis. Whoever loses has to take the other one out to dinner.'

She's started to enjoy being awake through all the quiet hours of the night, reading manuscript submissions or working on her novel, side by side with Angela. Not seeing the sun for two weeks as they prepare for tomorrow has been an odd experience, though. Spending so many of her daytimes dead is disconcerting, no matter how worthwhile she considers the spell. There are no dreams when she passes her days as Angela does, and there isn't any slow, gradual fade into sleep. Only a sudden drop into absolute nothingness until the sun goes down.

'I'm looking forward to seeing it,' Shelly says.

'Sorry?'

'The book,' she explains patiently. 'I'm looking forward to reading it when it gets submitted. Because I'm pretty sure it's going to get past the new Submissions Editor, for some reason.'

'Well, I mean . . . even if I get to the end of it anytime soon, it's still only going to be a first draft–'

'I'm an editor, Chloë. I understand about first drafts. Give me the book when it's done.'

'OK.' Chloë nods nervously and takes a slice of red pepper off the tray, mostly to have something to do with her hands. 'So, how have the holidays been treating you so far?' she asks, eager to change the subject.

'They've been weird.' Shelly leans back against the wall. 'We went to spend Christmas with Mike's family, and he finally decided to have the do-we-want-kids discussion while we were there.'

'Well, that's good, right?'

'Yeah. About damn time, though. It took a near-death experience on a road trip to make him think about the future. I guess better late than never, right?'

'That's for sure. So, uh, how did it go?'

'Well, apparently any kids would be . . .' Shelly glances around to make sure no one is listening. 'Unless we adopt or something, they'd be little werewolf babies, which means we'd need Mike's mother's help to raise them safely. And that woman is terrifying. I'm still mulling it all over.'

'Terrifying how?'

'I'm not a werewolf, but when she's mad, I feel like flipping on my back and pissing myself anyway.' Shelly shakes her head. 'But enough of that for tonight. It's a party. How much time do we have left until midnight?'

'Let me check.' Chloë stuffs the pepper into her mouth so she can get her phone out and flip it open.

Shelly raises her eyebrows. 'When did you get a cell phone?'

Chloë holds up a finger while she quickly chews and swallows. 'Angela pointed out that if any crazy dangerous shit ever goes down again, we might need to get in touch immediately. After everything that happened last month, it was hard to disagree.'

'Wonders will never cease. She's going to convert you to the cult of high tech one of these days. I'll look away for a minute and you'll suddenly have an MP3 player and a plasma TV and a PlayStation 2.'

'You're probably right. I might even like it.' Chloë glances down to check the time. 'Ten minutes to midnight. You should head to the windows. I'd better get Angela so we can pass around the champagne.'

She only makes it halfway to her girlfriend, however, before Esther intercepts her.

'So,' her many-times-great aunt says to her, 'your rental agent tells me you've had quite an exciting time of it lately.'

'Just to warn you, I'm pretty sure Moira's dead,' Chloë says. 'In case you were thinking of taking her back to your hotel room later.'

Esther gives her a reproving look. 'And what if she is? It doesn't make her any less charming. You're not the only one allowed to romance the unliving.'

'Touché. And you're right, she's nice. We wouldn't be having the party tonight without her help. She let us move into this place a few days before the lease officially starts.'

'Good to know that she comes recommended.' Esther takes a sip of her drink. 'It may be me going back to her place, though, rather than a night in a hotel. She says she has animals that need caring for.'

'Um . . . where exactly is her place?'

'Are we going to spend the entire evening discussing my love life?' Esther asks. 'Or are you going to tell me about your adventures?'

'Can I take a rain check on that, at least until after the fireworks?' Chloë hesitates, then adds, 'I learned a lot more about magic. I mean, about what I'm doing as a witch.'

'That's good.'

'It wasn't easy.'

'It usually isn't,' Esther says.

'I almost died of hypothermia, actually.'

'I'm not surprised.' Esther steps aside to let Chloë past. 'Passing very near to death is often the key to seeing beyond the border.'

'You know, you could have warned me about that,' Chloë grumbles as she goes by.

'Would it have helped?' Esther calls after her.

Chloë finally makes it all the way to Angela, greeting her with a quick kiss on the cheek. 'Hey, hon,' she says. 'It's almost time.'

Angela breaks off the conversation she's having with a man whose eyes are heavily rimmed with black liner. She turns to Chloë and smiles. 'Great. Let's get ready.'

The kitchen is a welcome respite from the people and the noise. It's only the two of them in there, practically the first chance they've had to be alone together all evening. Angela slips her arms around the back of Chloë's neck and leans forward to press their foreheads gently together.

'How are you doing, sweetie?' she asks.

'I'm having a good time,' Chloë says. 'What about you? Any problems with your allergies?'

'The pills are working about as well as they usually do. Entropy's dander and I are getting along fine so far.' Angela runs her fingers through Chloë's hair, toying with the curls. 'Are you feeling ready for the new millennium?'

'I thought that was last year.'

'Technically, the new century starts in 2001. So we'll get there on the stroke of midnight.'

'Well, then I'm looking forward to the next thousand years with you. Although I'm a little nervous about tomorrow morning.'

'Same here.' She steps away from Chloë and opens the fridge to get the champagne out. 'We'd better get a move on. You sure you don't mind watching the fireworks through the windows? Missing all the First Night stuff?'

Chloë shakes her head and grabs a stack of plastic cups. 'There's no place I'd rather be than here.'

She's already falling in love with their little Cambridge apartment, with its slanted ceilings and dormer windows. No more noisy upstairs neighbours for her; she'll be the noisy upstairs neighbour now.

Her home with Angela. Most of their stuff is still in boxes, and there's no furniture to speak of – Angela barely had any, and nearly all of Chloë's wasn't worth keeping. They'll get some soon enough. She's been mentally measuring the walls for bookcases since they moved in.

She's also been thinking about how to decorate the under-eaves space. They'll be spending a lot of time in there, after all. Just because they'll be dead when they're in it doesn't mean that it can't be cosy.

Once they get out of the kitchen, Angela opens the champagne with a resounding pop. They barely get the drinks distributed in time, filling the last person's cup the moment that Mike, the only one there with an actual watch, starts a countdown. The rest of the assembled guests chant along with him, even the corner-dwelling goths.

'Six! Five! Four!'

Chloë takes Angela's hand and squeezes it. Angela squeezes back. They both count out the passing seconds with everyone else. 'Three! Two! One! HAPPY NEW YEAR!'

Through the windows, they can see the fireworks going off over the Charles River, the glass-rattling booms following immediately after. Chloë drinks her champagne, and Angela pretends to drink hers. The noise of the fireworks is enough to startle Entropy at last, and he goes hurtling into the bedroom to hide among the boxes and coats.

'Want a kiss to ring in the new millennium?' Angela asks, already tilting her face up in anticipation.

'Yes,' Chloë says. 'Very much yes.'

CHAPTER FIFTY-FIVE

Excerpt From Chloë's *Gramarye*

The last of our guests have finally left. Some of them have gone home, some of them have gone downtown to see the ice sculptures, and some of them, possibly, have journeyed down to the underworld for a hook-up.

Angela and I will be heading out soon, too. But before we go, there's one last thing I need to do. Because if there's anything I've learned about magic, it's that spells are a story you tell the world. You create something that has shape and meaning, and hope the universe responds in kind.

A while ago, I was told that a certain story didn't exist. There is no book with exactly the right title, no folk tale with the perfect combination of characters and events, no myth or legend with the one particular slant on the subject that I need.

Which means that if I want it to exist, I had better write it.

The Woman Who Agreed to Break up With
Her Girlfriend After a Year
Because of the Biting
by Chloë Kassman

It's the oldest story in the world, even if you think you've never heard it before.

Girl meets girl. But then the first girl turns out to be a vampire, and they break up. But then the second girl discovers that she's a witch, so they decide to make a go of it, at least for a while.

If that doesn't sound like an old story to you, bear in mind that it's nothing more than a variation of a much, much simpler one:

Girl meets girl.

Girl loses girl.

Girl gets girl.

There's a fourth part of the story, though. One that the two of them haven't reached yet. It goes like this:

'And they lived happily ever after.'

Getting to that fourth part isn't easy. In the case of the two girls, one of them had to face psychotic vampires and her horrible ex-girlfriend – and in fact, her horrible ex was one of the psychotic vampires in question. The other girl had to deal with a dragon and a three-headed dog and a surprising amount of indecent public exposure, which turned out to be a lot less fun than you might think.

They couldn't have done it alone. They needed the help of a werewolf.

They needed a secret held by a trio of dead witches.

They needed advice from an imaginary talking lobster.

And they especially needed the great rebellious action of a long-enslaved vampire.

But more than anything else, they needed each other.

This coming morning, at a cold beach on the first day of the twenty-first century, the two girls are going to try to take another step closer to happily ever after.

They won't make it all the way there. The secret they never tell you about happily ever after is that you can't get all the way there until ever after has passed all the way by, and it never does. Happily ever after isn't the end of a story. It's a sequel. It's a series. It's your lives together. It's every day you spend happy together, or trying to be happy together, or sometimes even failing to be happy together. It's every night you spend doing your best to make things work. It's every hour you spend being in love.

Happily ever after is a journey of its own. And the only way to reach it is to walk through it, step by step by step.

CHAPTER FIFTY-SIX

San Francisco International Airport
31 December 2000

Meijing sets her magazine aside as the passengers come spilling out of the gate. The words on the page have been swimming before her eyes, anyway, unread and ignored. She hadn't expected to feel so nervous. But this will, after all, be a reunion with a person she hasn't seen in nearly three decades. They might be strangers to each other now, changed beyond all recognition.

'Mei!'

She stands up as she hears the shout, and finds a pair of arms being flung around her waist. After an instant of surprise she returns the embrace, resting her cheek against the side of Tess's temple.

How odd that the smell of the girl's hair is instantly familiar to her after all these years. Meijing feels her agitation dissipate as she inhales the scent.

She must stop thinking of Tess as a girl. No matter how young she appears to be, the woman holding her must be over fifty now, the days of her youth long past.

Tess pulls back to arm's length, her hands still lightly touching Meijing's sides. 'Look at you,' she says. 'You look exactly the same as I remember.'

'And you look entirely different,' Meijing replies. 'What have you done to your hair?'

Tess laughs. 'I never liked it brown. It made me look like a mouse. Had to go with a darker colour, though, because vampire hair doesn't bleach. Did you know that? I'm a snappier dresser now, too.' She gives a little half-twirl to show off her skirt's layers of black and ivory tulle. 'Not that it's hard to do better than the seventies. What the hell were we all thinking?'

'Are modern times an improvement? Bell-bottoms have made their comeback.'

'Ugh, don't remind me.' She motions behind her, and a young man steps forward wheeling a carry-on suitcase behind him. His hair is a bright green that contrasts pleasantly with Tess's dark red. 'This is Russell.'

'Ah, yes. Your beau.'

'If that's what you want to call it,' Tess says, smirking. 'Russell, come on, say hello.'

'Hi.' After this single syllable, he falls silent.

Tess rolls her eyes. 'I swear he's like a fucking mute sometimes.'

'Hello, Russell,' Meijing says. 'It is a pleasure to make your acquaintance.' She looks him over, taking in his slightly hunched shoulders and tight, anxious smile. She sees nothing prepossessing about him, but it's always possible that he has hidden depths.

The three of them follow the signs towards baggage claim, Meijing and Tess in the lead and Russell trailing along after them. They have to force their way through the crowds; the airport is packed tonight. A horde of travellers delayed by Midwestern snowstorms have at last reached their destination, just in time for the New Year's celebrations.

'Did you have a pleasant journey?' Meijing asks as they mount a moving walkway.

'It was only two hours in the air,' Tess says. 'Made it easy to find a night flight.'

'Any problem crossing rivers?'

'Maybe. I felt crazy nauseous every once in a while, but that could have been from being on a plane, you know?'

Meijing nods. 'I think you'll enjoy what San Francisco has become,' she says. 'We can go to the Embarcadero, perhaps. That's mostly new since you were last here.'

'Is it a lot different now? No more wandering hippies? Internet start-ups everywhere?'

'It's changed. It's the same city, though, nonetheless.' Meijing settles her hand on Tess's shoulder. 'Have you thought about what we discussed?'

'Moving back here? I don't know. Let me think about it for a while. I only just moved to a new house in Phoenix. And . . .'

'And you wish to be sure of me.'

Tess shrugs. 'Well, yeah. I mean, I don't *think* you'll use the vampire mojo on me, but it would be a hell of a risk to take. It was a risk coming to see you at all. I've taken steps to protect myself, of course.'

'Of course.' Meijing wonders if that's true. It's difficult to imagine what such precautions could possibly entail. Any secrets could be forced out into the open, if she were so inclined. But she is not. Tess does not elaborate, and Meijing does not press her. 'I hope I can earn your trust, in time.'

'Me, too. I'm glad you're free, Mei. I'm glad my plan worked.'

'Your plan,' says Meijing, in a genial tone, 'was barely worthy of the name. Had you been patient for a few years more, I would have had the strength to unbind myself. Your attempt to send me assistance was not merely unnecessary; it was ill-conceived, foolish, and very nearly resulted in my death.'

'Yeah, well, no one ever told me that we could order wolves

around, too. Chalk it up to my shitty education. It came out all right in the end, didn't it?'

'It did.'

Tess leans against her. 'Let's have a nice vacation for now, get to know each other again.' She grins. 'I want to be sure it's me you really want, and not Russell.'

'I am perfectly capable of finding my own meals,' Meijing replies stiffly.

'I know, I'm kidding. Feel free to make use of him while we're here, though. You still don't have anyone long-term right now, right?'

'No.'

'Well, I talked to him about it. He's cool with it.' Tess nudges Meijing with her elbow. 'And if you want to borrow him for anything else, I can probably talk him into that, too.'

'Tess!' Meijing is half scandalised and half amused. 'Is that the way I taught you to behave with your companions?'

'Nope. But I've put my own spin on a few things.' She winks at Meijing.

Baggage claim, when they get there, is a madhouse. They've arrived later than most, and there's a dense wall of bodies between them and the luggage carousel.

'I can see our bags,' Tess says, peering through a gap in the crowd. 'I think I can get to them. Wait here a minute.' She threads her small frame through the mass of passengers, slowly making her way to the front.

Meijing and Russell stand in silence, watching her. The lull in conversation stretches until it becomes uncomfortable. She's on the verge of asking a bland question, solely to make standing there less awkward, when Russell forestalls her by saying, 'Hey, um, can I talk with you about something?'

'Certainly,' she answers. 'What did you wish to discuss?'

Russell seems to be suddenly fascinated by his own toe. He does not raise his gaze from it when he asks, 'So, you know Angela, right? Tess's ex-girlfriend?'

'I've met her, yes,' Meijing says cautiously. 'And we talk, on occasion. She is the one who gave me your address.'

'Yeah. Well, when she came by last month, she said . . .' He takes a deep breath. 'She said that you don't always, you know, not everyone becomes a vampire. That some people die, and don't come back.' He finally looks up. 'So I was wondering, uh . . . I wanted to ask you, is that true?'

Meijing's eyes flick to Tess, hauling the suitcases off of the carousel, then back to Russell.

'I cannot imagine why she would have told you such a thing,' Meijing says. 'I do not think she likes Tess very much. Perhaps she sought to drive a wedge between you?'

'Yeah.' Russell's shoulders relax for the first time since Meijing met him. 'Yeah, that's what I thought, too.'

'You guys getting along?' Tess asks as she rejoins them.

'Splendidly,' Meijing says, taking one of the bags.

She will have to have a word with Tess about this sometime, she decides as they make their way to the taxi ranks. They need to have a conversation about the practicality of living as they have in the past, and whether it would be wise to change their habits.

Meijing wonders if Tess's decades as a *geong si* have not been good for her – if the power has exacerbated the ruthless streak that was always present. It is easy to slip further and further away from humanity, as Meijing well knows. Easy for *geong si* to forget that they were human once themselves, if there is nothing and no one around to provide an occasional sharp reminder.

She hopes it never becomes necessary to control Tess directly. That would sadden her.

But whatever Tess has told Russell during their time together is her own business, and Meijing is not about to interfere. And if, at some point, Tess needs assistance hiding Russell's body, Meijing hopes that she can be there to help. A daughter is a daughter, no matter what.

Russell, on the other hand, is no kin to her. Not yet. And most likely, he never will be. She does not wish him dead, but he does not merit any warning from her, either.

There are, after all, limits to honesty.

CHAPTER FIFTY-SEVEN

Revere Beach
1 January 2001

Angela pulls into one of the only remaining open parking spaces. There are a lot more people at the beach today than the last time they were here. Dozens of them gathering on the sand in the predawn twilight, shivering in boots and bathing suits, stomping around to stay warm. A bigger group is watching from the fringes, fully dressed, cameras at the ready. And is that a news van?

'What's going on?' she asks.

'Oh, damn it,' Chloë says. 'I completely forgot about this. It's a New Year's tradition. People throw themselves into the ocean on the first day of the year. I think it's supposed to be invigorating.'

'Wow. That's crazy. In kind of an awesome way, though.' It crosses Angela's mind to join in, but it feels like it would be cheating if she did it. She isn't going to get invigorated by freezing cold water; it won't even make her chilly. Besides, they've got other things they need to do here.

'Do you think we should have gone up to the mountains instead?' Chloë asks anxiously.

'No.' Angela shakes her head. 'The clearing would have been too far from the car to be safe. It's too late to get there now, anyway.

There's not a lot of time left before sunrise.' She gestures out at the growing crowd. 'None of them should see anything unusual, right?'

'Unless it doesn't work, and you catch on fire or something.'

'We've got a plan for that. All you have to do is throw me in the trunk.'

'Because that's inconspicuous,' Chloë grouses. 'And it'll only help if there's enough time to get you in there.'

'Tess thought I'd have a couple of minutes.'

That doesn't seem to calm Chloë down any. She crosses her arms and frowns. 'I don't think we should be taking everything Tess says as the gospel truth.'

'Chloë.' Angela tries to sound as reassuring as she can. 'This is going to work. We're prepared. You've spent two whole weeks staying up all night with me so you could build up to this. You've got more daylight hours stored up than we need.' She's been overdoing it, in Angela's opinion, although at least Shelly and Mike only had to cover for a couple of missed work days at the Compass Rose office. The holidays kept it from getting too out of hand. 'You know it's been having an effect,' Angela continues, 'because you've been spending half of your life dead, for goodness sake. So why are you so nervous all of a sudden?'

'Why are you not?' Chloë asks. 'It's your life we're putting at risk here, and you don't even trust magic.'

'You're right,' Angela agrees. 'I don't trust magic. It's weird and irrational and makes no sense. But' – she rests her hand on Chloë's hip – 'I do trust you. You told me what this spell is going to do. I believe you.'

'Oh.' Chloë blushes fiercely, her cheeks turning a deep red.

Angela's fangs spring out in response.

'Crap,' she says. The fangs are a visceral reminder that she has another pressing need. 'I haven't fed yet tonight. I thought we could do it out on the beach, but . . .' She glances out the windshield as a family of four jogs by the car, hurrying to join the others before the mad immersion gets underway.

'Should we put it off until later?' Chloë asks.

'I don't think I should, not on the new diet plan. I really can't let myself get back in the habit of delaying or skipping.' If she ever waits so long that the balance tips from hunger to uncontrollable starvation, the consequences could be dire. She doesn't intend to let that happen.

'All right.' Chloë tilts her head, exposing her throat. 'Let's do it while we're still in the car, then. Make it look like a kiss. I'm pretty sure no one's watching us too closely. The stuff on the beach has to be a big distraction.'

Angela nods. She takes a final look around before she leans forward and nips Chloë's neck, feeling her girlfriend's inevitable wince as the fangs penetrate her skin. When the blood trickles out, Angela takes a sip, no more, barely a taste, then pulls away and gives the puncture marks a quick lick to speed up their healing.

She misses the hot splash of blood in her mouth, more than she'll ever be willing to say. This is nothing in comparison, a nibble when what she wants is a banquet. Thirst is her constant companion now. She can ignore it, repress it, distract herself from it, and she does all of those things whenever she can, but it's always there. Urging her to drink more, drink deeper, soothe the maddening dryness in her throat, fill the gnawing emptiness she perpetually endures now. The craving can be close to overwhelming.

But she can never do it, never let herself give in. She can never falter or waver. Not even once.

Worth it, she thinks as Chloë turns and smiles at her, her mop of curls bouncing slightly. *Absolutely worth it.*

She comes to a decision about something she's been thinking over for some time.

'By the way, the answer is yes,' she says. 'I'll marry you.'

Chloë looks dumbfounded. 'What?'

'You asked me a while back, remember? That is' – Angela suddenly feels nervous – 'unless the offer has been rescinded?'

'No!' Chloë says. 'No, nothing's been rescinded. The offer still stands. I haven't, I mean, I wouldn't–'

'Good.' Angela smiles shyly. 'I'm . . . That's good.'

'Did . . . did you want to have a ceremony here? Or go to Vermont?' Chloë's tone becomes more and more enthusiastic as she goes on. 'Or if we can scrape together enough money to go overseas after we pay rent and everything, they're going to have the real thing in the Netherlands starting next year, or actually it's this year, I forgot we're in the new year already–'

'We'll figure it out.' Angela leans forward again, this time to do something with her mouth that isn't a bite. 'We'll get it all figured out.'

The conversation is replaced by other things for a while after that.

'I hate to be the one to put a stop to this,' Angela says when she finally gets the opportunity to speak again, 'but how much longer do we have? I'd rather be outside than in the car when it happens.'

'Right, of course.' Chloë takes a moment to get her breathing back under control. She checks the time. 'You weren't wrong. We've only got a few minutes left.'

'Then let's get ready.'

Angela pops open the trunk and steps out of the car. Chloë goes back to get the shopping bag, but doesn't close the trunk afterwards. 'In case we have to move fast,' she says pointedly.

Angela doesn't argue. There's no harm in being ready for the worst, after all. Although she's hoping for the best.

They walk a few paces out onto the beach, not straying too far from the Corolla. Chloë takes one of the honey-filled plastic bears out of the bag and pushes it down into the sand until it stands on its own.

'One measure of honey for all the gods,' she intones. She takes out the other honey bear and places it next to the first. 'A second measure of honey for the Mistress of the Labyrinth.'

One or two of the onlookers at the edges of the beach look over at them. A man in a parka takes a few pictures, apparently believing the honey offering is part of the festivities.

The little bears sit in the sand, not doing anything in particular.

'Are you sure that the measure of your measures was the right measure?' Angela asks.

'It shouldn't matter. It's more a courtesy than anything else. A way of saying thank you.'

'What would happen if you didn't say thank you?'

'I'm not sure,' Chloë admits. 'But in the myths, people who piss off the gods tend to get turned into spiders or monsters or suffer eternal torments. Poetic revenge for minor insults is kind of their thing.'

'Then I'm all good with putting out the thank-you honey,' Angela says. 'A thank you to whatever might be listening sounds like a great idea to me.'

'So much for atheism.'

'If I'm at risk of being turned into a spider, we've officially reached the point where I'll, you know, err on the side of agnosticism.'

The sky has been gradually lightening and looks pink at the horizon. The people milling about on the beach are beginning to organise themselves into a rough line.

In the pit of her stomach, Angela feels a lump of anxiety, her earlier calm evaporating. No matter how much confidence she has in Chloë, she's been avoiding the sun with so much care for so long that she can't quite quell the impulse to hide, get inside, get under cover before it's too late. Before she spontaneously combusts, or whatever it is that happens to vampires when the light hits them.

'How much longer is it going to be?' she asks.

'Any moment now.'

She takes Chloë's hand. Her girlfriend's tension is clear in the tight grip of her fingers. Angela is certain that her own nervousness is equally obvious.

No matter what happens in the next few minutes, some part of her life is ending this morning. But if it all goes well, it won't only be an ending. Two years and change after her death, she might finally be getting a second chance.

A sliver of sun peeks over the eastern horizon, and a wavery pathway of light spills across the Atlantic. With shrieks of joy and agony, the brave and deranged citizens of Boston plunge themselves into the sea.

It's the first glimpse of sunlight that Angela's had in more than two years.

'How do you feel?' Chloë asks, her voice full of concern.

'I feel fine,' Angela says. She entwines her fingers with Chloë's as she watches the sunrise. 'Just fine.'

EPILOGUE

Until You Die

CHAPTER FIFTY-EIGHT

Cambridge City Hall, Cambridge
17 May 2004

'Midnight,' Chloë says, looking up from the screen of her BlackBerry. 'It's time.'

Cheers erupt from outside the building, muffled by the walls, but loud enough to be heard, nonetheless. The long line snaking through the hallways echoes it back. Chloë and Angela join in, yelling at the top of their lungs.

When the noise dies down, Angela takes a quick glance up at the ceiling. 'No meteors.'

'And no earthquakes,' Chloë says. 'No floods. Not a single hurricane.'

'Amazing.' Angela laces her fingers together and stretches her arms over her head. 'It's almost like the world isn't going to end tonight after all.'

In fact, the weather's been beautiful, almost surprisingly so for spring in Massachusetts. Temperatures in the seventies, and not a cloud in the sky across the whole state.

Chloë puts the BlackBerry away, resisting the urge to check her e-mail again. No one's going to have sent her anything in the last five minutes. She shifts her weight from one foot to another, trying to soothe the aches that have come from standing in one place for far too long. The line might start moving now that the town clerk's office is open, but they're not going to get to the front anytime soon. As early as they got there tonight, plenty of couples arrived even earlier. It's a once-in-a-lifetime opportunity to be among the first. Well worth the wait.

As of a few seconds ago, for the first time ever in any US state, gay marriage is inarguably and unquestionably legal. In the People's Republic of Cambridge, Massachusetts, City Hall is opening for business at the first possible minute.

But at the first possible minute, Chloë's already been standing in line for three hours, and her shoes are really, really uncomfortable.

She doesn't regret wearing them, though, not really – they go with the tux. And it's been gratifying to learn that Angela has trouble keeping her hands off of Chloë when she's in a tuxedo.

The application for the licence isn't the same as the wedding itself, but Angela and Chloë had agreed that it was an occasion that called for dressing up. They aren't the only ones there who had the idea – about half of the people in line have come in their wedding clothes. Angela managed to find the gothiest wedding dress at the Filene's Basement Sale, cut low on the top and high on the bottom. Then she'd festooned it with black ribbons to goth it up further, until it was finally deemed acceptable to wear. Chloë was dubious about the process until she saw the result. It's gorgeous. So is Angela. It takes Chloë's breath away to see her wearing it, every single time.

'I still can't believe this is actually happening,' Angela says, shaking her head in a kind of stunned wonder.

'I know.'

'In George W. Bush's America, too.' A note of worry enters her tone. 'Do you think it'll last? They keep talking about using a constitutional amendment to ban it again.'

'I don't think they'll do it,' the woman standing in front of them says. She jiggles the dozing infant in her arms. 'I don't think they've got the votes.'

Chloë turns and nods. 'And from here on out, they'll have to unmarry people if they make it illegal. That'd be crazy, right?' She gives Angela's hand a reassuring squeeze.

They haven't talked much with the women immediately ahead of them, mainly because the other couple has been too busy corralling their children all night. One of them continues to be preoccupied with entertaining a bored and fractious toddler. But since the baby has fallen asleep for the moment, the other one is at least temporarily able to talk.

'I'm Jessie Nguyen, by the way,' she says. 'That's Jessica back there with the other kid, and yeah, Jess and Jess, we know. I'd shake your hand, but, baby.'

'I totally understand. I'm Chloë, and this is Angela. Nice to meet you.'

'Wait, Chloë?' Jessie's eyebrows go up. 'Are you Chloë Kassman, by any chance? The author?'

'Uh. Yes?'

'I thought you looked familiar. I know you from the book jacket photo. I really liked *Lovers and Lobsters*.'

'Well . . . thanks.' A year after the book came out, and she still stumbles over her tongue whenever anyone says anything about it. 'I'm surprised you've even heard of it.'

Angela gives her a gentle whack on the shoulder. 'You shouldn't be. Who did you think was going to read your gigantically lesbian book, if not the people we were going to meet here?'

'I do try to read everything gigantically lesbian,' Jessie says.

Chloë fiddles with her cummerbund and tries to think of a way to change the subject. 'So, how long have the two of you been waiting?'

'Only a few hours,' Jessie answers, puzzled. 'We got here right before you did.'

'No, I mean . . .' Chloë makes a gesture in the direction of the toddler. 'Have you been together a long time? How long have you been waiting for *this*?'

'Oh! About seven years. She proposed in 1997. In a parking lot.'

'A parking lot in a National Park,' her fiancée tosses in. 'It was a gorgeous parking lot. She always leaves that out.'

'We already had a commitment ceremony, but I'm going to marry this woman as many times as it takes. How about you guys?'

'Three and a half years,' Angela says. 'We thought about doing something earlier, but decided to wait it out.'

'Thirty-two years for us,' says a white-haired man behind them. His partner leans on a cane beside him; both of them are in matching cream-coloured suits. 'Since 1972.'

The chat continues as the line moves forward, inch by inch. The hours tick by. The baby wakes up and makes its dislike of waiting in line loudly known.

Chloë begins to wonder if either of them are going to make it in to work on time. She has to get down to Quincy in the morning, and Angela needs to be at the Center for Astrophysics on Garden Street, poring over her data in case a new planet unexpectedly emerges from it. At least the CfA is only one subway stop away.

They're going to be exhausted all day, but that's not unusual for a Monday. The changeover from night-time living to daytime living is always the most difficult part of the week.

In spite of Chloë's worries, when they make it to the front there are still a good many hours left before dawn. The clerk greets them with a tired smile and asks for their photo ID. After they fill out the paperwork and pay the fee, he pushes a small white card across the desk.

'There's a three-day waiting period before you can pick up the licence,' he says in a rote chant. 'Come back here with the card any time after that. The licence will be good for the next sixty days.'

'What about the marriage?' Angela asks. 'How long do you think that's going to be good for?'

'Until you die,' he answers without missing a beat.

Angela blinks, then laughs with delight, quick and bright.

As they wander towards the exit, she examines the card in her hand. 'It's so small. Such a tiny little thing. It feels like it should be something more grandiose.'

'Well, it's only the first step,' Chloë points out. 'We've got to have the wedding. And we need to *plan* the wedding, for that matter.' They've hardly thought about any of it beyond the licence and the clothes. It's been hard for either of them to trust that it would be real.

'You're right,' Angela says. 'We'd better start thinking about colour schemes . . . and flowers . . . and music . . .'

'There's a bunch of practical stuff to sort out, too. Some of our guests are going to require special considerations.' Mike could have a rough time of it if they pick a date near the full moon. Meijing needs advance notice for any cross-country trip. And Esther is spending most of her time in the underworld these days. How do you send a card there? 'I have no idea how we're going to find a venue in the next two months, either. Not with this many couples here at midnight on the first day. There's got to be even more people waiting until morning, or later in the week, right? Everywhere's going to be booked solid.'

'Well, it's Boston. Home of the Boston marriage. So many women were shacking up together here that they needed a name for it all the way back in the nineteenth century. Now that it's legal–' Angela stops short as they walk out the front doors and are greeted with a joyous roar.

The crowd is bigger than it was when they arrived earlier in the evening.

Much bigger.

There must be thousands of people in front of City Hall, thronging the hillside, crowding the steps, standing in the window embrasures. They spill out onto Mass Ave, across the street, all the way up to the walls of the YMCA on the other side of the road. Police in riot gear are keeping a pathway open to the door, but there doesn't seem to be any violence, or any threat of it coming. The few sorry protestors that were parading for the cameras when the night began are long gone.

Instead, there are Morris dancers. Drummers. Guitarists. People throwing rice. People holding up signs about equality, about love. Someone has a sign that just says 'YAY!' A new round of cheering starts up whenever it gets waved aloft.

'Kiss!' comes a shout as Angela and Chloë stand transfixed in the doorway. The crowd takes it up as a chant. 'Kiss! Kiss! Kiss!'

They look at each other, astonished.

'What do you think?' Angela asks after the surprise has had a moment to fade. 'Would you rather run away and hide, or give them a show? I'm fine either way; it's up to you.'

'I don't know what I'd do another time,' Chloë answers hesitantly. 'But, I mean, tonight?'

'Are you sure?'

'Yeah.' A grin begins to spread across Chloë's face, one that's quickly mirrored by Angela. 'Yeah, I'm sure.'

'Well, then. You're the one with the tux. Dip me.'

Chloë wraps her arms around Angela and leans her over backwards. Her girlfriend's back – her fiancée's back – arches as gracefully as a dancer's. The crowd erupts into thrilled and deafening noise. Beneath it, they can still faintly hear cries of, 'Kiss!'

And they do.

ACKNOWLEDGEMENTS

The earliest versions of Angela and Chloë appeared in a roughly scrawled plot outline that I jotted down in a notebook in the spring of 2002. Since then, both they and their story have grown and changed a great deal. I did not, for example, realise that Chloë was a witch until many years after that. And while Shelly was giving Angela a place to live and Chloë an ear to bend from almost the beginning, Mike didn't show up on the scene until 2014.

Their story wasn't the only one I worked on in all that time. But it was a story that I kept returning to again and again, tinkering with it and expanding it and sometimes drastically cutting it down. One way or another, whether they've been at the forefront of my mind or in the back of it, Angela and Chloë have been hanging out in my head for more than eighteen years. So while I don't think it's common practice to thank your characters in the acknowledgements, it seems only polite after all that time together. Thanks for everything, you two; I hope it wasn't too hard on you.

I'd also like to thank some people who affected my life in ways that helped me to create these characters and write these books.

One summer when I was reeling after an unspeakably bad break-up, Amy and Jon Herzog took me to my first goth club (and Amy lent me an appropriate skirt for the occasion). I'd never gone to a club of any kind before and was unsure about the whole thing, but the moment I walked in the door I felt like I had found My People.

A few years later, in that very same goth club, I fell into an intense conversation with a friend of a friend. A couple of days after that, we started going out. It's been two decades now, and Beth Biller and I are still together and still having that intense conversation.

While I usually don't put anyone specific directly into my books as a character, the Entropy in the story is for the most part indistinguishable from Entropy as he was in life. I miss you, kitty, and I hope that wherever you are now, the invisible monsters in the curtains have finally been found and slain.

The writing of *Bleeding Hearts* in particular was greatly assisted by insightful feedback and suggestions from Armarna Forbes, Whitney Curry Wimbish, Jack Jackman, Edinburgh Creative Writers, and Rogue Writers Edinburgh. Both Beth Biller and Amy Herzog also offered their brilliant advice on the book, and in any number of ways helped to improve the story that they also helped to inspire. Thanks as well to Paul Wong for his help with the Cantonese and Taishanese that appears in the book.

And of course, many thanks are due to my superb editors Jo Fletcher and Molly Powell, as well as Milly Reid, Ian Critchley, Emma Thawley, Laura Soppelsa, and everyone else at Jo Fletcher Books and Quercus.

Turn the page to see some of the authors
Ry Herman loves

Also Available from

Jo Fletcher Books

ROBERT JACKSON BENNETT

FOUNDRYSIDE

THE FOUNDERS TRILOGY BOOK I

'The exciting beginning of a promising new epic fantasy series. Prepare for ancient mysteries, innovative magic, and heart-pounding heists'

Brandon Sanderson, *New York Times* bestselling author of *Oathbringer*

She thought it was just another job. But her discovery could bring the city to its knees . . .

In the city of Tevanne, you either have everything, or nothing. For escaped slave Sancia Grado, eking out a precarious living in the hellhole known as the Commons, nothing is just one misstep away.

So when she is offered a lucrative job to steal an ancient artefact from a heavily guarded warehouse, she leaps at the chance.

But instead of a way out of Tevanne, she finds herself the target of a murderous conspiracy. Someone powerful wants the artefact, and Sancia dead.

To survive, Sancia will need every ally and every ounce of wits at her disposal, because if her unknown enemy unlocks the artefact's secrets, the world – and reality – will never be the same.

Jo Fletcher

BOOKS

LORD OF SECRETS

BREANNA TEINTZE

The Empty Gods Series Book 1

Magic is poison. Secrets are power. Death is . . . complicated.

Outlaw wizard Corcoran Gray has enough problems. He's friendless, penniless and on the run from the tyrannical Mages' Guild – and with the search for his imprisoned grandfather looking hopeless, his situation can't get much worse.

So when a fugitive drops into his lap – literally – and gets them both arrested, it's the last straw . . . until Gray realises that runaway slave Brix could be the key to his grandfather's release. All he has to do is break out of prison, break into an ancient underground temple and avoid killing himself with his own magic in the process.

In theory, it's simple enough. But as secrets unfold and loyalties shift, Gray discovers something with the power to change the nature of life and death itself. Now Gray must find a way to protect the people he loves, but it could cost him everything, even his soul . . .

With the humour of V.E. Schwab, the scale of Trudi Canavan and the deftness of Naomi Novik, *Lord of Secrets* is a heartwarming fantasy novel about saving the people you love without destroying the world (or yourself).

Jo Fletcher

BOOKS

This Is How You Lose the Time War

AMAL EL-MOHTAR

MAX GLADSTONE

'A fireworks display from two very talented storytellers'
Madeline Miller, author of *Circe*

Co-written by two award-winning writers, *This Is How You Lose the Time War* is an epic love story spanning time and space.

Among the ashes of a dying world, an agent of the Commandant finds a letter. It reads: *Burn before reading.*

Thus begins an unlikely correspondence between two rival agents hellbent on securing the best possible future for their warring factions. Now, what began as a taunt, a battlefield boast, grows into something more. Something epic. Something romantic. Something that could change the past and the future.

Except the discovery of their bond would mean death for each of them. There's still a war going on, after all. And someone has to win that war. That's how war works. Right?

THE
CHILD EATER

RACHEL
POLLACK

An ancient evil is on the rise. Children are disappearing. Only two boys, from different worlds, can stop it.

On Earth, The Wisdom family has always striven to be more normal than normal. But Simon Wisdom, the youngest child, is far from ordinary: he can see the souls of the dead. And now the ghosts of children are begging him to help them. Something is coming, something far, far worse than death . . .

In a far-away land of magic and legends, Matyas is determined to drag himself up from the gutter, become a wizard and learn to fly. But he, too, can hear the children crying.

Two vastly different worlds. One ancient evil. The child eater is coming . . .

'An intricately imagined Tarot-themed fantasy'

Guardian

Jo Fletcher
BOOKS

ASTRA

NAOMI FOYLE

The Gaia Chronicles Book 1

Is-land is a Gaian paradise in the middle of a blasted world – but its success comes at a dark price.

Like every child in Is-Land, all Astra Ordott has ever wanted is to get her Security Shot, do her National Service and defend her Gaian homeland from Non-Lander 'infiltrators'. But when one of her Shelter mothers, the formidable Dr Hokma Blesser, tells her the shot will limit her chances of becoming a scientist and offers her an alternative, Astra agrees to her plan.

Then the orphaned Lil arrives to share Astra's home and Astra is torn between jealousy and fascination. Lil's father taught her some alarming ideas about Is-Land and the world, but when she pushes Astra too far, the heartache that results goes far beyond the loss of a friend.

If she is to survive, Astra must learn to deal with devastating truths about Is-Land, Non-Land and the secret web of adult relationships that surrounds her . . . or her actions could bring the whole community toppling down.

Jo Fletcher
BOOKS

TOM POLLOCK

**'An impeccably dark parable,
endlessly inventive and utterly compelling'**

Mike Carey, author of *The Girl with all the Gifts*

**Welcome to the world of the Skyscraper Throne:
a hidden London that lurks just beneath the surface
of the city, full of marvels, magic . . . and menace.**

When seventeen-year-old graffiti artist Beth runs away from home, she doesn't suspect that beneath our London lies a hidden world of creatures who live off the city, nor does she expect to find Filius Viae, the Urchin, the Son of the Streets, or to drag her friend Pen along with her.

When war threatens to decimate this world, Beth must decide – fight, or flee?

**This trilogy includes *The City's Son*,
The Glass Republic and *The Skyscraper Throne*.**

Jo Fletcher
BOOKS

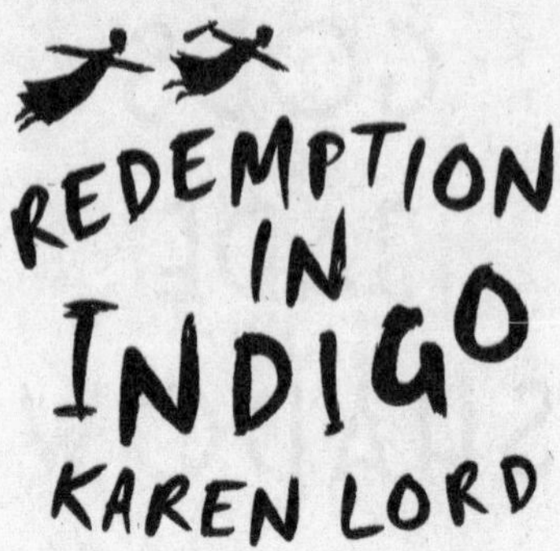

'A clever, exuberant mix of Caribbean and Senegalese influences'

New York Times

Paama's husband is a fool and a glutton. Bad enough that he followed her to her parents' home in the village of Makendha, but now he's disgraced himself by murdering livestock and stealing corn.

When Paama leaves him for good, she attracts the attention of the undying ones – the djombi – who present her with a gift: the Chaos Stick, which allows her to manipulate the subtle forces of the world.

Unfortunately, not all the djombi are happy about this gift. The Indigo Lord believes this power should be his and his alone, and he will do anything to get it back. Chaos is about to reign supreme . . .

'The perfect antidote to the formula fantasies currently flooding the market'

Guardian